Dear Gera

Loving you
Sunny We Stuck Here.
anyway Nice To work with you
and Thanking You your friendship.
Now Take Care OK   LOT OF ♡
                  X X X
                  O O O

              T☺N

              ☆☆☆

THE MASTER'S HORN

P A Fletcher

MINERVA PRESS

LONDON
MIAMI   RIO DE JANEIRO   DELHI

ISBN 0 75411 391 4

First Published 2001 by
MINERVA PRESS
315–317 Regent Street
London W1B 2HS

Printed in Great Britain for Minerva Press

THE MASTER'S HORN

Part One

Demons and Delights

An eerie wail echoed forth across the undulating downs of Marlford. Having broken from cover at the edge of the surrounding forest, this demonic call hauntingly carried itself across these soft flowing plains, over the high stone boundary wall and into the grounds of Carlile Manor, an imposing grey stone Gothic-style monstrosity set at odds with the picturesque scenery in which it reposed. The scenery constituted a panoramic banquet of autumn colours, the grounds filled with a burgeoning painter's palate of delicate hues of russet and gold. The ever-increasing autumn cascade of leaves from the resident mighty beech and oak trees heralded the forthcoming onset of winter.

Creeping with cat-like stealth, the sound penetrated the massive oak front door with consummate ease, continuing through the great entrance hall, up the grand staircase and along the darkened wood-panelled corridors. It brought a biting coldness to the air surrounding it, as it travelled with some demon possessed rite of passage, through and past, the labyrinth of passageways and rooms that this grand house possessed, into the expansive library, seeking out and finding its target as if it were the highly prized trophy of the hunt.

Its target was none other than the laird of the manor himself, Montague Alexander Carlile, who, on hearing this sound, was instantly transformed from the master of all he surveyed to a subservient serf-like creature at the control of the demons which were being unlocked from the innermost recesses of his mind by this insidious sound.

Bringing to the surface long buried remembrances and feelings, Montague sat transfixed, staring out of the book-encrusted library window into the brightness and beauty of a clear and unseasonably warm September day untouched by the peace and tranquillity of the scenery before his eyes, only feeling the sudden coldness of the air surrounding him in a lead-like blanket. His mind was a boiling cauldron of thoughts as he travelled back to times past…

The air had been bitingly crisp that twenty-sixth day of December in the Diamond Jubilee year in the reign of our gracious Majesty Queen Victoria. Montague and Catherine Carlile had, for one of the rare times in either of their lives, been experiencing a day of quiet pursuits cosseted in their Witton Place, Knightsbridge, home. They had bade farewell that morning to the last of their house guests for the Christmas Day celebrations and had packed off downstairs most of their household staff to enjoy their newly acquired Christmas gifts, having honoured the traditional Boxing Day rituals between master and servant within this peaceful London residence. They had just completed a splendid Boxing Day cold luncheon repast of hors d'œuvres variés, consommé à la julienne, filets de sole à la mayonnaise, petites crèmes de faisan, jambon de York à l'aspic, langue de boeuf, tartelettes de pommes, crème à la vanille, fromage and finally dessert which today had been specifically requested by Catherine to her aloof chef, M. Pavot, to be an English sherry trifle as this she knew to be Montague's favourite. Catherine had experienced much of European cuisine and loved it, her family having had a French chef since before Catherine's birth. Montague, on the other hand, although he had travelled extensively with his work and also had a great appreciation for the cuisine of Europe, had been troubled by his advancing years and mild disease of the digestion, which had left him intolerant of rich food, hence Catherine's desire to keep this menu relatively simple and behind the French table names essentially English!

'Thank you, my dear, for a most splendid repast,' Montague had said as he smiled lovingly at his wife across the vast expanse of the white damask, silverware and ceramics that constituted the dining-room table.

'I am so pleased that you were satisfied with the offering, my love. I am so very keen to make this holiday season very special for you, my new husband,' beamed Catherine.

'Do not concern yourself too greatly, my beloved. You must realise that whatever you do will always meet with my approval,' Montague had said, lightly reproaching his new wife for being a touch too sensitive and nervous of him and his requirements. Little did he realise that the words he had just spoken would one day return to haunt him.

'If you will excuse me, dearest sweet thing, I will with your kind permission take my leave of you, albeit temporarily, and escape to my library,' Montague had ventured.

'That will be perfectly fine, my dear. I, too, am escaping to my boudoir in pursuit of my motherly endeavours,' had cooed Catherine.

So it had been that Catherine had ventured forth to her boudoir in pursuit of her knitting and needlepoint, in joyous anticipation of the forthcoming birth of their first-born child.

Montague's mind, on the other hand, had never been far from the other great love of his life, his work as a banker in the city of London, so away to his library he had scurried, hopeful of an uninterrupted afternoon of perusing his papers and journals. As he settled himself behind his massive Georgian desk and commenced the perusal of his paperwork his mind had strayed to thoughts of his wife, upstairs. What a lucky man he had been, how proud she had made him feel and how thankful he had been that she, Catherine Elizabeth Bentley, as she had been, had agreed to become his wife just eighteen months previously.

He, Montague Alexander Carlile, had indeed been a fortunate man, having come from a meagre beginning, being the fourth son of an impoverished Scottish farmer. It had only been through the legacy bequeathed to him by a kindly, yet eccentric Scot, by the name of Ian McCabe, that had allowed him to escape his rugged existence in the highlands of Scotland to a new life in the hustle and bustle of London. Now, at this Christmas season, Montague had remembered the kindness that the fiery red-haired Ian McCabe had endowed to the poor children of the area, travelling around the frost-covered lanes in his fine carriage on Christmas Eve, throwing pennies to the children as they ran beside his carriage. Though a Scot to his very core, McCabe, through his many years of professional residence in London, had become accustomed through his long and varied associations with English colleagues in his world of finance to celebrating the Victorian traditions of the Christmas season. He likened himself in this simple act of charity to the benevolent Saint Nicholas and he was also mindful of the fact that Old Year's Night or Hogmanay, the rightful night of festive celebration for any true Scot, would see him through the necessity of his chosen profession once more resident far from his highland home.

Montague had also remembered the carriage stopping one year outside his parents' small thatched cottage, on its way home one evening from one such kindly adventure, and Ian McCabe calling to Montague, who had been standing by the door of the cottage, to come closer to the carriage so he may speak to him. How well Montague had remembered the fear which had risen in him as he stepped towards the fine black and red carriage. What had he done to deserve this treatment? He need not have feared, so much. All McCabe wanted had been to ask this eleven year old boy a question. Neither had realised at that time that the answer to the question would have such an effect on either of their ongoing lives to such a great degree. Montague had remembered Ian McCabe, with his shock of fiery red unruly hair, peering out from the open carriage door and beckoning to the boy to come closer to the vehicle so he may ask the question, 'What are you going to spend your pennies on, my wee lad?'

Montague had replied in a strong Scots accent, 'I'll no be spendin' these pennies now, sir, but will be puttin' them with the others I have hidden from last year and the years afore that, in a special place, to give me a chance of a better life.' Montague had hoped that his future life would, one day, include travel to London. To Ian McCabe this statement by a small boy of no means, whose name he did not even know but whom he would later find to be Montague Carlile, had a great effect on him. The child, a son of a poor crops' farmer, had been christened Montague Alexander, firstly in honour of his mother's much beloved and only uncle of the same Christian name, who had been tragically killed during the Crimea War, and secondly in honour of his hard-working father. So great had been this chance one-time meeting that very soon after, upon his death bed, McCabe, who had remained unmarried and without heirs throughout his long life, had bequeathed to Montague a legacy worthy of an only son. McCabe had instantly seen something of himself in

Montague, a look of determination. He had also sensed a longing in this boy for a chance to climb out of the mire into which birth had placed him. Ian McCabe had wished for this shared quality of fierce determination of purpose to live on in this wee boy.

As Montague had thought back, he had indeed been very fortunate. Without that legacy which he had received and which had been administered in his days as a minor through Donald McMaster of McMaster, McMaster and Willow, Ian McCabe's firm of solicitors based in Inverness, who had followed the instructions passed on to him by his client, there had been no way he could have attended the exclusive boys' school, Mendrew, situated in the border country between Scotland and England. He had spent a happy enough time there from the age of twelve. Montague had been noted by his subject masters as being a studious and solitary child, who completed the tasks set for him with a great degree of precision and dedication to detail; however, it was also noted that he had made no lasting friendships during the time that he had been in attendance at Mendrew.

During his final year at Mendrew, Montague Carlile had sat for, and passed with flying colours, the entrance examination for acceptance into Cambridge University, whereupon completion of his studies at Mendrew he had been duly enrolled and had taken his place with the aim and deepest held desire of completing the most relevant studies for his ultimate dream of a life in the financial heart of the city of London, as had been the life of his mentor, Ian McCabe.

Again, as at Mendrew, Montague's greatest claim of note had been the earnest desire and dedication to succeed at his appointed studies which he constantly had shown, much to the chagrin of some of his fellow students, whose nickname for him during those university days had been 'stick-in-the-mud Montie'. For him there had been no such thing as a social calendar; in his mind, within his life in university the all-encompassing, all-empowering need and desire had been the search for and compilation of the appropriate knowledge which would lead him further in his quest towards his ultimate goal, a new life in the City of London.

Thus, with this knowledge having been acquired and a degree

to his name, Montague Carlile had at last been able to make his triumphant procession into the city of his dreams – London. He had a letter of introduction signed by his beloved benefactor, the canny Scot Ian McCabe, which had been held in trust and passed on to Montague when the time had been deemed to be right by Donald McMaster, McCabe's crusty yet diligent solicitor. The astute Scot, McCabe, had the intuition from their chance meeting to believe fervently that Montague would one day be desirous of a position in his world of finance and banking. McCabe, to Montague's delight, had been found to be a man of major financial importance in this city of cities. Thereby, Montague finally had found himself with a position, albeit a junior one, of errand boy to one of the most prestigious financial houses in Europe, that of Barland Bank.

However, as Montague well knew, a good many years had passed by since these almost forgotten times and, having learnt the business from the ground up and watched and listened and held his tongue when he thought he knew better than his elders, he had become a member of the executive council of the bank with overall responsibility for the overseas investment department. This he had relished greatly as it had required him to travel extensively to such places as Paris, Milan and Vienna, which had, in turn, allowed him to indulge in one of his few non-business passions, that of the opera.

On some of these occasions, being able to have had Catherine accompany him on these business trips as his hostess, for the social entertainment he had been required to conduct on behalf of the bank in these foreign lands, had been the greatest relief to him. It had been the greatest comfort to him, as he had not been by nature a social creature, to be able to have looked down the dinner table and found her smiling and confident face beaming back at him like a lighthouse in a stormy sea of unfamiliar faces. When he had found himself away without her, he had felt lost in the hurly-burly of the social set, only feeling at peace and secure in the boardrooms and banking halls of these great cities.

It had been ironic to Montague that the first two loves he had experienced in his life, that of his work in the bank and that of the opera, would one day combine to give him the greatest love of his life, that of his wife, Catherine. It had been during one of these trips abroad to Vienna, at a March night at the opera, that he had first laid eyes on Catherine across a crowded foyer of the Vienna State Opera House during an interval in the performance. However, by the time he had extracted himself from the conversation he had been at the time engaged in with his host for the evening, naturally for Montague a banking colleague from their bureau in Vienna, and had made his way to where he had seen her standing with others, the bells had begun ringing summoning patrons to return to their seats, and the lady in question had moved away and had been lost in the throng of people returning to view the final act of that evening's performance, a performance of Wagner's *Tristan and Isolde*. How prophetic Montague once thought that had been, young lovers to be, watching young lovers that were.

The thought had run through Montague's mind as he returned to his seat and the company of his host, Life again has dealt me a blow in the affairs of the heart.

Life again had indeed appeared in Montague's opinion to have been unkind. His skill in attracting the attention and affection of a lady of similar habit to himself had to this time in his life never been greatly effective.

However, life indeed had in effect smiled kindly on Montague Alexander Carlile at this point in his life, for not five days had passed since he had glimpsed that radiant creature at the opera than he had come face to face with her across the dining-room table in the home of one of his few personal friends on any shore, an old college friend from his Cambridge days, Percival Groot.

How wonderful to see this goddess of beauty yet again! Montague had whispered to himself.

What heartfelt glee had filled his soul as, throughout the night, he had realised what a precious gem he had sitting before him. He must not let this jewel escape, though this fear of loss had appeared to be very slight. For, as time had gone on and the night had passed by, Catherine and Montague had become more and more engrossed in each other's conversation to the exclusion of all others in the room. They were, from this point on, observed by all as companions sharing a single soul for what had been equally judged by all to be the rest of their lives together.

'How has such a vision of loveliness come to be at this table?' Montague had queried. To which Catherine had gracefully replied that she was a school friend of Jane Groot, Percival's younger sister. Having recently lost her father – Catherine's father having been Sir Frederick Bentley, the wealthy industrialist renowned for his philanthropic endeavours – in a yachting accident during the Cowes Regatta, it had thus been decided for her, by her elderly twin maiden aunts, sisters of her late father, whom had moved uninvited into her London home upon their brother's death, that as she was now an orphan she had become their responsibility, having lost her mother, Christina Mary, at her own birth, though she had attained her coming of age the spring before and had thus been approaching her twenty-second birthday.

It had therefore been decided by Aunts Maude and Gertrude that, after the funeral, which had been conducted in St Paul's Cathedral, and the required period of mourning had been observed for the tragic and untimely death of their dearly loved and deeply missed brother, Sir Frederick George Bentley, Catherine would partake of a trip away in an effort to ease the pain and grief her mind and body had been experiencing at this extreme and sudden loss. Sir Frederick had slipped from the deck of his yacht, the *Christina M*, off the coast of the Isle of Wight during the concluding day of the regatta. He had bumped his head and had fallen in a state of deep unconsciousness to an instant death in the waters of the Solent.

The decision had therefore been made by Maude and Gertrude Bentley and arrangements had been organised for Frederick's only child and their only blood relative to visit her school friend Jane Groot at her paternal grandmother's ancestral home in Vienna. Catherine's elderly Yorkshire maid, Gladys, had alone accompanied her on the trip as her two aunts, having never had a day of real illness in either of their long lives, had agreed between themselves that they both had been too close to their own earthly demise to contemplate a journey abroad such as the one they had totally organised for their niece.

So it had come to be that Catherine Bentley had been duly

organised, packed and transported to Vienna in the strict accompaniment of Gladys. Catherine was of a cheerful and warmhearted disposition and it had not been in her nature to respond angrily to this uninvited and at her age unwarranted intrusion into her life by these seldom seen sisters of her late father. Furthermore, the sudden and untimely loss of her dearly loved father had sent Catherine's inner mind reeling into a state of temporary imbalance. Everything around the home that she had shared so happily with her father had reminded Catherine of him and intensified the heartfelt pain that she had experienced, having lost the one person in the world who truly loved and believed in her.

Catherine had felt lost in her own home which had become a monument to her father's death and not the accompaniment to his life that it had always been. This home that they had so contentedly shared, being draped in mourning, had oozed death from every pore of its being. That had repulsed and frightened Catherine to the extent that for the first time in her life she had been grateful to her meddling aunts for their intrusion into her affairs and their insistence that she went to Vienna.

It had, therefore, been with a sense of relief that Catherine had journeyed away from this place, her home, which for so long had been a sanctuary away from the day-to-day trials of her young life. With her father, as an abbot to a monastery, her confidant, guide and protector through life, Catherine had felt secure and confident to take on life as it confronted her, but now that sense of confidence had been threatened by this tragic loss. Having never truly experienced the loss of her mother, being a newborn babe at the time of her death, this had been the first time that she had felt such a sense of emptiness in her life. It had frightened her not to have had control over her feelings and emotions at this time.

So it had been that Catherine had been in the loving protection of the Groot family that March evening when Montague had first laid eyes on his 'Goddess of Beauty' as he would be heard to describe her. This vision of ivory skin and ebony hair, resembling in appearance a delicate figurine of the finest porcelain imaginable, who to Montague had appeared to float across the room on a cushion of delicacy, had a radiance about her as to pale into insignificance all those about her.

As the dinner had progressed to its conclusion, these two dinner companions each had become more and more convinced that, out of loneliness and tragedy, the hand of fate had dealt them both an ace. The dinner ended but not their time together, as by this great stroke of good luck they had both been house guests of the Groot family and would share the next couple of days in the gracious company of this most loving and accommodating of families. In the following days, Montague and Catherine had shared a common delight in more dinner parties and luncheons, visits to the numerous museums and art galleries this glorious city had had to offer, carriage rides and times of simple amusement in the many parks such as the renowned Prater, under the ever-watchful eye of Gladys as chaperone and, of course, more of their beloved opera together now in the generous company of their hosts.

Montague well remembered how the hours had flown by and soon it had been time for him to return to London and the business world of high finance. Never had he felt a sadness and a sense of loneliness before at the act of returning to what had always been his lifeblood. However, it had been with a strange feeling of emptiness that he had returned to his office in the city of London. The only consolation which had eased his heart had been the assurance he had received from Catherine that they would continue their new-found friendship upon her return to London in a month's time. His parting assurance to Catherine had been that he would be waiting for her on the platform at Victoria.

Within Montague's mind, he still kept a remembrance of how slowly that time away from Catherine had passed by and how lifeless his work suddenly became. His dedication to his work had still been evident, only due, however, to his strong sense of loyalty and commitment to the firm which had allowed him to achieve so much in his career.

The fellow members of the Sovereign Club, the gentleman's club situated in the prestigious area of Pall Mall in the heart of London, of which Montague had been a highly esteemed and long-time member had noticed a change in his general demeanour since his recent return from Vienna, almost having become reclusive in his manner towards his brother members. This club had been dedicated to the particular wants and needs of the bankers and financial merchants of this industrious capital, and had been patronised by the heir to the throne of Britain and its Empire, hence its regal and solvent double play name. Montague Carlile had always been described by his fellow members as a 'man's man' in this elite club dedicated to finance and banking, who had enjoyed to the fullest extent the company and activities provided by the club's secluded nature, activities such as educated discussion of world affairs away from the social constraints applied in mixed company, enthusiastic involvement in the time-honoured gentleman's pursuits of billiards and whist and a haven for quiet contemplation of the passage of his life.

It had been this last aspect of club life which had encapsulated Montague and had held him up to ridicule upon his return from Vienna. Although it had been a thoroughly male-dominated club, it had not been above the womanly pursuit of gossiping within its ranks, which it had commenced to do from the instant Montague had crossed its threshold the first night after his return from abroad. Montague remembered well having been greeted at the main door of the club by Jenkins – the rotund and completely bald doorman, resplendent in the club's livery of dark green tailcoat with gold buttons which had been embossed and gave the appearance of the sovereign, coin of the realm, from which the club had taken its name, black trousers and a black top hat – with a cheery welcome which had been indicative of this man's general disposition.

'Good evening, Mr Carlile. Had a very successful trip abroad this time, I hear, sir,' Jenkins had stated with great purpose.

Montague instantly had realised there had been more meant in that statement than just in a business sense; however, he had responded with nothing more than, 'Thank you, Jenkins. Yes, my business was conducted very successfully.'

With that simple reply Montague had entered into the main body of the club, into the atmosphere of fine cigar smoke and old leather, which he had always found so comforting, to be con-fronted by a hushed silence as he entered the smoking room. It had been, as Montague now sat and remembered, extremely disconcerting to him, as he walked towards the card tables to enquire with regard to the likelihood of a game of whist, that a general buzz of voices had started to echo around the room, snippets of which Montague had caught as he had moved through the room and past the already occupied tables.

'By Jove, here comes Montague Carlile, sly old fox. I heard he achieved more than just a successful business deal on his recent foray to Vienna,' had said one merchant banker from a somewhat dubious establishment.

'Yes, wonders will never cease, but will they make it to the church or will the lady in question see the error of her ways before it is too late,' his playing companion, a person whom Montague had previously considered to be a loyal colleague, had replied.

'He may have money and nobody in this room would dispute his ability to keep a wife, but surely this parvenu has left his run too late to think of fathering any children, which the young lady must be desirous of at her tender age,' had espoused the gentleman of dubious professional pedigree.

Montague had been dismayed and had stood for a moment in this sea of common dissent of his actions, aghast at the thought of his personal affairs having become the current topic of conversation, and thus public property, in this his cherished haven. Unable to quickly summon to mind a suitable response or retort, Montague had turned on his heels and fled out of his club, never to return again.

As he walked the streets of London, having brushed aside the offer of a cab proffered by Jenkins, in an effort to clear his head of all the anger and pain he had been feeling, he had realised just how lost and alone he had suddenly become, lost in this great city of London which had always felt like, and been, home to him during his adult life and, suddenly, greatly desirous of another person's company – that of Catherine's. Where throughout his life he had craved no other intimate company but that of his books and his work, there had now appeared a void which had only been able to be filled by the radiant presence of this precious creature. As he had walked distractedly in the direction of his Belgravia home, he had looked upwards towards the myriad of stars residing in apparent peace within the heavens and had all but silently uttered the plea,

'Please God, may this union have your divine blessing, for ever.'

Finally the time had passed and Catherine had returned to London, having rested her mind and body from the turmoil which had blanketed her upon the death of her father. She had again become the radiant and confident young woman of whom her late father had been so proud. The only cloud on her horizon had been the thought that had kept plaguing her mind during the journey back to London on the train, that the blossoming friendship with Montague had been but a passing infatuation and that his thoughts had once again returned to his world of high finance to the exclusion of her. These thoughts, Catherine some time later had revealed to Montague, the remembrance of which he had consigned along with his own on the matter to be locked away in the depths of his mind.

Oh, how very far from the truth Catherine's thoughts had been. This had proved acutely evident when the boat train had pulled into the station. As Montague had promised, he had been waiting on the platform with his strong as iron coachman, Barnes, to greet Catherine and her dour-faced Yorkshire maid, Gladys, and subsequently had conveyed them in his grand black and grey carriage, which had on this instance been pulled by two fine dapple grey geldings, to Catherine's Witton Place, Knightsbridge residence.

The fear of being exposed to Catherine's aunts at this early stage of their relationship had been minimised by the nature of their early arrival into the city and in the knowledge that the aunts had not been predisposed to rising from their beds before the clock had struck eleven in the morning.

Gladys, Catherine's short and stout Yorkshire maid, had not been of a mind to tattle to anyone either above or below stairs of her young mistress's affairs, and what she may or may not have observed of her actions during their recent trip to Vienna, as she had always had, behind that dour and somewhat foreboding countenance, a secret soft spot in her heart for this young lass, since the time she had been Catherine's nursemaid as a newborn baby. There having been no further issue, due to the previous mistress's tragic death at Catherine's birth, Sir Frederick Bentley, as time had passed and Catherine had grown into a young girl, had requested Gladys to stay on within the household in the position of personal maid to the blossoming Catherine. This loyalty and affection which Gladys had felt had only been heightened by the ongoing tragedy of her family life and any happiness she could help Catherine to achieve, Gladys thought had been good for all their hearts, hers included.

So it had been, as the weeks and months had passed by, that Montague's and Catherine's friendship had turned into a true relationship, and finally into a fully blossoming romance which had deepened more and more until it had come to that point in time for all such intense relationships such as theirs that it had had to come into the open completely, and Montague's and Catherine's participation in each other's lives had had to be formally acknowledged by each other in the form of a proposal of marriage. This had come in the guise of an invitation to Catherine by Montague to be one of a number of guests at a weekend house party in September at his country estate of Carlile Manor in the countryside of Marlford. Catherine had been able to accept what for her part had been this most gracious and innocent invitation under the cover of accompanying Percival and Jane Groot, thereby minimising any inappropriate thoughts on the part of Catherine's aunts.

The weekend had been spent very pleasantly with the gentlemen of the party having availed themselves of horses from the extensive stable of animals Montague had possessed and participated in the local meet of the Marlford Hunt. The ladies of the party also had participated as interested spectators from the safety and relative comfort of hunting traps placed at strategic points around the hunting grounds. This, the first meet of the new season for the Marlford Hunt, having come to a successful conclusion, with the bagging of a strong dog-fox, the party had adjourned back to the manor house in preparation for the festivities of the Hunt Ball that night. It was a sumptuous affair of dancing and a magnificent buffet supper which included the likes of devilled lobster, fillets of sole in aspic, and galantine of turkey followed by oranges in jelly, French pastries and meringues with vanilla cream and had been accompanied by a refreshing selection from the house cellars, with all the participants of the day's hunt and their partners for the evening having been invited to the Master of the Fox Hounds, Lord Rupert Henry Penman-Smythe, The Right Hon. the Eighth Earl of Marlford's country home, Beeches Hall.

It had been as part of these festivities that Montague had found himself dancing around the floor of the grand ballroom with Catherine in his arms. What a splendid couple they had made, he in his hunting pink dress tail coat and black trousers and Catherine in a gown of emerald green silk which Montague had thought highlighted wonderfully those milk green eyes of Catherine's which he had adoringly become mesmerised by that night of all nights in Vienna. As they had waltzed around the floor to the musical accompaniment of the violins playing in the background, each completely captivated by each other's presence, Montague had bent forward towards Catherine and had whispered softly into her delicately sculptured ear the words she had so longed to hear, 'Catherine, my dear, will you do me the greatest honour of becoming my wife?'

To which Catherine had immediately replied without the least sign of hesitation, 'Montague, my love, I would be truly pleased and honoured to accept your proposal of marriage.'

With the completion of these words of acceptance by Catherine, Montague had produced from his waistcoat pocket a small black ring box, which he had then passed into Catherine's hands. As he had, Montague had opened the box's tiny lid to reveal a magnificent diamond and emerald engagement ring. Montague had seen from the expression of joy and exquisite pleasure on Catherine's beautiful face that the ring had met with her approval and he had slipped it from the box having taken Catherine's tiny left hand delicately in his own large muscular one and had placed the ring on her third finger, thereby sealing this most important of life's decisions.

Catherine's aunts had noticed a change in their niece since her recent return from Vienna and, more markedly, after her recent return from her autumn weekend away with members of the

Groot family, but had thought that she had been just passing through a period of readjustment in her life without her beloved father. Little did they realise that they themselves would soon go through a very drastic readjustment in their own lives.

It had, therefore, been quite a shock to both these maiden aunts when Catherine had requested and received their blessing to invite to tea – a Spartan affair of late in this house now consisting only of Dundee cake and China black tea, due to the austere attitude of these miserly ladies – a newly acquired friend from her recent time in Vienna and unknown to them the host of her recent trip to the country. Catherine, and subsequently her aunts Maude and Gertrude, had bade welcome Montague Alexander Carlile into the drawing room of their Knightsbridge home that chilly autumn afternoon in late September. Montague well remembered how tasteful to the eye the view of this elegant drawing room had been, decorated in a golden hue of painted plaster work and silk wallpaper with its centrepiece of the clean-cut lines of the stark pure white carved marble chimney-piece and associated gleaming blacked-leaded grate. The thought had crossed Montague's mind how this room had stood as testament to the exceptional taste and high position held by the Bentley family and it had pleased him greatly.

Montague, not being a man to play with his words, straight away that afternoon, after formal introductions and social pleasantries had been dispensed with, had announced to the assembled party his intention of asking for the Misses Bentley's blessing to take Catherine's hand in marriage. Though their courtship in most part had been kept secret from the world, had been brief by most standards, that of only six months, and had been conducted in the most unusual of circumstances, Montague believed both their commitments to this lifelong partnership had been strong and as Catherine had been of age the aunts' approval had not by law been required. Montague had, however, asked on Catherine's and his behalf for their blessing, issuing forth the following heartfelt request.

'It would give Catherine and myself great pleasure and peace of mind if her two remaining blood relatives could find it in their hearts to cast their blessings upon this union.'

Initially, the two aunts had appeared surprised and shocked by the thought that, unlike themselves, Catherine had found love and the prospect of marriage without their interference and control in the matter. The other consequence of the prospect of Catherine's and Montague's marriage, which had affected the aunts directly, had been that, upon the marriage taking place, they no longer would have residence in what had been their late brother Sir Frederick's, then by virtue of his will Catherine's home and finally Montague's property without his consent, and it had been highly unlikely that a newly-wed couple such as Catherine and Montague would wish to share their home with a pair of grey-haired, wizened, old spinster maids.

Having quickly realised the true position Maude and Gertrude had found themselves in, they had had no alternative but to cast their blessings upon the couple who had stood before them that cool September afternoon by uttering – as if by some intuitive gift of knowing each other's thoughts granted only to twins – together the words still long remembered by Montague:

'Only God may control such actions. May it be his blessing which shines upon you.'

The forthcoming marriage had duly been announced in *The Times* as follows:

Mr M A Carlile and Miss C E Bentley

The engagement is announced between Montague Alexander, son of Mr and Mrs Alexander Carlile of Invercarvan, Scotland, and Catherine Elizabeth, daughter of the late Sir Frederick and the late Lady Christina Bentley, formerly of Witton Place, Knightsbridge, London.

The plans for the wedding and reception had been discussed between themselves, the church, the organist, the bishop and his ministers and the caterers. It had thus been decided that they would be married in the June of the new year, thereby giving themselves nine months of engagement in which to organise all the relevant details of this most special of personal life events. The church had been decided upon. It was to be St Paul's Cathedral, that being the final ecclesiastical resting place in the city of

London of Catherine's much loved and sorely missed late father in the form of his heavenly spirit, and she had truly felt that this spirit would be with her there to comfort and guide, as he had always done, on that most special of days. A function room at the Savoy Hotel had been organised for the reception, which had included as invited guests family and friends to the number of two hundred and fifty.

With the timing of the wedding service to finish mid-afternoon, it had been decided by the young couple that, as well as wedding cake and champagne to toast and celebrate their marriage, the guests at their reception would be exposed to the simple joys of a very special high afternoon tea as the basis to their wedding reception fare. By not being totally tied to dictated table seating, both the young couple and their guests could mingle more freely and experience a more relaxed social encounter, with no official speeches and less ceremony.

The carriages for the transportation of the bride and her party to the cathedral had been provided by Montague, as his personal carriage had been more spacious and easier to access for the bride in her gown than any other carriage available in London at the time.

The lingering question and persistent worry in Catherine's mind with regard to her forthcoming marriage had been, in the absence of her beloved father, who before the eyes of God and the congregation of the church would give her away. Thankfully Montague had come upon the perfect solution.

'Why did Catherine not ask Thomas Groot, Jane and Percival Groot's father to take this most important role in their service of marriage?' he had suggested.

As it had been through his generous nature that their union had come to be, Catherine believed this to be a most wonderful idea. Subsequently Thomas Groot, the portly and jovial father of their two friends, had been approached on this matter and had joyously accepted the duties of this most sacred task with the simple exclamation of, 'By Jove, what a surprise! I would indeed be very honoured, my dears, and will by all means accept the duties of this most distinguished role. Thank you.'

Weeks travelled on into months and so the time had come to

that special day in June on which Montague and Catherine were finally to be through with waiting and become husband and wife. The day had dawned bright and dry. There would be no worry of rain in London on this day of days. Montague and Catherine had breakfasted lightly in their respective London residences, though each had had no real need for mortal sustenance as their minds and bodies had gravitated to a higher plane of consciousness at this point in time. Both Montague and Catherine had methodically revised their last minute plans during the morning; then, by the time of luncheon, Catherine with the aid of her faithful maid Gladys had been dressed in her late mother's cream silk and lace wedding gown and accompanying pearl-inlaid train with the crowning glory of a Limerick lace veil decorated in delicate floral motifs and secured in place by a garland of imitation orange blossom. This beautiful ensemble had by some great divine coincidence fitted Catherine to perfection. With the final touch of a calf-length cascade of cream lilies which had formed Catherine's wedding bouquet, the bride had completed her dressing.

Meanwhile, Montague had himself been assisted into a superbly tailored black dress suit with an accompanying white silk waistcoat, being an intermediate between morning suit and evening dress, by the man who had performed these duties for him since his time at Cambridge, that of his loyal and trustworthy butler and valet, Collins. As he had been assisted to dress into this immaculately cut Savile Row tailored suit, Montague had tested the waters of his valet's final thoughts on the prospect of his master's forthcoming marriage by issuing forth with the statement, 'Well, Collins, we have been together for a great many years now, have we not, my good man?'

To which the cadaverous Collins had replied without any outward show of emotion, 'Yes, sir, since your student days at Cambridge, and may I take this opportunity to express on behalf of all your household and myself our good wishes to you and through you to your new wife-to-be on this the occasion of your wedding day.'

Montague had accepted Collins's good wishes with the words, 'I am sure I may speak on behalf of Miss Bentley and myself in expressing to you our heartfelt thanks for all the assistance this house has given us in this, the event of our marriage.'

In line with these thoughts, Montague had been interested to gauge the feelings of below stairs of the effect of this day on his staff. It had been decided by Catherine and Montague that, upon their return from their honeymoon, their two respective households would combine under the one roof, that of Catherine's Witton Place residence due to its substantially larger size than his Chaster Square home and it already having held the position of a lavish family home as they had both wished it again to become.

Montague had quietly continued with the question, 'Today, we join two households to form one, a marriage of sorts in its own right, you might say. As you know yourself, Collins, this house will no longer be home to any of us after today, a new beginning so to speak. Do you foresee any problems?'

To which Collins, in the style of the polished performer, reciting the lines he knew the audience would want to hear, had replied succinctly, 'I am not aware of any problems in the forthcoming execution of this union, sir.'

Well, Collins may not have been consciously aware of any problems on that day but time would come to show him that, in fact, he may well have intuitively felt that there would be problems in the future of this household, and not all below stairs.

This would indeed be a wedding with much involvement on the part of the Groot family, with Thomas Groot giving the bride away, his daughter Jane acting as Catherine's sole bridesmaid and his son Percival acting as Montague's best man. This involvement by the Groot family had essentially been taken for granted by both Catherine and Montague, as they had looked upon their respective friends as always having been the only candidates for these most important positions, always having looked upon them as extensions of their own family.

Having been a guest overnight in Montague's Chaster Square, Belgravia, residence, Percival, his friend and mirror image in appearance, apart from his hair which had been as dark as Montague's had been fair, and his manner to such an extent that they had often been referred to as brothers by strangers during their university days, had come together with Montague in the drawing room in final preparation before departing for the cathedral.

'Well, old man, the time has finally come to cast away your bachelor life and take unto you a wife. Are you quite sure, now that this day has finally arrived, that you are totally ready to make this great change to your life?' had queried Percival with considerable seriousness of mind, wishing to test his old friend's state of certainty in his decision of this most momentous matter once more before it became law.

To which Montague had quickly replied in an even and calm voice, 'Yes, my dear friend, thank you for your most sincere concern. However, I do not believe I could do anything better in my personal life than to take my dearly beloved Catherine as my wife.'

With this exchange completed Montague and Percival had departed for the cathedral. Their subsequent journey there had been uneventful and without any loss to the planned timings of the day.

Meanwhile, Catherine had experienced no problems in the events of this most special day in her life. As she had descended the main staircase of her home in Witton Place, Knightsbridge, the servants of her household had been assembled at the bottom forming a guard of honour, each so pleased to see their new mistress in such a serene and confident frame of mind on this, her wedding day. The true head of their household had finally taken her rightful place since the untimely loss of the old master and the long-awaited demise and withdrawal from all their lives of Maude and Gertrude Bentley, who had slipped quietly away to reside with an elderly lady acquaintance at her small private hotel in the seaside resort of Brighton.

Thomas Groot had been momentarily left speechless, as he would later recount to Montague, by the vision of beauty who had floated down to stand beside him at the bottom of the grand marble staircase. He had turned towards Catherine, smiled and extended his arm towards her which she had gracefully accepted. They had then moved together, with Jane in assiduous attendance, through the front doors and into the sunny brilliance of this glorious June afternoon.

As Catherine had commenced to enter the carriage, which had been waiting patiently at the side of this tree-lined street, she had momentarily stepped back, turned and moved towards Gladys, who had been among the senior servants who had been allowed to spill out on to the footpath outside the house to watch the carriages depart for the cathedral. Catherine had stepped up to Gladys and had lightly placed her arms around this faithful maid's waist and had gently and quickly hugged her. With this humble action and the whispered words of 'Thank you' from her lips had come the confirmation to all present that, without Gladys's help and blessing, this whole situation in Catherine's relatively young life would not have come into being. With the completion of this simple gesture of love and respect, Catherine, again with the constantly present assistance of Jane, the demure golden-haired friend from her time in a Swiss finishing school, had ascended the steps into the carriage and seated herself beside Thomas Groot for the journey to the long-awaited service of marriage vows to Montague.

During this journey, as she would later relate her thoughts of this great day to Montague, Catherine had thought of the life she had been about to commence with this man called Montague Alexander Carlile. How happy she had been to be entering into this life journey with such a kind and generous man, however, also a man of great determination of spirit. On reflection, how much like her dearly departed father Sir Frederick Bentley had Montague been in nature and manner. Perhaps those had been the attributes which had attracted her to him in the first place, but there had been more to it than that. They had so much in common.

However, there had been one stumbling block to the public face of their marriage, that being the difference in their age, with Catherine at twenty-one years of age being a mere slip of a girl and generally regarded, due to her previously cosseted life away at school and in her father's house, as naive in the ways of the world, in the eyes of polite English society. Montague, at the age of thirty-nine at the time he first had laid eyes on his goddess of beauty, had been viewed as a man of experience, whose interest in ladies should have, by most accounts, from his world of finance and his club, been placed in a partner of greater age and experience to suit his position in European society. Montague had brought to Catherine's attention what he had explained as his painfully remembered nightmare at the Sovereign Club. This troubling thought had lingered in Catherine's mind as she had travelled along the cobbled streets of London that June afternoon, but only long enough to register and acknowledge its existence as a current social comment on their marriage by narrow-minded and hypocritical individuals who would either never find love or marriage, or both, as she and Montague had, and had been bitter and tormented enough to wish that these two relatively young people would not be granted their wish of a happy and fruitful life together.

The carriage had rolled on past street scenes of a bustling and industrious city, a city for the greater part unaware and uncaring of the great importance and significance of this day in the lives of these two people. The traffic of horse and cart and carriage had ebbed and flowed, just as the mighty river Thames, until it had delivered the small procession of carriages to its bank outside the Cathedral of Saint Paul. As Catherine had alighted from her carriage, the sun had burst into its own song of brightness as if the heavenly hosts had already been showing this time, place and act with their holy blessing.

As she had ascended the steps of this impressive stone monument to the worship of God, Catherine had turned her face towards that of Thomas Groot on whose arm she had gracefully reposed. Through her delicate lace veil he had instantly observed and been impressed by the view of calm serenity in her milk green eyes, a serenity which he only wished could have been in him at this time, as at no other time in his life to date had his mind and body been such a sea of nervousness at the part he had been playing in this most important of days in the lives of two of his children's best friends. However, it had not been only a calmness born of the serene feeling that all had been going well that Thomas had seen in Catherine's eyes but also a confidence that the actions that she and Montague had been about to enter into for what apparently would be the rest of their lives together had been right for them, no matter what the public opinion on this most private issue might have been.

Having paused briefly upon the threshold of this magnificent church for Jane, her ever-diligent bridesmaid, to assist Catherine to undo the button of her left-hand glove, so it had been that the bridal procession had made its resplendent entrance through the main door into this powerful cathedral of the Church of England to the accompaniment of *The Bridal Chorus* from Wagner's *Lohengrin*, and viewed the scene which had opened itself before them, following the scarlet line of carpet which traversed the journey from the main front door at which the party had stood to the high altar. Catherine's eyes had stolen a glance at the view of Montague Carlile standing at the base of the steps which had led to the high altar, with his head turned watching and waiting for the procession of his bride's party down into the body of the cathedral and onwards towards him. How happy and proud he had looked at this moment. The procession had travelled on up the long, red-carpeted centre aisle, with Catherine, her head reverently lowered and her hand resting peacefully on the arm of Thomas Groot, taking the lead, then Jane Groot her best friend and now earnestly fulfilling the role of her bridesmaid and finally Sarah and Josephine Miller, the two flower girls who had been the twin god-daughters of Catherine's late father. Momentarily, the procession had come to rest beside Montague and Percival at the base of the steps leading to the resplendent high altar, then having gathered the bridegroom and best man into the party and Jane in passing having accepted Catherine's wedding bouquet for safekeeping, had ascended to the high altar for the commencement of the service.

Time had appeared to all concerned to fly by, as if in a dream; one moment Montague and Catherine had been completely separate individuals, the next they had been husband and wife, joined by a common name and a common desire for a new life together. Montague's remembrances of his wedding service had all but been lost to the annals of time and life by the state of intense and, for him, unnatural disarray of the mind he had suddenly felt upon reaching the high altar. He had been aware of what had been going on around him and his participation in those affairs; however, it had been as though he had been separated from the control of his own actions.

Snippets of phrases returned to Montague's consciousness as though now showing him that indeed the demons had lain in wait for him for many years.

'Wilt thou have this woman to thy wedded wife, to live together after God's ordinance in the holy estate of matrimony?... To have and to hold from this day forward, for better for worse, for richer for poorer, in sickness and in health, to love and to cherish, till death us do part, according to God's holy ordinance; and there to I plight thee my troth... With this ring I thee wed, with my body I thee worship and with all my worldly goods I thee endow... To love cherish and to obey... Those whom God hath joined together let no man put asunder...'

Needless to say, the wedding ceremony in its own good time had wound on to its conclusion. Having exchanged vows and rings and signed the register, Montague had turned with Catherine now on his arm and had descended the steps into the body of the cathedral and through the congregation as they had retraced the steps Catherine had taken earlier with Thomas Groot, now together to the strains of the *Wedding March* from Mendelssohn's *A Midsummer Night's Dream*. They had paused briefly in the aisle opposite the plaque commemorating Sir Frederick Bentley where, as a mark of respect, Catherine had curtsied and Montague had bowed. Then, they continued to their waiting carriage, which had on this day been pulled by two fashionably grey horses, and away to their wedding reception.

The day's passage had moved on to mid-afternoon by the time the wedding party and their invited guests had assembled in the Savoy Hotel for the wedding reception. It was an understated yet sumptuous affair of fine Veuve Clicquot champagne and a three-tiered wedding cake creation comprised of a mixture of rich dark fruit cake, apricot jam, marzipan paste and royal icing which had combined to create a true culinary triumph worthy to toast this great occasion. As well as this crowning glory, the guests had indulged in such delights as cold roast chicken and spiced beef pigeon pie, tongue and ham, lobster salad, cream cakes and meringues, strawberry tarts with custard and cream and fresh fruit.

For the enjoyment of the assembled wedding party and their guests, a melodious string quartet had entertained from a raised platform in the corner of the room. This gentle music had provided a pleasant background to the hum of conversation which Montague now remembered had echoed around the room. Having dispensed with the only ceremonial duties for this part of their day, that of the taking of the official photographs and the cutting of their magnificent wedding cake, which had both been gifts to the now newly married couple from Montague's and Catherine's respective households, Montague and Catherine had been left free to mingle and converse with their guests in an informal and comfortable manner for the rest of the afternoon, until the time had come for them to make their preparations for departing this glorious gathering for the commencement of their honeymoon.

The hotel, as part of the services it had provided to the young couple on this day, had set aside two adjoining suites of rooms for the use of the bride's party and the groom's party respectively to change into their travel clothes which Montague and Catherine had taken advantage of, particularly Catherine who, with the combined help of Jane Groot and her ever-faithful maid Gladys, had relieved herself of her most glorious but to some degree cumbersome wedding gown and had replaced it with a most modest and practical grey linen travelling ensemble.

Along the corridor in the next hotel suite, Montague had disrobed from his black dress suit with the assistance of his shadow-like manservant Collins into an equally elegant travelling outfit of black frock coat and trousers, black and grey striped cravat accompanied by a diamond stick pin, black top hat and the final addition of his black gloves and his ever-present black and gold gentleman's stick, a treasured legacy of Ian McCabe. Montague had thus been ready to again step out into general company to await his new bride. This act, he remembered, he had done with a new-found passion for life and an intense desire for this, their new life together, to begin as soon as possible. As he had emerged, Montague had turned his attention in the direction of Catherine's suite to be pleasantly surprised by the sight of her emergence from her suite. How delightful it had been to have found a companion who had been as quick at hand with the essential elements of life as Catherine had appeared, Montague had thought.

As Montague had approached, he had smiled warmly at Catherine and had said, 'You are a complete vision of loveliness, my dear.'

To which Catherine had replied, 'Thank you, my dearest love. How handsome you also look.'

Montague Alexander Carlile had indeed been, at this time in his life, a handsome man standing of six foot in height within a thin yet erect frame and possessed of a full and extremely well-coiffured head and beard of sandy-coloured hair which had of recent times started to grey slightly. His face had been a picture of his ruddy good nature and his dark brown eyes had shone with happiness on this special day.

'Are you ready to take our leave and journey to Victoria, my new wife?' Montague had enquired.

'Yes, Montague dear, as soon as we have concluded the social requirements with our guests downstairs,' a radiant Catherine had replied.

'Very well, my dearest love, we will continue downstairs to our guests, who no doubt will bid us a fond farewell and a safe onward journey to Venice upon our honeymoon,' Montague had beamed at his new bride of but a few hours.

So it had been that Montague and Catherine had ventured forth back to the great function room of this grand hotel. This had been a most picturesque room having been decorated in peach and white lilies in keeping with the pastel colour of the bridesmaids' and flower girls' gowns and indeed the floral arrangements in the cathedral itself.

With all the social requirements completed, the guests had processioned the newly wed couple to the main entrance of the hotel where Montague's carriage had awaited and had sent them on their way in a hail of rice and a shower of good wishes for their honeymoon and their forthcoming life together.

Once they had settled themselves in the carriage and been on their way, the thought had occurred to Montague that this had been the first time since he had met Catherine in Vienna, all those months ago, that he had ever been allowed time with her completely alone. This time in itself, however, would be short-lived as in the carriage following behind had been their ever-present servants Gladys and Collins who would accompany them on this most personal of life's events – their honeymoon. However, such had been the convention of the times in which they had lived and who would Montague have been to try and change that. Indeed, would he really have desired to anyway? He had thought not.

As they had travelled through the London early evening traffic towards their target of Victoria Station, there had lingered in Montague's mind a doubt which had had its birth that torturous night at his gentleman's club when the topic of his fathering a child had so impolitely been raised by some dubious members of the Sovereign Club. The greatest wedding gift which Catherine could have bestowed upon him had been to allow him to become a father at the earliest opportunity. This Catherine had led him to believe, in the most discreet of terms, had also been her dearest desire. The remembrance of this assurance instantly had laid to rest any melancholy thoughts Montague may have held on this matter and had brought him once more back to the world around him and the beautiful lady who had sat so composedly beside him.

The carriage, having fought its way through the fierce London traffic, had finally arrived at its destination, that of the bustling convergence that was Victoria Station. As Montague and Catherine had alighted from their carriage, the carriage which had been following closely behind throughout the journey from the hotel had been reined in behind and their travelling party had been made complete by the inclusion of Gladys and Collins into their lives. Both Catherine and Montague had been once again thrown into this hubbub of life, after the comparative silence of their recent carriage journey.

Montague had at once sent Collins in search of a railway porter to convey to their appropriate place the numerous pieces of baggage which they had required for this momentous journey, whilst Catherine, on the other hand, had requested Gladys to go in search of, from the railway bookstall, the various newspapers and journals both Montague and herself had required to occupy their free time on the train journey to Venice.

Having duly found the bookstall and the railway porter (who in turn had consigned most of their leather-clad luggage to the care of his attendant junior and forthwith onwards to the porter's van at the rear of the train for the duration of the trip), the small party had proceeded forth speedily under the direction of this most efficient porter to their allotted compartments aboard this most magnificent of current-day railway engineering achievements. Catherine and Montague had adjacent compartments with a connecting door in one of the first-class sleeping cars and Gladys and Collins each had a shared sleeping compartment in one of the second-class sleeping cars. Montague still remembered how gleaming and new everything about this impressive brown and beige train had appeared. Indeed, it had been on the rails for only a short time and had been discussed in the recent press as the benchmark upon which all subsequent railway services would be judged for many years to come.

As he had settled himself into what had been about to be his home away from home for the next few days, he had remarked to himself how full of class and refinement the accoutrements of this sleeping compartment had been. It had a very comfortable saloon chair and table which, upon the time arriving to retire to bed later in the evening, had been folded away by the steward to reveal an equally comfortable bed with full linen and bedding requirements in position. Also, for his personal comfort, Montague had found a folding washstand and upon further investigation of the carriage the most modern of public conveniences in such a mode of transport as this, a water closet. Montague, his Scottish thrift still evident all those many years since his departure from his highland home of youth, thereby had felt assured that the high price he had had to pay to secure this passage to Venice for Catherine and himself had been well worth it. Here had been a train in keeping with their shared station in life.

As the time had neared for the train to depart, Montague had finished the organisation of his own private travel affairs from his valise and briefcase and had gently knocked upon the connecting door, bidding Catherine to allow him enter her compartment.

Immediately, from within, had come the refined response of 'Come in' from Catherine's delicate lips, which Montague had responded to rapidly by pushing down on the doorknob and quietly opening the door to reveal the view before him of Catherine seated serenely beside the compartment window looking devotedly in the direction of the opening door.

'Have you completed the organising of your travel requirements, Catherine, my dear?' Montague had enquired in the most loving of tones.

'Yes, thank you, my darling. All is in its proper place in this our little home away from home. Anything more to be attended to, I am sure I may leave in the ever-capable hands of my maid, Gladys,' Catherine had replied, aware of the immense pride which had been contained in Montague's voice as he had spoken to her.

'I, too, shall leave any further attendance to my travel affairs to my man, Collins. That being the case, would you care to take a stroll up to the saloon car and partake of an aperitif before we return to our respective compartments to dress for dinner?' had enquired Montague of his beautiful wife of but a few hours.

Catherine had been astute enough to realise that this enquiry had been more by way of a request on Montague's part to be allowed at the earliest opportunity to be seen with and to exhibit Catherine in the fondest possible way to the public at large, as one would any precious and sparkling jewel, for this had been how Montague had viewed the addition of Catherine to his life.

'That would be most enjoyable, my dear,' had been Catherine's enthusiastic reply.

With that, they had made their way out of Catherine's compartment along the narrow carriage passageway through the door connecting their carriage with the next carriage, which by good fortune had contained the saloon and across the threshold into the luxurious surroundings of this car. An atmosphere of true beauty and refinement had greeted their senses as they had moved further into the body of this car, with a mixture of intricately carved wood panelling and inlaid engraved mirrored sections on the walls giving greater depth and creating an ambience of lightness and life to what could have been a dark, dead den.

As they had settled themselves into the plush and deeply cushioned chairs which had been arranged around a large, glass-topped table situated beside a large carriage window, the engine of this majestic train had fired into action effortlessly and relatively quietly moving this huge snake-like train away from the platform and out of Victoria Station.

Noting the movement of the train, Montague had turned in his seat taking his vision away from the kaleidoscope of views which had been his beloved city of London and had said to Catherine, 'Well, my love, at last we are on our way to Venice.'

To which Catherine had replied joyously in almost childlike awe and wonder, 'What a lovely trip lies in store for us, from London through Paris, Zurich, Innsbruck, Verona and finally on to Venice,' reciting almost in a parrot-like fashion the travel information she had devoured from the brochures which Montague had obtained from Cook's.

'Yes, Catherine, my dear lady, it will, I hope, only be in keeping with the fine life we are going to enjoy together,' Montague had replied with a degree of feeling which had appeared to come from the deepest recesses of his heart.

While they had both sat briefly contemplating their private views of what their new life together would hold, Montague had registered a slight movement at his elbow and had looked up to find an immaculately liveried steward standing beside their table waiting zealously to take their request for refreshments,

'May I be of assistance, sir, by offering sir and madam some refreshments from the bar?' the steward had eagerly enquired of Montague.

'Yes, thank you, steward,' Montague had replied and, turning towards Catherine who had been seated across the table opposite him, had enquired of her, 'What would you care to drink, my dear?'

'I would appreciate greatly a small glass of Madeira, thank you, Montague,' had replied Catherine in the most genteel of tones, to which Montague had gallantly responded, 'Very well, you shall indeed have as you request, my dear,' and turning his attention once again towards the attentive steward had issued, in his usual businesslike manner, the following order,

'Steward, please bring my wife a glass of Madeira and a single malt with a dash of water for myself.'

'Very good, sir,' the steward had simply answered and, briskly turning on the heel of his highly polished black leather shoes, had immediately returned to behind the long glass and brass bar which had been positioned along part of the opposite wall of the carriage, poured and concocted their refreshments and had returned post haste. Having deposited the glasses deftly on the silver coasters in front of each of them the steward had again silently and briskly departed upon his numerous other appointed duties within the seemingly spacious car.

Montague had then focused his attention on the discreet observation of the other occupants of the saloon car. Within the car, there had been a dozen or so tables with their accompanying chairs assembled at equal intervals along the length of one side of the car, the bar facilities having taken up half of the opposite side of the roomy car, with the remaining space beside the bar taken up by an array of individually positioned plush and thickly padded chairs for those patrons who had required a more intimate or solitary atmosphere in which to consume their refreshments.

It had thus been observed by Montague that, at this time in the early evening, apart from Catherine and himself, there had been five other people in this first-class saloon car. An elderly gentleman of retired military appearance had been seated by himself in one of the solitary plush chairs engrossed in his own thoughts and the enjoyment of what had appeared to Montague to be a rather large gin and tonic; further along the car Montague had observed the four other occupants who had been seated together at a table two away from Catherine and himself. To Montague's keen eye, they had been two sets of middle-aged couples who had known each other and had either been travelling together or, by some coincidence, had found each other on the same train; in any case, pleasingly to Montague's ever-watchful and keen gaze, they had all given the appearance of great wealth and position, having been happily engaged in the consumption of a bottle of fine champagne during the witnessed exchange of views in an apparently animated conversation.

Having established in his mind and been pleased with the

social standard of the company that he and Catherine would be travelling in for the next few days, Montague's attention had again returned to that of his new wife who, during his time spent quickly reviewing the other passengers, these strangers who would now play the somewhat intimate role of their travelling companions for the next few days, had sat with her glass of Madeira in hand looking out of the expansive glass window beside her at the ever-changing views of a rapidly disappearing London.

'You look positively radiant, my dearest love, you do not appear to be showing any signs of tiredness or strain from the effort of the proceedings of today,' Montague had espoused with great depth of intense feeling in his strong, deep voice which had still held the lilt of a Scots accent.

'Thank you, Montague, for those most kind words. I fear, however, that the same cannot be said on my part, as to my eyes, you appear somewhat tired in body if not spirit. Would you care to return to your compartment and partake of a short rest before dinner?' had queried Catherine with guarded concern, having been aware at this point in this most emotional day of the obvious difference in their age and state of well-being.

'Yes, thank you, Catherine my dear. I believe I will, with your kind permission, avail myself of the luxury of a short rest before the proceedings of dinner,' Montague had quietly responded.

'You will not be too bored by my absence from your side, I hope, my dearest,' Montague had further asked, a touch concerned that he may have been seen by Catherine as abandoning her too soon into their married life.

'No, Montague, I will appreciate the time to commence with the correspondence of letters of thank you to our wedding guests for their treasured company on this most auspicious day and, of course, their fine gifts and the good wishes they showered us with,' Catherine had diplomatically responded.

With that exchange of thoughts and deeds on the respective parts of this newly married couple, they had risen from their table, exited the saloon car and made the return journey along the narrow carriage passageway back to their adjoining compartments and their separate pursuits...

Time travelled on in Montague's mind. How well he remembered the joy which he had experienced during the train journey. The admirable food and wine and the excellent company of their travelling companions he had found in the other passengers had been heightened by the ever-caring and constant companionship and affection of Catherine.

The hours had passed by rapidly, as had the panorama of the cities they had travelled through, cities such as Paris with its numerous churches and cathedrals, such as the Cathédrale de Notre-Dame, the Cathedral of Paris, and the Basilique du Sacré-Cœur or Basilica of the Sacred Heart of Jesus, Zurich with its shimmering waters of the Lake of Zurich, Innsbruck nestled in the Inn River valley and surrounded by the Austrian Alps, Verona with such noteworthy architectural landmarks as the Gothic Dominican Church of St Anastasia along with many other fine examples of medieval and renaissance architecture and the ever-changing and picturesque countryside the train had passed through on its swift passage onwards to its destination in the glorious city of Venice.

Having arrived in Venice late in the afternoon of the fourth day since leaving their home city of London, both Catherine and Montague had been grateful to bid farewell to the relatively closed confines of this most magnificent example of mechanical engineering and had looked forward expectantly to experiencing the splendour that Venice had held in store for them. Again, Montague had offered up silent prayers of thanks and had been grateful for the position in life he had found himself, having had the finances and knowledge to make reservations for his party at one of the finest private hotels in Venice situated on the picturesque Canale di San Marco, overlooking the Isola di San Giorgio Maggiore.

Having left the transportation to the hotel of their baggage in the capable hands of Collins and Gladys, Montague and Catherine had decided to take the first opportunity which had presented itself to them to explore this city of enchantment that had been Venice by partaking of a gentle stroll from the railway station to their hotel. Upon leaving the station, both Catherine's and Montague's initial reaction to the scenery that had greeted their eyes had been one of sheer delight at its colour and beauty. The couple had strolled through the myriad of narrow streets, filled to overflowing by shops and markets with vendors all plying their wares to the passing throng of residents and visitors alike, unable to take in at once all that their senses had been experiencing. Their stroll having taken them past and through such landmarks as St Mark's Square and Basilica, the Ducal Palace and the Bridge of Sighs had finally delivered them to the Riva degli Schiavoni and the grand entrance to their hotel which had been proclaimed to all by two immense ornamental winged lions, the emblem of Venice, crafted in pristine white marble.

As they had entered, Montague had resumed his businesslike manner once more and had escorted Catherine with great mindful purpose and an air of incalculable pride across the expanse of the hotel foyer to the reception desk to be greeted cheerily by the clerk behind the counter with the response of, 'Buon pomeriggio, Signor e Signora.'

To which Montague had responded, 'Good afternoon, my good man, do you speak English?'

The clerk having responded in the affirmative, Montague had replied in his strong commanding voice, 'My name is Carlile, Montague Carlile to be precise. Have the rest of my party arrived from the station yet?'

'Si, yes, sir, your valet and lady's maid are awaiting your arrival in the suite we have reserved for you, which is situated on the first floor overlooking the lagoon, the Imperial Suite.'

With that exchange and the subsequent signing of the leather-bound and gold-embossed register completed, the dark complexioned clerk had tapped a small silver bell over which his hand had been hovering for part of the previous conversation and a young boy attired in hotel livery rich in gold braid and tassels had appeared at Montague's side. The clerk behind the desk having quickly issued instructions to the boy in his native tongue had turned his attention once more towards Montague and Catherine and had said, 'Mr Carlile, if you and your wife would please follow this boy, he will show you to your suite.'

To which Montague had replied, as he had moved away from the carved dark wood desk to escort Catherine in following this hotel pageboy, 'Thank you, my man.'

Montague always having been mindful of his humble begin-ning in life had been ever ready to thank the people around him for the successful completion of any task required of them by him.

Having followed the young boy away from the reception desk Montague and Catherine had found themselves again traversing the foyer toward its central feature, that of an imposing pink and green marble staircase which in a dramatic curve had swept upwards from the middle of the foyer to the first floor in a lavish display of the Venetian opulence which had been the hallmark of this lagoon side hotel.

As they had ascended the staircase, Montague had again been struck with a sense of great pride and wonderment at the position in life he had now found himself. As he stole a glance beside at the lady Catherine, his new wife, the thought had crossed his mind, had this really happened to him or had he to wake soon and find that all had been a wonderful dream, for here he had been with this goddess of beauty on his arm in the city named in honour of the goddess of love about to participate in the most intimate of life's pleasures, their honeymoon.

Montague had quickly been returned from his private thoughts by the thin voice of the young pageboy, 'Per favore, Signor e Signora,' as he had beckoned to Montague and Catherine to enter through a doorway, having led them from the staircase along half the length of a red-carpeted hallway to an impressive teak-coloured door which upon it had been emblazoned in gold letter the pronouncement of it to be the entrance to the Imperial Suite. Having bade Montague and his new bride entry, the young boy had passed a gold key to Montague and had disappeared as silently as he had appeared.

The massive dimensions of this, their lodgings for the next week, had become apparent as they had moved further into the suite. For within these walls had been housed palatial sleeping quarters for Montague and Catherine which had consisted of a shared bedroom containing among its accoutrements a seven-foot brass bed and a private balcony which had afforded them some of the most magnificent views of Venice and its life on the water.

Placed on either side of this room had been adjoining rooms which had formed Catherine's private boudoir and Montague's dressing room, each with separate day accommodation and the most modern of toilet facilities. Adjacent to this main bedroom had been the respective bedrooms for their attendants, Collins and Gladys, all these rooms having taken up half of the total space within the suite, the other portion of space had been taken up by a moderately sized private dining room and serving pantry and an equally moderately sized drawing room with a balcony, access to which had been gained through a pair of intricately engraved Venetian glass doors.

This balcony overlooking the Riva degli Schiavoni with its waves of promenading couples had acted as a magnet to Catherine. It had been to this balcony situated off the drawing room that Catherine had eagerly ventured, again demonstrating an almost childlike wonderment and uncharacteristic disregard of everything around her as she had called back over her petite shoulder towards Montague who had remained to this point within the genteel and protected confines of the suite.

'Oh, Montague, my dearest love, come and view this most glorious of scenes,' she said.

Caught up in a wave of infectious enthusiasm which had appeared to have been generated by Catherine, Montague had willingly joined his wife on the balcony to view this passing parade of Venetian life which somehow appeared to his mind to have had the effect of filling him with a sense of energy and joy of life he had not previously felt. From their balcony, as dusk had been rapidly descending, they had viewed the magical lifescape of Venice, the flotillas of gondolas in their somewhat solemn black livery plying back and forth across the lagoon from the islands, maybe going to Murano, renowned for its glass works since the late 1200s or, on a more sombre note, the cemetery island of San Michele and directly adjacent to their view from the hotel, the island of San Giorgio Maggiore with its striking white palladian church of San Giorgio.

'This is the most enchanting of views, my dearest. How very pleased I am that we chose Venice to place the final seal upon our marriage through the enjoyment of this, our honeymoon,'

Catherine had espoused with great sincerity and warmth of feeling.

'It pleases me greatly that you find this city so much to your liking and so soon into our time here, Catherine, my dear,' Montague had replied as he had adroitly escorted Catherine away from the balcony and had returned them both to the warmth and security of the suite, mindful of the rapidly descending night air and fearful of the effects of its coolness upon his young bride's health. How ironic Montague now thought it had been of his predisposition to worry so of Catherine's health over and above that of his own, how the years had come to show the error of his ways.

How well Montague now remembered the pleasure both he and Catherine had experienced during their all too short stay in this city of Venice which they, themselves, came to refer to in later days as the Jewel of the Adriatic. The days had flown by having been filled with numerous walking tours, as, with guide book in hand, this newly married couple had taken in the splendours of this city upon the waters. Landmarks which they had passed by on their initial stroll the afternoon of their arrival in Venice had been revisited in more detail as the week had progressed, such points of interest as the Piazza San Marco, more commonly known as St Mark's Square, the mighty open-air meeting place for the citizens of Venice with its dramatic white pavement design dating back to 1723, St Mark's Basilica, more commonly referred to by the populace of Venice as the Basilica di San Marco, with its colourful and detailed mosaics decoration built in 829 to house the earthly remains of St Mark the Evangelist who had become the patron saint of this unique city, the glorious treasures of the Palazzo Ducale or ducal palace with its famous Venetian marble work facade and the intricately worked Ponte dei Sospiri, or Bridge of Sighs, which had led from the Prigioni della Paglia or prisons to the Palazzo Ducale; the name had been said to be derived from the prisoners' sighs as they had passed over the bridge on their way to or from the Inquisitors. Another of the many pleasures of their honeymoon had been the experience of a magical gondola ride across the lagoon and the viewing of the glass-blowing artisans of Murano. Accompanying their sightseeing endeavours, Catherine and Montague had filled their days and nights with sampling the finest cuisine that Venice had to offer with the resultant flavours and aromas of the various seafood dishes alone having been unlike anything either had experienced before.

They had partaken of coffee on the final morning, seated at a small white marble table, under a white canvas awning on their drawing-room balcony, overlooking the passing parade of pedestrians promenading along the lagoon-side pavement under a radiantly clear blue sky as it had been for the entire week. Catherine had turned to look at Montague who had also been seated so as to observe this vista of passionate life which they had come to realise had been at the very heart of this pulsating city.

As she had looked across to Montague, Catherine had said in her whisper of a voice, 'My dearest Montague, what a wonderful time we have spent here in this Jewel of the Adriatic. I almost wish that our time here would not come to an end. It has been like an enchanted dream from which I do not wish to wake.'

'Yes, my dear, it has been a most enchanting time spent in this most glorious of cities, which for myself has been heightened so much by the exquisite pleasure of your company and the blessed realisation that this is but the first taste of what our life together shall be,' Montague in his sonorous Scots timbre had passionately replied.

This final day had passed by, as had many of the others of this mystical time in this the city of love, with Catherine and Montague strolling arm in arm through the maze of alleyways festooned with numerous and varied hanging baskets of flowers resplendent in delightful colour. Everything about this city had impressed upon these visitors the vibrant nature of its heart, a vibrancy which had had its effect on Montague, dispelling from his mind any previously and privately held thoughts that this marriage may have been a mistake on his part. Had he indeed been in some form of dream state induced by the magic of this most romantic city, only time would tell and how it had told only too acutely.

With their final hours having flown by, Catherine and Montague had returned to their suite within the hotel and had made their travel preparations for departure from Venice on that evening's train. These preparations had as usual been conducted with the assistance of their ever-devoted servants, Collins and Gladys who had, during this time away from London, themselves enjoyed a certain relaxation in the formal state of their position and duties, having been granted permission from their master and mistress respectively to venture forth from the confines of the hotel in each other's protective company and had experienced much of the atmosphere of this most peculiar of cities. The appreciation of this action on the part of their employers had had the usually emotionless Collins animatedly espousing to his master as he had conducted the time-honoured duties of valet under Montague's watchful eye in the confines of his dressing room that June afternoon. As protocol and position had dictated, Collins had waited for his master to open the conversation which Montague had done with the words, 'The mistress and I sincerely hope that you and Gladys have found pleasure in the activities you have experienced in this most curious of cities.'

'Most assuredly, sir, I think I may speak on behalf of Gladys and say that this has been an experience neither of us will ever forget. We are both most grateful for the opportunity that you and the new mistress have granted us in requiring our services for this most important time abroad,' Collins had enthusiastically replied.

'It pleases me greatly to hear that you have both found enjoyment in the simple pleasures of this beautiful city and might I add in each other's discreet company. To the mistress and myself it is very important that our newly united household performs its duties harmoniously,' Montague had tactfully replied, eager to gauge the initial feelings of the head of his about to be changed domestic household, having now spent some time in the company of what would be a valued member of the inner circle of senior servants residing below stairs.

'May I say, sir, that having spent most of this time abroad in the company of Gladys in either a professional or a discreetly personal capacity, I have found her to be a most diligent and honest person possessed of a compassionate and kindly nature who, I feel sure, will be of continuing great assistance to the new mistress and thereby to me in the smooth management of your household,' Collins had replied with words which had held an unmistakable undercurrent of newly discovered affection and respect for this stout Yorkshire maid.

With the conclusion of this exchange of observations, the travel preparations had been completed and the travelling party had again re-grouped in the drawing room of the suite in readiness for departing the hotel and retracing their steps to the train station.

Montague had again resumed his most businesslike demeanour, issuing forth the following requests and commands to his staff, 'All the preparations for our return journey this evening to London have been completed have they not, Collins?'

With this request from Montague, Collins for the first time as a senior servant in his master's household had had to look towards another for confirmation that all had indeed been in order as he had quickly passed an enquiring glance in the direction of Gladys who, with the slight inclination of her flaxen-haired head, had assured Collins that all had indeed been in order in her mistress's affairs.

'Yes, sir, everything is indeed in order for our return to London tonight,' Collins had replied with resolution.

Montague had then turned his attention towards Catherine who, during Montague's discourse with Collins, had been standing at the glass doors which had given access from the drawing room to the balcony taking one final look at the dusk-lit cityscape which they had come so clearly to know as Venice.

'Are you ready to venture forth to the station now, my beloved?' Montague had lovingly enquired of this woman who had showered upon him during their most intimate times together as husband and wife such a level of passionate pleasure during their honeymoon as he simply as a man had never ventured to dream of experiencing.

'If this time must come to an end then, yes, I am ready to return to London consoled in the knowledge that this has been but a taste of what our life together shall be,' Catherine had replied eager to express to this her new husband of but a few days the profound joy she had experienced in Venice in his most protective and loving company.

With these words and a nod of acknowledgement towards

Collins, Montague had escorted Catherine from the suite, negotiated the grand pink and green marble staircase and had conducted his concluding business with the clerk behind the reception desk. Having left the transportation of their luggage and their staff in the capable hands of Collins, Montague had then gently guided Catherine through the impressive entrance and past the winged lions in their act of silent sentry duty of the hotel to the quayside where a gondola and its master the gondolier had been waiting to ferry this loving couple on a leisurely candlelit ride through the network of canals to their destination of the train station.

'What a truly fitting way to bring to its conclusion this most marvellous of times, my love,' Catherine had beamed, completely enraptured by the deep and singular consciousness of thought for her exclusive pleasure and well-being that Montague had displayed throughout this time together.

'It is only right and proper that one so full of beauty, love and romance such as you, my dearest sweetness, should be conveyed in the most romantic means available,' Montague had replied simply as they had settled themselves into the gondola's comfortable seats and their cruise had begun.

As they had proceeded along the darkened canals, the light escaping from the windows of the houses they had passed had enshrouded Catherine and Montague in a pulsating mist of light that had to Montague resembled the action of a massive heart pumping its blood of life energy around the body which had been – this Jewel of the Adriatic – Venice. Catherine and Montague had become part of this body, if only temporarily, and now had appeared as it had been to have received as its parting gesture to them, the final injection of enthusiasm for life that this city could offer them.

Upon completion of this rare experience, Montague and Catherine had found Collins and Gladys awaiting their arrival at the station, Collins having arranged the storage of the luggage and the travel requirements of his master and Gladys that of her mistress within their adjoining first-class sleeping compartments. Both had conducted their duties with the consummate ease that their years in service had afforded them. Montague had subsequently dispatched Collins and Gladys to take their respective positions in their second-class cars, as he had politely escorted Catherine to their sleeping quarters for the return journey home to their beloved London.

This journey had been uneventful, with both Catherine and Montague having been intent upon gathering their own respective and private thoughts of the organisation of their soon to be newly shared home and domestic household. The hours dashed by with great rapidness until the moment had come that they had been greeted upon their arrival again at Victoria by the ever dutiful coachman, Barnes, and had been conveyed back to what had now constituted their shared home in Witton Place. In their absence abroad, Montague's Chaster Square gentleman's residence had been cleared of its contents and most of its staff except for a caretaker in preparation for its sale, the couple having decided to keep only two properties operational. That of – prior to her marriage and now subsequently Montague's possession – Catherine's Witton Place, Knightsbridge, residence as their London city address and Montague's country estate of Carlile Manor, Marlford, as their country seat.

As they had ventured across the threshold of their London home, Catherine and Montague had been greeted by the assemblage of their newly united domestic household which had stood as a credit to both Montague's and Catherine's organisational and diplomatic skills. With both Montague's and Catherine's stubborn spirit of determination, self-evidenced by the fact that none of their loyal and devoted staff had had their services terminated, some of the staff however had been given the option of transferring to the country estate while others had chosen at their time in life to retire from service, unable to cope with what they had described as the stresses placed upon the mind by this new regime. Thus, before Montague and Catherine had stood a happy yet respectful group – their household – which had consisted of the following:

Butler/valet – Collins (from Montague's old household)
Housekeeper – Mrs Burns (from Catherine's old household)
Lady's maid – Gladys (from Catherine's old household)

Footman – Joseph (from Montague's old household)
Coachman – Barnes (from Montague's old household)
Parlourmaid – Mary (from Montague's old household)
Housemaid – Alice (from Catherine's old household)
Chef – M. Pavot (from Catherine's old household)
Kitchen maid – Helen (from Catherine's old household)
Scullery maid – Annie (from Catherine's old household)
Bootboy – Tommy (from Montague's old household)
Groom – Harris (from Montague's old household).

Mrs Burns, the angular-faced housekeeper, having been the senior member of staff left in attendance during Collins's absence abroad, had stepped forward and issued forth with the following words, 'Welcome home, sir and madam. We trust that you had a pleasant and safe time abroad and we wish good luck upon this house and all who live under its roof.'

To which Montague had responded in a warm rich voice, 'Thank you, Mrs Burns, for your good wishes and your kind words of welcome. Both the mistress and I wish you all to look upon this house as your home and all who live in it with you as your family. May this again be a house filled with immeasurable joy and happiness for all.' How prophetic those words now appeared to Montague. Had he somehow placed a curse upon his own life by the disclosure of these passionate thoughts.

So it had been with a feeling of great expectations for their life ahead that Catherine and Montague had settled into this house. The weeks had flown by as Montague had returned to his formal work habit within the city and Catherine had busied herself with the fine adjustment of her household.

All had appeared to have settled into a smooth working routine. Catherine and Montague had been joyously happy in their life together until a day about ten months into their married life when, upon rising from her bed one morning, Catherine had collapsed, suffering an acute sensation of lightness of head. Being only a momentary lapse, she had thought nothing more of it until the same sensation had afflicted her in Montague's presence. One evening, upon mounting the stairs to retire early to her bed, having spent an exhausting day amidst the hustle and bustle of

Regent Street shopping, Catherine had again been overcome by an intense feeling of dizziness. If not for Montague's quick presence of mind in supporting Catherine in his strong arms, serious harm may have come to her in the form of a nasty fall upon the solid white marble staircase.

Having carried Catherine to her boudoir, Montague had enquired, with great concern edging his deep masculine voice, 'Has this type of attack afflicted you before, my dearest?'

Catherine had replied in a slight whisper, 'Only once before, my love, the morning after the late evening we experienced at the opera last week. I reasoned it to be a slight case of exhaustion and thought nothing more of it until now.'

'You must go to bed and rest, my dear. I will ring for Gladys to come and assist you. Further to that I will send Collins to fetch the doctor in the morning,' Montague had commanded with an unmistakable air of authority in his deep voice which had left Catherine in no doubt as to his control of the situation and her own response to that control.

'If you think it will be best, Montague, my dearest. I will do as you command,' Catherine had replied meekly.

So it had been that Catherine had, with the ever-dutiful assistance of Gladys, been helped to her bed to endure a somewhat fretful night's sleep. With the morning had come the arrival of Dr Morris, the man possessed of an ever-cheerful disposition, who had been Catherine's physician since her birth.

After his examination of Catherine, he had sought out Montague in his library and had opened the conversation as follows, 'If I were to wish you congratulations, my dear fellow, I would not be out of order.'

Montague had looked up from his desk with a somewhat bemused look upon his face and had replied with a touch of fire in his voice, 'Congratulations for a wife who is ill in bed, that, sir, I find a very strange form of response from such a highly credited man of medicine as yourself.'

'Calm yourself, man, do I have to spell it out for you in plain English. Your dear wife is with child, your first-born child and the heir to all you command. There, does that allay your worst fears for the safety of your beloved wife?' the patient Dr Morris had responded.

'Oh, Doctor, what wonderful news. I do so apologise for my lack of mental capacity in this matter, but the night has hung heavy for me with worry, and the thought of possibly losing my beloved Catherine,' Montague had proffered as his excuse for his apparently mindless conduct.

'Think nothing more about that, my dear fellow. Catherine is essentially fit and well for a woman in her position. However, now that you are aware of her condition it would be best if she were convinced to limit the activities she enters into for the time being at least, until her body has come to term with what is happening to it,' Dr Morris had intently requested.

'Rest assured, Dr Morris, I give you my word that Catherine will not be allowed to overtire herself again,' Montague had forcefully responded.

So, having bade farewell to Dr Morris with heartfelt words of thanks for all his assistance, Montague had rushed to the bedroom he had shared with Catherine, dispensing with the normal protocol of knocking before entering. Montague had flung himself upon his knees on the floor at Catherine's bedside. Having lovingly taken her two small hands in his, kissing each in turn, Montague had turned his head so as to look directly into her milk green eyes and had said, 'My dearest love, Catherine, how proud you have made me on this day, no more precious gift could you have bestowed upon me as this, the prospect of our child.'

Catherine had responded lovingly, 'Oh, Montague, my darling, what joy it gives me to see you so happy this day…'

With those words still freshly revolving in Montague's mind, a sharp sound had pierced the security of his reverie, a sound which had returned him from his altered state of consciousness. Quickly, his mind had recognised the sound and immediately had responded to the knock upon his library door, this his sole domain, by bidding this intruder entry with the unusually curtly spoken command, 'Enter.'

With the issuing of this command, the library door had flung open and upon the threshold of the room had stood the very plain parlourmaid, Mary. In a slightly dishevelled and upset state she had stepped forward and had opened her large rather coarse-looking mouth to speak, only to have a jumbled cascade of words pour forth from her lips.

'Sir, Mr Collins sent me to tell you. He would have come himself, but he had to go with Barnes to fetch the doctor,' she said.

In his slightly confused state, Montague had not at first grasped the full meaning of these words, evidenced by him somewhat coldly asking, 'Is someone ill below stairs, partaken of their Boxing Day festivities a little too heartily, perhaps? If so, why do you bother me with these household problems, Mary? I am sure Mr Collins and Mrs Burns are quite capable of taking care of the situation,' he said.

To which Mary, having been fully aware of her position in the house, had politely replied to her master, 'Oh no, sir, I must have said things the wrong way. It is nobody downstairs that is sick. It is the mistress herself that is taken ill. Mrs Burns and Gladys say that the baby is coming, so they sent Mr Collins off to fetch Dr Morris, quick smart like. They are both with the mistress now. Even as they say that this is no time for a husband to be poking his nose in woman's business, they sent me up here to tell you anyway.'

As if in a dream, Montague had not truly heard, let alone comprehended what this slip of a girl had just told him, a fact which had been blatantly apparent by his response of, 'It surely cannot be the baby coming yet. The doctor told the mistress only last week that it would be another two weeks at least.'

To which Mary, as she had prepared to take her leave of Montague, had replied with words of experience far beyond her apparent years, 'The baby will come in its own good time, whatever the doctor has said on the matter.'

With that, Montague had instructed Mary to inform Collins when he returned from fetching the doctor that he wished to be kept informed of proceedings and he had sent the parlourmaid on her way back downstairs. The time had dragged on, hour after hour, with Collins ferrying reports from Dr Morris to the effect that all had been proceeding slowly but surely on its way until, finally, there had come again a knock upon the library door and there upon it being opened had stood Collins in stern accompaniment to Dr Morris.

'Dr Morris wishes to speak with you, sir. May I show him in?' Collins had queried in his usual calm and emotionless voice, thereby not disclosing to Montague any hint of what the state of affairs had been with the mistress of the house.

'By all means, Collins, show the good Dr Morris in immediately,' Montague had stated in a voice cracking with rich emotion.

As the doctor had stepped across the threshold of the library, he had thrust out his hand grasping and shaking Montague's vigorously and with a broad smile appearing upon his cheerful face had issued forth with the words, 'Congratulations, Carlile. You are indeed a very fortunate man. Catherine has delivered unto you this day a healthy, baby boy. Mother and son are a picture of health…'

Part Two

Danger and Despair

As Montague now sat looking with unseeing eyes at the view displayed from his library window of the splendid September day which beheld itself to his unwanted pleasure, the demons possessing his mind returned his thoughts to another September day some fifteen years previously...

'Carlile, Montague Carlile, my dear friend, how good it is to see you again. It seems much time has passed by since we have had the pleasure of your company in the country and more particularly at the hunt,' had been the opening response from Lord Rupert Penman-Smythe, as he had recognised and acknowledged Montague as they had passed in the teak-panelled corridor of the London office of Barland Bank.

'Your lordship, how pleased I am to see you once more and yes, it is some considerable time since my family and I were last in residence at Carlile Manor. The only excuse, on my part, I can offer to you in my defence is extreme pressure of work, having spent much time of late abroad dealing with the ever-expanding business of this most buoyant financial institution. With my extended absences from home, my wife Catherine prefers to remain resident in London. Further to this, whilst our young son, Reginald Alexander, is still within his formative years, Catherine is most adamant that his private tutoring in his studies must take precedence over all else without, in her opinion, any unnecessary distractions until his eventual and, again in Catherine's opinion, unwarranted departure to my old school, Mendrew,' Montague had tactfully explained.

'That may be all well and good in a woman's eye. However, it is my considered opinion that it does not do a boy good to be too cosseted in his mother's affections,' Lord Rupert had boomed in his foghorn-like voice, a constant reminder to all of his former military life.

'Too much book learning and too little fresh air and open space can do harm to the growth of a boy,' his lordship had proffered as his 'expert' opinion on the raising of boys having had only one girl of his own.

'Where is his father's love of the hunt, the thrill of the chase, the wind blowing in your face and your favourite hunter safely beneath you?' Lord Rupert had further queried.

Montague had not had time to reply before the booming voice had let forth once again with the following question, 'Are you free of social activities and commitments the weekend after next?'

Quickly Montague had retrieved his diary from the sheaths of papers he had been carrying to his office and having consulted the relevant dates he replied in the following words, 'Yes, your lordship, it would appear that my family's social calendar is vacant for that weekend.'

'Good, then I suggest that for the good of all concerned, myself included, you retain that weekend for the September Hunt across the downs of Marlford and the subsequent Hunt Ball at Beeches Hall. I seem to recall that it was at one such ball, some years previously, that you proposed the act of marriage to Catherine. May I suggest that your assistance in the remembrance of the fact by your good lady wife should be enough to encourage her no doubt romantic nature to agree to this country encounter. It would also give your boy his first taste of real country life and further to that it would clear your head of all its boardroom stuffiness; indeed, I believe it would be good for your health.'

Good for your health, how these words would in the years to come return to Montague's mind as a constant reminder of the curse this man had placed upon his beloved family.

'Very good, your lordship, rest assured I will do all in my power to ensure our attendance at Carlile Manor for that weekend,' Montague had eagerly responded, keenly aware of the hidden inference in Lord Rupert's request, Montague being in full realisation of the financial power the Earl had wielded within the bank, Lord Rupert being one of its major shareholders.

With the final words of 'Good man', the Right Hon. the Eighth Earl of Marlford, Lord Rupert Henry Penman-Smythe, had withdrawn his rather nondescript frame down the corridor and out of view from Montague, leaving Montague with a rather cold feeling of foreboding which he had not comprehended then but, later, had seen as an ominous premonition of what life had held in store.

Upon returning to the Witton Place residence he had shared as man and wife with Catherine for the past ten years or so, Montague had been greeted at the opening of the black front door by his ever dutiful butler, Collins, whom he had greeted with the same words he had used each evening for all of those many years, Montague having been a creature of extreme habit.

'Good evening, Collins, is all well in my household tonight?' Montague enquired as he divested himself of his briefcase of banking papers to its usual resting place beside the hall table, as had always been his custom.

To which Collins, with his same lack of any outward sign of emotion which he had displayed throughout his many years of faithful service to Montague, had replied in his monotonous voice which had to Montague always resembled that of an undertaker, 'Good evening, sir, all is in order in your household tonight. The mistress is in the drawing room, awaiting your arrival home from the city. Master Reginald, no doubt, will be found in the school-room about to complete another day of studies with his governess.

'Thank you, Collins,' Montague had replied as he had handed the outer trappings of his gentleman's apparel of hat, stick and gloves to his faithful manservant.

With these familiar actions and responses completed, Montague had left Collins standing in the entrance hall of this fine London home, attending personally to the brushing of his master's newly acquired top hat. As Montague had ascended the massive white marble staircase to the first floor, home of the golden hued drawing room, the room which had so impressed him upon his initial entrance into this house, his thoughts had returned momentarily to those years before when, on that similarly chilly September afternoon, he had informed Catherine's now departed aunts of his bold intention of marrying their only blood relative, without their permission but hopefully with their blessing, which he had now recalled had never really been given by that crusty pair of old maids.

Why, he had wondered, would thoughts of such long gone times catch in his memory now and send a cold chill through his body, as he had now experienced for the second time that day. He had brushed aside these thoughts as he had reached his destination and what would be the loving embrace of his dearest wife, Catherine. As Montague had opened the drawing-room door, the image that had befallen his eyes had instantly taken his mind back in time again to his wedding day when he had quietly opened the door connecting their two compartments on the train taking them to their honeymoon in Venice; that same picture of serene radiance which had sat as an aura around Catherine had again encapsulated her. To Montague, his wife's delicately beautiful appearance had not dimmed throughout the passage of time.

As Montague had stepped across the threshold into this tastefully decorated room and had moved in the direction of Catherine, who had been seated upon a single straight-backed chair in the occupation of some fine needlework as had always been her fancy as relaxation, towards his own favourite, old, green, leather-clad wing chair situated by the hearthside opposite her, Montague had opened the conversation gently with the following words, as he had bent in passing to place a kiss upon Catherine's ivory cheek.

'Hello, my dear, how good it is to be residing within the four walls of my home once more and how positively radiant you look this evening.'

'Good evening, Montague, my darling, thank you for those kind words. Have you had a successful day of toil in the city, today?' Catherine had enquired with due wifely concern for matters which she did not fully understand.

'Yes, thank you, my dear. My meetings today bore great fruit for the bank. Speaking of the bank, you will never guess who I passed in the corridor outside my office today, the Earl of Marlford, Lord Rupert Penman-Smythe; you no doubt remember him, my darling, for it was at his country residence, Beeches Hall, that I offered you my proposal of marriage, which you so graciously accepted,' Montague had discreetly offered as his reply.

'It would be terribly remiss of me to have forgotten the Earl or that encounter would it not, Montague?' Catherine had replied with a slight hint of lovingly applied reproach in her voice for having had it thought by her husband of all people that she might have forgotten that most important period of time in her life.

'Indeed, point taken, my love. In passing, his lordship enquired as to whether we might have a free social calendar for the weekend after next, to be in residence at Carlile Manor for the inaugural meet for this season of the Marlford Hunt and subsequently the Hunt Ball. The thought did pass my mind that you may enjoy participating in these festivities in part as a celebration of our union which, as you so well remember, was set in motion officially the night of one such ball,' Montague had tenderly stated.

Further to this Montague had quickly added, 'Furthermore, I truly believe, my dear, that the time has finally come when Reginald should partake of a little more of outdoor life, much as I understand and agree with his studies being of utmost importance to his life and future, as indeed I saw mine at the same age. At this age, I also believe we should assist him in cultivating an appreciation of some of the finer country pursuits. The young fellow is a fine rider, as you well know, having accompanied him and his riding master on many excursions to Hyde Park and the Row and I feel very strongly that he would, I am sure, benefit from the experience of entering into the festivities of his first hunt,' Montague had stated to Catherine with all the passion of a barrister at law pleading his case to the all-powerful judge.

With a look that had held within it an expression of intense trepidation, Catherine had replied, 'If you truly believe that the time has come for this pursuit to be encouraged within the heart of our treasured son, then, as your dutiful wife I must respect you as my husband and thereby accede to your wishes in this matter. However, if you wish to know my own heartfelt thoughts on this affair, then I must say to you, Montague, my husband of so many happy years, that I do not believe that our son, our only child, for that is all he is, a mere child, should be encouraged in what I feel is a most foolhardy and unnecessary adventure.'

'Calm yourself, my dear. With the assistance of Old Ben, my head groom, on the Marlford Estate and myself, also in attendance, I assure you that no harm will come to our son. If it will allay your fears a little, the boy will only stay out in the field for the first half of the day's proceedings,' Montague had comfortingly compromised.

Registering that she would not be able to dissuade Montague from this newly formed course of action involving the life of their beloved son, Catherine had meekly resigned herself to this fact and had replied, 'I must as your wife follow your wishes in this matter. Let us leave it at that, Montague.'

'My dearest, have we not forgotten the most important point in this whole matter? We have not as yet asked the young master in question, himself,' Montague had calmly retorted.

Upon the utterance of these words, as if by some divine command or demon coincidence, the drawing-room door had burst open and in had rushed a small, thin boy of almost ten years in age, possessed of a luxuriant head of ebony coloured hair. The boy, being none other than Montague's and Catherine's son, Reginald Alexander Carlile, had moved with great speed of foot in the direction of Montague's chair and, in one swift movement, had launched himself into Montague's lap and in the process had wrapped his two thin arms around his father's neck in a most affectionate hug of greeting.

'Oh, Papa, how good it is to see that you have returned home from the city at last,' Reginald had enthusiastically greeted his beloved father.

'Reginald, my dear boy, seeing you makes your old papa's heart fill with joy,' Montague had returned as his loving response to his son's greeting, in the process returning the intensity of embrace in a rare public display of the deep-seated love and respect he had felt for this, his only child.

Returning his son gently to stand on the floor before his chair, Montague had looked into Reginald's trusting, dark green eyes and had asked of him the question, 'Reginald, my son, what would you say if I were to suggest to you that the opportunity to experience a little of country life has presented itself to our family?'

Reginald's answer to his father's question had come in the form of a rather blank and uncomprehending look upon the young lad's face.

Montague had instantly realised the need to simplify his question and had, after rephrasing his words within his quick mind, calmly asked, 'Reginald, would you like to accompany your mama and I to our country estate for a short holiday the weekend after next?'

In response to these words, Reginald's eyes had lit up as though it had been Christmas morning and all the presents beneath the tree had been his. His attention had then turned to that of his mother, who, seated in her chair, had remained silent throughout this exchange between father and son. Reginald, then, with the true wonderment of a child evident in his small, timid voice had asked politely of his mother, 'Mama, may I put my studies aside for a short time and enjoy a holiday in the country with you and papa?'

To which Catherine, in her voice of but a whisper, which Montague had come to realise through their years together had always been reserved for times when she had felt intense emotions, had replied, 'It is your papa's wish that we undertake this adventure, so there is nothing more to be said on the matter.'

Oblivious to the deep feelings his mother had just expressed, Reginald had been totally and instantly engrossed in his own world of thoughts and expectations as to what this adventure had held in store for a boy of his tender years and experience. Reginald had again turned his attention in the direction of his father and, with an expression of intense enrapture covering his fair-skinned cherubic face, had asked of the most important man in his life the question which had held the greatest importance to him at this special moment.

'Papa, I read in the newspaper yesterday, with the help of Miss Laycock, that the weekend after next will herald the start of the hunt season. Does that mean that you will be riding to hounds that weekend?'

'Yes, Reginald, my boy. By chance I met the Earl of Marlford in the city this morning and he expressly requested my attendance at the inaugural hunt of the season, he also requested another member of this family to attend,' Montague had cryptically replied.

Reginald, with a certain downcast expression suddenly invading his previously happy countenance, had turned to his mother and said, 'Mama, if you will be accompanying Papa at the hunt, I do not think there is much point in my going. All I will do is sit in a cold, old trap with a lot of gossiping ladies all day.'

To which Montague had quickly replied with the hint of a laugh creeping into his sonorous voice, 'Your mama is a very fine rider. However, your mama is indeed not the other member of this family to whom I referred earlier, Reginald, my dear sweet boy. It is of you, Reginald Alexander Carlile, whom the Earl spoke this morning. It is his desire to see you attend your first hunt upon this appointed weekend.'

The expression of these words by Montague had again rapidly sent Reginald's mind into a whirling sea of thoughts as had been evidenced by the changing array of contortions which had been displayed upon his face. This kaleidoscope of intense thoughts and feelings had then erupted forth in an explosion of questions and replies directed towards his father.

'Oh, Papa, how wonderful! Will I be allowed to ride beside you during the hunt?' Reginald had breathlessly requested of his attentive father.

'Your mama and I have agreed that you may attend the first half of the day's proceedings. This way, the day will not be too tiring for you. Old Ben, my head groom at Carlile Manor, will be in attendance to chaperone you from the manor to the meeting point outside the village inn, where I will be waiting to accompany you in the hunt proper. During the hunt, Old Ben will follow behind and when I deem that you have had enough, he will travel the return journey with you to the warmth and security of the manor and the, no doubt, proud embrace of your dear mama,' Montague had sternly replied in part to calm the still apparent fears of Catherine who, to Montague's keen gaze, had sat ringing her thin delicate hands in her lap throughout the previous exchanges.

'What horse will I ride, Papa? The only one I really know is Midnight, the park hack I ride here in London,' Reginald had eagerly requested.

'I will correspond with Old Ben for his thoughts on the matter. However, if my memory serves me correctly, Sterling, the placid grey cob, would be extremely suitable for your needs, my boy,' Montague had happily replied.

'What horse will you be riding in the hunt, Papa?' Reginald had enquired intently interested in the response from his much loved father.

'I will take the opportunity to be aboard my newest acquisition from Germany, a fine three year old gelding who, I have been assured by the breeders, has a heart of fire and is from all accounts extremely fearless in nature, so that is what I have named him, Fearless,' Montague had replied, his eyes twinkling at the thought of this forthcoming challenge of wills between horse and man.

'Fearless by name and fearless by nature, eh, sir! I do hope that I will not hold you back too much, Papa,' Reginald had ventured with a slight tentative edge to his young, thin voice.

'Do not worry yourself, Reginald, my dear boy, you will acquit yourself admirably. I am told by your riding master, Herr Muller, that you are a keen and able student who shows a high degree of capability and courage in executing the directives given to you,' Montague had stated encouragingly.

'But, Papa, riding in the exercise pavilion and the park is one thing, but riding to hounds is a very different situation. I would not wish to bring discredit to our family name by not riding well,' Reginald had responded earnestly with the childhood concern instilled in him for the honour of his family name.

'No harm or discredit could come to our family name through any actions of yours, my dear boy. I would not consider it appropriate for you to enter into this activity if I thought you were not ready to participate. Brush all such concerns from your mind from this instant forth and enjoy all the preparations for this momentous day,' Montague had stated emphatically.

'As you command, Papa, I will concentrate on my preparation for this grand adventure. However let me assure you now, sir, that I will do all in my power to make you proud of my efforts on this most special day,' Reginald had said in a most conscientious manner belying his tender years.

Upon Reginald uttering this statement in the most earnest of tones, a knock had come upon the drawing-room door and admittance had been granted to none other than Gladys who had, in conjunction with her duties as Catherine's lady's maid, resumed her original position of nursemaid which she had so lovingly been to Catherine all those years before. Gladys now, in turn, had taken on the responsibility of Reginald, Catherine's dearly beloved only child, as her charge.

'Good evening, sir and madam, if it pleases you, it is young Master Reginald's bedtime,' Gladys had politely ventured.

'Thank you, Gladys, the young master is well ready to take to his bed, are you not, Reginald, my boy? Remember, my lad the first rule of a good horseman is to rest his body well in preparation for the trials of the hunt,' Montague had gently ventured as ample reason for Reginald retiring to his bed without protest.

'Yes, Papa, good night, Mama, good night, Papa,' Reginald had meekly responded.

'Good night, Reginald, my dear son, may your dreams be sweet,' Catherine had ventured in her most motherly of tones.

'Sleep well, my boy,' had been Montague's simple farewell to his son.

The demons which thoroughly possessed Montague's tortured mind now moved his thoughts further along their doomed path to the day imminently preceding that weekend adventure.

Montague now remembered how impressed he had been with the smooth running of his household. How well all his staff within his London residence had worked together, in conjunction with his estate household, in the preparation of all that had been required to be transported to Carlile Manor for his family's enjoyment of this most special weekend. Most of the staff from the Witton Place residence had remained in London performing limited duties in the absence of the family.

Friday afternoon had seen Collins, as Montague's trusted valet and as had always been the case on trips away from London, custodian of the luggage and Gladys, as Catherine's lady's maid and subsequently as Reginald's nursemaid travelled down to the family's country estate in discreet accompaniment to Montague and his family. The family and servants occupied first- and second-class seats respectively aboard a train of the same regional

railway which had so ably serviced the route between London and
Marlford for many a long year. Montague had decided that the
services of Barnes, his burly coachman of old, who had since
become the household's chauffeur with the addition to the
London 'stable' of a gleaming young thoroughbred of the
mechanical variety, a Rolls Royce 'Silver Ghost' automobile, and
his assistant/mechanic, Harris, who had previously held the
position and duties of groom, had not been required that weekend
as the journey along roads that had been nothing more than
glorified cow paths, Montague had deemed, would have been far
too distressing and time-consuming for his family.

As the train had travelled along its snake-like lines hurrying on
to its appointed destination with an air of mindful purpose, the
peace of one of the first-class compartments had been shattered
by a deafening noise.

'Ahchoo, ahchoo, ahchoo,' Montague had sneezed uncontrollably.

'My dear, I wish you would have seen sense and taken the very
sound advice of your physician to remain in your bed for this
weekend. It is a most dreadful case of influenza that you have
contracted during your recent business trip to Paris. What you
need is complete rest, not to go galloping across the countryside
in what it appears will be atrocious weather,' Catherine had said,
expressing her views on this matter with great intensity of feeling
as she had turned from viewing the emerging scenery of a windy
and miserable London through the rain-splattered train window.

Catherine had further added passionately, 'I truly believe, deep
in my heart, that your actions show to me an immeasurable sense
of foolhardiness which is so uncharacteristic of your true nature.
In my opinion, unwarranted as you may deem it, you have been
drained by this sudden illness of the strength required to complete the strenuous activities of this weekend without some form
of harm coming to you. I fear deeply for your safety, my darling.

'Do not trouble yourself, Catherine, my dear. All I require is a
good night's rest with a change of air and some good country
food. I will be fine for the weekend's festivities. What do physicians know? This is but a slight chill that I have as a result of
being caught a little unprepared by a shower of rain whilst

walking the boulevards between meetings in Paris earlier this week. All will be well this weekend, my dearest love. Do not fret yourself unduly. This weekend must continue as planned, for I cannot disappoint Reginald. It would indeed be dreadfully hurtful to him to dash all his expectations, just because of a slight malady on the part of his old papa,' Montague had replied in but a whisper of his usually strong voice.

Behind these words had remained in Montague's mind the fervent belief that Reginald must not be made to go without any activity by virtue of his father's advancing age and, at this particular point in time, failed health. Montague had intensely wished to be a companion to this his most cherished only child and son.

As Montague had sat looking out the train window at the disappearing grey cityscape that had been London on that chilly, wet September afternoon, momentarily his mind had filled with thoughts of his life, how often the phrase 'a fortunate man' had he expressed to himself with regards to his own life. He had indeed been granted a fortunate life, with a position of strength and power within the society of London, a beautiful and competent wife and, as the crowning glory, a son to carry on his name. The only cloud within this golden sky had been the realisation that no further issue from this union of man and wife would be possible. As Montague had well remembered, Catherine had experienced a painful and protracted labour, bearing Reginald's entrance into this world and, though her health and well-being had quickly returned, for some unfathomable reason, unknown to her own physician or to the best minds of Harley Street, the rigours of Reginald's birth had left Catherine barren of any further issue.

This had been a painful blow at the first realisation of this fact. However, time and the intense love that had been shared between the proud parents and the rapidly growing child had dispelled the pain and heartbreak and had turned it equally on the part of all participants into a strong bond of love and mutual respect. Again Montague's mind drifted to bygone days. What heartfelt glee and deep pride this man had experienced as he had stood in escort to his beloved Catherine with Jane and Percival Groot, their loyal friends – again in attendance, this time in the role of godparents – gathered around the font in the Cathedral of Saint Paul in celebration of their new bairn on his day of christening. How exquisite had been the pleasure Montague had felt as the Bishop of London had uttered the words, 'I baptise thee Reginald Alexander...' Reginald meaning strong ruler and Alexander meaning defender or helper of men – strong names for the wee bairn he hoped would grow into a strong and dependable man.

Montague had been returned from his reverie by the sudden opening of the compartment door and the entrance of the subject of his recent remembrances, that of his small, thin son, Reginald Alexander Carlile, in the accompaniment of his ever-watchful nursemaid, Gladys. To which Catherine, in the role of the ever-concerned mother and mistress of the household, had asked of her devoted servant, 'Is anything the matter, Gladys?'

'No, madam, nowt is wrong, only that young Master Reginald here was getting mite concerned about his papa and I thought best to allay his fears and bring him along for short visit,' Gladys had responded in the polite tones which had been indicative of her many years in service.

'Thank you, Gladys, your actions were correct,' Catherine had quietly responded, then had turned in the direction of Reginald and had issued him with the following stern directive, 'Reginald, my dear son, you may stay in company with us for a short time. However, you must not tire your poor papa too much, for he is quite ill.'

'Hush, now, Catherine, do not alarm the boy with false tales of my state of health,' Montague had wheezed.

'Oh my poor, dear papa, it concerns me greatly, sir, to see you in this state with the heavy burden of knowing that, in part, it is my fault that you are in this grave condition,' Reginald had intently stated.

'How do you fathom that it is in part you who is responsible for my condition, my son?' Montague had asked, displaying great effort in uttering this request.

'Well, sir, if it had not been for my expectations of this week-end, I dare say you would have cancelled your acceptance of the Earl of Marlford's invitation to the hunt,' Reginald had quietly issued forth as his explanation.

'Young sir, if anyone is to shoulder blame for this situation, it must rest upon the demons of fate for dealing us this wild card,' Montague had responded in the lightest of tones in an effort to allay his son's feelings of ill-founded guilt.

'Now away with you, Reginald, and allow your papa his much needed rest,' Catherine had burst forth in uncommonly stern tones.

'Oh come now, Catherine, my dear, it is but a relatively short time until we will be arriving at Marlford station and I spend so little time with this young chap as it is. It will do no harm for the boy to remain with us for the rest of the journey,' Montague had stated insistently.

'As you wish, Montague, I am but your poor devoted wife and as such must obey you directives. However, Reginald, I must impress upon you once again, you must remain as quiet as possible to allow your papa his much needed rest,' Catherine had replied in her usual whisper of a voice signifying her inward intense disapproval of these actions on the part of her stubborn husband.

To which Reginald, turning his face, which had given the appearance of having been cast with angels as the model, to look concernedly at the now prostrate form of his father, had submissively replied, 'Yes, Mama, I will be as silent as a mouse.'

So, Gladys had been sent back to take her seat yet again in the second-class carriage for the relatively short remainder of this train journey while Reginald had taken his seat beside his mother and opposite the man whose well-being had been of paramount importance to both as Montague had drifted in and out of a haze of sleep. Time had swiftly travelled on, as had the train, to its appointed destination until the party had found itself re-grouped upon the station platform cloaked in its pre-dusk light and held within the polite yet welcoming embrace of Old Ben, the head groom, and George, his junior from Montague's country estate.

'Welcome to you, sir and madam, and not forgettin' the young master. It is so good to have you in residence at the manor again,' Old Ben, this man of diminutive stature yet mighty strength, had cheerily bade the party welcome.

'Thank you, Ben, I believe it will do my family good to reside again if only temporarily in the heart of this most beautiful countryside,' Montague had graciously responded in a faltering whisper which had born little resemblance to his normally rich strong voice.

Noting Montague's rapidly failing strength, Catherine had astutely stepped forward and had issued with a degree of calm determination the following instructions.

'Let us not stand here a moment longer. The air is damp and cold and will do the master's health no end of harm. Ben, show us to the carriage immediately, if you please.'

Then, turning towards Collins and Gladys, Catherine without pausing to draw breath, had further instructed, 'Gladys, you may accompany us in the carriage with young Master Reginald. Collins, you will see to the swift transportation of our luggage and yourself to the estate in the trap with George.'

To which Old Ben, Collins and Gladys had responded in unison with the words, 'Yes, madam.'

So the party had dispersed to its appointed duties. Montague, Catherine, Reginald and Gladys had duly been escorted by Old Ben to their waiting carriage for the short journey to Carlile Manor. Upon entering the carriage, Montague had instantly been reminded of his wedding day, as he had recognised the gleaming black and grey carriage as that which had conveyed Catherine and him from the cathedral as newly proclaimed husband and wife, all those years before, its days of work in London now gone. With the advent of the mechanical horse and carriage, which had subsequently come to reside in the mews of his Witton Place home, Montague had had this fine example of the coach builder's art dispatched to his country estate where he had deemed its services to have been of a more appropriate nature.

As they had travelled along the, at times, uneven path which had masqueraded as a major road in this West Country hamlet, Montague had surreptitiously viewed Catherine through half-closed eyes as she had sat opposite him. The view which had greeted these red and watery eyes had been of a face completely absorbed in thoughts of concern and fear for the safety of what had been her dearly loved husband, as Catherine had alternatively viewed the passing mist-shrouded rural scenery displayed through the carriage window and to her eyes the continually deteriorating condition of Montague. As Montague had allowed his act of observation to become apparent to Catherine, she had immediately ventured forth with her own passionate observations of the situation.

'Montague, I do so wish that we had not ventured from London for this weekend. I have a feeling that, like the present weather, there is a cloud of doom hanging over this family. Your appearance to me has not withstood the arduous nature of the train journey at all well and it will only be worsened by the combined stresses and strains of tomorrow's hunt. I beg of you to communicate with the Earl this evening. Send him your apologies and defer from the morrow's meet. If it is our boy's feelings of disappointment that weigh so heavily in your thoughts, I feel sure that, as his mother, I may speak on his behalf in this matter and say that he would prefer the loss of such an opportunity to the loss of his father.'

'Hush now, Catherine, please do not demean yourself with such a public display of unfounded emotion as to give yourself the appearance of one of those cheap music hall performers whom I so detest. When do you produce your crystal ball to tell my future? All you will achieve by the continuation of these comments will be to worry yourself into a state of malaise and procure for yourself no happiness from what should be a pleasant and proud time with your family. Further to this, your actions will only take Reginald's thoughts from his role in this, his first hunt, thereby endangering his safety. I will not have you raise this matter with me again. Thank you, Catherine, all will be fine my dear,' Montague had uncharacteristically exploded with considerable feeling, little knowing how soon Catherine's plea which had rung in his ears would later return to haunt him.

With that, the party had travelled on in silence until the carriage's arrival at the heavy black iron gates which had signified the point of official penetration of the stone wall that had defined the extensive estate grounds of Carlile Manor. Old Ben had reined in the two black geldings which had pulled the carriage on this particular journey and alighted from the coachman's seat high at the front to assist Samuel, the gatekeeper, in the opening of these massive iron barricades. As Old Ben had regained his seat and had moved the carriage slowly through the gateway, Samuel, as a mark of respect to his laird and master, had bent his head and doffed his tweed cap in the process uttering the words, 'Welcome home, sir.'

To which Montague, as had always been his polite manner when dealing with the servants in his employ, had responded, 'Thank you, Samuel, it is good to be home, if only for a short time.'

With the utterance of those words, Montague had suddenly been reminded of his own humble country origins, the thought of which had bestowed upon him an uncommon and previously unperceived sense of peace, as though he had truly been coming home to stay.

By the time Montague had returned his thoughts from those of his childhood, the carriage had swept up and around the curved gravel driveway and had brought its passengers in view of the manor itself. Before their eyes had stood Carlile Manor in all its glory and symmetry. This fine example of the stonemason's art had stood at this point in its history at peace and in harmony with its surroundings. As the carriage had continued up the central drive, flanked on each side by a row of mighty English elm trees, down between the two protruding wings of this U-shaped house and into the security of the central courtyard and the main entrance, Montague had again been pleased with the purchase he had made all those years ago. To his mind, such a feeling of strength and power had exuded from this imposing, grey stone structure.

Finally, the carriage had come to rest, adjacent to the massive, oak, front door which had, without prompting, been decorously opened by Hopkins, the elderly butler, to reveal to Montague and his party his entire manor household solemnly waiting to bid a respectful yet cheery welcome to their returning laird and master within the lavish surroundings of the grand entrance hall with its fan-vaulted ceiling. Assembled in dutiful order of seniority had been the following collection of loyal servants:

Butler – Hopkins
Under butler – Gilbert
Master's Valet – Collins

Housekeeper – Mrs Booth
Lady's maid/Nursemaid – Gladys
Footman – Donald
Footman – Cedric
Footman – Angus
Housemaid – Emma
Housemaid – Charlotte
Housemaid – Ruth
Cook – Mrs Christian
Kitchen maid – Lily
Scullery maid – Grace
Bootboy – Bertie
Estate agent – Thompson

Having ushered the party into the warm confines of this, their country home, Hopkins, with the assistance of his junior, Gilbert, had relieved Montague and his family of their heavy travelling coats, in the process uttering the words, 'Welcome home, again, sir, to you and your family. We were so hoping that the weather would have been better for your weekend activities.'

To which Montague had philosophically replied, 'Thank you, Hopkins, it is a pity that God does not appear to be smiling upon our endeavours for this weekend. However, I have found that one must take the cards the hand of fate deals for you and work them to your own advantage, or be lost in a sea of self-pity.'

How prophetic those words of wisdom which Montague had endowed to his assembled servants would soon become to all concerned. What indeed did the hand of fate hold in store...

The following September morning had dawned cold damp and foggy; Montague had frustratedly registered this annoying fact as he had sat alone – as had been his desire upon this particular morning having retained this weekend excursion to their country home purely for his family's pleasure by not having extended invitations to their friends as had been his usual custom – at the head of the damask-clad breakfast table, consuming a cup of steaming hot coffee as his only attempt at the early morning repast, which had been a hearty affair with the likes of porridge, poached eggs on toast, sausages, grilled bacon and stewed kidneys, readily waiting to be accompanied by copious amounts of hot buttered toast and marmalade and washed down with an ocean of piping hot tea or coffee. Montague's general condition had not improved with the previous night's rest. Whilst endeavouring to clear his head by the imbibing of this hot, strong liquid, Montague had become aware of a movement at his side and had looked up through his congested haze to see the ever-immaculate Gilbert standing beside him; a silver slaver had reposed in his long sinewy hand as he had bent courteously towards Montague and had issued forth with the following explanation for his appearance beside his master at this early hour of the day, 'Good morning, sir, a hand-delivered message from his lordship, the Earl of Marlford, has just arrived.'

Without his customary good-natured and thankful reply, Montague had speedily taken up the envelope-clad message and had unceremoniously disrobed it. The mental digestion of its contents had left him in no doubt of the required course of his actions on that day. As his mind had fought for clarity in this sea of illness-induced fog, Montague's attention had intently passed again to the figure of the willowy young man who had remained standing at his side, and he had commanded moodily, 'Has Master Reginald risen from his bed this morning yet, Gilbert?'

To which Gilbert had impassively replied, 'I believe, sir, that Donald is in the process of dressing the young master for the hunt at this precise moment in time. Master Reginald no doubt will be descending for breakfast imminently, sir.'

'That will be all for the moment, Gilbert,' Montague had curtly replied.

To which Gilbert had replied ever dutifully, 'Thank you, sir,' and had left Montague alone, again.

As Montague had sat within the presently dull expanse of what had usually been a light and most inviting room, with the incessant sound of the pitter-patter of the insidious and unrelenting rain hammering upon its large French windows – which, in finer weather, had usually been open to allow access to the terrace and the luxuriant lawns beyond – his face had been a mirror of the darkened thoughts which had fought for supremacy in his clouded mind…

A bitterly cold west wind had slapped aggressively against Montague's weakened frame, encased as it had been in his pristine hunting attire of sturdy black velvet cap, stout 'pink' coat closed by a row of silver MH hunt buttons, white breeches, mahogany top boots with white garter straps and blunt spurs and white gloves, bidding him a most unkind welcome to this day as he had ridden out from the relative warmth and safety of the manor's stables upon his appointed route to join the other members of the Marlford Hunt at their time honoured meeting place outside the Horse and Hound Inn. As he had ridden alone and with great difficulty, wrestling with his newly acquired mount for control of the situation, along the network of lanes, the thought had occasioned into Montague's mind of how welcome that customary stirrup cup, the alcoholic offering of goodwill extended to the participants of the day's hunt by the landlord of this free house, would be.

His mind momentarily had returned to earlier that morning and Montague's first introduction to what had been his mount for the day's sport. This fiery specimen of Germanic equine breeding, a massive Hanoverian gelding of jet black colour standing sixteen hands, was possessed of an unnaturally tempestuous disposition, as evidenced by the dramatic display of smoke which had appeared to belch forth from his flaring nostrils, his breath having condensed upon touching the cool air as he had cavorted around the confines of his stall. It had been only with a great deal of effort on the part of Old Ben, Montague's head groom, and the assistance of two stable boys, that this seething mass of highly strung emotions encased in a Pegasus-like skeleton had been brought to some form of order by its saddling and bridling before Montague's blurred gaze.

The passing comment had been made of this glistening creature by Montague with a hint of trepidation in his faltering voice, 'By Jove, Ben, this horse truly has an uncommonly fearless and fiery nature.'

To which Old Ben had breathlessly replied, 'Yes, sir, he is unlike any animal I have ever dealt with before in all my years as a groom. I believe he has a soul possessed by demons. He may well be a fine example of horse flesh. There is no disputing his blood line, but to all who have to deal with him he is nothing more than a bugger of a horse. I am aware, sir, that you paid very good money for him but, if you were wanting my opinion on this animal, you would do well to rid yourself of him. He will bring you no happiness, especially today with you not at your best. Will you not consider riding another horse for today's sport, sir, or at least travel to the meeting place in the dog-cart and my boys could follow with the horse?' Old Ben had pleadingly completed his response.

'Thank you for your concern, Ben. However, I must see for myself what the situation is with this beast as soon as possible. Anyway, I cannot disappoint his lordship, the Earl of Marlford. He has been looking forward with great anticipation to viewing this animal participating in all the thrill of the chase. This point he has made most apparent by his communication with me this morning, no less, his lordship having seen mention made in the local newspaper of this recent acquisition on my part. How would it look to him to see me arrive as an old woman would? It would not do well to incur his wrath,' Montague had meekly ventured as a reply.

'As is your wish, sir. Now, you would be requiring the mounting block this morning, sir, would you not?' Old Ben had quietly enquired of his master in the full knowledge of the affirmative nature of the answer to this enquiry, having rapidly assessed the hazardous condition of his master of so many years upon first laying eyes on him that morning.

'Yes, Ben, I believe I will avail myself of the luxury of using the mounting block this morning. I fear that my age is starting to catch up with me,' had been Montague's rather lame attempt at a light-hearted reply to the look of concern etched upon the face of his loyal servant.

'Right you are then, sir. The boys and I will endeavour to walk this tiresome creature to the mounting block, if you care to follow. However, might I suggest, sir, that in following us you remain at a safe distance behind during this action. For this horse, as you can see, is dreadful flighty in the confines of these stables. I fear only God himself knows how it will perform in the field,' had been Old Ben's final words on this troublesome situation.

Montague well remembered the feeling of sheer exhaustion which had greeted his tortured body upon the execution of the simple act of taking his place securely upon the back of this, his mount for the day's sport. How his body had ached and his mind had longed for the comfort and ease of his bed, even at this early stage of the day's proceedings as, having climbed the stone steps of the mounting block, he had unceremoniously pulled himself upon the writhing back of this black demon of a horse. It had only been with the devoted and painstaking attention to his duties exhibited by Old Ben, this short powerhouse of a man, that had averted an early calamity with him adding his substantial strength and stability to that of his weakened master's and had hoisted him into the saddle while his two patient stable boys had valiantly held the head of this vexatious horse.

'Thank you, Ben, for all your efforts in assisting me this morning,' had been Montague's breathless response to the combined actions of his staff.

'I am sure Master Reginald will be along presently, after he has breakfasted well as all young boys of his age are prone to do. Remember, Ben, you are to accompany him to the meeting point. Remain within view during the hunt proceedings, awaiting my signal to come forward to escort the young gentleman safely back to the manor,' Montague had strictly reiterated the instructions he had already issued in the preceding days to his dedicated and caring head groom.

To which Old Ben had dutifully and simply replied, 'Yes, sir, I will take good care of the young Master Reginald.'

Montague's parting remark, which had been left ringing in the ears of his head groom as his master had manoeuvred his unwilling mount out of the close confines of his extensive stables and into the treacherous conditions which had laid ahead, had been, 'I wish this day, the first of many hunts to come, to be memorable for my dear son. However, his safety must be of paramount concern to us all'

Little had Montague realised how his own safety would come into dramatic question before the sun had set upon this day's festivities…

A sudden movement of his hands and thrust of his already cold, racked body in the direction of the ice hardened ground below had returned Montague's thoughts back to his immediate task at hand, that of the control of this worrisome equine spirit which, at this precise moment, had shied violently sideways, the result of the passage of a brown hare across its path and beneath its blackened and shining hooves. How glad Montague had been at this moment as he had become aware of his bearings and had realised his approach to the top of the soft flowing hill which had announced to the travellers of these lanes their imminent arrival at the outskirts of the hamlet of Marlford. With infinite care, Montague had reigned his worrisome mount down the gentle hill and into this picturesque little village, past its row of neat High Street cottages and had joined the throng of horses and riders milling about outside the stone and slate Horse and Hound Inn.

From this throng of colour and noise had rung out the clear foghorn voice, the identity of whose owner even through his illness-induced haze Montague had well recognised. The rather nondescript figure, with silver stirrup cup in hand, that had approached attired in the finest hunt livery Savile Row could provide and astride a magnificent dark bay hunter had been none other than the Master of Fox Hounds, Lord Rupert Penman-Smythe himself.

'Carlile, Montague Carlile, you received my note, I see, good man. I thought it best to let you know that the day would proceed as usual. We will not have a spot of inclement weather spoil our fun, will we?'

As usual, not allowing his companion time to answer, Lord Rupert had further espoused in his booming voice to all in the immediate area, 'Cannot abide by these fellows who will not go out in the field if there is a touch of rain and wind about, nothing but Mama's boys in my opinion. Best rid of that sort out here. Elements, such as we have today, in my humble' – which Montague had long realised had been anything but – 'opinion, only add to the thrill of the chase and the excitement of the day.'

Lord Rupert, throughout these highly opinionated words, had

remained mindlessly oblivious to the already deteriorating condition of his newly acquired companion as he had bellowed forth his following command to Montague and then had fallen silent.

'You will be in for the full day's activities, I trust, Carlile. It would please me greatly if you would stay close at hand during today's proceedings. I do so wish to see this, your new equine acquisition, in action. What a fine specimen he appears to be. By the way, where is your young son? He will be joining us this morning, I trust.'

To which Montague, having finally had a chance to respond to all that had transpired in the previous few minutes, had quietly replied in a shadow of his normally sonorous voice which had held just a trace of sarcastic annoyance in it, 'Good morning, Your Lordship, so good of you to let me know that all was proceeding as usual today and of your ardent desire to view this, my fine, new addition to the stables at Carlile Manor;' – Montague having indicated with a wave of his crop over the neck of the malevolent animal of which he had quickly come to realise had been his misfortune to have been astride – 'it would indeed have been such an unconscionable waste to have not carried on. What, as you say, is a little pelting rain and biting wind and penetrating cold. May I say, Your Lordship, what a fine figure you cut astride your most impressive mount this morning. In answer to your most gracious request, I will ride within your view today and, yes, my son, Reginald, is being escorted from Carlile Manor as we speak and will be here with us very soon.'

'Good man, Carlile. Now, if you will excuse me, I must attend to a matter with my kennel-huntsman about one of the hounds,' Lord Rupert had boomed again as loud as any field cannon, as he turned his steed in the direction of the huntsman and his accompanying pack of hounds which had been gathered at the edge of this ebbing and flowing river of colour with black, grey, chestnut, blue-roan, bay, brown, dapple-grey, strawberry-roan and liver-chestnut horses milling beneath an equally colourful display of riders covering a wide spectrum from the authoritative pink through to hues of blue, black, green and brown indicative of their position in the hunt and life in general.

As Montague had sat observing the passing parade of country life, a familiar and welcome voice had roused him from his thoughts with the question, 'Good morning, Mr Carlile, would you care for a draught, sir?'

Upon hearing these words, Montague had looked down through streaming eyes to see the cheerful round face of Joe Cotton, the landlord of the Horse and Hound, beaming up at him. A silver stirrup cup, fashioned to resemble a fox's head, full of a potent mix of cherry brandy and port had been proffered in his hand.

To which Montague had readily responded affirmatively, 'Morning, Joe, yes, thank you, I believe I will need more than one of these cups to keep me going today. Age appears to be catching up with me these days,' in an attempt to allay any concerns on the part of this quick-witted publican.

Joe, through his many years behind the bar, had become a good judge of a man's condition and had issued forth concernedly the observation,

'You do not appear, to my eye, to be your usual self this morning, sir. Is it entirely wise for you to be engaged in these activities in your apparent condition, Mr Carlile?'

'Life must go on, Joe,' had been Montague's succinct response as he had downed a second cup in a vain attempt and valiant effort to ward off the combined effects of life and the elements.

As he had passed this second emptied cup into the careful custody of this most gracious and generous landlord and had observed Joe's silent passage back into the throng of seething horseflesh, Montague's cold numbed mind had gradually been made aware of a presence on the opposite side of his mount to where Joe, mindful of the obvious temperamental nature of Montague's mount, had carefully stood. In answer to this awareness, Montague had turned his attention in the direction of this newly registered presence and had been greeted for his effort by the sight of the smiling face of his treasured son, Reginald, in the stony-faced accompaniment of Old Ben.

'Good morning, Papa. Oh what a glorious day this will be!' had been Reginald's opening overture to his father, oblivious to the highly inclement condition of both the weather and of his beloved papa. Reginald had been completely absorbed into the circle of gentle country life which had been revolving around him.

Not wishing to detract any possible enjoyment of this important day from the life of his cherished only child, Montague had valiantly struggled with the demons of illness which had beaten mercilessly against his weakened body, digging deep within his reserves of faltering strength to maintain the appearance he had so fervently wished to display at this point in time to the most important person in his life, his son. The appearance that Montague had hoped he had succeeded in projecting had been one of strength and stability, for it had been the exhibiting of these attributes of his character which he had believed Reginald would come to rely upon, for example, during the passage of the day's events.

This he had appeared to have succeeded in achieving in the eyes of his young son, by issuing forth with the light-hearted response, 'Good morning, Reginald, my dear boy, I thought you were never going to arrive and thereby miss all the festivities of this momentous day.'

To which Reginald had respectfully replied, by way of an explanation for his tardiness, 'I am so sorry, Papa, but it was the cook's, Mrs Christian, fault. If she had not laid such an extensive table this morning, I would have been here much sooner. There was just so much to choose from. I could not make up my mind quickly. Further, Papa, remember, it is you who have always told me that a hearty breakfast is essential before a day's hunt to sustain body and mind through the rigours of the day's chase.'

This response from Reginald had calmed Montague's mind to some extent, having indicated to him his apparently normal appearance in the eyes of his son, and he had replied in the lightest of tones, 'May you enjoy this day to the fullest, my dear boy.'

However Montague's deteriorating health had not passed without notice by his astute head groom, Old Ben, who, upon laying eyes on his master, had uttered the words, 'You will still be requiring me to remain within sight today, sir, will you not?'

To which Montague having transferred his feeble gaze away

from that of his son, whose attention had again been absorbed into the throbbing mass of humanity which had milled around this little group, and returning it to that of his assiduous servant Old Ben, had replied haltingly, 'Thank you, Ben, yes, given the conditions for today's activities, it would, I think, be best, as this is his first hunt, if the young master does not stay out too long. As I have instructed, you will remain close at hand, waiting for my signal and when I so indicate, you will escort this young man safely home to the manor.'

As Montague had issued this confirmation of his orders, the word 'safely' had caught and subsequently lingered meditatively in his mind. How well Montague now realised that this word had been an omen of what life had held in store...

Upon the Master's instructions, the horn had sounded clear and strong, issuing to all the assembled party, horse and rider alike, the need to ready themselves for the imminent initiation of the day's anticipated proceedings. Montague, on hearing this call to order, had proudly turned towards Reginald mounted on his trustworthy grey cob and had lovingly whispered in a cracking voice, 'We are about to be off on our day of great fun, Reginald, my boy. How proud you make your old papa feel to have you beside me today. To wish to share in one of my few pleasures is truly one of the greatest gifts, you, my only son, could bestow upon your father. How handsome you look astride your steed.'

Indeed, the young boy had cut quite a dashing picture in his well-tailored hunting ensemble of dark green hacking jacket and accompanying cream-coloured breeches, long brown leather boots with matching garter strap, brown knitted gloves and a sturdy mud-coloured cap, the total image of which had, to Montague's eye, accentuated his already strong resemblance to Reginald's dear mother, Catherine.

Suddenly upon the recollection of Catherine to his mind, Montague had wished that his departure from his much loved wife earlier that morning had been on more harmonious terms. With Montague having risen from their bed at such an early hour to make preparation for this day of days, he had left Catherine still sleeping, in part not wishing to have to bear the brunt of another of her emotional diatribes as had been his fate earlier in the course of this excursion to the country. However, now as the horn had sounded its final call to arms and the combatants for today's battle had commenced their procession through the cobbled High Street of this sleepy West Country village, towards the battlefield of the surrounding downs and woodland forest, Montague had been seized by the remembrance of Catherine's expression of fear for the safety of her family in what she had viewed as a foreign and hostile environment, and he had wished he had made his peace with this woman whom he loved as he would no other…

The Earl of Marlford's head gamekeeper, in the role of earth-stopper, had distinguished himself well in the performance of his duties in the night preceding this day by having precluded the foxes return to their burrows after their nocturnal foraging expeditions. It had been in the direction of these stopped earths and the adjacent thickets that the hunt and its pack of hounds had been directed. The equally enthusiastic riders and horses had assembled at the ready in the neighbourhood of the coverts, with the meet gathered in earnest anticipation of the coming day's sport. The hounds had been 'thrown off' and encouraged to seek out the fox from his temporary lair with the Master and his associated assistants of huntsmen and whippers-in following the pack. 'Browncap', the old hound with markings that had resembled that of a monk's tonsure about his fine intelligent head, had that day acted as leader of the pack. As he had heralded the presence of the fox by his telltale whimper, the cry of 'View halloa', the warning cry, had echoed forth as the fox had been seen to break cover and the day's sport had commenced. With that cry had come the subsequent call of 'Tallyho' and the horn had again issued forth its mournful command to the pack to be about its appointed task. The hounds had, with great speed, settled to their work and the pack accompanied by the Master and his diligent attendants together with the assembled riders had soon been in 'full cry' after the quarry.

The riders and horses had settled into their rhythmical union in the contented knowledge of a full day's pleasure in the thrill of a fine chase of what had been described, in passing, by the rider who had issued forth with the earlier cry of 'View halloa' as a strong, dog fox. Reginald, who had sat in awe at the colourful nature of the proceedings which had so far been played out before his young eyes, had turned a beaming face to his father. Montague, who had been seated none too comfortably on his mount, which at each call of the horn had become increasingly bad-tempered and harder to handle – beside that of his son's own equally placid steed – had noted in his son's countenance the true unblemished wonderment of the mere inexperienced child that Reginald had been. The thought had run through Montague's fatigued mind of how he had wished he could have returned that instant himself to those carefree days of childhood when his mind and body had worked in unison for his pleasure and not, as today, in battle.

The day's sport had continued to increase in excitement with the chase leading the Master, Lord Rupert and his following hunt over mile after mile of countryside, some his own estate and some land owned by other participants in this day's sport including those fertile and extensive lands owned by Montague himself. As the hunt had breached the low stone wall, which had officially defined the boundary of the estate of Carlile Manor, and had paused briefly to settle themselves and their mounts once more to the chase, Reginald had quietly requested of his father the answer to the following question.

'Papa, do you think that Mama will have accompanied the other ladies in the trap and will be able to view my riding as we travel across our own home grounds?'

Not wishing to dishearten the boy's enthusiasm for the obvious pleasure he had been attaining from the day's proceedings so far by repeating truthfully to him his mother's negative views on his participation in the day's sport, Montague had lightly replied, 'I am sure your mama will enwrap you with great pride of your riding ability when you are reunited with her later today, my son.'

Appearing content with this answer, Reginald had been seen by his father to return to his thoughts and concentration to the immediate task at hand, that of the control of his steed, which in passing Montague had proudly noted he had been accomplishing with a notable degree of inherent skill. How happy Montague had been to see this, his son and heir to these lands traversing them with the skill and courage of the laird of the manor which he would one day be.

It was more than could be said for Montague himself. For, as the day had progressed and more and more miles had been covered through the gusty wind and the pounding chilly rain which had been relentless, each jump over fence, gate or obstacle had appeared to reduce his strength and the arduous and apparently never-ending battle for control he had fought with his mount over this slippery, mud-covered countryside had whittled away at his stability in the saddle. The pain of his aching body and pounding head, Montague had felt sure, had commenced to become mirrored upon his weary face. In an effort to avert any undue concern on the part of his dearly loved son, Montague, with what remaining presence of mind he had left in his control had quickly signalled to the shadowing presence of Old Ben to come forward – at what by careful consultation of his watch had been the approximate halfway point in the day's proceedings which had found the hunt on the far northern boundary of this extensive estate many a mile from the warmth and security of the manor – during a break in the continuity of the chase as the hounds had been called 'at fault' having temporarily lost the scent of the fox.

Having beckoned to Old Ben to come forward, Montague had turned his sweat-covered face towards Reginald and said, 'My dearest son, it has been the greatest of pleasure to me, your old papa, to have had your delightful company today. You have made me very proud by your conduct today, my dear sweet boy. However, I believe this to be a most opportune time for you to retire from today's proceedings and, with Old Ben here as your careful escort, return to the manor and what I have no doubt will be the loving and proud embrace of your dear mama. Now I want no objection on your part, my young man, as it would indicate to me a definite lack of good grace and sportsmanship on your part which are qualities the lack of which I will not tolerate in a gentleman of any age.'

Having been made succinctly aware of his father's decision and subsequent opinion on the matter, the young lad had had no option but to agree without complaint, not wishing to anger his strict yet loving father and thereby jeopardise any future chance of a repeat invitation to such festivities as he had been so graciously been allowed party to.

'Thank you, Father, for your most kind invitation to today's proceedings and, as was our gentleman's agreement, I shall happily return now to the manor and Mama to await your arrival home and your tales of the day's final conquest. May the victor's laurels of head, pads and brush of today's lively quarry rest securely in your hands when next we meet, Papa,' had been the polite reply from Reginald's brightly flushed lips, a result of the elements and emotions he had been subjected to during this thrilling day.

Montague had nodded his acknowledgement of these fine words on the part of his adored son as he had again signalled, with a wave of his trembling hand, to Old Ben to commence his escort homeward to the manor. What a strange combination of pride and relief had filled Montague's heart as he had watched the retreating view of his son accompanied by his loyal servant.

As his thoughts had lingered happily on this rapidly disappearing sight, that easily recognisable boom echoed through Montague's pounding head as the Master, Lord Rupert, had steered his still fresh looking steed through the once more milling horses and riders and, coming to rest beside Montague, had boomed forth the following observation, 'Young lad of yours had enough has he, Carlile? I must say that is a bit of a shame; thought he would be made of tougher stuff than that and see the day to its end. Did he not like the day's proceedings? I thought he was acquitting himself very well. He has the makings of a fine rider. Cannot fathom these young ones of today,' the Earl had rattled on in his usual bombastic style, dogmatic in his belief of his own opinion being the only one of any merit.

With as much tact as he in his diminished state of health had been able to muster, Montague had diplomatically replied, 'Thank you, Master, for your kind words of praise with regard to my young son's riding ability. I am sure he will be greatly encouraged when I repeat them to him later. He is very fond of riding and will, of course, place great importance on your magnanimous words of wisdom and approbation.'

Thankfully, with the uttering of that reply, the attendant huntsman had suddenly requested the Master return his attention whence it had come, ensuring no further tirade on the issue of modern-day child raising issuing forth in Montague's direction.

Upon being granted this lapse into silence and relative solitude for the first time in this day's busy events, having gratefully relinquished the responsibility for his son's safety and bid what he had known would be an all too temporary farewell to the unwanted attention of the Master, Montague had attempted to take some little comfort and relief from the despondently dark and cold weather and his continually deteriorating state of health by taking from his kit his leather-cased silver and glass hunting flask which he had now gratefully acknowledged having personally filled with fine brandy from the tantalus in his library before leaving the manor that morning. Unwittingly, Montague, by the performance of this simple act, had brought into play a chain of events whose climax had had dramatic consequences for all parties concerned. How well Montague remembered the warming relief the liquor had quickly imparted to his cold battered body and also how equally quickly the liquid had flowed and had been gone.

Whilst in the action of replacement of the flask to its appointed resting place in his kit, a small woodland creature, a wood mouse or suchlike, had darted before the front legs of the temperamental steed with whom Montague had battled wearily all day. Having been caught off his guard as he had bent to replace the flask, Montague had thereby not been in a position of control over his mount. This black demon of a horse, as on an earlier occasion during this day, had shied violently sideways and then thrust its head forward, easily shaking the rain-soaked and slippery reins from Montague's weakened and trembling hands. Thankfully, Montague had thought for all concerned that he had been positioned at the back of the field some distance from the point of action and whilst awaiting the resumption of the day's sport had taken protection from the blustering gale in the lee of a copse of trees on the edge of the forest woodland which bounded the northern front of this his extensive estate.

Montague, being the horseman that he had been, or would have been in better health, had felt sure he would be able to regain control of this drastic situation quickly without any undue concern for his own or anyone else's safety. However, he had not bargained for the horn to issue forth its command once more to the combatants in today's battle to rejoin the chase. As Montague had all but grasped hold of the reins in his cold, numbed fingers, the mournful wail of the horn had infused his horse's spirit with an almost Pegasus-like action – which gave to look as though it had actually been flying across the ground – and had taken flight.

With the mournful sound of the horn ringing in his ears and a fit of sneezing racking his already fumbling body, Montague had been propelled violently forward at the mercy of this uncontrollable demon equine spirit, cutting a swathe through the assembled riders and horses, past the Master himself and onward into the misty and increasingly foggy bleakness of this mud-covered countryside.

As Montague and his mount had, in their lonely battle for control, been about to jump a mighty oak tree which in the previous year's violent storms had been struck and felled by lightning, the beast, having still remained in its highly agitated state – generated by what Montague in his tortured state now registered as an insidious sound alike the booming voice of its instigator – had lost its footing in a patch of oozing mud in the act of lifting its heavy yet muscular body off the ground. With the haunting refrain of the Master's horn still ringing in his ears, Montague had been propelled from his never too stable seat in the saddle towards the frozen earth and had crashed heavily upon this steel-like ground. In the process, Montague's head had thumped down violently against this solid plain, the action of which had instantly conveyed him into a state of deep unconsciousness.

'I am afraid, madam, only time will tell to what degree Mr Carlile will recover. I have mended all I can, now it is left in God's care and his own courage as to what he makes of the rest of his life. He is a fortunate man even to be alive, a lesser man would surely have died in the field. There is definitely something to be said for the cast-iron constitution of a Scot. However, may I warn you now, his days of an active life are over. Mark my words, he will see out the rest of his days as nothing more than a twisted cripple. Further to this, in the time to come, he may well wish that upon that day, as had the fox, he had not been spared his own death, and so may you.'

These had been the sobering words whispered by the somewhat familiar voice of the person he had later recognised as Dr Mathews, the village doctor, which had brutally ushered Montague's mind back into consciousness. How well Montague remembered the waves of excruciating pain which had greeted his senses upon regaining his awareness of his surroundings, surroundings which he had slowly come to recognise as familiar, as his current resting place had been that of a bed in his ground floor smoking room within his own home of Carlile Manor. This room with its ox-blood painted walls, deep cushioned comfortable leather chairs and still lingering aroma of fine cigars had always held in Montague's heart and mind the special position of his own private masculine haven away from the somewhat feminine inclination of the rest of the house. The feeling of warmth and safety had always been heightened by the roaring fire which had constantly burned within the impressive fireplace and the centre point of the room of the magnificent portrait in oils of his long gone benefactor, Ian McCabe. To those gathered around him, Montague had heralded his return to cognisance by the uncontrollable release from his swollen lips of a moanful groan.

Upon hearing this sound, which to the assembled group and Montague's ears alike had resembled the desperate cry of a trapped and tortured creature of the wild, the tall dark frame of Dr Mathews had turned from his position in whispered conversation with Catherine at the foot of the bed and had moved to come more distinctly into Montague's rather blurred field of vision, taking up a position at Montague's bedside.

Whilst undertaking this movement, this competent and much liked country physician had issued forth in his usual bright, yet calming voice, with the words, 'Decided to join us again in the world of the living I see, Mr Carlile. Do not try to talk, my dear fellow. You are damned lucky to be alive. Not many a rider survives their mount rolling on them the way I have been informed your steed appears to have done, then lying for all that time on the cold damp earth before the hunt was able to locate you in the fog that had rolled in. You may not believe it now, but you are a very fortunate man. No doubt you are experiencing a degree of pain. I will try and ease that for you, now that you have regained sentience once more.'

Through dark, pain-filled eyes, Montague, his head swathed in bandages, had looked up towards the clearing view of Dr Mathews' calm face and had queried in an almost indistinguishable mumble, 'How long have I been here like this? I must return to London as soon as possible. There are important matters awaiting my confidential attention in my office in the city. Dr Mathews, how long will I be laid up in this structure which is masquerading as my bed? Could I not return to convalesce in a proper bed at my London residence?'

To which this diligent, yet kindly purveyor of medical care, had calmly replied, 'The accident occurred on Saturday afternoon. Today is the following Friday morning. As to your request for an answer to when you may return to London that will all depend on how quickly your injuries mend, sir. However, you must keep in mind they are not of a minor nature and you are not the youngest of men. So time is what will be needed here. It is most important that you remain as quiet and still as possible for at least the next few weeks.'

From the direction of the foot of the bed had then come yet another familiar voice, that of Catherine, which had issued in the most soothing of tones the following plea, 'Montague, my darling, your recovery from this most unfortunate and untimely accident is of the utmost importance to all those gathered here about you, above and beyond any secondary concern for your work in the city. Please rest your mind of all its fears and let the good doctor here assist you to rest your wounded body.'

This Dr Mathews had succeeded in accomplishing by the administration of half a grain of morphine by means of a hypodermic injection. Having executed this task with a dexterity born of a true vocation held to this privileged position and patiently observed Montague again drifting back into a state of pain-relieved sleep, he had once more turned his attention in the direction of Catherine. Montague, as he had drifted off in a cloud of peaceful rest, had overheard but not fully comprehended in his drug-induced sleepy state the physician's words.

'What Mr Carlile needs now is plenty of peaceful rest. I will return later today to administer another dose of pain relief. However, in the meantime, I believe it would be advantageous for you to organise the employment of the trained and professional services of a nurse, if not two, to share the full-time duties of caring for this man, your husband of so many years and now my patient of but a few days. In addition to this, it is my considered opinion that you should communicate with Mr Carlile's London office as soon as possible words to the effect that he shall no longer be able to retain his position in the bank. They may well wish to send his private assistant down here in the days and weeks to come to commence the termination and subsequent transfer of his authority and duties, for he will not be able to move from within these walls for some time, if at all.'

To which Catherine's petite voice had been heard to reply, 'Very well, Dr Mathews, I will obviously be guided by your learned opinion and make the necessary arrangements for my husband's care. Is there no possibility that my husband will be able to return to London and his position in the bank at some time in the future?'

Immediately, the reply to this concerned enquiry had issued forth from the good doctor's thinly sculptured lip.

'My dear lady, as you no doubt realise, in the last few days since the hideous accident which brought Mr Carlile into the position of being my patient, I have been in constant communication with my esteemed medical colleagues in Harley Street and have conveyed to them in the most minute detail the serious nature and detailed extent of your husband's numerous injuries. Even with this intense scrutiny of Mr Carlile's current medical condition by the top men in their field, we have been unable to gauge with any confidence what effect prolonged movement in any form of transportation would have upon his shattered body. With regard to your enquiry of his returning to his office at some future time, in association with what I have just explained to you, it is our considered medical opinion that, due to the severity of the injuries incurred by Mr Carlile, he will never regain the use of his legs. Therefore, it would appear that his world of activity will be forever limited to the access granted to him by a wheelchair. It is also doubtful to what extent his mental capacity has been effected by the injuries his head sustained in the fall. His mind, along with his body, may never again truly express the thoughts and feelings of this fine man in same way as before this fateful day. My final words to you now, Mrs Carlile, must be not to expect much improvement from what you see before you today. It is my own opinion that Mr Carlile will see out the rest of his days, however many that may be, in the relative peace and security of this, his country home.'

Upon the conclusion of this lengthy discourse on the part of the earnest Dr Mathews, Catherine had appeared almost unable to comprehend the words this kindly doctor had desperately tried to impart to her as gently as possible, with her only response, which upon overhearing had lingered in Montague's battered mind as he had drifted fretfully back to sleep, having been, 'Thank you, Dr Mathews, all we can do is wait and see.'

So having endured the subsequent hours of that day which had passed through fitful passages of sleep accompanied by horrific nightmares, Montague had again woken with the immediate awareness in the pre-dusk light which had filtered through half-closed curtains into this his temporary resting place of a presence at his bedside. Raising his eyes, his gaze had again been greeted by that of Dr Mathews, true to his word with yet another painkilling injection. However, this time his companion at the foot of Montague's bed had not been Catherine, but instead the rather pathetic and anguish-raked persona of his cherished son, Reginald.

'Found this young man loitering outside your door. I thought it best for all concerned if he came in and spoke to you for a short time,' had been Dr Mathews' meaningful explanation to all present of Reginald's presence at the foot of the bed, as he had administered the injection which would see Montague through the rapidly approaching night's rest.

Upon receiving the injection, Montague had speedily thanked Dr Mathews and had sent him on his way, eager to converse with his frightened son for the first time since the accident. Montague had feebly beckoned to Reginald to come closer to him by taking the place that the physician had discreetly just vacated beside his bed. Immediately Montague had noticed a degree of trepidation and a certain reluctance in Reginald's process of passage to his father's side and had held out his trembling hand as a sign of welcome to the boy. With that simple action, Reginald had swiftly moved forward and grasping that outstretched hand in his own small hand had bent his head and kissed it, thereby renewing the bond of deep love and respect between this idolising father and his equally devoted son. With the completion of this action working as a catalyst, a cascade of words filled with the emotion of tears which had by manly convention been forced to remain buried inside this young boy for what had been all those long days had finally flowed freely.

'Oh, my dear papa, how much it saddens me to see you suffering so and to know that it is, in part, my fault. For, if it had not been for the great desire I displayed to you to experience my first hunt, it is quite probable to my mind that you would not have taken part in it in the first place. We, as a family, would have remained in London as Mama had requested us to do. I am so very sorry, sir.'

Wishing to relinquish responsibility for this horrendous situation from the shoulders of his fine son, Montague had quickly but painfully replied through swollen and cracked lips, 'Do not trouble yourself, Reginald, my dear son. For if anyone must shoulder the responsibility for what transpired at the weekend, it must to my mind be anyone or anything but you, my precious, sweet boy. Your actions during the hunt brought nothing but pride and honour to your mama and myself. The Master himself praised your riding prowess personally to me after your return home that day. So please, my boy, let these words from your old papa's lips ease your mind of its troubles.'

'Thank you, Papa. Does the doctor know how long it will be before you are well enough to return to London? Mama says that I must return very soon to my studies, but how can I think of those with you, my poor papa, so ill in your bed,' had been Reginald's response, his young cherubic face a mirror of the worry which his anguished mind had held for his beloved father.

'Reginald, you must not concern yourself too intently with the affairs of my health. It is, however, most important that you treat your studies with the respect and dedication that I expect a son of mine would show. Unfortunately, it would appear that it will be some considerable time before I will be able to return to London. My bones, I fear, are not as young as they used to be and it will take some time for all my injuries to heal. However, I see no reason why your governess cannot be brought down from London. I will speak with your mama on this subject in the next few days,' had been Montague's loving, yet increasingly painfully mumbled reply.

With the completion of these kind words on the part of his still courteous father, Reginald had noticed Montague's eyelids gradually closing, with the doctor's injection having started to take its effect upon his pain-racked body and mind.

In turn, Reginald, in an obviously relieved frame of mind, had hazily been observed by the contented Montague. As the boy had quietly taken his leave of his beloved papa, Montague had floated yet again into a sea of drug-induced, turbulent sleep with the hope of some much needed rest.

So the routine of his new life had been established. With Dr Mathews as a regular and welcome visitor to his bedside, Montague had endured the subsequent days that had passed through erratic passages of sleep – made possible only by the regular administration by the diligent country doctor of the powerful drug morphine – and equally disconcerting passages of wakefulness. Montague had gradually groped his way tenaciously back to total consciousness of what he had still thought to be his temporary surroundings and his own disbelieving rejection of the drastic situation in which fate had placed him.

As the days had passed, his strength had grown and his health had improved such that the point in time had been reached where, with carefully chosen words from Catherine's lips, Montague had gradually been made aware of the passage of events which had caused his now painfully apparent – to all but Montague himself – permanent demise. His own mind had gradually restored to him the blurred remembrance of the instant when he had fallen towards the ground. Catherine had, like bricks in a broken wall, subsequently filled in the missing spaces, the facts of his newly altered life.

How well Montague now remembered that particularly sunny October morning as he had lain in his bed in quiet appreciation of the warmth emanating from the robust fire which had blazed in the grate positioned to the side of his bed. He had become aware of a faint knock upon the heavy smoking-room door. Upon readily bidding this visitor entry to his lonely domain, Montague's effort had been rewarded by the view of his ever-caring and radiant wife, Catherine. Quietly and floating on the same cushion of delicacy which had caught his eye all those years ago in Vienna, Catherine, like a ministering angel, a picture of heartfelt wifely concern, had glided effortlessly to rest upon a straight-backed chair which had been positioned at the side of Montague's bed and had uttered the following opening greetings and requests.

'Good morning, Montague, my dearest husband, I hope you slept a little better last night. Are you comfortable? I do hope you are not in too much pain!'

'Thank you for your concern, my dear. In answer to your request, yes, I did sleep rather better last night than any previous night, although I cannot say that I do not miss my own bed and your most intimate affection and marital companionship. No, I am not in any notable pain at all this morning, testament, I should think, to the most capable skill of Dr Mathews. The pain does appear to be diminishing slightly as each day passes, which I hope means I am recovering more rapidly than was first hoped and I indeed will soon be able to return to London and thus resume our life together as a true family once more,' had been Montague's pleasant and naive reply to what had appeared to him the face of his understandably concerned wife.

'Montague, my dearest love, the time has unfortunately arrived when it has been suggested to me by Dr Mathews that you must be made aware totally of what occurred on that fateful day last September and, consequently, what your subsequent injuries were and their effect on your and our future life. You have made it known that you were aware at the time that your mount had lost its footing upon the approach to jumping a fallen tree.

However, in reality, that terrified mount having indeed lost its footing had actually fallen on you, stunning itself into unconsciousness in the process, crushing your body and limbs and pinning your already illness-racked and weakened frame upon the cold damp earth beneath its massive bulk. There you remained for some considerable time as the fog had rolled in obscuring the view to the participants of the hunt – which in passing, might I tell you, was abandoned at this point in the day's events – who valiantly searched for you, their task made even harder by the fact that your mount, in the process of falling, had hidden himself and consequently you in your position beneath it from their view, behind the immense fallen tree. Your injuries have thereby been extremely serious with' – and, at this point in Catherine's monologue of doom she had paused and taken a deep breath before continuing – 'both your legs severely, and I am devastated to say, irreparably twisted, a deep gash to your thigh, a number of your ribs were broken and from where your head had hit the iron-like ground a large bump and open gash on the side of your forehead resembling the imprint of a horseshoe, a broken nose and a badly swollen face. Your condition was further aggravated by the severe chill you had been battling prior to that weekend.

'The hardest realisation for you, my dearest love, Montague, will be the fact, which has been made discouragingly apparent to me by Dr Mathews and now through me, as I hope, his gentle emissary, is that the wonderful life of finance and banking you have experienced in your beloved London and throughout the civilised world must, I am regretful to say, be over. Dr Mathews, in detailed association with his eminent Harley Street colleagues, has been unable to say confidently what effect prolonged movement in any form of transportation would have upon your broken body at this immediate point in time, or at any point in the foreseeable future. It is their learned opinion for your own safety and security that your new life must be spent in the relative comfort of this, your country home. It is therefore with a very heavy heart that I must impress upon you this realisation that your future life will be lived in the shadow of possible early death if you do not abide by the instructions of your physicians,' Catherine had tearfully stated.

In recognition of the intense pain she had also felt, Catherine had further quickly added, 'Oh, Montague, what a shock it was to me when the huntsman came that cold, wet, windy day with word that there had been a dreadful accident during the proceedings of the hunt. My mind immediately thought of Reginald who, at that stage, had just arrived home to the manor. Subsequently, the thought ran through my mind of how grateful I was that Reginald had not been witness to some poor soul's pain and suffering, not realising for the briefest of moments that it had been you, my dearest love, Montague, who had come to grief. I truly believed that the huntsman had come to our home only for the reason that this was the closest residence, not because it affected us so personally. It was not until Hopkins came to me in the drawing room and informed me that the trap, with Old Ben in command, had been sent to the northern boundary of the estate and his junior, George, had been sent to fetch the village doctor. Innocently, before Hopkins had had time to take a breath and continue with his tactful words of explanation of the events of the hunt as told to him by the huntsman himself, and his own actions in rendering assistance, I had immediately requested of Hopkins if he had known the identity of the poor unfortunate rider.

'What a shock it was to my mind, the name which greeted my ears being none other than yours. I sent word immediately below stairs for Reginald who, at that precise time had been in his bedroom in the process of changing from his mud-splattered riding attire, to be distracted away from what I well imagined would be quite gruesome proceedings, having in my time witnessed many a rider come to grief with dire consequences. All then I could do was make ready for your arrival by organising this bed here, in your smoking room, having wished to minimise the risk of any further injury by your prolonged carriage up the steep staircase to our bedroom, and wait. Oh, Montague, it seemed like an eternity before Old Ben returned home to the manor. As I watched from the drawing-room window, I viewed with extreme trepidation the sight of the slowly approaching trap with your seemingly lifeless body laid out in the back. Simultaneously to your arrival had been the prompt arrival of Dr Mathews, the

Marlford village doctor, escorted by George, the groom. As Collins, Gilbert, Old Ben and George, under Dr Mathews' strict supervision, had carried your limp and bloodied body from the trap on an old door, the thought that you were dead had sprung into my mind and must, I feel, have, by the look upon my face, become apparent to Dr Mathews, for he had momentarily turned his attention from his intense concern for you as his patient and had quickly affirmed to me your hold on life and that you were at present in a deep state of unconsciousness.

'Montague, what a dreadful sight beheld itself to my eyes as I came to your side. As upon my direction, acceded to, I might say, by the good doctor, the servants placed you dressed still in your mud-caked, hunting attire upon the crisp white sheets of this bed. Your face streaked not with the blood of the fox that you had set forth that morning to hunt but your own precious life's blood, the dreadful gash upon your forehead still oozing rich and red. It was, however, to all concerned blatantly obvious that, although this wound was serious, it was not the one which gave most concern to Dr Mathews, for as you had been laid out it was made dramatically clear to all by the white of your breeches now so heavily stained red that your legs were a mangled and twisted shadow of their former dependable and muscular self with much of their framework contorted and lying askew from their proper place.'

With that, Montague had burst forth angrily. His words issued through clenched teeth, tears had welled in pools in his tormented dark eyes and in the process he had thumped the bed fiercely with a closed fist.

'Stop, Catherine, stop, I do not wish to hear any more. If what you say is true, and I do not believe that in a matter of such gravity you would be at all flippant, then I might as well have been left to perish upon the cold, damp ground that calamitous day. My life, it would appear, is over. What pray tell is left to me? The life of a twisted cripple shut away in nothing more than a prison, banished from what little peace and pleasure I may have been able to secure in my beloved London. Why did I not listen to your words of advice and now disastrously apparent wisdom and remained secure in our home at Witton Place that weekend? The only issue which gives me any degree of comfort in this whole dreadful matter is the knowledge that Reginald was not exposed, at his tender age, to the horrific sight of the happenings of that fateful day.'

To which Catherine had seized upon the subject most dear to both their hearts, that of the welfare of their only child, Reginald Alexander Carlile, rallying forth with the following carefully pondered over and eloquently spoken words.

'I too, Montague, am eternally grateful that Reginald was spared the horrific sight of his cherished father, a battered and broken shell of his former self, being so ungraciously returned to our home. As his mother, it now falls to me to guide and protect his interests and his balanced development. To this end, I do not believe that it is within those best interests for him to remain within these walls so filled with pain and suffering. It is my considered opinion that he should return to London and the continuation of his studies. The time is fast approaching when he will travel away to Mendrew, as has always been your wish for his future education. So, I truly believe he must have a period of stability and strict routine in his home prior to this important stage in his life. This he will not achieve if he remains here. To this end, I have instructed Gladys to make herself ready in the next few days to make the return journey to London, as protective escort to our son.'

Montague's eyes had again welled with tears at the thought of losing the treasured companionship of his much loved son, but he had realised the helpless position in which fate had now placed him, having forced him to relinquish the control of his own and that of his family's life into the hands of others. He had meekly replied, 'Every other pleasure in my life appears to have been wrenched from my grasp, so I suppose it must be in keeping that what small pleasure I may have obtained from Reginald's young and bright company will also be denied to me. As you have so eloquently revealed to me, I have lost control of all that was mine and must now be helplessly reliant on the pity-filled services of others for the rest of my so-called life. Reginald, I fear, will be bitterly disappointed with this decision. However, as you have previously stated, it is now you who have responsibility and therefore control over his best interests and it is painfully obvious that I am now in no position to effectively countermand your decisions, so there it is.'

'Please, Montague, try and understand that my decision to send Reginald back to London has been made with his best interests at heart and not intended in any way as yet another blow to you personally. He is our son, our only child, and I am sure that deep in your heart you want only the best for him now and in the future, whatever that may hold. To that end, he will return to London with Gladys at the end of the week,' had been Catherine's defiant reply.

Then, quickly following on, she quietly continued, 'Further to this subject of changes within the household, tomorrow will herald the arrival in this house of two new faces, those of day nurse Curtis and night nurse Ballinger whom I have engaged from a most reputable agency in London. They both come to us with an excellent training record and, from what I have ascertained from that agency, impeccable references for this type of nursing. The engagement of their services, I truly hope, will give you more comfort and security in this your new life. In association with this changed life, Godfrey Simpkins will also be arriving in the morning from London to finalise the transfer of control of your professional responsibility in Barland Bank.'

To which Montague had in all but a whisper replied, 'What life changed or otherwise, this is but a tortured existence. No care will ease the pain within my heart and mind now that I am to have ripped from my grasp the first love of my life, my occupation, no vocation, within the domain of the bank. It is of no further concern or interest to me the happenings of life which continue around me. Conduct the affairs of this house and your life as you wish, Catherine, I do not wish to be privy to them ever again. I see myself now as nothing more than a convict seeing his sentence of life imprisonment slowly to its timely and inevitable conclusion...'

So it had been that the resignation of this sentence of an altered life having been passed upon the rest of *his* life had come finally to Montague, with the punctual arrival at Carlile Manor the following morning of the two new members of Montague's household in the form of day nurse Curtis, a tall slim-framed dark-haired woman in her late thirties and night nurse Ballinger, a woman as short in stature as Curtis had been tall with auburn-coloured hair and a countenance which had mirrored her gentle yet determined nature. Montague had quietly but curtly accepted the introduction of these nurses into his new life simply as a practical aid to his physical, if not his mental, comfort.

With words of introduction having been issued from Catherine's lips of, 'Montague, my dear, here are Nurse Curtis and Nurse Ballinger, of whose arrival I spoke to you yesterday,' as the party of three had quietly invaded the last remaining sole domain of the smoking room and had stood before him at the foot of his bed.

Montague had observed this view through dark, emotionless eyes as he had responded coldly, by saying, 'We will soon find out if you know your duties as well as you profess to. This will not be an easy time for either of you. However, that is what you are being paid what I presume must be very good money for, is it not?'

To which the diminutive yet senior member of the new duo, Nurse Ballinger, had indicated to all the strength of spirit and determination to see a job done well which she had held within her reserved personality by quickly retorting, 'Mr Carlile, I believe I may speak on behalf of my colleague Nurse Curtis and reply to your enquiry by saying that we are both highly trained nursing professionals and, if we had wanted an easy life, we would have chosen it by remaining in the civilised atmosphere of London. As you can see, we are both here. The task before us, that of your complete medical care, is here, and here we will both remain until that task is concluded one way or another.'

Well Montague knew that indeed they had both stayed and had indeed been proved to be a valuable combined inclusion into his diminishing household, having both considerably eased the physical pain of his life in the most gentle and methodical of manners.

However, with the subsequent arrival later that same October day of the ever personable countenance of Godfrey Simpkins, Montague's personal assistant from the London city office of the

Barland Bank, into his fractured existence, had come crashing within Montague's beleaguered mind the final stone-cast realisation of this sentence having indeed been for the term of his earthly life with no apparent likelihood of his return to any form of an active professional occupation or, as Montague had always had the conviction of it, a true vocation. This morbid realisation had been heralded by a distinct change in what had always been Montague's crowning glory, his kindly disposition towards his junior colleagues in his domain of the bank and its accompanying affairs. As the softly spoken Simpkins had industriously sorted and catalogued the relevant papers and files to be transported back to London, having already completed the same exercise at Montague's London home and his city office, Montague had moodily lain in obdurate accompaniment offering no assistance to this young man's unpleasant endeavours. Montague's only acknowledgement of the process going on around him had been the curt and uncalled for taunt, to whom Montague had previously always referred to as a most affable and conscientious young man of, 'If you must conduct these actions then at least, man, get on with it as quickly and quietly as possible, then be gone from my sight for ever.'

The request of this manoeuvre from his former superior, Simpkins had readily and speedily acceded to.

As if all that had transpired in these recent days had not been enough for Montague to have had to bear, there had been one final heart-wrenching act which he had had to endure, that of bidding farewell from his life of the gentle and respectful companionship of his son, Reginald. The act of his return to London had confirmed to Montague his own apparent loss and Catherine's subsequent gain of power and control within this family, a taste of which Montague had already ironically silently observed and meekly acceded to upon their initial arrival at the station in Marlford, never having realised how soon that this temporary reversal of roles would have become a permanent arrangement. How well he still remembered the pain, more excruciating than any he had so far experienced in this whole bloody fiasco, which had cut his heart to pieces as cleanly as any dagger. As on that Friday morning, so long gone in time, he had embraced within his withering arms his young son for what both had thought would be the last time.

With both participants in this poignant life scene on the verge of emotional collapse, Montague had struggled valiantly to maintain his composure as a last display to his son of the conduct expected always of him by his father, by extending to Reginald his final thoughts on the matter as followed.

'It is your mama's considered opinion that you should return to London today to continue earnestly your studies in preparation for your eventual and rapidly approaching departure to Mendrew. Reginald, my dear boy, you are aware I know of my ardent wish that you carry yourself favourably at my old school and that you find as much pleasure in the art of learning as I did at your age. Within the confines of my newly altered life, the only pleasure I will ever again achieve will be through your fervent endeavours. So do not think badly of your dear mama, for it is only through the deep love she holds in her heart for you, her only child, that she commands what appears to be such a terrible act in your young eyes.'

To which Reginald had weepingly replied, 'Oh, Papa, I wish so to please you and bring vast honour to the family name of Carlile by my achievements but I do so wish that it could have been you and Mama accompanying me back to London, and that none of these terrible events had happened.'

'We all may wish those thoughts, my son. However, fate has dealt us this hand and we must play it as best we can. The most important issue for you is a sense of stability and strict routine in your young life. Now, my boy, it is time that you go in search of your mama, who will accompany you to the station, and Gladys, your travelling companion, and be on your way. May God grant you a safe journey home to London,' had been Montague's caring words of farewell to his beloved son.

As Reginald had turned from Montague's bedside and quietly departed this room, which in its former life as the smoking room had been the bastion of masculine good cheer and now had established itself morbidly as Montague's prison cell, the word 'routine' had caught in Montague's bedevilled mind. What sort of routine did he have to look forward to? The routine of the bedridden cripple, consumption of the likes of beef tea, chicken broth and fish soup as his daily sustenance, round the clock invalid nursing of a most invasive and dignity-destroying nature and the destruction of his prized world of money and power, together with the disintegration of his family life. Oh, how he had cursed then, as he would time and time again over the years to come, that weekend, that hunt, and most of all that man, who in Montague's eyes had instigated the whole chaotic chain of events which had caused his demise – the Master – and in accompaniment to him – the Master's horn...

Weeks had followed on into months and finally years, the frustration of this new life having taken its toll on all but one of the participants in this drama, Reginald having been the only one spared. Having been returned to London, he had prospered in the relieved atmosphere of his Witton Place home under the austere tutorship of his governess, Miss Laycock, into a very capable and determined scholar. Time had swiftly moved on and he had soon departed to Montague's old school of Mendrew, where he had derived a degree of peace of mind in the tranquil and scholarly surroundings of this old and prestigious school. Along with his mental advancement had come his physical development into a tall young boy, not unlike his father in build yet who had also retained the dark hair and dark green eyes so characteristic of his mother. Together, all these attributes had combined to produce a handsome cherubic-faced boy, possessed of a gentle and compassionate nature which had in turn been steeled by the inheritance of his parents jointly held attribute of iron-fisted determination. This inherited determination of mind and spirit had been constantly directed towards his studies, much to the satisfaction of his tutors and his parents alike, as the various and numerous achievements of this future laird of the manor had constantly been communicated to the pleased and proud inhabitants of Carlile Manor both above and below stairs. However, this limited experience of joy at his son's achievements had been the only pleasure allowed to Montague in his constrained existence.

As fortune would have it, that same atmosphere of peace and tranquillity in which Reginald had so prospered at Mendrew had not by any stroke of the imagination been observed to settle once more in the surroundings of Carlile Manor. Indeed, relations between those under the roof of this impressive country house as time had worn on had become more constrained to the point where, on a particularly sunny day in June, the following cloudy storm burst directed towards Catherine had issued forth from Montague's tangled mind, through the action of his unmerciful lips.

'Why do you stay with me, Catherine? I am but a shell of the man you married all those years ago. I am no use to you any more. The only thing which holds you to me now is the commodity of money. Your daily presence with its still youthful vigour in this, my house, fills me with nothing more than frustration and pain. Further to this, your constant journeys to London and further afield to Mendrew to visit Reginald may well fill your life with pleasure. However, to me this is a constant and degrading reminder of my own loss of mobility and freedom of action. I can only think that you somehow gain a sense of power from this situation and thereby some perverse sense of pleasure in this whole ghastly situation. It has thus come to the point in time when I can no longer tolerate this presence in my tortured life. I desire to recapture a degree of authority and power in my own home and the only way I can achieve this is by your complete and permanent banishment from these confines. It is therefore my wish and further my command, as your husband and laird of this manor, that you move out of my house and my life forthwith.

'You shall return to Witton Place immediately and henceforth reside there permanently. The London household, which I shall supplement with the addition of Gilbert, as a replacement for the services of Collins, whom I shall retain with me here and Donald, who will also return with you to London as a replacement for the services of Joseph whom I seem to recall some time ago terminated his employment within the London household due to the sudden and untimely death of his father and the subsequent need of assistance by his ailing mother in operating their confectioner's shop back in Leeds, will be at your discretion, as will the motor. As for Gladys, she's yours anyway! It would appear that you wish to spend as little time as possible under the same roof as myself.

That being the case, I have with these directives made it unnecessary, dare I say unwarranted, for you to spend any further time here. You, shall, as is your right, as my legal wife, continue to receive an adequate allowance to cover your various expenses and I shall obviously continue to support Reginald's education as is his right as my son and heir. However, Reginald's day-to-day requirements I shall leave in your hands as his mother, as it is blatantly obvious that I am in no position to see to these myself.

'This situation will remain in force until our inevitable deaths, for I do not wish the scandal of any divorce proceedings broadcast to the rumour mongers of London. I have had quite enough of the likes of them and their gossiping ways, with regards to our personal affairs, as you shall no doubt remember. However, should I have cause to question your discretion in the conduct of your personal life in London, I shall show no hesitancy in altering these arrangements with great expediency. I have my nurses to competently attend to my physical needs. We have nothing left to share together. Our married life died the day of the accident when you banished me from our bedroom and marital bed to this room and poor excuse for a bed, and our life as a family died the day you so callously banished Reginald away back to London.' With these final words so filled with pain and hatred for the woman he had once loved so dearly, Montague had fallen silent with the apparent appearance of having been both physically and emotionally drained by this outpouring of bitter recriminations.

Grasping this opportunity of momentary silence on the part of Montague, Catherine having quickly gathered her thoughts had replied in her familiar whisper of a voice which had to Montague always indicated a heart full of deep emotion.

'Oh, Montague, how can you choose today of all days to issue forth with such a vitriolic tirade of words. Do you not remember what day it is today? It is obvious by your words that you do not. It is our wedding anniversary, my husband.'

'It matters not to me that it is that day, or any other day. However, it is perhaps fitting that I should choose this particular day. The act of marriage which we entered into so long ago no longer has relevance in our now quite separate lives. Indeed, perhaps I should have followed the counsel offered to me at the time and never have entered into this state in the first place. However, I wish no longer to play this macabre game of masquerade, as it has become apparent to me we cannot, or more accurately, do not wish to share any longer in each other's lives as true husband and wife. It is therefore my wish, no my command, to be left in the solitary confines of this my prison,' had been Montague's acrimonious reply which he had fired from his thin pale lips as surely as any shot from a rifle and having found its target deep within Catherine's shocked and stunned heart as evidenced by her meekly framed reply.

'If that is your heartfelt wish, Montague, then may I say that if I have learnt nothing else during our many years together, I have learnt that you will not be swayed from this desire and I must regretfully accept it. It is with a very heavy heart that I will make arrangements as soon as possible to return to London and thereby accede to your request by withdrawing myself totally from your life. Before I take my leave of you, may I say that in all things to this day before and after the unfortunate accident, I have always thought of you as my treasured husband. I have thought that I indicated to you the deepest and most intimate love, affection and respect and the enduring wish to continue to endeavour to provide you with the highest levels of physical care through the provision of those dedicated nurses you have just spoken so highly of and mental companionship by relating to you the happenings of our scattered family. My numerous journeys to Mendrew were in my thoughts only to act as a link between yourself and Reginald and to fulfil the responsibility – which I must in my own defence state was thrust upon me by your own foolhardy actions – of solely supervising the upbringing of our son.

'Further, I must say that it was not I who banished you from the comfort and intimacy of our bed, but rather the very nature of the injuries you sustained that dreadful day, and my fervent wish to prevent any further exacerbation of your pain and suffering by prolonging your movement any more than was entirely necessary. I am indeed so sorry for you, if that is not the impression that these combined actions on my part gave to you. You have made it painfully apparent that my love for you means nothing and that you no longer wish to remain as true husband and wife. In parting, I hope you will find the peace in your solitude which you appear to so desperately require. You may rest assured, Montague, that I shall do nothing in my own future solitary life to bring discredit to the family name of Carlile, which I shall still bear proudly,' had been Catherine's emotion charged reply.

Upon its utterance, with pools of tears welling in her milk green eyes, Catherine had turned on the heel of her Italian leather shoes and had fled from Montague's domain and his life.

So with this intercourse of reflections and deeds, Montague had passed upon himself a sentence of solitary confinement within these cold stone walls. His only true companion in this life's struggle had been that of his allegiant manservant Collins, who had chosen to remain with his increasingly ill-natured and perplexing employer through what had turned out to be many a long and unpleasant year. During this time, the thought of this, his home, as a prison had burned deep into Montague's demon-possessed consciousness, to the point where instructions had been forwarded to the relevant estate workers, the commission of work of raising the height of the existing low stone boundary walls which enclosed this massive estate to a height such as to form an impenetrable barrier to the outside world, thereby eliminating the opportunity for access having been granted to the subsequent hunts of any further seasons. Aligned with this new regime of total confinement, had also come the decision by Montague to change for ever the architectural character of what had, in times past, been noted by many as a magnificent example of symmetry and grace into a monstrosity of gargantuan proportions, strangely at odds with the countryside in which it reposed; by the addition to the once refined line of the roof of a series of Gothic style watchtowers and battlements.

Slowly Montague's war of solitude had wound its way along the road of time seemingly untouched by the happenings of the world around him until one cold, damp and miserable September day when Montague's life had again been touched by the demonic hand of fate. As he had sat at the selfsame desk, at which he now reposed in his library, he had been handed by his ever-dutiful butler Collins a black-edged telegram, the contents of which had turned his blood cold and his mind into a sea of hazed thoughts and images as his lips had read aloud the words so starkly printed on the page that he had held in his trembling hands.

'It is with the deepest sadness that I regretfully must inform you that your son, Lieutenant Reginald Alexander Carlile, has been posted missing in action, presumed dead, during a particularly aggressive offensive in the area of the Somme River in France...'

Montague's mind had turned to thoughts of his beloved son. Upon completing his studies at Mendrew, he had followed his own heart and determined mind and had not followed in his somewhat disappointed father's footsteps into his world of finance and banking. By the scanty and infrequent letters he had received from his son since the all but legal dissolution of his marriage to Reginald's mother, Catherine, he learned that Reginald had obviously been so impressed by the stories of the achievements of the regimental fathers of his school chums during those formative years at Mendrew and apparently did not wish to have to endure the likely comparison to his father if he had taken up a career in the city. Instead, he had chosen a military career with its crowning glory having been his graduation from Sandhurst and subsequently his appointment as a commission officer to a battalion of a Guard's Regiment. Oh, how Montague had wished that he had insisted upon his son following him into the secure atmosphere of his former world of money and power, money and power which would have seen this adored lad kept safe from harm. Montague had finally appeared to have lost the last thread which had connected him to any form of pleasure from the life which had existed outside his stone confines. Only time would show how this war to end all wars would in the years to come again impinge upon his own bloodthirsty war with surprising consequences for all concerned.

So it had been that morbidly Montague had continued to endure the years that followed his accident. His injuries had in part slowly mended, his broken nose and ribs had set well, the gash upon his forehead had healed, leaving an almost indistinguishable scar just below his still thick though now totally greyed hairline. His upper body had somehow been granted a renewed

modicum of strength and stamina, allowing him, with Dr
Mathews' permission as his continuing medical consultant, to
extend his range of habitation within the manor via the means of a
wheelchair which with Montague in majestic residence had been
at his command and whim of mind physically manhandled by
Cedric and Angus up and down the grand staircase at any time of
the day or night. However, those had been the only joys within
his physical recovery. Montague's formerly dependable and
muscular legs had, to his abject dismay, followed the route of
recovery which Dr Mathews had initially encouraged him to
believe in those first few weeks after the tragic accident and had
not throughout the many years that had followed regained any of
their former use, having left Montague trapped like some caged
and wounded animal within the domain which his wheelchair's
available access and his renewed strength had allowed.

His mental recovery and readjustment to his altered state of
life had, on the other hand, been all but non-existent with the
frequent recurrence of nightmares and headaches due to the
severe blow to the head Montague had sustained upon that fateful
day, impeding any chance of acceptance of his enforced change of
life on Montague's part. This pain and bitterness directed towards
life and its remaining participants had only been intensified by the
apparent permanent loss of Reginald from Montague's life.
Montague still remembered the hatred which had filled his heart
as he had consigned that telegram upon its onward journey to
Catherine still solitarily resident in their previously shared Witton
Place, Knightsbridge, residence with the simple inscription across
the bottom of its page of, 'May this grievous and soul-destroying
loss be upon your head and his precious blood upon your hands,
MAC.'

The only emotion which had sustained and steeled Montague's will to continue this wretched existence had been that of
deep-seated revenge, the ice cold and calculating thought that one
day he, Montague Alexander Carlile, may have been able to reek
his long savoured after revenge upon the one and only true
person in his eyes and consequently at whose feet he had always
placed the total responsibility for the fateful events of that cold
September day those many years before, the Master Lord Rupert

Penman-Smythe. Revenge, how sweet this deliverance would be, how long the demons of his mind had longingly waited for their intensifying thirst to be quenched. Finally the climax of their passionate work had come through this trance-like meditation of his life as the ultimate and decisive commitment to this act of revenge and had been induced by the eerie wail of the Master's horn...

Part Three

Death and Deception

Montague's body shook uncontrollably from the effects of the cold air which surrounded his frail body, as control of his senses returned and his mind was finally released from the trance-like state as strong as any medium's power to full realisation of his immediate surroundings. This feeling of intense cold which surrounded Montague was not the effect of the weather, as the day was unseasonably warm for the month of September. It was in point of fact a sense of shock which Montague's body and mind were now experiencing at the decisive cognisance of the path he now believed in so fervently and had committed upon this day in his life to take. The path of long-awaited revenge was to Montague's mind paved with rightful endeavours on his part.

The only question which lingered pensively now within the grey matter of Montague's brain was how this process of retribution would be achieved. As he sat pondering this dark question, his eyes cast downwards from the twilight vista that his eyes beheld through the library window – in the process registering in his mind the passage of time which must have elapsed while he had been held within this demon's spell cast over him by the call of the Master's horn – towards the desk top in front of him, strewn with papers, books and newspapers. His attention was caught by the front page headline of the local newspaper, the *Marlford and District Herald*, which lay as yet not scrutinised by the laird of the manor having been delivered to Montague by his diligent and long-suffering manservant Collins, just as he had settled himself in his current position and prior to the commencement of his trance-like meditation. Clutching up the paper in his shaking hands, Montague read aloud, though he was quite alone in the expansive room, the headline and accompanying article as follows:

Earl of Marlford Makes Welcome Return to Country Seat

It is with much pleasure that we, the editor and staff of the *Marlford and District Herald*, extend our most warm wishes of welcome to The Right Hon. the Earl of Marlford, Lord Rupert Penman-Smythe, upon his recent return to his country home, Beeches Hall. We are sure that we may speak on behalf of all our readers when we say how pleased we are to see His Lordship returned safely to English shores once more, having completed his extensive trip abroad to oversee his vast diamond mining interests in South Africa. May we also express our hope that he will remain in this community's company now for an uninterrupted and extended period of time.

There before Montague's dark and glistening eyes, as if by some act of gift giving by Satan himself, lay the chance of accomplishing his demon possessed act of vengeance upon this pillar of the community. With the Earl's recent return from abroad so publicly documented, Montague was granted the perfect opportunity to bid Lord Rupert, his old and dear friend, his own 'welcome home', thereby having the perfect reason to bring the target of his vengeful intentions within his sights, as a spider would woo its prey towards entrapment and death within its web, by proffering the invitation for Lord Rupert to visit Montague here in his own domain of Carlile Manor. Now Montague's intellect must be put to furious labour to provide the means by which this act of retribution would take place.

The thoughts ran rapidly through Montague's haunted mind as he whispered, as though sharing an important secret, again to the empty room, 'Much careful planning and a good deal of dedicated contemplation must be given to this whole process. I have waited so long now to have rough justice act in my favour. I must not rush in my actions or show my hand too soon. Concealment of these most deep-seated desires is of the essence. All must see my actions as those of one dear friend to another.'

Upon rousing himself from these musings and once more realising the passage of time blatantly apparent by the darkness which greeted Montague's eyes as he gazed again through the library window, his hand stretched out and pressed aggressively and urgently the button positioned at the side of his ponderous dark-coloured wood, brass and leather desk which, when activated, summoned the required help needed to move Montague's wheelchair from where it now rested in the library situated on the first floor to the dining room which occupied a ground floor position in this expansive country house.

No more than a few minutes elapsed before a familiar knock responded upon the library door and, upon being granted entry, Collins, in strict supervision to the accompanying Aryan-featured Cedric and Scottish-born Angus, crossed the threshold. Fully aware what his master's request would be, having taken into account the time of the day, the hall clock having just chimed seven, Collins had taken the liberty of bringing his two juniors with him in the full knowledge that his master would be requiring to be moved directly to the dining room downstairs, Montague having dispensed with years ago the time-honoured gentleman's ritual of changing for dinner. His questioning and rebellious logic having been, for whom would he be dressing! With no family left in residence, it would only be for honouring the wishes that convention placed on him by virtue of his position as laird of the manor and, to his mind, it had been the honouring of someone else's wishes namely the Master Lord Rupert Penman-Smythe which had placed him in the crippled position life found him now.

Having been aided downstairs by the customary careful assistance of his dutiful yet gradually diminishing household staff, Montague consumed in an unusually hearty manner his invalid's dinner which consisted of the likes of oyster soup followed by mutton cutlet with mashed potato and Brussels sprouts, chicken soufflé and semolina cream. This meal he devoured with an enthusiasm and a sense of obvious enjoyment not noted in his behaviour since before the accident, his usual manner having always been to pick distractedly at the food placed before him. He also heartily consumed the accompanying beverage concoction of port and egg as prescribed by the ever-patient and conscientious country physician, Dr Mathews. He subsequently retired to bed in the ground floor smoking room which had, after his accident, initially been thought of as a temporary repose. However, as time had moved along its course and Montague's life had been moulded into its altered pattern and routine, he had taken this room which had always been his own masculine domain within this house permanently as his sleeping quarters. Although his strength had been regained to the point of extended access to his house being granted by his wheelchair and the combined efforts of his dedicated staff allowing him to return, if he had so desired, to his old bedroom, the same bedroom he had shared in happier times with Catherine, Montague had had no desire to be haunted by yet more demons of the past. It was thus to his bed beside the hearth that he was aided where he endured a fitful night's sleep, his mind a sea of thoughts and possibilities for the successful accomplishment of his desired endeavours…

The morning brought the initial step in the plan into being. Having consumed a nourishing breakfast of porridge, poached eggs on toast and a cup of weak yet warming coffee, Montague issued the instructions to Collins – who recently had assumed the duties of butler within this household upon the timely and well-deserved retirement of the failing Hopkins – to place a call through to his Lordship's residence. The invitation was extended by Montague via the means of the telephonic system of communications which Catherine, against Montague's strongly held opinion of the waste of good money, had insisted upon the need to have installed in the manor, as what she had declared as a most necessary aid to the manor and its inhabitants, retaining a link with the world outside its confines.

'Good morning, Your Lordship, this is Carlile, Montague Carlile here. I observed in the local newspaper yesterday that you have recently returned from South Africa and again taken up residence at Beeches Hall. I thought you might like to come over to Carlile Manor some time soon for a drink to welcome you home, one old friend to another, so to speak,' Montague tactfully forwarded as his reason for this unheralded communication.

'That's very good of you, Carlile old boy. I would like nothing better than to take a drink with you, my dear old friend. Unfortunately, I am forbidden by my quack physicians to drink any alcohol since, during my recent trip to Africa, I contracted a particularly virulent bout of ague which has, as a consequence, left me unable to tolerate in my system alcohol, of any form, to the point where those Harley Street witch doctors believe that ingestion of the smallest amount of alcoholic substance could indeed be fatal. As one man of the world to another, I would appreciate it if the knowledge of this fact goes no further than this conversation between two old friends, as I have been at pains to keep this information a secret from the family. A somewhat bitter and silent pill to have to take, but then all of us have some cross to bear, do we not?

'Speaking of crosses to bear, I didn't think you had visitors these days. I had heard through the grapevine that you had become a bit of a recluse since the accident all those years ago. I must have heard wrongly. Mind you, I haven't been around here much since my wife Emelia passed away, not long after your accident if my mind serves me correctly. I took myself off to Africa quick smart after the funeral. It was the best thing a man could do in the circumstances, I thought. What with Isabella, my daughter, away at school in Switzerland at the time, there was no use in my remaining here in England and just moping around the place. Speaking of Isabella, she is home now to stay, I hope. You no doubt know she saw service as a nurse in an army field hospital in France during the war. I am immensely proud of all that she achieved in such appalling conditions, especially for a woman of her tender disposition. She stayed on to the end out there, saw some ghastly sights and was truly heroic in her endeavours towards her patients from what I have been told by her superiors.

'Isabella voluntarily extended her tour of duty in part due to a young chap who was brought into the hospital during one particularly bloody offensive in June 1917. From what Isabella has discreetly told me, there was very little of this young man's face left intact. His uniform was all but unrecognisable as it hung in ribbons and he bore no form of identification upon his battered and bloodied person. The surgeons did not believe that he would see the night out let alone go home. He did both, primarily due to the assiduous care showered upon him by Isabella, as she remained constantly by his side. They came home together to Beeches Hall, which, in my absence in South Africa, I allowed to be thrown open as a convalescence home for returned combatants of all regiments, where he remains still. All but inseparable they are those two. A most unfortunate situation for all concerned, as the poor chap has no recollection of who he is, where he comes from, who his family are or during the war what rank or regiment he served as, or with, to the point where he does not even know his own name.

'The hospital staff in France unceremoniously christened him for want of a better name, John Smith, and that it has stayed to this day. The best medical minds in this country cannot say if this situation will be permanent for this poor wretched young man but Isabella has got it into her sweet head that whatever happens she wishes to remain with him permanently, which means of course her eventual marriage to this hapless chap. I cannot say, Carlile, that I greatly approve of this action on her part and I have, I must admit, on countless occasions since my return, told her so in no uncertain terms. However, Isabella informs me that her mind is made up and that she will not be swayed on this most important issue. Much as I like the chap, and he probably would in time make a decent husband to some young woman, he is not what I had in mind as the future husband to the woman who, at my passing, will inherit a large and extremely valuable estate. I must do something about my will if that happens,' was Lord Rupert's familiarly long-winded reply to the extended invitation.

'A very sad and courageous story, Your Lordship. Might I be so bold as to suggest to your lordship, if you would prefer, the Lady Isabella and her young gentleman friend are most welcome to accompany you here to Carlile Manor and we could all take tea together, and perhaps, later, enjoy a spirited game of whist,' was Montague's remarkably diplomatic and quick-witted response, not wishing to allow the target of his revenge for all these years to disappear from his sight without a fight.

'That Carlile, would indeed be a splendid idea and I feel sure I may accept this most gracious invitation on behalf of Isabella and her young companion. The young man needs to be taken out of himself a little and this outing will be, I think, just what he needs,' Lord Rupert loudly enthused.

'So it will be. Today is Monday. Would Friday afternoon at three o'clock be convenient to you and your party, Your Lordship?' Montague tactfully enquired as he fleetingly remembered with a stinging poignancy someone else long ago who the Earl had insisted needed taking out of themselves and the resultant drastic consequences.

'I have no reason to believe that that would not be so, Carlile. However I will enquire of Isabella of her proposed movements for that afternoon and if it is not convenient I will let you know by tomorrow evening. Thank you again most sincerely. Forgive me, for I must close this conversation now. I look forward to seeing you on Friday. I have so much more to tell you of my life since we last met. Goodbye for now,' Lord Rupert boomed down the telephone line and was gone, leaving Montague to sit once again in blissful silence gathering his perfidious thoughts.

Two dark figures, one tall, the other equally short, silhouetted in the gentle hue of the pre-dusk light, approached the massive oak front door of Carlile Manor having just alighted from an equally dark and, in the last hint of sun, shiny black cab. Upon reaching this entranceway the shorter of the two shadow-like figures requested entry to this grand country home by pressing impatiently upon the highly polished brass doorbell positioned in the stone wall to the right of the door. They waited silently in the rapidly descending darkness for their request to be answered. All but a few moments passed. The impressive wooden barricade was creakily pulled aside and the two shadows became three.

The taller of the two new visitors who now stood on the threshold to the invitingly warm entrance hall spoke enquiringly with a ring of authority which his many years in a senior position gave to his deep and educated London voice.

'I take it, young man, that you are the local village constable who reported this apparent murder to us at Scotland Yard earlier this afternoon?'

To which the young man who stood before his now superior officer nervously replied, 'Yes, sir, I am Constable Stevens from the Marlford Police.'

'As you would probably be aware, my name is Inspector Dentworth and this is my assistant, Sergeant Jones. You will from this point on until further notice be under my immediate direction and orders, Constable. Well, men, let us not stand here in the cold all night. We have a murder to investigate. It has taken well and truly long enough to get down here in that old rattle trap they dare to call a train,' the authoritative voice of law and order commanded sternly of his subordinates, having not in the least been impressed by the stop, start, slow nature of the stopping at all stations market-train journey, which he and his junior colleague had just endured.

In Inspector James Dentworth stood an impressive example of the methodical art of criminal detection and investigation, possessed as he was of a keen mind and dedicated work habit. Rare were the occasions when this man dubbed by his superiors 'the Pride of Scotland Yard' did not get his man and he fully intended this not to be the case in this current investigation. He was blatantly aware of the seriousness of the investigation he was about to commence, with the murder victim being none other than the Right Hon. the Earl of Marlford, Lord Rupert Penman-Smythe.

'Constable Stevens, please enlighten us with the most relevant details of this enquiry which you have collected so far,' Inspector Dentworth quietly yet firmly commanded of this sandy-haired and rosy-cheeked young example of the honest and hard-working village policeman as the party ventured deeper into the grand entrance hall.

Constable Stevens quickly and clearly replied to his newly acquired superior along the following lines.

'The deceased is one Rupert Henry Penman-Smythe, the Right Hon. the Eighth Earl of Marlford, who had accepted the invitation extended to him by the owner of this property, Carlile Manor, one Montague Alexander Carlile, to take tea with him at the appointed time of three o'clock this afternoon, the invitation having also been extended to His Lordship's daughter, the Lady Isabella Emily, her gentleman companion whose name I have yet to ascertain correctly and the village doctor, Dr Robert Douglas Mathews. As the assembled guests and host had settled in the drawing room and were in the process of finishing partaking of the said tea, a knock had come upon the French windows which led from the drawing room to the terrace and the grounds beyond. The butler, who had at that point in time been engaged in the supervision of the tea things, upon answering the knock had found the head groom in an extremely agitated state of mind and body who had subsequently requested the services of Dr Mathews as an accident had occurred down at the stables involving one of the stable hands. The butler had subsequently been sent to retrieve the doctor's bag from his automobile, as the doctor himself had hurried with the head groom directly to the stables. The Lady Isabella and her gentleman friend had just stepped out into the garden to take a breath of fresh air, having finished their tea more rapidly than the older members of the party, leaving Mr Carlile and His Lordship still in the drawing room engaged in what has been described to me as quite animated conversation. As the young couple promenaded around the lawns, they observed Mr Carlile alone on the terrace. Oh, by the way, Inspector, Mr Carlile is an invalid confined to a wheelchair. Having seen to the injuries of the stable hand, the doctor returned to the drawing room as did the other guests, in the process discovering what appeared at first sight to be the sleeping form of His Lordship. On further, more detailed investigation, the doctor realised His Lordship was in fact dead through what he saw as extremely unnatural circumstances.'

With that, Inspector Dentworth halted the young constable in his monologue of the events succinctly with the words, 'That will do for the present, thank you, Constable Stevens. Have the guests been retained and has the body of the deceased been left un-touched?'

To which Constable Stevens promptly replied, 'Yes, Inspector, all the guests are waiting in the ground floor dining room and the body of the deceased has been left as we found it in the drawing room, which is adjacent to the dining room. I have been informed by those persons present this afternoon that no one moved the body or disturbed anything in the room itself after the discovery of the death of the Earl.'

'What about the servants of the household?' enquired the inspector, eager to have no loose ends at this early stage in the investigation.

To which Constable Stevens, wishing to be seen by his superiors as a capable officer, at once replied, 'The servants of the house have been requested to remain within the servants' hall downstairs until further instructed. Further to this, the estate workers have been gathered in the stables.'

'Good man, Stevens. Now, I think it is time that we saw the scene of this apparent crime for ourselves, if you would be so kind as to show us the way to the drawing room,' Inspector Dentworth politely yet firmly instructed his newly acquired subordinate.

With the utterance of that command, the party of three, under Constable Stevens's stewardship, traversed the grand entrance hall and walked briskly yet remarkably quietly along the wide, wood-panelled and parquetry-floored corridor which gave unrestricted access to the rooms which occupied the ground floor of this impressive country house. Finally, the party stopped at a pair of ornately carved teak doors, at which point Constable Stevens politely stood aside issuing the words, 'This is the drawing room, Inspector.'

Coming to a halt before these imposing examples of the wood carver's art with their swirling curves and intricate chisel work, Inspector Dentworth, his grey eyes shining with the challenge of this new puzzle of death, turned to his companion in this mission and many before like it, Sergeant Charles – Charlie to his numerous chums in the force – Jones and said, 'Well, Sergeant Jones, are you ready to once more do battle with the dastardly instigators of crime to bring true and fair justice to bear?'

To which Sergeant Jones, a man of relatively short stature and solid build, possessed of a head of thinning brown hair now becoming generously speckled with grey as testament to his advancing years, set above a kind yet intelligent face, rapidly and with a force and character to his voice born of the true conviction he held within his heart of the rightfulness of the actions he was about to once again enter into, in the performance of his duties as a veteran member of the country's elite police force, replied to his superior colleague in cases such as this for the last eight years, 'Yes, sir, I am ready, to see once more that justice is done to all.'

Satisfied with this assurance of his subordinate's continued dedication to his duties, Inspector Dentworth turned his attention once more towards the drawing-room door. He grasped the thin, shining, brass door handle in his long, willowy fingers and in the enactment of this process he pushed down and inwards upon the paired doors of the drawing room, thereby having gained for himself and Sergeant Jones their first observation of the apparent murder scene. The view which beheld itself to their eyes as Inspector Dentworth noiselessly opened the large double doors was one of a most tastefully decorated room, indicative of the obvious wealth and position with which the owner of this fine home was endowed.

As his eyes carefully scanned across this refined and orderly panorama, from the fern green painted walls scattered with a striking collection of oils by many renowned European masters to the intricate Venetian glass chandelier, his gaze finally settled upon the comfortable setting of chintz-covered, deeply cushioned armchairs positioned at the centre of this room. For within one of these luxurious chairs reposed a man of advanced years, clean-shaven except for a well-clipped military style moustache, with a head of dishevelled silver-grey hair and a face tanned by sun more fierce than any experienced in England. His frame was well covered as befitting a man of wealth who, at first sight, might well have been thought to be blissfully asleep. Yet upon careful observation, the expression of horror which shrouded this poor soul's contorted countenance left Inspector Dentworth in little doubt that his had been no natural decline into death. Beside the victim, on a small occasional table, sat a half-empty teacup slightly askew in its resident saucer and beside it the accompanying plate with a few crumbs the only visible indicator of the repast which this man had consumed.

Inspector Dentworth looked towards the sideboard positioned along the back wall of this harmonious room. Upon it, he observed the remnants of the day's fare. A large silver teapot reposed regally in accompaniment to a pair of equally majestic multilayered cake trays, on which lay a partially depleted variety of cakes, sandwiches and pastries. Beside these, sitting with an apparent disregard for their place in the order of the day, were the equally gleaming silver milk jug and sugar bowl, along with the cups, saucers and plates which had been gathered by the butler prior to the intrusion by the head groom and now sat methodically stacked within a glistening silver tray upon the highly polished sideboard.

Turning his attention from this initial observation of the victim and the scene of the crime, Inspector Dentworth spoke again to the two officers in his control who now stood side by side before him.

'Constable Stevens, is there another room close by this room that may be placed at our disposal for the purpose of conducting our interviews?'

'Yes, Inspector, prior to your arrival, I requested that information of the butler and, having been informed that at the end of this corridor there is the now rarely used billiard room, I have viewed the said room and had it prepared for your anticipated requirement. I feel sure the room will suit your needs,' Constable Stevens dutifully replied.

'Good man, Stevens, that is what I like to see in my men, some initiative,' the inspector replied encouragingly to this instantly likeable young lad.

'Jones, please go to the dining room and ask the village doctor to come in here. Constable Stevens, I want you to go down to the stables and bring the head groom back to the billiard room. Right, you have your instructions, man, now hop to it, quick smart, and let us get this investigation under way,' Inspector Dentworth snappily commanded.

With the departure from the room of his two men, Inspector Dentworth again engaged himself in the observation of the scene of the crime as he ventured deeper into the bowels of the room. As he prowled keenly around its plush confines, the questions revolved unceasingly within this hound of detection's methodical mind. Who had brought about this man's untimely death? By what means and when had it occurred? For what reason? Who would benefit by this man's death and how? Who, if any, were his enemies and, for that matter, his closest friends? These were the questions which must in the hours, days and possibly weeks to come be resolved to a fruitful conclusion. Whilst deep within this contemplation of the multitude of currently unanswered questions, a sharp knock upon the drawing-room door smartly brought the inspector back from his intense meditation, prompting him to instinctively bark out the command, 'Enter.'

To which the drawing-room door slowly opened to reveal the sight of Sergeant Jones accompanied by a tall dark-haired man seemingly of middle age who appeared to the inspector, at this first sight, pleasingly to carry with him an aura of alertness tinged with benevolent kindliness as befitting a man of his chosen profession.

'Thank you, Sergeant Jones, I will need you now to take notes for me. I think it best if you sit on the chair over by the French windows,' Inspector Dentworth espoused as he indicated to Jones the straight-backed chair beside the window.

With a nod of acknowledgement between the two men, Jones deftly moved into his requested position. In doing so, he took from the left breast pocket of his crisp police uniform his trusty black leather-clad police issue notebook and seated himself ready for the initial interview in this investigation to commence.

Inspector Dentworth motioned to the doctor to take his seat upon yet another of these solid-form chairs which were grouped around a green baize-covered card table positioned in front of the French windows. The doctor readily accepted this direction, promptly placing himself opposite the inspector at the table which still lay with the pack of cards ceremoniously at attention in the centre, ready for the intended game of whist which, with the tragic passage of events, had never eventuated.

In opening the enquiry, Inspector Dentworth, his grey eyes penetrating from behind his wire framed round spectacles, cordially instructed, 'Sir, for our records please state your full name, address and occupation.'

The reply came from the interviewee immediately and with a natural degree of ease, Inspector Dentworth dully noted.

'Certainly, Inspector, my name is Robert Douglas Mathews and I reside at Apple Tree Cottage in the village of Marlford. My occupation is that of village doctor which, may I say, is a position I have competently held for a good twenty years.'

'Thank you, Dr Mathews, for that information. Now, if you could in your own words and good time tell me of the pertinent events leading up to and of this afternoon, as they appeared to you,' Inspector Dentworth further quietly commanded.

'Yes, Inspector. Well, to begin with, Mr Montague Carlile, the owner of this residence, Carlile Manor, contacted me on Wednesday night last, informing me that he was holding afternoon tea at this said residence on Friday afternoon at the time of three o'clock to bid 'welcome home' to the Earl of Marlford who, you may not know, had recently returned to his country estate, Beeches Hall, having spent an extended period of time in South Africa overseeing his mining interests there. Further to this point, Mr Carlile enquired if I might also like to accept an invitation to take tea at the appointed time, day and place and later to participate in a friendly game of whist with the other members of the party, those members being Lord Rupert Penman-Smythe, his daughter the Lady Isabella, her young gentleman friend whose name I believe is Mr John Smith, and Mr Montague Carlile. I accepted most readily this invitation, as I was happy to see Mr Carlile finally becoming interested in life outside the solitary confines of these grey stone walls once more, after many years as a virtual recluse brought about in part as a result of a most tragic riding accident which occurred many years ago. I was also keen to hear His Lordship's impressions of life in the wilds of South Africa and the thought of an enthusiastic game of whist was further music to my ears.

'So I gratefully accepted Mr Carlile's most gracious invitation and presented myself here at the appointed time of three o'clock this afternoon, having driven myself over from my cottage in Marlford in my newly acquired Austin Seven. The other guests, having arrived only moments before me, were still in the entrance hall in the process of divesting themselves of their heavy motoring coats when I, too, crossed the threshold of this outwardly grotesque country home. Now, as one party, we were subsequently escorted by Collins, the butler, to this, the drawing room, to be greeted with a most animated welcome by Mr Carlile in the obviously happy role as our host for the afternoon. We were at this point formally introduced, I myself knowing the Earl only in the role of the doctor who administers to his household, but not himself, his needs of a medical nature being catered for by my most esteemed and senior colleagues in Harley Street.

'However, I had never formally met his daughter or her companion previously, the Lady Isabella also having spent a good deal of her relatively short life abroad from where I am of the understanding that she made the acquaintance of her gentleman friend. With formal introductions having been conducted, we settled upon these most comfortable, upholstered chairs' – Dr Mathews nodding in the direction of where the deceased now reposed – 'and were in the final proceedings of having enjoyed a most sumptuous high afternoon tea or should I say banquet, the likes of which I personally have not seen since prior to the war. The Lady Isabella and her young gentleman friend, having both finished their tea more rapidly than the more elderly members of the party, had expressed their wish to take a breath of fresh air, even though it was indeed fresh September air, and had in due course proceeded to promenade around the spacious grounds.

'It was at this point that an urgent knock had sounded upon the French windows which, as you can see, lead from this room to the terrace outside and beyond to the lawns and gardens and further still to the grounds and outbuildings of this still quite vast estate. Upon opening the window, Collins, the butler of long standing in this household, had been confronted by an obviously distressed expression and appearance upon the sweat-covered face and about the bloodstained clothes of Old Ben, the head groom. After quick consultation between these two long-serving and trusted employees of our host, Collins left the groom standing as was his place to remain on the terrace, came to his master's side as he sat in his wheelchair positioned between myself and His Lordship and whispered discreetly in his ear, to which Mr Carlile whispered an unheard reply.

'Mr Carlile then turned sharply to me and explained the issue of these two men's concern being that one of the stable boys had sustained a nasty gash to his arm which was bleeding quite profusely, the result of the flailing hooves of a particularly recalcitrant horse as the lad had tried to move him into his stall down at the stables. Old Ben, as he is known by all around here, had had the presence of mind to dash up here in the knowledge that, having seen me arrive earlier, I would be able to attend promptly to the lad's injuries. I subsequently requested that Collins be sent in search of my medical bag which was at the time residing in my motor, the said mechanical steed I had parked myself in the garage upon my arrival earlier. I hurried off to the stables accompanied by Old Ben who, in passing, I noticed was awash with dried blood. Not waiting for the return of Collins with my bag, as with this quite obvious evidence that the lad was indeed bleeding quite badly, I wished to stem the flow as quickly as possible. As I now remember, Collins would have been only a few steps behind myself and Old Ben when we reached the stables where he remained holding my bag and assisting me while Old Ben held the lad and his arm steady.

'I first stemmed the flow of blood which was extremely difficult and quite time-consuming. In the process I was able to calm the lad's pain by the use of a hypodermic injection of morphine, then, finally, the point was reached where I sutured the deep crescent-shaped wound to the lad's right forearm. Strangest thing though, with the bandaging of the wound in its final stages of completion, Collins left me in the stables without any words of explanation. I literally turned from my patient in the act of imparting some words of advice to the assembled group to find him missing, all but spirited away. It must have been that he felt compelled to report to his master that all was now again in order in the stables. It had taken some considerable time to quench the bleeding and attend to the wound. However, when I returned alone across the grounds whence I had come, I observed the young couple, the Lady Isabella and Mr Smith strolling up the grounds in the now faltering light in the act of returning to the house.

'Their explanation, as voiced by Mr Smith to me of their actions, had been that upon moving closer to the terrace they had each time heard His Lordship and Mr Carlile in animated conversation and did not wish to interrupt and thereby disturb these two old friends in what had appeared to them to be high-spirited banter. As I cast my gaze in the direction of the house, my eyes were caught by a movement and I noticed Mr Carlile sitting alone at the edge of the terrace under the now unwarranted protection of a small gazebo. I thus suggested that it might be a suitable time for all to return to our host and the festivities of the afternoon, whereupon we rejoined in the gazebo Mr Carlile who had discreetly explained to me his presence there as having also required a short breath of air and silence away from what had apparently developed in my, and the young couple's, absence into the never-ending and monotonous monologue of His Lordship's life in the wilds of South Africa. Mr Carlile's excuse for his departure from His Lordship had been whispered to me. Then also in his daughter's hearing it was to request the returned company of the Lady Isabella and her friend. Having joyously found all the missing members of the party together, we returned to the drawing room, whereupon we discovered His Lordship at first sight apparently in gentle slumber. However, upon further more detailed investigation on my part, I was shocked to find His Lordship was indeed dead. I, therefore, in the role of local medical officer, instructed that nothing be touched and that Mr Carlile should contact the police immediately. That, I think, brings us clearly to where we are at present, Inspector,' Dr Mathews stated determinedly, finally bringing his testimony to its methodical conclusion.

'Thank you, Dr Mathews, for that most detailed observation and recitation of the events as they appeared to you. I have only a couple of further questions to put to you. If you would please rise now and accompany me over to where the body still lies,' Inspector Dentworth again authoritatively commanded of the extremely compliant country physician, as indicated by the good doctor's quick movement to accompany the inspector, as both men rose from their seats in one fluid movement and moved to stand before the purple-faced and slightly slumped figure which had previously formed such a dynamic part of this modest hamlet's life. As the inspector and the doctor stood looking down at this morbid sight of a life cut prematurely short, the inspector again spoke.

'As you may well know, in cases such as these, the services of the police doctor are brought into the operation. However, in this instance, Dr Scott, your police counterpart, will not be arriving here until later tonight as he has been unavoidably detained in London on other police matters. With this being the case, I would be obliged if, in your capacity as local village doctor, you could give me some relevant medical information.'

To which Dr Mathews, his face a picture of professional dili-
gence, eagerly agreed to this request by the simple nod of his
intelligent head.

'Right then, Doctor, firstly, is it possible for you to deduce
from your observations of the body of the deceased an approximate time of death and, secondly, again from these observations,
could you give me any thoughts on the matter of how that death
might have occurred?' The inspector calmly asked the questions
which had been burning within his mind as the good doctor had
reported his recollections of this tragic afternoon. However, as
was his method, Inspector Dentworth always allowed the subject
of his interviews full and uninterrupted rein in such dissertations
as these.

'Well, Inspector, as I have just informed you, the visiting
party's arrival was at approximately three o'clock. We subsequently spent about an hour partaking of the sumptuous
afternoon tea. Further to this, it was, as I now recall from my
memory, a few minutes after four that the knock came upon the
French windows heralding the news from the stables. I remember
this quite precisely as I had just replaced my watch into my
waistcoat pocket having wondered how long we had been
subjected to the seemingly endless monologue of His Lordship's
exploits in South Africa. Further to this, having completed my
administrations down at the stables, I again consulted my trusty
timepiece and was surprised to observe that such time had flown
by so rapidly, for it was approaching five o'clock. In passing, may I
make the observation that only a few minutes were taken up in
conversation between Mr Carlile, the Lady Isabella, Mr John
Smith and myself at the edge of the terrace before we returned to
the drawing room and found His Lordship in such a tragic
condition. Upon examining him, I found no pulse and further
registered no heartbeat or sign of breathing. The skin of his hand
was cool, but not totally cold to touch and obviously at that point
in time, no signs of rigor mortis had set in. Therefore, from all
these observations, both human and medical, it is my considered
opinion that Lord Rupert Penman-Smythe's death occurred not
long before his party's return to this room, that is to say some
time between four and five o'clock this afternoon.

'As to your second request, Inspector, again having viewed the body in limited detail, not wishing to disturb the scene to any great degree, I can only make the following observations – as duly noted down in Sergeant Jones's regulation police issue black leather notebook:

'1. The death occurred suddenly and insidiously, as witnessed by the lack of movement of the deceased from where he had previously comfortably reposed. There was no apparent signs of injury to the body in keeping with any physical struggle having taken place.

'2. The purple discoloration of the face and the bluish hue taken on by the lips, ears and fingernails of the deceased indicate to me that he may well have been asphyxiated. This theory is I believe compounded by the further observation of the deceased's eyes which have begun to bulge, the tongue which has been forced outwards from its normal position in the mouth and the appearance of small amounts of froth around the nose and mouth. However, this is not to say that he was strangled as you can clearly observe no marks of rope or hands upon or around the area of the deceased's neck. Upon opening this poor soul's mouth, I observed that the tissue at the back of the throat was severely inflamed and the airway appeared to be totally constricted. The man's throat and airway having been in this condition had, I feel sure, restricted completely the flow of air in and out of the lungs. This situation would have caused immediate loss of consciousness and the rapid onset of death.

'3. Finally, in conclusion, it is my firmly held belief that Lord Rupert Penman-Smythe indeed was the victim of foul play by means of some extremely fast-working chemical agent or, might I even suggest, poison which he ingested or was administered to him in some form without any apparent knowledge on his part until it had had its effects and death had come all but instantaneously.'

Upon this methodical conclusion having been reached by what the inspector pleasantly noted to himself as the astute and concise observations of this keen-witted country physician, Inspector Dentworth brought the interview to its close, issuing forth the following final directives to the man who stood before him.

'Thank you, Dr Mathews, for your assistance in this most tragic matter. If you would now please return to the dining room and rejoin the others of the party for the time being, I will endeavour to retain you there for as little further time as is possible. By the way, Doctor, as a final comment on this matter from you at this point in these proceedings, did you observe during the time you were present in the drawing room taking afternoon tea this afternoon all the participants in the festivities partake of all the food and drink that was on offer?'

'As far as I am aware, Inspector, everyone present this afternoon was served a cup of tea from the same teapot and partook of milk not lemon from the same milk jug at the same time, both of which now reside still on the far sideboard. As for the food which was consumed I could not be entirely sure if everyone sampled all that was on offer. In all honesty, I must for my part say that I myself did not partake of all. There was just too much to choose from upon the generously laden cake trays which Collins dextrously proffered to all the assembled guests. The only definite observation I can make on this question is that, prior to my leaving the drawing room to attend to the problem at the stables, the Earl and Mr Carlile had not completed their enjoyment of this fine fare. Nevertheless, the Lady Isabella and Mr Smith had, to my recollection of the passage of events, finished their tea and had indicated their wish to take a stroll around the immediate grounds, as I have previously described,' Dr Mathews replied in most earnest tones, his dark features a study of the professional concern he held deep within his being for the conveyance of the truth in this matter of such a catastrophic nature.

'Thank you again, Dr Mathews, for all your assistance in this matter. Naturally, you would be aware that a coroner's inquest will be required to be held at some time in the forthcoming proceedings, at which the evidence you have given here today may well be again requested. For now though, as I have indicated, would you please rejoin the other members of the party in the dining room,' Inspector Dentworth again reiterated to the compliant man of medicine who, upon being issued with this final command, swiftly rose to his feet and uttered this final comment.

'Certainly, Inspector, I will naturally be available to aid in any further police matters in the coming days.' He then walked briskly across the room to the ornate panelled doors from whence he had previously entered what had always, previous to this day's tragic occurrences, appeared to him a most serene room, and adroitly manipulated the shining brass door handle, thereby silently securing release for himself from this modern-day inquisition.

Having watched intently the withdrawal of Dr Mathews to its absolute finality, ever mindful of any clues which could be gained by the observation of any slip in the normal appearance of the players in this drama, Inspector Dentworth again turned his attention and himself – as he returned to seat himself once again at the card table – in the direction of the remaining occupant of the room, his colleague Sergeant Jones, who, throughout the previous interview, to the untrained eye had appeared to remain stolidly intent upon his appointed duty of recording the pertinent facts of this case – evidenced by the apparent flurry of the short black pencil held in his large stubby-fingered hand across the pages of his well-used notebook – to the exclusion of all other actions on his part. Yet, with the ingrained intuition of his many years on the force, Sergeant Jones had indeed been actively employed in the intense observation of this tragic drama which was unfolding before his experienced and well-trained eyes. With this knowledge in mind, the inspector initiated the following exchange of views and observations, the first in a long line of such discussions, which these two men would engage in before this investigation would be brought to what both would hope to be its fruitful conclusion.

'Well, Jones what do you make of the good country doctor? Is he, in your opinion, keeping in mind the fact that he professes by his vocation to be a man of science? May we also believe him to be a man of truth, whose evidence we may indeed rely upon in this instance?' enquired the inspector of his associate whose behaviour in cases such as this were likened by his brother officers at Scotland Yard to that of a determined and feisty terrier – as efficient as any bred by the good Parson John Russell for his beloved hunt – who, once upon the trail of his adversary in crime, would not be shaken by any amount of effort on the villain's part from his assigned role as an officer of the crown.

'Sir, it is my considered opinion that Dr Mathews is indeed a man of great intellect. It is also my belief that his complete consciousness is given totally to the fulfilment of his duties to the sick and ailing of this community, to the exclusion of all other thoughts on his part,' Sergeant Jones replied with true sincerity ringing out in his soft, clear voice.

'Glad to hear you say that, Jones. Those indeed were also my impressions of the true character of that most affable gentleman. He may well be of more help to us before this ordeal is over. Now, let us adjourn from this room and go in search of that young constable I sent to fetch the chap from the stables. Let us hope we find them both waiting for our arrival in the billiard room so that we may indeed continue this investigation as speedily as possible,' requested Inspector Dentworth, a touch distractedly as he rose to his feet, having in passing taken from his nose his reliable wire-framed spectacles and commenced to clean them methodically with the white handkerchief which he removed from the breast pocket of his well-cut, dark blue jacket, as was his habit when wishing to cogitate earnestly the issues placed before him.

'Yes, Inspector, I am sure that young lad will have found the target of his endeavours, for his heart truly appears to be deeply in his chosen profession,' Sergeant Jones tactfully yet meaningfully replied as he rose and readily followed the inspector in the path that the doctor had taken only a few moments earlier, and departed the room, which to his heightened senses hung almost tangibly with the intense aura that an apparently pointless death as this brings with it…

'Sit down here, my good man,' instructed Inspector Dentworth of the short and thickset little man with the crop of snow white hair – the only true indication of his advancing age – who stood before him now in the billiard room, his cloth cap respectfully clasped in his strong bony hand as the inspector indicated one of a group setting of leather-clad wing chairs situated at the far end from where all had entered this most dignified example of the Victorian gentleman's retreat. The massive billiard table, a true credit to the master craftsman, John Thurston himself, with its twelve feet by six feet green baize playing surface – though now shrouded in an expanse of cotton dust cover, a barrier to the perils of the years of disuse – still stood in majestic command in the centre of the room; its intricately turned and highly waxed legs just visible beneath the voluminous cover stood testament still further to the apparent wealth and position of the owner of this house. Inspector Dentworth was again pleased by the forethought of actions the young constable was continuing to display to his superiors as the inspector in passing looked towards the hearth situated in the wall around which their chairs were grouped and the warming fire which lay within it, in the knowledge that its setting had been at the country constable's instigation. This same young man whom he had found in the corridor moments before at the entrance to this room in stern accompaniment to the requested target of his endeavours, the head groom, dutifully awaiting his superiors arrival, had forthwith been sent back in obvious eager anticipation of the quest before him to the stables to take the relevant statements from the gatekeeper and the staff of the stables.

'Sergeant Jones, be seated here,' Inspector Dentworth briskly instructed of his respected colleague, indicating the chair which placed him to the left of his superior who had taken for himself the central position between foe and friend.

'Now, my good fellow, for our records please state your full name, address and occupation,' the inspector calmly requested as all parties seated themselves in their respective chairs.

'Yes, sir, my name is Benjamin Alfred Middleton, but everyone around these parts just calls me Old Ben. I live with my good lady wife of twenty-five years in the same cottage that my dearly departed father and mother lived in before me, where I was born many a year ago, that of Horseshoe Cottage here on the estate. It is the cottage which comes with the job of head groom. As you see, sir, my father was head groom here to the previous owner of the estate before me as I am now to Mr Carlile and as I'd hoped my son would one day be to the next owner, Master Reginald, after me and the missus have gone to our graves in the churchyard. However, seeing as how Mr Carlile's only son was lost in the war as was our brave lad Alfred, there will be no family left on both our parts to inherit this place when Mr Carlile and us are gone,' replied Old Ben a touch long-windedly as the experience of being the centre of attention was a novelty that he did not wish to relinquish quickly.

The inspector wishing to cut short any rambling monologue on the part of this friendly yet, in the obvious circumstances of his participation in this interview, still respectfully sombre servant, adroitly intervened as Old Ben paused to take a well-needed breath of air, with the command, 'Now then, Old Ben, in your own words tell me about the events at the stables this afternoon?'

'Well, sir, it was like this. As usual, at a quarter to four in the afternoon at this time of the year, the lads commenced moving the horses from the fields where they had spent most of the day grazing and frolicking as is their way, back into the stables before the night air started to roll in. Life being what it is, the older lad, Jimmy, who should in fact have known better, happened to get a mite too close to the hind quarters of our problem horse as it came his time to be brought in. A little after four o'clock as he was walked into his stall, a hoof lashed out and caught him a nasty blow on the arm, split the flesh right to the bone and what a torrent of blood poured out. As I came from the tack room, I knew straight away that it was going to need more than just a bandage. So I called George, my right-hand man, who had been dealing with a merchant in the feed room at the time of the accident, to help me make Jimmy as comfortable as possible. The poor lad was writhing around on the stable floor in agony and we tied as many clean pieces of cloth and handkerchiefs as we could find around his arm to quench the flow of blood which had, I might say in passing, started to cover his own and in part my clothes as you can plainly see. (Old Ben having gestured to the bloodstained waistcoat and breeches in which he still sat.)

'Knowing that the good doctor was up at the big house for tea, I left George in charge and I scurried up there as quickly as my old legs could carry me to tell the master what had happened and bring the doctor back with me. Dr Mathews came back with me straight away. He did not even wait for his bag. He said he could start without it. Collins, the butler, followed close behind with it, as I remember. When we reached the stables again, the poor lad was in a sorry state with his clothes completely drenched in his blood. I took over looking after him and keeping him as still as I could while George finished seeing to the stabling of the horses with Will, the other lad. Collins stayed and held the doctor's bag and passed him things from it. It took some time for the doctor to stop the bleeding. I remember he first gave Jimmy a needle in the arm. He said it would deaden the pain and make it easier for all, which, true to his word, it did. Still, it did take ever such a long time before the doctor was finished stitching and bandaging. It was near on five o'clock by the big round clock over the stable door, but that runs a mite bit fast, when the doctor closed his bag and issued the instructions that the young lad should be helped to his lodgings and put to bed as soon as possible where he was to remain quiet and not be disturbed until the doctor calls again, tomorrow. Strange thing though, Inspector, as the doctor was finishing up, Collins just seemed to disappear without a word. He must have decided to go and inform the master of all that had happened, though I thought at the time it strange that he said nowt to anyone as he went. He just seemed to spirit himself away. That as may be, that is the events of this afternoon as I remember them, Inspector.'

'Thank you, my man, for that account. By the way, you spoke of the horse at the centre of the catastrophe as a problem horse. Is it normally hard to handle?' the inspector enquired in passing.

With his face becoming a sea of blackened consternation and his dark eyes shining fiercely, Old Ben replied adamantly, 'That horse, sir, Fearless is its name and its nature, has been nothing more than a bugger of a horse since it arrived here back in 1907. It might be an old horse now, going on eighteen it is now, but it still has the heart of a demon beating inside it, a demon that, it would seem, will never die. Why the master ever bought him I don't truly know. Even more so, I cannot understand why he kept him after everything that happened. You may not know, sir, but the master was crippled in a hunting accident the first time he rode that same maniac horse. I pleaded with the master from the day that horse first arrived to now, to get rid of him. But for some unknown reason he would not then, and will not now, listen to reason. I never could understand it and I never will.'

'Thank you, my good fellow, that will be all for the moment, you may return to the stables and continue with your duties there,' Inspector Dentworth quietly instructed of the sprightly yet ageing man who, upon hearing this instruction, gave a sharp nod of acknowledgement of his white head, rose rapidly to his feet, silently traversed the runner-clad, bare, wooden floor and disappeared behind the billiard-room door back to his domain of horse and cart.

No sooner had the billiard-room door closed than a knock, clear and crisp of character, resounded forth from its outer surface echoing through the room to the ears of the inspector who responded in his usual businesslike manner by barking out the command, 'Enter.'

This command was greeted by the appearance around the edge of this solid wooden barricade by the fresh face of Constable Stevens.

'Excuse me, Inspector, but I have just completed taking the statements from the relevant persons down at the stables. Do you wish me to hand over that information now, and what further duties do you require of me?' the young policeman possessed of average build and height with a high forehead set between a pair of twinkling blue eyes and a generous head of straw-coloured hair, nervously proffered as his reason for this intrusion into his superior's sphere of activity.

'Come in, Stevens. We are most interested to hear how you progressed down at the stables. Have you been able to take statements from all the relevant parties present there this afternoon already?' enquired Inspector Dentworth in a voice rich with sincere interest in this young man's exploits, eager to indicate to him his superior's rapidly formed yet highly regarded opinion of the bright future which lay in store for him.

'Yes, Inspector, I was able to extract statements from most of the relevant parties present, all except the unfortunate fellow who incurred the injury to his arm, as the village doctor had left strict instructions that he was to be put to bed in his lodgings in the stables and was not to be disturbed until Dr Mathews visits him tomorrow morning,' Stevens enthusiastically replied, the hint of a smile appearing upon his plain yet honest face, the only outward indication of his inner recognition of his superior's opinion of his speedy professional efforts.

'Well, come, lad, and let us hear of your findings,' instructed the inspector as he beckoned to the young constable to abandon his position at the door, indicating to him to take residence in the chair which had only recently been vacated by Old Ben.

'Right, sir,' was the simple response from Stevens as he deftly made his way across the expanse of wooden floor and took up his position in the cluster of chairs grouped around the invitingly warm hearth.

'Now, Constable, what new information have you been able to glean from the workers on the estate?' Inspector Dentworth quietly enquired as he settled himself more comfortably into his luxuriantly padded green leather chair in the apparently experienced anticipation of an extended oration on the part of this, his junior country officer. As the inspector prepared to listen intently to the evidence gathered, as was his habit in times such as these, he took from his long thin nose his glistening glasses and proceeded to polish the already spotlessly clean lenses, this simple act allowing his sharp mind to focus its attention more keenly upon the matter at hand.

'Well, Inspector, the facts are as follows' – having produced his own police issue notebook from whence he read – 'the gatekeeper of more than twenty years, a man by the name of Samuel Isaac Ibson, who resides in the gatehouse cottage, states emphatically that the motor car belonging to His Lordship requested entry at the estate gates at precisely ten minutes to three. In passing, he stated that he did not take any great interest in the occupants of the motor car only to say that there were three passengers as it swiftly passed, but recognised the vehicle on sight as that of His Lordship's regal black Hispano Suiza. He further stated that he had just closed the gates, as is his master's dictum that they may not remain open apart from allowing entry to now rarely invited guests to the estate, when the doctor's motor with Dr Mathews at the wheel had come into view. It was stated further by this man that, to his recollection, no more than five minutes elapsed between both parties passing rapidly through the gates,' Constable Stevens stated in his most solemn policeman's voice.

With Stevens halting slightly at this point in his official monologue, Inspector Dentworth nodding knowingly in the direction of Sergeant Jones ventured forth the statement, 'Ah, now that confirms the statement made by Dr Mathews as to the time of arrival of the two parties this afternoon. Please continue, Constable.'

'As you wish, Inspector,' was Stevens's simple yet polite reply and he set forth once again with the inspector and sergeant as his interested observers on his journey of discovery and disclosure of the events of the afternoon,

'Whilst at the stables, I interviewed the stable boy who this afternoon was employed in the duties of caring for the movement of the horses from the exercise fields back into the secure confines of the stables in accompaniment to the young lad who sustained the injuries in the accident. The lad's name is William John Nettleford. He has been in Mr Carlile's employ for the past three years in the post of junior stable boy and resides in lodgings in the loft above the stables. He states determinedly that the accident occurred at a few minutes past four o'clock as he recalls hearing, on the breeze, the village clock in Marlford strike the hour as they had approached the stable buildings. He further stated that Jimmy had only that afternoon reminded him, the new boy, of the danger of the horse as they were endeavouring to move it from the field back to the stables, this job always taking two stable boys at least to handle this particular beast, when, with a burst of fury, the horse lashed out, striking Jimmy a painful and serious blow to the arm. He further stated that Old Ben, the head groom who had been occupied with other duties in the tack room, had, upon hearing the moanful cry from the young lad, immediately acted to help the lad by bandaging the arm with what clean cloths as could be found and then running for help to the big house to fetch the doctor.

'Further to this, the young lad stated that within a matter of minutes Old Ben had returned with the village doctor, Dr

Mathews, with Mr Collins the butler following behind carrying the doctor's bag. Old Ben then sent George and this lad Will about their duties of attending to the stabling of the remaining horses and took over looking after the injured boy and aiding the doctor in his duties of care. Subsequently the doctor attended to the injuries and Will finally saw first Mr Collins leave, then, some ten minutes later, Dr Mathews left the stables moving in the direction of the house. That concludes the statements from those pertinently involved in the proceedings of the accident this afternoon, namely, the gatekeeper and the other stable boy, with the exception as I have previously stated of that of the stable boy who incurred the injuries. His name, by the way, is James Walter Moore, known by his fellow workers as Jimmy, and he has been an employee of the estate for the past ten years, holding presently the position of head stable boy and residing as his position dictates also in lodgings in the stables.' Constable Stevens, having finally come to the end of his lengthy dissertation, sat back slightly in his chair, anxiously awaiting the response to his earnest endeavours from his superiors.

'That is all quite interesting, Constable. It would appear that we do have a certain degree of continuity in the evidence given by all parties so far in this investigation, wouldn't you say so, Sergeant Jones?' Inspector Dentworth ventured enquiringly as he replaced his spectacles once again on the bridge of his thin, sharp nose and turned his attention once more in the direction of the round and pleasant face of his professional ally in many such campaigns as this, one Sergeant Charlie Jones.

'It would appear to me, Inspector, that certain aspects of this case are already requiring further investigation and confirmation,' Sergeant Jones cryptically replied.

'That indeed would appear to be the case, Sergeant, yet there will be time enough for further fine tuning of this case as the days progress. Let us push on now with our initial enquiries, shall we?' responded the inspector, his grey eyes glinting as strongly as any precious gem as his mind quickly evaluated the evidence so far presented and thereby the future path which this investigation must take.

'As you instruct, Inspector,' was the simple yet dutiful response from the slightly portly yet notably astute Sergeant Jones.

'Now, Constable, I have two further duties for you to perform. Firstly, please be so good as to go now and inform Dr Mathews that he is free to leave and return to his administering duties, bearing in mind that he must be available for the inquest and, secondly, inform Mr Carlile that we request his presence and escort him or should I say assist him back here,' Inspector Dentworth solemnly commanded.

'Yes, Inspector,' Constable Stevens replied as he quickly rose from his chair, deftly navigated a course across the room avoiding the massive majestic obstacle of the billiard table which held such a regal position in the centre of this impressive male domain and disappeared from view behind the solid billiard-room door.

'There goes a young man with a bright future in today's force,' espoused the inspector in passing.

'Indeed, Inspector,' Sergeant Jones succinctly replied.

The brightness from the electric light which perfused the dining room and enveloped its occupants in a golden haze could easily have led to the misplaced belief that time had stood still and that indeed daylight still reigned supreme in the environs beyond, thereby creating an impression of security which had been further heightened by the warming fire which blazed modestly in the hearth of the room around which the group gathered and intensified a feeling to those present that somehow they had all been caught in the same drastic dream from which all would subsequently be released to return to the normal routine of their assorted lives. However, that misplaced conception was irrevocably shattered for all concerned by the arrival before the assembled group's gaze of the unmistakable symbol of the afternoon's catastrophic events in the person of Constable Stevens.

As Constable Stevens ventured into the depths of this light and comfortingly warm room from the relative coolness of the bare panelled corridor, he in passing observed the expressions on the faces of the people who sat in silent contemplation before him. Dr Mathews sat at the centre of the group, his finely boned hands stretched slightly out in front of him in the act of absorbing the warmth being generated from the hearth. His head was lowered, his face a picture of introspective contemplation as his eyes gazed reflectively downwards into the flickering flames. To the doctor's right sat the young couple, the Lady Isabella and her gentleman companion, Mr Smith, their gloved hands discreetly joined and resting on Mr Smith's knee. As Constable Stevens gazed momentarily at the face of the victim's only child, he observed the stains of freshly shed tears upon the finely chiselled and delicately powdered features of this most beautiful example of young womanhood. In contrast, the war-tortured face of her companion, Mr Smith, showed a battle-hardened disregard of the importance which had been placed upon this death, as he sat with a noticeable degree of boredom evidenced upon his scarred features. The final member of this quartet, Mr Carlile, sat in his wheelchair to the left of the good doctor, an old scarlet rug draped over his withered legs.

Constable Stevens again tactfully observed the expression on the face of this final occupant of the room. In so doing, he was filled with an unexpected feeling of great depression and total disregard for mankind and life which was accentuated when he looked briefly into this man's steely dark and cold eyes which appeared to look lifelessly straight through him. Having rapidly made these mental observations of each of the individuals who presently resided in this room, Constable Stevens moved closer and spoke to those assembled, directing his words of instruction to the appropriate persons as he had been requested to do by the Scotland Yard inspector.

'Good evening, Your Ladyship and gentlemen, I come on behalf of Inspector Dentworth of Scotland Yard with instructions. Dr Mathews, the inspector wishes me to tell you that you are free to return to your medical duties. However, the inspector has further instructed me to remind you that you must remain available to give evidence if required at the coroner's inquest when it is held,' said Constable Stevens sternly.

The doctor's response came immediately, with him rising quickly from his straight-backed dining suite chair and moving in the direction of the partially open door. In enacting this motion, he said as he came level with the Constable, 'Thank you, Constable Stevens. Certainly, as I have told the inspector earlier today, I will by all means retain myself available as a witness if required at the inquest, when it is called. Until such time, I will bid everyone here goodnight.' And with these words, the doctor continued speedily upon his route across the room, smartly disappearing behind the dining-room door.

With the withdrawal of Dr Mathews from the room completed, Constable Stevens turned his attention once again in the direction of the remaining occupants and more specifically that of the morose and crumpled figure of the owner of this house, Carlile Manor, that of Mr Montague Alexander Carlile. Constable Stevens spoke again with a new found ring of authority to his mellow voice.

'Mr Carlile, the inspector wishes me to request, on his behalf, your presence in the billiard room, if you would accompany me there now without any undue delay please, sir.'

Having moved his gaze from that of the fire, which lay unseen in front of him, to the constable, in his role as pillar of police authority in their small rural community, Montague Carlile now looked Constable Stevens squarely in the face and replied in the broadest of homeland accents, his voice a mere whisper unheard by those seated beside him, a result Constable Stevens believed of the trauma of the day and the subsequent lapse in his usual clear composure.

'I dunna ken why he needs ta speak ta me, for I'll no be able ta tell him anythin', but if it'll make ye happy, young un, I'll go with ye. Mind, ye'll need ta give me a hand.'

'Mr Carlile, rest easy, sir, we will take it nice and steady for you,' replied Constable Stevens in most assuring tones.

His composure somewhat restored, Montague's speech regained its regular educated articulation, born of years in a society far divorced from that of his native homeland.

'Thank you, Constable Stevens, for your timely consideration of an old cripple,' was Montague's sardonic tinged reply.

However, as Montague and Constable Stevens prepared to depart the dining room, the determined movement of a small hand gloved in cream silk halted the constable immediately in his appointed task.

'Could you tell me, Constable, how much longer will we be

required to be detained here? As you may well understand with the tragic happenings of this afternoon, I have many and varied arrangements of the late Earl's affairs which must be attended to as soon as possible,' enquired the Lady Isabella in the most respectful yet determined of tones, leaving none in doubt of her position in the life of this community.

'Rest assured, Your Ladyship, the investigation is moving as quickly as possible, but I will convey the concerns you have just expressed to my superior upon my return to the billiard room,' Constable Stevens reverently replied as he turned again and dextrously manoeuvred the chair in which Montague Carlile languidly reposed through the now open dining-room door and out into the wide corridor which led directly to the billiard room, their prompt progression along this dark-panelled passageway being conducted in silence on the part of both parties. On reaching the plain wooden door of the billiard room, Constable Stevens knocked crisply upon this solid barricade, thereby requesting acknowledgement from his superiors of his expeditious return. This acknowledgement came promptly in the form of a sternly barked out command of, 'Enter.'

Upon heeding this instruction, in escort to the still silent Montague Carlile and entering once again the warmly comfortable confines of this sturdy room, Constable Stevens was further commanded.

'Constable Stevens and Mr Montague Carlile, I presume? Come in, gentlemen. Constable Stevens, be so good as to move this chair away so as to wheel Mr Carlile's chair to sit beside me here.' Inspector Dentworth's long thin hand indicated the thickly padded wing chair to the right of his own. Having adeptly achieved this desired objective, settling Montague Carlile in the position as indicated by the inspector, Constable Stevens stepped back to face this well-known bloodhound of Scotland Yard fame, eagerly awaiting his further instructions, which, having consulted his gold pocket watch, came via the inspector's strong calm voice, as follows.

'Well done, Constable Stevens. Now I want you to go to the front door and await what should be the imminent arrival from London of the police surgeon, Dr Scott, for it is my understanding that he would arrive on the twenty past seven train from Paddington. At such time as he arrives, you will escort him to the drawing room and assist in his investigations in any way in which he so directs you to do. Further to this, after Dr Scott has concluded his examinations in the drawing room, you will subsequently escort him back here to the billiard room. Is that understood, young man? Do you have any questions with regard to this investigation so far, Constable?' Inspector Dentworth enquiringly concluded, having noted the slightly troubled expression on the face of his young charge since his recent return from the dining room.

'Yes, Inspector, I understand what is required of me. As for any questions, the Lady Isabella has just voiced her concern at the time which it appears to be taking before she may be free to be allowed to organise her late father's affairs. I informed her that the investigation was moving as speedily as possible and that I would convey her concerns to you personally,' was Constable Stevens's respectful reply.

To which the inspector replied contemplatively to his conscientious constable, 'Thank you, Constable Stevens. We will indeed deal with the Lady Isabella all in good time. However, your response to her enquiry was quite correct. Your county superiors will indeed hear of the great assistance you have been to our investigation. Now be about your duties, my lad,' at which Constable Stevens sharply turned on the heel of his brightly polished boot and swiftly retired from the room upon his appointed task, leaving Inspector Dentworth and Sergeant Jones free to interview methodically the man who sat amongst them, that of the instigator of this afternoon's festivities.

With an all but imperceptible nod of acknowledgement to his colleague, Charlie Jones, as a signal of the commencement of the interview, Inspector Dentworth turned his sparkling grey eyes upon the heavily lined face of the man who was seated beside him to his right and said, 'Now then, sir, for our records could you please state your full name, address and occupation.'

To which the man, in a rich, deep, resonant voice which belied his advancing years and long ago Scottish rearing, rapidly without a hint of emotion, replied, 'My name is Montague

Alexander Carlile and for the last fifteen or so years I have permanently resided here at Carlile Manor. My occupation, if you can call it that, is one of a retired banker in the City of London.'

'Thank you for that, Mr Carlile. Now, I would like you to tell us, in your own words and good time, of the events of this afternoon as they appeared to you, if you would be so kind, sir,' Inspector Dentworth graciously requested of the laird of the manor.

So it was upon this command from the power of the moment that Montague commenced his own personal dissertation on the subject of the afternoon's events as his eyes and mind had observed them. Slowly he began.

'Well, Inspector, may I initially say that my recollections are those of an old and as you can plainly see a crippled man. I do not hear and see as well as I used to and my mind sometimes plays terrible tricks on my memory, courtesy of the injections of morphine that I must administer to keep the severe pain I constantly suffer at bay. However, as you direct, I will endeavour to tell you all that I believe I observed this afternoon, in what I have just explained as my limited capacity.'

Inspector Dentworth endeavoured to encourage this crumpled man who sat imprisoned in the wheelchair beside him, by soothingly responding with the comment, 'Please, Mr Carlile, take your time, my dear fellow. Rest assured, we do not wish to rush you in any way.'

To which Montague, having momentarily been enveloped in a sea of meditative thought, rallied himself again to the task at hand.

'Thank you, Inspector, for your consideration. The events of this afternoon were, to my mind, as follows. As far as I am aware, courtesy of information relayed to me by my butler Collins, both parties, that is to say, Lord Rupert Penman-Smythe, his daughter, the Lady Isabella, and her gentleman companion, Mr John Smith, as one party, and Dr Robert Mathews as the other, arrived almost simultaneously here at approximately three o'clock this afternoon. I had extended the invitation to Lord Rupert's party on Monday morning with the proviso that if the arrangements were not suitable for the Lady Isabella and Mr Smith His Lordship would subsequently contact me by the following evening. Having received no further communication from the Earl, I, in turn, subsequently contacted Dr Mathews on the Wednesday evening last, extending a similar invitation to him. All these communications, I might say, were conducted via the means of the telephonic device. The object of this invitation was to wish His Lordship a 'welcome home' to his country estate, Beeches Hall, and indeed to England itself, when I realised upon talking to His Lordship that not only had he recently returned from abroad, Lord Rupert having spent an extensive period of time overseeing his mining interests in South Africa before, during and after the war, but that his daughter the Lady Isabella had also recently returned from her extended time in Europe, having seen service as a nurse in the French campaign.

'I extended the invitation to include the Lady Isabella and her apparently constant companion the gentleman who is known by the name of John Smith whom I have been told the Lady Isabella nursed back from the brink of death and whom, I have been reliably informed, she intends to marry next summer. With the nature of the party being mixed, I thought it best to make the invitation for afternoon tea with a possible game of whist to follow. Therefore, I also extended an invitation to the village doctor of at least the last twenty years, Dr Mathews, whom I knew to be an avid enthusiast of a lively game of cards and also in the knowledge that he would find the inevitable dissertation by His Lordship on his exploits in South Africa interesting. The first I actually saw of my guests was when my butler Collins escorted them from the front entrance hall to the drawing room where I was eagerly waiting to greet my guests. Upon their arrival in the drawing room I welcomed them all and, having seen to the required formal introductions, I asked them to take a seat upon the most comfortable drawing-room chairs; whereupon on a nod from myself, Collins proceeded to serve us the afternoon tea. I might say here that my old cook, Mrs Christian, did herself proud with the spread of fare on offer.

'You may in passing wonder why, Inspector, I had my butler Collins serving tea unassisted by his junior staff. Well, sir, my reasoning is quite simple. I am a man who has lived for the majority of these past fifteen years in peaceful solitude away from the social restraints required by the act of a woman of position residing in my house. It is therefore my desire that my surroundings be complimented by what I have found to be the stable influence of men exclusively serving at my table. Further to this, indeed Collins in normal circumstances would have been aided by either of his juniors, Cedric or Angus; however, as fate would have it, Cedric had unfortunately been sent to his bed on the orders of Dr Mathews suffering from a severe case of back strain, while Angus on the other hand had been in the days preceding sent to tend to the affairs of his dying mother in Swindon. It was as such that Collins stood adequately alone in his duties this afternoon for I am a man of habit; thus, in my house no change of circumstances will come to change the rhythm and order of my surroundings.

'However, I digress a little too far from the required train of thought. Now, where was I? Yes, to my eyes, Lord Rupert who, I might add here, has been a treasured friend of mine for many years both in a professional and personal capacity, appeared to my eyes to be in the best of health and mood this afternoon. During the enjoyment of the tea, he kept all amused by his lively dissertation on his bold exploits in South Africa and he appeared to consume the same general assortment from the array on offer as did everyone else present. As I am sure you are aware by now, Dr Mathews was called away at approximately a little after four o'clock by my head groom, Old Ben, to attend to one of my stable boys who had been kicked by what I myself must admit as my most burdensome horse. A moment or two prior to this time, the Lady Isabella and her gentleman friend, Mr Smith, had completed partaking of their refreshments and had expressed the wish to leave the gathering temporarily and take a stroll around the immediate grounds while the older members of the party conversed of times past in the completion of their own slowly consumed refreshments.

'So it came to pass that I was subsequently left alone in the company of His Lordship having sent Collins to retrieve the doctor's bag from his automobile, which Dr Mathews had earlier stated to me he had housed himself in the garage at the back of the house, follow him to the stables and while there assist the doctor in any way possible. Lord Rupert and myself enjoyed some time renewing remembrances of times long gone, our conversation becoming quite animated at times, I must myself admit. However, our peace was yet again disturbed by the intrusion by way of a knock again upon the French windows leading from the terrace and the subsequent admittance of Thompson, my factor, or I should say, estate agent in charge of all my dealings with my tenant farmers. He was unaware of the fact that I was entertaining guests and had come, as was the usual routine on a Friday afternoon, to enter into discussion of the affairs of the estate. Again, in passing, might I add that the estate had been recently experiencing some problems with the new batch of tenant farmers, who are returned servicemen and their families who had taken up the land at the end of the war in place of the poor unfortunates who enlisted and tragically lost their lives in the service of their country, as did my beloved son, Reginald Alexander, who was lost in action in the region of the Somme River in 1917.

'However, I digress again, for which as a sad old man, I apologise. Now, as I was saying, Thompson arrived in the drawing room at about a quarter past the hour of four and, due to the serious nature of the problems we have been experiencing with these farmers, I begged His Lordship's indulgence in this interruption. Then, with Thompson's assistance, we moved from the drawing room to the smoking room where we spent a short time, maybe the next half-hour or so, of this fact I could not be entirely sure, discussing the state of affairs on this diminishing estate, what with the increase in taxes and the gradual decrease in good staff available since the war. However, that is my concern, not yours, Inspector. With the completion of our talks, Thompson, before leaving Carlile Manor overnight to attend to some ongoing estate matters in Swindon, assisted me on to the terrace where he left me to take a short breath of fresh air before I returned to Lord Rupert.

'From where I sat on the terrace, I immediately noticed the young couple strolling back up the grounds in the direction of the house. So I wheeled myself slowly, with, I might add, the grateful help of the natural slight incline the terrace has in the direction I wished to travel, to the end of the terrace to where a small gazebo stands in the hope of attracting their attention and to join me. As I reached this structure, I happily observed that Dr Mathews had joined the young couple on his apparent return journey from the stables and had registered my presence in the gazebo, having indicated this to his newly reacquainted companions by a wave of his thin arm in my direction and had then ushered them towards me. Upon their arrival at the gazebo I indicated privately to Dr Mathews that I was taking a breath of fresh air and a time of silence away from the constant drone of His Lordship's ramblings. However, my discreet excuse for my presence on the terrace to the Lady Isabella had been that I was indeed in the act of requesting her party's returned presence to the drawing room. With these explanations accepted by all, it was readily agreed to by this newly re-formed party, that we should return post haste to the company of Lord Rupert in the drawing room and the continuation of the festivities of the afternoon. We all did so in a spirit of joyous anticipation of the pleasures to come, with Mr Smith being so kind as to push my chair for me. Upon our return to the drawing room it was observed that His Lordship appeared to have fallen blissfully asleep. However, upon further investigation on the part of Dr Mathews, it was discovered that Lord Rupert was indeed, dead. Whereupon, on Dr Mathews' instruction we informed the local police and they in turn contacted Scotland Yard and hence commissioned your services.'

'Thank you for that most comprehensive information, Mr Carlile. Further to all that you have told us, was there anything else that you saw or heard which you thought was at all unusual during this afternoon's proceedings?' enquired Inspector Dentworth, taking those idiosyncratic spectacles from his distinguished face to polish absently with gentle care their crystal clear lenses as he awaited the reply from this invalid of a man who sat beside him.

'Well, Inspector, strange that you might ask that question as indeed I did observe something quite unexpected during this afternoon's happenings. It was while I was seated in the smoking room talking to Thompson. I glanced out of the window and happened to see Mr Smith on his own, moving up the slope towards the terrace and disappearing out of view in the direction of the drawing-room window. For some reason, I instinctively glanced at the mantel clock as I observed him pass by and noticed that the time was half past four; subsequently some time appeared to elapse, perhaps five or ten minutes, before I again observed him retracing his steps to apparently rejoin the Lady Isabella in the garden. That, Inspector, was the only unusual occurrence during this afternoon's now tragic proceedings,' Montague stated with a degree of intense determination, indicating to all his wish that his words be taken as the truth.

'Again, Mr Carlile, thank you for your assistance in our enquiries. There is just one further question I wish to put to you at this time and that is, what were your instructions to your butler Collins in the act of assisting Dr Mathews in his tending to the unfortunate young lad at the stables this afternoon?' Inspector Dentworth, with an expression of mild curiosity upon his lean face, distractedly enquired as he returned his spectacles to their appointed place upon his rather stern face, in the process making a mental note of the observed lack of any visible response to this request upon the haggard face of Montague Carlile.

The laird of the manor quietly replied, 'Certainly, Inspector, when I was informed of the accident by Old Ben through Collins, and subsequently informed Dr Mathews of the situation which existed down at the stables, he informed me of his eagerness to tend to the young lad as quickly as possible. He asked that Collins be directed to his motor, which, as I have mentioned previously, he himself had garaged upon arrival this afternoon as was always his habit when visiting this house, to retrieve his medical bag and follow the good doctor down to the stables to assist along with Old Ben in treating the boy. These ardent requests on the part of Dr Mathews I conveyed discreetly in whispered tones so as not to upset the intense and animated pleasure which His Lordship was deriving from his boisterous dissertations on the topic of his life in South Africa. I was able, at the completion of a particularly intense remembrance, to satisfy his belated curiosity as to the departure of the doctor as a mild ailment in the household. I informed Collins at this time, before he left the drawing room to fetch the bag, that he was to be at the service of Dr Mathews in any way in which the doctor requested until such time as the doctor had completed his administrations. Was there some problem, Inspector, with the way in which my man, Collins, conducted himself while in the service of Dr Mathews this afternoon?' Montague enquired with a growing expression of consternation appearing upon his deeply and now permanently furrowed brow.

'Do not concern yourself too greatly about this matter, Mr Carlile. If you were to know me better, you would understand that I am known down at the Yard as a disciple of method and order in my investigations. Further, it is my belief that it is better to have too much information to consider than not enough in cases such as this. Is that not right, Sergeant Jones?' Inspector Dentworth replied lightly, a mischievous twinkle playing in those clear grey eyes as he turned his attention in the direction of Sergeant Jones for the expected steady and emotionless reply of, 'Indeed, that is always the case, Inspector.'

With that confirmation of the inspector's methods from the chubby lips of his long-serving companion in such investigations, Montague Carlile's countenance appeared to clear quite visibly and his demeanour to improve to almost a state of jocular bonhomie as he said, 'It is my sincere wish, Inspector, that your endeavours will bring to justice the scoundrel who so callously took the life of my dear old friend, Lord Rupert Penman-Smythe, a man who had the rare honour of having throughout his long and illustrious life cultivated many friends but not one enemy.'

'Rest assured, Mr Carlile, that I and my men will do all in our power to apprehend this devious person. Now, if you have nothing further to add to what you have already told us, we for our part have no further questions to put to you. At this point, I would ask you to return to the dining room for the moment, please, sir. Having said that, do you require assistance in making that journey, Mr Carlile?' the inspector enquired with distinct concern etched in his rich educated voice of this apparently frail shell of a man.

'No thank you, Inspector. Let it not be said that Montague Alexander Carlile held the police from their appointed task for his personal comfort,' replied Montague in tones of subdued politeness as he grasped the large wheels of his cumbersome chair and commenced to push himself with what appeared to be an insurmountable degree of difficulty across the smooth and perfectly flat polished floor of the billiard room. Montague's endeavours, however, halted momentarily as Inspector Dentworth's solid voice rang out across the room commanding the following of his now slowly withdrawing witness.

'Mr Carlile, when you have returned to the dining room, would you be so kind as to request the Lady Isabella's presence here immediately, please, sir.'

With a noticeable caustic edge to his cracking voice, as he manoeuvred his chair to the edge of the fully barricaded billiard-room doorway, Montague turned his twisted body slowly within his chair to look back awkwardly in the direction of the inspector, and replied, 'I shall endeavour to be as fast as these old hands and arms will allow me to be, Inspector. I will certainly deliver unto you the Lady Isabella to play her part in this modern-day inquisition as soon as possible. With a view to this endeavour, might I request the assistance of Sergeant Jones in opening this door for me, please, Inspector' (Montague having in the process nodded sharply in the direction of the closed billiard-room door).

'By all means, Mr Carlile. Sergeant Jones, please go and open the door for Mr Carlile immediately,' was the inspector's snappy response which, in turn, placed a hint of a regal smile upon the laird's haggard face as he viewed the act of rightful servitude on the part of these usurpers of his power and position within this, his home and castle.

'Thank you so very much, Inspector, for your extreme consideration of such an old man as me.' These words constituted Montague's final personal comment on the day's proceedings as he continued on his way out of the door and beyond the view of his two inquisitors.

With the departure of this increasingly caustic witness and the subsequent return of Sergeant Jones to his chair by the fire, Inspector Dentworth sat motionless and silent for a moment, meditatively contemplating all the evidence which he and Sergeant Jones had been subjected to in the course of the investigation so far. The prominent thought which ran through the inspector's mind at this early stage was the intense feeling that all was not as it appeared. With this thought lingering in the back of his mind, Inspector Dentworth again rallied himself to the cause – in the process registering to himself the distant and muffled buzz of the front doorbell indicating the expected arrival of Dr Scott – directing his attention and the following enquiry towards his brother officer who, during this slight interval in the proceedings, had been engaged in the earnest perusal of his notebook and its rapidly mounting pages of evidence.

'Well, Jones, what do you make of our last witness? What are his true feelings on the untimely death of what he so publicly purports to be his dear friend, the Earl of Marlford? I, myself, have been left with a decided feeling of uneasiness after that last interview,' the inspector candidly stated to his junior officer.

To which Sergeant Jones raised his well-shaped head and replied intuitively, 'Mr Carlile does appear to me to be a very strange old beggar, a man who truly does not have any feelings of real compassion for anyone but himself, Inspector. It has also come to my attention that, slow though he might be and giving the impression of great frailty, he is not perhaps as confined in his movement in that chair and as frail in his actions as he would have us believe. Upon observing him discreetly at close range whilst we were all seated by the fire, I noticed the development of the muscles in his upper body to be quite strong.'

'You noticed that, Sergeant. Thought I would test him out to see how much of a cripple he truly was. Glad you cottoned on to what I had in mind and didn't venture your services until requested. As you say, he is a very strange chap. Only time will tell what role, if any, he indeed played in this afternoon's events,' replied the inspector philosophically as, again, a light knock was heard upon the billiard-room door.

The inspector responded to this request for entry by barking out the familiar single word of command, 'Enter.'

As this word resonated across the room to its furthermost reaches, the door opened to reveal to the inspector's eyes the view of a tall, willowy young woman of exquisite beauty and consummate grace. As she paused beside the now opened door – her gloved hand gently grasped the thin brass handle as if in an attempt to steady herself before her passage into the room proper – the inspector noticed even from this distance the mark of wealth and power which stamped this woman as the true blue blood that she was from the cut of her expensive European-styled clothes and finest Italian leather shoes to her immaculately coiffured head of auburn hair.

'Thank you, Your Ladyship, for gracing us so promptly with your presence. If you would be so kind as to join us here please,' Inspector Dentworth ventured in the most polite of tones as, in the act of the gentlemen that both he and Sergeant Jones were, they rose to their feet at the swift, yet graceful approach, of the Lady Isabella, Inspector Dentworth indicating the chair which Sergeant Jones had just replaced to its position beside him.

As all parties seated themselves again in their respective chairs, the inspector was once more taken aback by the delicate features possessed by this demure young lady, the high cheekbones and noble nose, the clear and piercingly blue eyes and the rich and full lips now discreetly covered with the thinnest coating of the highly fashionable blood red shaded lipstick.

'May I, before we commence this interview, extend to you, Your Ladyship, on behalf of Scotland Yard our most sincere condolences at the most tragic loss of your father, the Earl of Marlford,' stated Inspector Dentworth respectfully.

'Thank you, Inspector, for your kind words of condolence at this my inestimable loss,' the Lady Isabella replied quietly. These words, however, appeared to the inspector to be edged with intense and sorrowful emotion and required great effort on the part of this young woman to project successfully.

'Now, if you are quite comfortable, Your Ladyship, I will begin by asking you to state for our official records your full name, address and occupation,' the inspector in a return to his typical methodical manner sternly requested of this his new witness.

The Lady Isabella responded quickly by emotionlessly stating, 'My full name is Lady Isabella Emily Penman-Smythe. I am currently residing as a guest in my late father's country home, Beeches Hall. However, my permanent address is that of 22 Oak Park Gardens, Chelsea, and my occupation is that of a lady of independent means, having recently returned from an extended period of living in Europe having seen service in the nursing corps during the war.'

'Right, let us move on, for the time is rapid in its passage and I have been made duly aware of Your Ladyship's wish to attend to your late father's affairs as soon as is possible. Therefore, I will now ask you to tell us as succinctly as possible, in your own words, your observations of what has transpired to be the tragic course of events which occurred this afternoon,' the inspector requested calmly of yet another witness in this horrendous drama.

'Thank you, Inspector, for your consideration. I will for my part endeavour to remember the passage of events as concisely as is possible. Now, let me commence by saying the invitation was extended to our party through a telephone conversation between my late father and Mr Montague Carlile on Monday morning last. I think at this point it best that I clarify who I mean by our party, the members of which being those of my late father, the Right Hon. the Eighth Earl of Marlford, Lord Rupert Henry Penman-Smythe, myself and my gentleman companion who is known as Mr John Smith. As I was saying, the invitation was extended and duly accepted to take tea here, at Carlile Manor, at three o'clock this afternoon. We three motored across from Beeches Hall in my father's automobile with His Lordship himself at the wheel, and regrettably at whose wheel I shall have to be for the solemn return journey, being granted admittance to the great hall by Mr Carlile's butler, Collins, punctually at a few minutes before three. I know that we were a little early, as I remember glancing at the long case clock in the hall as we stepped through the main portal into this grotesque yet imposing house, and observing that it was three minutes to three o'clock. As we stood divesting ourselves of our heavy driving coats, the front doorbell rang and Collins, having dextrously retrieved and hung our coats speedily in the small cloakroom beside where we stood, stepped forward and opened the front door, in the process cheerfully extending a greeting and bidding entry to a tall man with dark and ruggedly handsome features whom my father instantly recognised and greeted as the village doctor.

'Upon the doctor having been divested of his driving apparel and initial social pleasantries having been seen to, we as a newly extended group were ceremoniously escorted by Collins to the drawing room, where we were informed our host for the afternoon's festivities was eagerly awaiting our arrival. As the drawing-room door opened, the gracious and friendly countenance of our host, Mr Carlile, beamed upon us from where he reposed most decorously seated in his wheelchair at the centre point of a cluster of chintz-covered chairs under the glistening hue of the giant crystal chandelier. He encouragingly beckoned us to join him which we, as a group, readily acceded to, quickly moving to join him by seating ourselves in the vacant chairs gathered around him. Having seen us settled comfortably and after social pleasantries had been exchanged, I noticed Mr Carlile nodding to Collins who then commenced to serve the afternoon tea. Oh, Inspector, I must say here that to call this fare just afternoon tea is to do the kitchen staff of this house a grave disservice. I do not think that, even as a small child with all the associated wonder that that time in life bestows, I ever felt such a feeling of childlike enchantment at the sight, smell and taste of the exquisite delicacies that were on offer this afternoon.

'With this spectacle so clearly at hand, had instantly come to mind the thought that indeed, Mr Carlile, was the dear and treasured friend as had been the way my now dearly departed papa had always spoken of what appeared now to me to be a most generous and jovial host. Having both rapidly, as is the curse of youthful vigour, consumed our fill of this fine food and tasteful tea and wishing to give the older members of this party a little time alone to reminisce, Mr Smith and myself begged the party's indulgence to part with our company for a time, venturing as our excuse for this disappearance as the desire for a breath of fresh air, which I must now admit was in part true, Mr Smith having found the warmth generated from the roaring hearth a little too sapping of his still limited strength. With the group acceding to our wish, we proceeded forthwith from the well-padded chairs, out through the French windows, across the terrace to the gardens beyond. There, we commenced to promenade quite determinedly around the still beautiful grounds now adorned in their autumn tones of russet and gold, happily making numerous circuits in a spirited manner during which we conversed on matters of, might I say, a most intimate and personal nature.

'Each time we ventured within earshot of the drawing-room window, we heard the quite determined voice of my now dearly departed father still entertaining most enthusiastically his host and remaining guest with his exploits from abroad. During one of these early circuits, we strolled to the furthermost point of the immediate grounds and were in the process of turning when we both noticed a short stocky man dressed in the clothes of a stableman hurriedly making his way in the apparent direction of the main house. We thought nothing more about it, as we had by this stage reached a small stone summer house situated at a point where the manicured lawns and gardens meet the natural woodland and downs. Mr Smith having expressed a wish to rest for a time, we sat there alternating between revelling in the peace and tranquillity of our own thoughts and contemplation of our lives past, present and future and engrossed in a most animated conversation unnoticed by, and unresponsive to, the events which we were later to find out had been unfolding around us. The passage of time must indeed have been swift, for some forty-five minutes had elapsed when Mr Smith roused me from what to my mind had been only a short period of tranquil reverie with the suggestion that, in my relaxed and obviously comfortable state of mind and body, I had nodded off to sleep. This suggestion of my actions I accepted as highly likely as, since our recent return to Beeches Hall, I had not slept at all well. It was then agreed by both of us that we should return immediately to our host and the other guests in the drawing room of the manor.

'Upon venturing forth from our retreat and proceeding across the lawn in the direction of the house, we observed the figure of Dr Mathews returning from the direction of the stables. Having noticed our approach, he slackened his step and we caught up with him, whereupon he informed us of the accident at the stables. We all agreed that we should return to the manor as soon as possible. Upon resuming our steps in the desired direction, Dr Mathews noticed a movement in the gazebo at the side of the terrace. To our surprise upon further investigation, we found it to be Mr Carlile himself who, upon our approach, offered to us the excuse for his present position as that of having come in search for myself and Mr Smith to bid our return to the festivities. This, we as a renewed group, with the unexpected addition of Dr Mathews, his administrations at the stables completed for the time being, acceded to readily, with Mr Smith diplomatically offering to push Mr Carlile up the slight incline on to the terrace, which our host accepted most thankfully.

'It was, therefore, as a reunited and happy group that we came upon what was at first sight thought to be the sleeping figure of my poor papa, still seated quite peacefully in his chair in the drawing room. However, it quickly became apparent as we moved further into the room and closer to his slightly slumped form that he was not merely asleep but was, in fact, dead. The confirmation of this fact having come rapidly, as Dr Mathews adeptly drew from the medical bag which he had carried back from the stables himself the necessary tools of his trade, and plying his art had turned to the assembled group with the most unpalatable pronouncement of death upon this upstanding and outstanding figure of a man, whom it was my indescribable pleasure to have as my father. Yet, I waver slightly from the point. Subsequently, the village constable was contacted through Mr Carlile at Dr Mathews' instruction, and upon his arrival we were directed to gather and remain in the dining room until the arrival of an inspector from Scotland Yard. That, as far as I can remember, Inspector Dentworth, is the passage of events as they appeared to me,' concluded the Lady Isabella appearing noticeably drained by the concentrated act of relating this information which she had just endured.

'Thank you, Your Ladyship, for that most detailed account of this afternoon's proceedings. I will not detain you very much longer. However, I do have a couple of further questions which I would like, if I may, put to you at this time?' the inspector diplomatically requested.

'Certainly, Inspector, I wish to help in any way possible to catch the fiend who took the life of my much loved father,' the Lady Isabella responded, her blue eyes blazing with a light as fierce as a priceless sapphire.

'I will therefore ask you to explain to me in your own discreet terms the nature of the relationship between yourself and the man called John Smith?' commanded Inspector Dentworth, his face a picture of confidential fatherly encouragement.

'If that is of importance in this case, which you obviously deem it must be, then I will by all means, Inspector, tell you all you request in this matter,' replied the Lady Isabella. The slight hint of a blush rising in those finely chiselled cheeks as she continued, 'The relationship, as you so eloquently describe it, is that of my fiancé. Notwithstanding, I think it best if I return to the beginning of our acquaintanceship. As I have previously informed you, I saw service in the last war in the position of a nursing sister initially in a casualty clearing station some miles behind the battle front in France. During my tour of duty, a particularly aggressive offensive took place in the region of the Somme River. There were many casualties brought in on one particular day, one of which was a young man, who first caught my eye and to whom I was inexplicably drawn when I saw him lying unconscious on a stretcher, one of a long line of waiting patients in the muddy hospital compound. It was instantly apparent, as I bent to assess his wounds, that he had been caught in one of the many barrages of fire of this campaign, with his head completely swathed in a sea of bloodstained and mud-splattered bandages. Much of his clothing had been torn from his body in the blast, to the point where his identity was marked as unknown on the paperwork which had accompanied him down the line from the regimental stretcher bearers who had brought him bloodied and all but unconscious to the regimental aid post and on to the main dressing station which had initially tended his atrocious wounds.

'As fate would have it, when his turn finally came to be attended to by the magnificent surgeons, it was to the table at which I was assisting that this young man's stretcher was directed. Once the surgeon had worked patiently and removed the grimy bandages, it was horrifically obvious to all the serious nature and extent of the injuries to this poor young man's face. Suffice to say, that if you had drawn a line down the centre of this poor fellow's face from top to bottom, there was not much left intact on the right side. His right eye had been blown out and lost as indeed had been his right ear in the initial blast with the rest of the flesh of that side of the face having been sliced away from the associated bones, this damage, as clean as any butcher's knife, having been inflicted by razor-sharp flying shrapnel, sulphur burns then finishing off the job by burning deep into the remaining flesh of the rest of the face and up into the hairline cutting a zigzag swathe, as a scythe through a field of wheat, through his luxuriant head of thick black hair.

'Having done all that they could, the surgeons placed very little measure in the thought that this poor young fellow would indeed see the night out. They could not be sure, together with the obvious external injuries he had incurred indeed, what internal injuries they had not been aware of, let alone the thought of the onset of infection the likes of gas gangrene which, in a case such as this, was more than likely. However, as fortune would have it, he did see out the night and several subsequent nights until, it was into my face, he blearily peered upon regaining sedated consciousness. As you see, Inspector, for some reason known only to God in heaven, I was again drawn to this shattered young man and his plight, being rostered to care for his every need. It was, and still is, beyond my understanding why, from the hundreds if not thousands of poor young souls I cared for in these terrible times, I should so determinedly be drawn to this particular, wretched fellow, but I was indeed.

'A deep and unprecedented bond developed between nurse and patient in the days after this tortured soul's admittance to our facility. His road to limited recovery was very slow, with him at times becoming extremely frustrated by the added problem of suffering from severe amnesia to the point of not remembering a thing about his previous life leading up to the blast. With his identity a mystery to all around him it was decided that he should take the name of the regimental stretcher bearer who found him in the field of battle and brought him to safety. Obviously, his name was John Smith. The only thing which he could believe as being constant in his tormented existence was my attendance and support which I gladly gave partly as my professional duty, but also, as even in the brief time he had been in my care, I saw in him a man of great determination and spirit for whom I personally had begun to feel deeply. We quickly became all but inseparable within the confines of my other duties in my nursing role at the clearing station and when the time came that he was repatriated on to a base hospital on the coast of France for further treatment and convalescence, I requested transfer to this establishment.

'The armistice came and went. We remained in Europe, with Mr Smith transferred yet again to a private hospital and, entrusted to the best European medical minds and hands, he regained the physical strength required to undertake the journey back to England. With the knowledge that my father had opened Beeches Hall as a facility for recuperating soldiers, we returned to my tranquil childhood home. With the strength of my fairly substantial finances behind us, I put to work, as I had done in Europe, the finest medical minds in the country to assist Mr Smith in any way possible to regain the highest level of mental as well as physical recovery. Sadly, however, no more can be done for his physical well-being and none can say if the poor fellow will ever regain his memory or any more of his shattered mind, for he is still prone to bouts of confusion and dark depression. It would appear, though extensive investigations have been carried out through the Ministry of the Army, that he will remain a man without name or family. In conclusion though, I must state that he will not go through life alone, for it is my fervently held wish and determined intention to marry this intelligent and courageous young man in the summer of next year,' the Lady Isabella stated emphatically, finally coming to the end of her heartfelt dissertation.

'Thank you, Your Ladyship, for that most graphic and detailed account,' Inspector Dentworth said, his voice indicative of the high regard he placed in the past actions of men such as had been the subject of the last discourse.

He continued again in his most businesslike policeman's manner by briskly asking, 'To your knowledge, Your Ladyship, did Mr Smith at any time this afternoon leave your presence?'

To which the Lady Isabella, turning her now cold blue eyes to stare squarely at the inspector's placid face, instantly and quite determinedly responded, 'No, Inspector, Mr Smith was in my company at all times this afternoon, that is to say of course up to the point where I was requested to come here to speak with you. It would be out of character for him to go anywhere in public without me. He is, as you might well understand, extremely reliant on my help in his life.'

Still looking straight into those mesmerising sapphire blue eyes, Inspector Dentworth, his terrier instincts coming strongly to the fore further doggedly enquired, 'You mentioned yourself, earlier, Your Ladyship that you drifted off to sleep whilst seated in the summer house. Could Mr Smith not have moved away from you during this lapse into unconsciousness on your part and been back in that time before he awakened you himself?'

'I would find that very hard to believe, Inspector, as Mr Smith suffers from an inability to see in limited light and as has been noted the sun was well and truly on its way to bed at the time in question,' the Lady Isabella, noticeably taken aback at the insinuation of some form of guilt on the part of her intended by the sharp-witted inspector, responded defensively. The inspector in passing mentally noted the ferocity of her response and defence of this man, likening it to that of a lioness protecting her cub.

'I have just a couple of further questions to put to you at this time, Your Ladyship, and those are: one, to your knowledge did His Lordship have any personal and or business acquaintances who would in your opinion wish to do him any harm, and two, to your knowledge was His Lordship in good health since his recent return from South Africa?' Inspector Dentworth steadily enquired of the now somewhat discomposed creature who sat before him, her hands wringing nervously in her lap.

As she passed a comforting hand across her auburn locks which had been stylishly cut in a bob form, accentuating her willowy features, the Lady Isabella quietly yet with a surge of heartfelt emotion replied, 'Firstly, there is no one, Inspector, whom I can think of at this time whom I would consider would wish to do harm of any kind whatsoever to my now dearly departed papa and, secondly, as far as I can say, Inspector, my father was in excellent state of health for a man of his age and position. He complained to me of no feelings of discomfiture since his return from South Africa. However, if you wish to confirm his recent state of health, to my knowledge, his physician is Sir Garfield Pembleton, naturally of Harley Street.'

Wishing now to bring this witness's testimony to its conclusion, Inspector Dentworth requested a final reply to the following enquiry.

'Thank you for that information, Your Ladyship. That, you will no doubt be pleased to hear, brings us to the conclusion of the questions I wished to put to you at this time. Oh, by the way, Your Ladyship, just in passing, how did your father greet the news of your forthcoming marriage to Mr Smith? Indeed for that matter, how harmoniously did His Lordship and Mr Smith reside under the same roof?' The inspector, having made this enquiry as he sat with his head lowered in a somewhat offhand manner as if more intent on scanning the papers he had just taken from his inside coat pocket and now held intently in his long sensitive hand than the answers to the questions he had just asked.

With a light yet still noticeable touch of nervousness in her voice, the Lady Isabella replied, in but a whisper, 'My late father, the Earl of Marlford, and my fiancé, Mr Smith, were men of two different ages and worlds, Inspector. Both had experienced much of life, yet in totally diverse realms. It was, therefore, unlikely that they would see eye to eye on very many matters. After all, the one issue they were united in was their deep respect and concern for my constant well-being and my future happiness. Now will that be all, Inspector?' the Lady Isabella enquiringly concluded.

The inspector, placed a little ill at ease by the sudden reversal of roles and command, sternly replied, 'That will be all, for now, Your Ladyship. May I remind you that a coroner's investigation into the late Earl's death will be required to take place at a date and time in the near future. Your attendance at this inquest may well be required. So I would appreciate it, if you are planning on returning to your London residence at any point in the next few days, that you advise myself or my personnel of these travel plans. Apart from that, you are at liberty to go about your business. You will, of course, be notified as soon as we have completed our examinations of Lord Rupert's body which should be within the next day or so. If you have nothing further to add to the information you have so far given us, then I suggest you return to the dining room, as I gather from what you have previously told us that you would not wish to return to your country home without the companionship of Mr Smith. By the way, Your Ladyship, as you are returning now to the dining room, would you be so kind as to inform Mr Smith that we require his presence here immediately?'

The Lady Isabella, with the definite signs of relief etched into her handsome features that this immediate ordeal was moving to its close, replied breathlessly as she rose from her chair, 'Thank you, Inspector, I will send Mr Smith to you as soon as possible. Might I suggest, in parting, that you treat him with a certain degree of gentle consideration, Inspector, for he still suffers a substantial level of physical pain from the drastic wounds he incurred, a pain, I might add, which is kept at bay only by the administration by myself or Mr Smith of hypodermic injections of morphine on a regular basis. This medication, in turn, tends to heighten his already present state of confusion.'

Along with those words and not waiting for a reply which may retain her a moment longer within the confines of this harrowing room, this elegant member of the landed gentry swiftly disappeared from view. With the genteel fragrance of a lady's fine perfume lingering softly in the air, the two men were left to ponder all that had come to light so far...

A subdued warmth greeted the Lady Isabella upon her return to the hushed confines of the dining room. As she resumed her seat before the lightly glowing hearth, she turned her attention towards the gentleman seated beside her who, in her absence, had remained silent apparently lost in an ocean of black contemplation as evidenced by the deeply furrowed brow which beheld itself to her gaze. It was from this trance-like state that the Lady Isabella endeavoured to rouse her companion with the following sternly spoken words.

'John dear, the inspector wishes to ask you a few questions about this afternoon. He has asked me to convey his wish for your presence immediately in the billiard room.'

Having taken some time for these words to have registered in the young man's apparently addled brain, Mr John Smith turned a deeply confused and still trance-like gaze upon the alert blue eyes of his beloved and replied slowly in a muffled voice.

'Why does he want to talk to me? I could not help the man being killed. He was just one of many. I could do nothing about any of them. The good Lord knows I tried to help I am sure but then the blast came and I was gone myself. Life is so cheap... such a dreadful waste... so much blood...' His words trailed off into the darkness surrounding the flickering flames of the fire into which he absently returned his unseeing gaze.

'Oh, hush now, John, please. You are home in England now. The war is over and you are safe. It is the death of my father that is in question now, not one of your pals at the front. The inspector wishes to speak to you now in the billiard room. You had better not keep him waiting. If you turn right as you leave this room, the billiard room is at the end of the corridor, the last door on the right,' the Lady Isabella declared authoritatively, issuing her directives as that of a mother to a wayward child.

As John Smith rose stiffly from the seat in which he had reposed for what had seemed like many hours and moved awkwardly across the room, a voice issued forth from the direction of the dappled light at the edge of the hearth with the simple words of encouragement, 'Be fearless, my boy.'

With the utterance of these words, John Smith turned his head instantly in the direction of their speaker, Montague Carlile, and with his face aglow with previously unseen emotion plainly obvious to all present he replied with some effort as he slowly retreated from the room, 'Fearless by name and fearless by nature, eh, sir.'

Leaving both Montague and the man called John Smith with a cold feeling of uneasiness and a faint remembrance of times past...

'Now, sir, for our records would you please state your full name, address and occupation,' had been the familiar and methodical request by Inspector Dentworth which commenced yet another testimony in this first day of the investigation, he having settled comfortably the young man called John Smith in the chair beside him.

John Smith, his words having come slowly and haltingly with

great labour of effort in their enunciation on the speaker's part, frankly replied, 'Well, Inspector, I am sure by this stage in your enquiries... you know my past history, for what it is worth. My name, I don't really know. Since returning from that ghastly war... I have taken the name John Andrew Smith, after the regimental stretcher bearer... who found me and brought me to safety... from that bloody battlefield and indeed saved my life. As for my address... I must in all honesty say... I have no home of my own. Due to the generous nature of my fiancée, the Lady Isabella, and her now late father, the Earl of Marlford... I have since our return from Europe... been resident in his country home, Beeches Hall. Finally, in answer to your question of my occupation... my service in the war and the subsequent injuries... I unfortunately and obviously incurred... put paid to any chance I had of enjoying... a prosperous life in the workforce... of this country. With no apparent financial position of my own... I am, in fact... a destitute cripple... at the generous mercy of strangers.'

'Thank you, Mr Smith, for that most earnest reply. Further to these investigations, would you now, in your own words and good time, tell us of the chain of events of this afternoon as you observed them,' Inspector Dentworth calmly requested in the most reassuring of tones possible, conscious of the increasingly anxious attitude the gentleman beside him was adopting at the apparent prospect of having to converse further.

'As you instruct, Inspector. I will attempt to remember... what happened this afternoon. We arrived here at about three o'clock... having been invited to take tea with the owner, Mr Montague Carlile... through an invitation extended to His Lordship... via a telephone conversation held on Monday morning last. Upon arriving by motor from Beeches Hall... we were greeted at the front door by the butler... whose name I believe is Collins. While we were taking off our heavy driving coats... the doorbell rang and a tall distinguished gentleman was bade welcome... and in passing, introduced to us... by Lord Rupert as the local village doctor by the name of... Dr Mathews, I believe. We were then, as a group... stewarded by Collins to the drawing room... where, he had informed us, our host for the afternoon's festivities... was awaiting our arrival. Upon entering the drawing room, we were greeted... most graciously by a gentleman of advancing years... who reposed quite sedately within a wheelchair... positioned at the centre of a grouping... of thickly padded lounge chairs.'

At this point, John Smith paused to take a much needed breath and then laboriously ventured on, 'He beckoned us to him, instructing that we take a seat... in the chairs positioned around him, which we readily did. Having formally introduced all those present to one another... afternoon tea was commenced by... what I noticed was a nod of acknowledgement... between master and manservant. The afternoon tea was a lavish affair... which I must admit both the Lady Isabella and myself... consumed with great relish and relative to the other older participants... great speed. I must, at this point state, Inspector, that... I was already beginning to find the very warm confines of the drawing room... too overpowering and restricting to my impaired breathing. Since returning from the war, I find it very hard... to remain enclosed for extended periods of time... much preferring the open space. Having registered my increasing unease... the Lady Isabella begged the indulgence of our host... to allow us to take a stroll around the impressive grounds... while the rest of the party were completing this afternoon's repast. Agreement to this request... came readily on the part of the remaining elderly gentlemen... who had appeared to be totally engrossed... as Lord Rupert continued his monotonous monologue... on what to the Lady Isabella and myself was... the frequently heard topic of his recent exploits in South Africa.

'Mr Carlile suggested that he would send for us... when we were required to return for the planned game of whist... following the tea. It must, by my reckoning... have been approaching four o'clock... when we left the drawing room. As we strolled about the grounds, I noticed... and mentioned to the Lady Isabella, in passing, the sight of what appeared to me... an elderly groom, hurriedly moving across the lawn... in the direction of the main house. We thought nothing more about it, as by this stage... I had begun to tire slightly and suggested to the Lady Isabella... that we stop and rest for a time in the discreet seclusion... and relative comfort of the stone summer house situated at the far end of the grounds... at a point where the garden meets the surrounding cultivated woodland... and rolling downs. This, the Lady Isabella agreed to quite readily... neither of us wishing to rapidly return... to those stuffy and boorish confines from which we had just escaped... and what we both knew would be the continuous droning... of that foghorn voice and bombastic manner... of Lord Rupert Penman-Smythe.'

John Smith again paused, took a few deep breaths and continued, 'I must in all honesty, Inspector, say at this point that it was only out of polite respect... to His Lordship and our host Mr Carlile that the Lady Isabella and myself... accepted this invitation. As we sat, in the cool peace and tranquillity... of our chosen retreat, we revelled in the simple pleasure of each other's company... at times deep in our own contemplation, at others joyously laughing at a shared comment... on some of life's happier experiences. Time passed by rapidly... it was only the onset of fading light which triggered me to consult my pocket watch... whence I was amazed to see that the time was fast approaching... towards five o'clock. As I turned to speak to the Lady Isabella... I observed that, during what had been a period of quiet reflection... on both our parts, the Lady Isabella had drifted off to sleep, from whence I sadly had to awaken her. Having informed her of the time... it was agreed that we should return to the main house immediately... which we proceeded to do. As we ventured across the lawn towards our target... we, or I should rightly say the Lady Isabella... for with only one eye left to me to use and it not being very useful in darkening conditions... such as those experienced at this particular time... in the afternoon, noticed the approach of a figure... which the Lady Isabella astutely recognised as that of Dr Mathews... moving also in the direction of the main house, from what we gathered by the grouping of buildings... to be the stables. Having noticed our approach, he slackened his hurried pace... meeting us in the middle of the lawn and explained concisely the passage of events in our absence.

'Dr Mathews then suggested that we join him in returning... to the manor, of which, we informed him... had indeed been our intention prior to his arrival. As Dr Mathews turned to resume the trek back to the rest of the party... he acknowledged to us the presence of Mr Carlile... residing in the gazebo at the far edge of the terrace. We subsequently strode out a course towards this structure... and our awaiting host. Upon reaching him, Mr Carlile ventured as his reason for residing in the gazebo... as twofold, in the Lady Isabella's hearing... that of wishing to hopefully find us and bid us return... to the drawing room for the continuation of the festivities... and, secondly, in what he thought was Dr Mathews' discreet and solitary hearing... which by chance I overheard in doing so... take a much deserved rest from the booming noise... which constituted His Lordship's voice.

'Having easily found all the missing members of his party, the suggestion was thus made... by our quite jovial host that we should return to the drawing room... forthwith to which we, as a reunited group, readily agreed. To my eye, Mr Carlile appeared to be looking a little tired... so, having in myself felt to have regained a little of my own strength... in the pleasant distraction of the garden and the Lady Isabella's delightful company... I forwarded the suggestion that he may like me to assist him... by pushing his chair which he speedily agreed to. We then ventured, as a quite friendly group... back into the confines of the drawing room where we immediately observed... what all at first thought was the slightly slumped form of Lord Rupert... apparently reposing in blissful slumber. However, as we moved closer to this seemingly peaceful figure... Dr Mathews shot forward in the process... informing all to stay where they were.

'His medical astuteness became apparent, as he was seen by all to rapidly examine... the recumbent form before him. It was then, with a brow as dark... as the worst thunder clouds of any severe storm, that he slowly raised... himself from the position that he had assumed... kneeling before His Lordship, and turning to the assembled party... had informed us that the Earl of Marlford was dead. In a most calm and businesslike manner, Dr Mathews took control... of this most serious situation by issuing the instruction... that Mr Carlile should contact the police. This Mr Carlile speedily attended to as I, for my limited part... attempted to comfort the Lady Isabella. Communications were made with the local police... in the form of Constable Stevens and subsequently your arrival here... from Scotland Yard,' John

Smith breathlessly arrived at what he hoped would be the conclusion of his statement of events.

'That is all very interesting, Mr Smith. Further to what you have told us, there are just a couple more questions which I wish to put to you at this time, if I may?' Inspector Dentworth nonchalantly in an air of light-heartedness requested of the young man who still nervously reposed beside him.

As the inspector paused briefly to focus the thoughts within his methodical mind, he glanced – for the first true time, having during the previous dissertation by this witness been intent upon watching the rhythmical flickering of the flames within the hearth – surreptitiously sideways at the subject of his present thoughts. The view which beheld itself to his keen grey eyes was of a physically battered and mentally scarred young man. The inspector thought sadly to himself, here should have sat a man in the prime of his young life but for the horrific intrusion of the war. What a handsome specimen of manhood he would have been; as traces of his former masculine beauty were still visible from behind his now grotesque mask-like features, features which caught and held the observer's eye in a vice-like grip of macabre attraction, from the solemn black patch covering the spot where his right eye should have reposed in gentle companionship to the remaining emerald green and penetrating member of the pair, the obvious loss of flesh and action of the cheek and lips as evidenced by his laboured and muffled enunciation, the dark hair now streaked prematurely with wisps of grey and its zigzag pattern of burns induced baldness stretching from the right side of his high, intelligent forehead through the forest of his otherwise dense hair disappearing from view over the crest of his crown, and finally to the ear that would no longer hear the call of the first cuckoo in the spring. The depression and sadness felt at this sight was to the inspector's mind further heightened by the knowledge that this poor soul had not only lost his body, but also his mind. Inspector Dentworth sadly noted the way in which John Smith sat staring into space, his fingers twiddling nervously back and forth in his lap. It was from this trance-like state that the inspector now raised himself and his subject by the utterance of the following series of questions and responses.

'Firstly, Mr Smith, did you at any time this afternoon leave the company of the Lady Isabella, for any reason?' the inspector quietly enquired as he shuffled absently the papers that he held in his hand.

Noticeably taken aback slightly, Mr Smith remained silent for a moment before he replied, 'I find it very difficult, near impossible... to move around alone, Inspector, especially in the subdued light conditions... such as we had late this afternoon.'

Noting the tinge of defiance creeping into the subject's voice, the inspector stoically pushed on in his quest for answers, by sternly requesting, 'Secondly, and I expect you will be glad to hear finally for now, may I ask you, Mr Smith, how well did you and the late Earl reside under the same roof and, for that matter, what was his response to your forthcoming marriage to his only child?'

The response to these intrinsically linked enquiries came cryptically from the mangled lips of John Smith.

'Well, Inspector, Beeches Hall is an extensive residence and we resided... quite amicably together within its many walls. As for my forthcoming marriage... to the Lady Isabella, we are both adults who have seen much more of life's joys... and sorrows than most people around here... including the late Earl and are not greatly concerned by the attitudes... or, might I say, the narrow-minded opinions... of those around us.'

'Very well, Mr Smith, that will be all for now. You may rejoin the Lady Isabella in the dining room and subsequently are free to accompany her home to Beeches Hall. I have completed my questioning of you both for the time being. However, as I have informed the Lady Isabella, a coroner's inquest will be required to take place at a date and time yet to be set and your presence there may well be required. With this fact in mind, I would require you to inform myself or my staff of any travel plans you may wish to enact in the foreseeable future. Apart from that, you are free to go about your business,' Inspector Dentworth sternly commanded, thus signifying to all that this interview had been terminated.

Comprehending this fact, Mr Smith rose slowly and silently from his seat and made his way stiffly across the room, the time spent in the chair beside the hearth having had a not so beneficial effect on his already cramped muscles. With the disappearance from view of Mr Smith behind the now partly closed door came a crisp and clear rap upon this sturdy barricade.

Having barked out his barrack room retort of, 'Enter,' Inspector Dentworth was greeted for his effort, upon the further opening of the door by the sight of Constable Stevens standing before him in accompaniment to the familiar, tall, thin figure of Dr Edmund Scott.

'Oh, Stevens, it is you. I see you have Dr Scott with you, good man. Well, do not stand there on the threshold for ever. Show him in here, young lad. I hope, young man, you have been of help to this fine gentleman. You would do well to take note of the attention to detail that Dr Scott exhibits in the performance of his duties and the conduct of his occupation,' Inspector Dentworth commanded earnestly of his young subordinate as he extolled the professional virtues of the man now seating himself in the chair, as indicated to him by the ever-polite young constable, beside that resided in by the inspector.

Turning to look directly into the studious yet handsome face of Dr Scott, the inspector issued forth a most hearty welcome with the words, 'Hello, Dr Scott, glad to see you were able to make it down here at last. Good to know that you will be working on this case with us. It deserves nothing but the best and with your dedicated help that is what it shall have.'

The inspector finished these warm words of praise, which Dr Scott acknowledged by a simple nod of his lozenge-shaped head and the words, 'Hello, Inspector Dentworth, good to see you again and, yes, this young man is a credit to the force.'

Inspector Dentworth turned again towards Constable Stevens who, during this time, had stood before his respected superior absorbed in his words of almost fatherly advice and patiently waiting his further instructions in the course of what had from the outset appeared to be a most fascinating case.

'Now, Stevens, while I am conversing with Dr Scott here, I want you to go down to the servants' hall and escort the butler, Collins, back up here. There are a few questions about this afternoon's proceedings I wish to put to him before we conclude our investigation for this evening. The hour is growing late and all concerned are, I am sure, becoming a touch tired, myself included. I know I will not be sorry to go to our lodgings at the Horse and Hound soon, but enough of that now. Away with you, young man, let us see this day out as we began,' these words having been spoken as the inspector consulted his polished silver pocket watch – a gift from the force for twenty-five years of unblemished service – registering the rapid passage of time; the hour approached that of ten.

With the disappearance from view, yet again, of this most eager young man upon his appointed task, the inspector turned his attention once more towards the man who sat quietly beside him. A man of comparable age to himself and possessed of a similar diligent nature, Dr Edmund Herbert Scott, with his head of still thick black hair and equally thick and bushy moustache was an easily recognisable figure in the corridors of Scotland Yard.

'Right now, Dr Scott, what can you tell us of your findings so far in this most important case?' Inspector Dentworth enthusiastically enquired, eager to inject some fresh information into what had appeared to him to be a somewhat stagnating case.

'Well, Inspector, to start with, it would indeed appear from my preliminary examinations to be a case of murder which we are looking at. However, further investigations will have to be made into the general health of the victim to rule out any form of natural seizure which sometimes mirrors certain forms of poisoning, the effects of which I have duly observed and documented on the deceased. I will, by the way, make the necessary arrangements for the transportation of the body back to London for further testing. Nevertheless, it is my belief that the victim was indeed murdered by some form of fast-acting poison being introduced into the food or drink that he consumed this afternoon. This belief is further strengthened by the remains of food, I discovered, which had been hidden from immediate view clenched behind the fingers of his right hand. Needless to say, I have taken this, and the remains of the tea held in his teacup, together with other samples for further analysis, back in the laboratory in London to which I will return immediately. I am of the understanding, from the stationmaster at Marlford, that the last train to London departs at twenty minutes to eleven and with nothing more that I can add to the information at hand for the moment, I wish to be on that train,' concluded Dr Scott leaving none present in any doubt of his wish for his future actions that evening.

'Thank you, Dr Scott, you will of course keep us informed of your findings in this matter. As is your suggestion, further enquiries will be required to be carried out in the rarefied atmosphere of Harley Street after our return to London tomorrow evening. In passing, it may interest you to know that the medical requirements of the now late Earl were handled by the eminent physician, Sir Garfield Pembleton. I must in all honesty say that I do not relish having to question one of these highbrow members of your own profession. They always leave me feeling as though I drew the short straw in intelligence and that it is their God-given right to show me the fact,' Inspector Dentworth confidentially replied.

As he paused to take a needed breath before continuing, Dr Scott all but yelled out in uncharacteristic boyish excitement the following words, 'Oh, Inspector, if you feel that strongly about speaking to the likes of Sir Garfield Pembleton, I, myself, would be most happy to undertake this task on your and, of course, Scotland Yard's behalf. If you are agreeable to this situation, I will most readily make the necessary arrangements to speak with him at his earliest convenience on the matter of His Lordship's state of health prior to this afternoon.'

'That, Dr Scott, would be a most generous and welcome offer on your part on behalf of myself and my men. You will, of course, as I have mentioned before, keep us informed of your findings in this matter. However, for now as you have indicated was your immediate wish, I will have Constable Stevens upon his no doubt speedy return with the butler arrange for your transportation to the station,' Inspector Dentworth replied, an extremely relieved tone etching his noticeably tired voice.

With the inspector's last words still ringing across the expansive room, and before Dr Scott could again respond, the now familiar knock resounded forth from the direction of the billiard-room door, to which Inspector Dentworth jovially stated to those present, 'Speak of the devil. This young man is bound to succeed in today's force.' In a somewhat milder volume than usual –

indicative of the late hour of the day – Inspector Dentworth yet again barked out his command of, 'Enter.'

Upon treading the now well-known and equally well-traversed path to stand before the inspector, Constable Stevens on this occasion brought with him into the assembled party's view a cadaverous man who, as a product of the advancing of his years, had developed a quite predominant stoop.

As he came to rest before his superior with his companion of the moment, Constable Stevens, taking the initiative, spoke out in his clear, strong voice.

'Inspector Dentworth, this is the butler, Mr Collins.'

'Thank you, Constable Stevens, I have but a couple of further orders for you this evening. As you came here this afternoon on your police bicycle – I observed it beside the front door as we entered the house earlier today – you cannot personally afford the good doctor a means of transportation to the station. It is, therefore, my request that you escort Dr Scott to the front hall and arrange for his immediate and speedy transportation to the station for what I have been reliably informed to be the last train back to London tonight. Then, having seen him safely on his way, you will return to the dining room and inform Mr Carlile that he is free to go about his business. Following that, you are free to go home. I will take this opportunity to thank you now, Constable Stevens, for all the assistance you have rendered to both myself and Sergeant Jones in our investigations today. I do not believe we will require your services any further in this matter. It would indeed be remiss of me to take you from your duties to your community for an extended period of time. Rest assured, you have been a credit to the force you so aptly serve and it is this view of your abilities I will be forwarding to your immediate superiors. Now, off with you, Constable, and be about your tasks,' the inspector instructed firmly, in the process placing a good deal of emphasis on the importance of these tasks being completed as speedily as possible by this competent young man.

'Straight away, Inspector. If you would like to come with me, Doctor, there is a telephone in the hall from which I will ring for a vehicle to take you to the station straight away,' Constable Stevens respectfully requested in an even, strong voice which, in its strength and nature, did not reveal the surge of deep-seated pride which had engulfed his whole being at the sound of the intense praise from his current superior.

'Goodbye, for now, Dr Scott. I will be in contact with you again, in a day or so, to see how you are getting on. Please let me know if any new information comes to hand before then. Now, if you will go with the constable here, he will see that you do not miss your train,' the inspector courteously said.

'Thank you, Inspector Dentworth. Rest assured, it is my intention to leave no stone unturned so to speak in the conduct of my part of this investigation,' was the final, determined reply from Dr Scott as, in accompaniment to Constable Stevens, the pair disappeared out of sight, leaving the inspector and his companion, the sergeant, to turn their attention upon the final witness to be interviewed on the first day of this investigation, Collins, the butler, who now stood languidly in front of them awaiting their instructions.

Noting the apparent fragility of this elderly manservant, Inspector Dentworth immediately issued forth with the following request.

'Come, man, sit yourself down here,' the inspector said, indicating in a compassionate tone of voice to the frail butler the comfortable chair by the hearth.

As he settled himself by the warmth of the fire, the old man replied in a cracking voice, 'Thank you, Inspector, I am sorry to say that my old frame does not hold me up all that well these days by this time of night.'

Having nodded acknowledgement of this comment by the walking skeleton of a man who sat beside him, the inspector, in a return to his most businesslike manner, ventured forth once more in the ongoing investigation by calmly requesting, 'Now, my good man, if you are comfortable we will continue our task at hand. To begin with, for our records, would you please state your full name, address and occupation?'

'By all means, Inspector, but may I first express this household's deep shock and sadness at the happenings of this afternoon. In my long experience in service, nothing like this has ever happened before, except perhaps the loss of young Master

Reginald in the war. In answer to your question, my full name is Wilfred Harold Collins. I reside, as I have done for the past fifteen years or so, under the roof of this house. My present lodgings are that of the butler's pantry below stairs, as I have held the position of butler in this house for the last ten years, since the timely retirement of my predecessor, Mr Hopkins. Previous to that, I resided in London, as butler to Mr and Mrs Carlile. That was in much happier times, before the master's tragic accident which left him a virtual prisoner down here,' Collins replied, sharply coming to a close, mindful of his position and his tendency in old age to waffle on when given the opportunity.

'So, is there a Mrs Carlile?' the inspector suddenly interjected.

'Yes, sir, but she has lived in London permanently these past ten years or so,' Collins succinctly replied.

'I am keen to hear a little of the history of this family and its relationship to that of His Lordship, so please, if you would be so kind, go on, old fellow,' Inspector Dentworth gently encouraged this so far co-operative witness.

'Oh, as you wish, Inspector. Well, to go back to the beginning, I came into Mr Carlile's employ when both he and I were really just boys. He was about to go to Cambridge and my services as his valet were, to my understanding, organised by a firm of Scottish solicitors who handled his affairs at the time. I have been with him ever since. I have seen him rise through the ranks of the Barland Bank to become one of its senior men. I was there when he married Mrs Carlile. Oh, what a beauty she was, too. Life was so good and it only seemed to get better with the birth of young Master Reginald. Those indeed were happy times, seeing the young babe grow into a fine young man. The family was complete and happy even though the mistress could not have any further issue, women's problems if you know what I mean, but that just seemed to make them all so much closer as a family.

'Then the master gets it into his head to come down here for a weekend of gentlemen's pursuits, riding to hounds and all that it entails. He thinks it is time for young Master Reginald to enjoy a bit of country life for the first time in his young and somewhat sheltered life. The mistress, Mrs Carlile, was none too happy about coming, seeing as how I remember Mr Carlile had caught a very bad cold during a trip to Paris on business during the week before and was, in the mistress's opinion, in no fit state to be anywhere else but tucked up in his bed in London for the weekend. Well, the master is nothing if not determined in his pursuits and insisted that the family would still travel to the country. It is my later understanding that the Right Hon. the Earl of Marlford, Lord Rupert Henry Penman-Smythe, was really behind this blatant insistence on the part of the master. As fate would have it, the weather was wet and windy when we left London and only got worse as we travelled to Marlford, as too did the master's state of health.

'It was cold and miserable on the following morning when the master set off from the house aboard that troublesome and flighty horse, Fearless, the selfsame bugger of a horse as Old Ben, the head groom, has always described him as caused the trouble down at the stables today. The actions of man and horse truly ruined the lives of all under this roof from that moment on as, during the course of the day, in the increasingly wet and muddy conditions, the master lost control, with his horse slipping in the mud and falling on him crushing his body and, in my opinion, breaking his spirit. Mr Carlile has never been the same in mind or body since that dreadful day. A poor, tortured and pain-racked cripple, he never came to terms with the tragic accident and the added loss of his life's work at the bank in London.

'He all but sent the mistress mad with his black moods. The more she tried to comfort him, the more he pushed her away until one day, their anniversary to be exact, he ups and tells her to go back to London and leave him in peace, his sentence of punishment to her, I suppose, for her sending his beloved Master Reginald away back to London, as I remember in preparation for his long-awaited departure to the master's old boarding school, Mendrew. Mr Carlile became a total recluse turning this house into a prison, for the best doctors in the land could not at that time tell how fragile his spine was, so forbade the exertion of his moving back to London, so here we stayed. By the time he regained his strength to a degree to be able to take some enjoyment again, he had by his own hand lost his family as surely as he had lost the use of his legs. The strange thing though, to my mind, has always been, Inspector, the fact that the master has never, throughout all these long and trying years, laid any of the blame for his predicament at the feet of His Lordship.

'It has always been the people closest to him who have born the brunt of his anger and frustration and who in turn have had to pay the price. For years, it has been a solitary life for all concerned, with life becoming even worse upon the loss of young Master Reginald in the last war, until today's festivities, when it was suddenly as though God in His Heaven had finally lifted the curse from this man, only to have this happen!' Collins exasperatedly concluded.

'Yes, from what you have just told us it would appear that this family was indeed cursed,' the inspector agreed.

'Now, Collins, what can you tell me of the tragic chain of events which occurred here today?' Inspector Dentworth enthusiastically enquired wishing at this point for the flow of this witness's testimony to remain unimpeded.

'Well, Inspector, things happened like this. The Earl's party consisting of His Lordship, Lord Rupert Penman-Smythe, his daughter, the Lady Isabella and her gentleman companion, a Mr Smith, arrived by motor from the Earl's country home, Beeches Hall, a little before the appointed time of three o'clock. I remember this, as I consulted my pocket watch as I climbed the stairs from the servant's hall in response to the front doorbell being pushed. As I was assisting the group from their driving coats, the doorbell rang again and, upon opening the door, I bade entry and welcome to Dr Mathews the village doctor from Marlford, who was the other invited guest for the afternoon. Having relieved the doctor of his outer apparel, he also having motored from his cottage in Marlford, I conducted this group as had been my master's instructions to the drawing room where Mr Carlile was eagerly awaiting their arrival.

'Upon this group's arrival in the drawing room and having settled themselves in the most comfortable chairs which were gathered about Mr Carlile's wheelchair, some time was spent in the act of proper social introductions, as not all present had previously met formally. With these social pleasantries attended to, Mr Carlile indicated to me by a nod his desire that I commence to serve the afternoon tea, which I proceeded to do. I might say, it was a delight to have some young people, such as the Lady Isabella and that young Mr Smith, in this house again with their happy voices and hearty appetites. They did appear to enjoy the marvellous spread that the cook, Mrs Christian, had provided. Their consumption of this fare was, in comparison to the others, quite speedy, with them both having their fill long before the remaining more elderly gentlemen of the party. I noticed, too, that Mr Smith was developing a real rosy hue in his pale cheeks and a somewhat distressed look upon his face which the Lady Isabella also noticed.

'It was at this point that this most genteel young lady demurely requested of her host, Mr Carlile, that she and her young companion should be allowed to take a stroll around the garden until such time as the rest of the party had completed their repast. This request was agreed to readily by Mr Carlile, as those remaining had already been absorbed in the talk by His Lordship on the subject of his recent time in South Africa overseeing his mining interests there, this afternoon tea having in fact been intended as a ceremony of 'welcome home' to the Earl on the part of his old and dear friend, Mr Montague Alexander Carlile. Only a short time elapsed from when we watched this charming young couple disappear out of the French windows to when a knock rang out on those selfsame windows.

'I immediately went to the window and opened it to find, to my surprise, Old Ben, the head groom on this estate, standing on the terrace with blood all down the front of his waistcoat and breeches and with a very anxious expression on his blood-streaked face. He straight away launched into his explanation for being on the terrace, telling me that there had been a dreadful accident down at the stables and asking if Mr Carlile would allow the doctor, whom Old Ben knew was taking tea this afternoon, to come and see to the stable boy who had caught a hoof from "that bugger of a horse, Fearless" leaving him with a very nasty bloody gash to the arm. I left Old Ben standing on the terrace, as was his proper place, and straight away informed the master as discreetly as possible of the happenings down at the stables and of Old Ben's urgent request for the doctor's assistance in this matter. Mr

Carlile then turned to Dr Mathews, who was seated beside him, and quickly informed him of the problem. Having instantly comprehended the seriousness of the situation, Dr Mathews then requested that his medical bag should be fetched from his motor in the garage, while he would make his way with Old Ben down to the stables straight away not wishing to waste any time waiting for the return of his bag, which he further asked to be brought to him there.

'There being no other manservants available, seeing as how both my juniors were either incapacitated or absent, and the fact that I had all but served the tea, Mr Carlile commanded that I fetch the doctor's bag from his automobile, take it to the stables, and remain there to assist the doctor for as long as was necessary. So it was that the doctor accompanied Old Ben back to the stables and I, having quickly retrieved the required bag from the doctor's motor, the garage being but a few yards from the back corner of the house, followed within sight of the good doctor all the way down to the stables. What a bloody mess met my eyes when I reached there, with the young stable boy writhing around on the cold, cobblestone stable floor, obviously in a great deal of pain and attempting to be held still in the arms of George, the groom. Dr Mathews worked feverishly to stem the bleeding and ease this young lad's discomfort. All of us worked together, with Old Ben taking over from George, so he could finish seeing to the stabling of the horses with the remaining stable boy, Will, and I assisted by handing the doctor various things from his bag seeing as how his hands were covered in the boy's blood. We all kept to our tasks, but it took ever such a long time until Dr Mathews had finished his work and we all returned to our appointed duties.' Bringing his testimony to its close, Collins suddenly fell diplomatically silent, awaiting further direction from the inspector.

This was immediately forthcoming in the form of the direct enquiry, 'Did you accompany Dr Mathews on the return journey back to the house, Collins?'

Having paused for a moment in an obvious effort to gather the thoughts now spinning wildly in his head, Collins replied in but a whisper, 'No, I returned to the house alone, Inspector.'

In response to these words of respectful yet bewildered reply, the inspector, his grey eyes now blazing, let forth a bombardment of questions as fierce as any cannon volley imparted at the front upon this seemingly unsuspecting witness.

'Is it not true, Collins, that you left the stables and your so-called appointed duties before Dr Mathews had actually completed his work? Why was that? Did you report back to your master, Mr Carlile, or were your intentions of a more sinister nature? Perhaps you yourself saw the late Earl as the instigator of your master's and consequently your life's misery?'

Unable to sustain this continuing onslaught any longer, Collins cried out, 'Stop, Inspector. Stop! Yes, it is true that I left my post at the doctor's side a little before the task at hand had been entirely completed but, upon secretively consulting the clock in the stables, I had noted that the time was rapidly approaching five o'clock. This should have been my afternoon off but, seeing as how both my juniors, Cedric and Angus, were incapacitated or absent, my privileges were suddenly revoked by the master upon Cedric having been sent to his bed late yesterday by Dr Mathews, suffering badly from a bad back. Seeing as how the master will not allow women to serve at his table, my services were unfortunately retained for this afternoon's festivities. May I state simply that I had to meet someone at the railway station at Marlford this afternoon and leave it at that, sir,' Collins pleadingly concluded.

However, as was his terrier instinct, Inspector Dentworth could not leave it at that and aggressively blasted out the words.

'No, Collins, we will not leave it at that. A man lies dead in this house and it is my appointed task to find the person, or persons, who committed this heinous crime. You will therefore tell us, please, who it was that made you leave your duties this afternoon, Collins? The hour may well be growing late, but I assure you we will remain here until I have received a suitable reply. I am sure that your master, Mr Carlile, would be very interested in knowing that the most trusted member of his household was derelict in his duty.' These final words left Collins in no doubt of the path his further actions must take.

As Collins appeared to crumple in a heap in his chair a broken man, he quietly replied, 'Please, Inspector, I beg of you do not tell the master. I am sure I would lose my place in this household. Positions in service are hard enough for a young man to find in these days since the war, let alone a man of my advancing years. As you command, Inspector, I will tell you of my actions this afternoon. The person that I left my post to meet at the railway station this afternoon was a dear friend from my past.'

'Right, now we are getting somewhere, Collins. What was the name of this dear friend from your past and why was it so important for you to meet him this afternoon?' came the further enquiry from the inspector, not wishing to release his presently ruffled quarry from his powerful jaws for the moment, at least.

'If you must know, Inspector, the person in question is a lady friend of mine from London. We were in service together in the employ of Mr and Mrs Carlile in those happier times I spoke of earlier when we all lived as a happy and secure family in our London residence. The lady had been with Mrs Catherine Elizabeth Carlile (née Bentley) since the mistress's birth, first as her Yorkshire nursemaid, then becoming her lady's maid and subsequently upon Master Reginald Alexander's birth, his nursemaid as well. When Master Reginald returned to London, this lady accompanied him expecting to return soon to her mistress again here, but it was not too long before the mistress returned to her in London permanently. This gentle woman remains in Mrs Carlile's employ to this day.

'In the previous few days this lady had developed a bad cold in the head as a result of all the rainy weather being experienced in London at the moment, and was ordered by the family physician to take the fresh country air and sunshine for a couple of days. It was therefore decided between us that the lady would come down here and stay at the local inn, as her identity would not be known by the new landlord and his staff and I could visit with her there in peace and private. Having realised the passage of time, while I was down at the stables and seeing that Dr Mathews was all but finished in his work, I quietly slipped away from the group and scurried along the right of way footpaths across the fields between the manor and the hamlet of Marlford where I was just in time to meet the train from London and assist the lady in question to her lodgings at the inn. By the time I returned to the manor, His

Lordship had just been found dead in the drawing room and the master was calling for a telephone line to be put through to the police,' Collins responded placidly, wishing this ordeal to come as quickly as possible to its close.

'That is all well and good, Collins. However, I assume this lady does have a name. What might it be?' the inspector further enquired now tempering his barrage having achieved the desired result.

'The lady's name, Inspector, is Miss Gladys Agatha Quimby and if it is her statement of affairs that you are wanting, you will, true to my word, find her tucked up in her bed in a room at the Horse and Hound Inn,' Collins crustily replied.

'Thank you, Collins, that will be convenient, for it is to that particular inn that Sergeant Jones and myself will soon venture to rest our weary bones and minds for the night. The hour is indeed late. If you would be so good as to call what masquerades in these parts as a cab to take us to this local hostelry, then that will be all for now, Collins. The only further duties I have for you at this time, my good man, is for you to inform the cook, Mrs Christian, and the land agent, Mr Thompson, when he returns from his overnight stay in Swindon, that we require to speak with them at some time in the morning. Apart from that, the household may go about its normal affairs as best it can in the circumstances. Finally, may I inform you that a coroner's inquest will be required to be held into the circumstances of the Earl's untimely death, at which your testimony may be required, so I must request that you retain yourself available in the event that you are indeed required for this forthcoming inquiry,' Inspector Dentworth sternly, yet cordially, stated, in the process with a wave of his authoritative hand, dismissing what had in finality been a most enlightening witness.

'Yes, Inspector, I will inform both Mrs Christian and Mr Thompson of your wishes and make sure that they are available at your command in the morning,' stated Collins, resuming his usual emotionless demeanour once again as he rose decorously from his chair and slowly manoeuvred across and floor and towards the door.

'Oh by the way, Collins,' Inspector Dentworth suddenly

called, bringing the old man again to a halt, 'how did you get down to the station and back again to the manor so quickly that nobody was really aware of your absence?'

Turning to face the inspector, Collins crustily replied, 'A bicycle, sir. I might be old and decrepit but I can still ride a bicycle. How else does one get around this godforsaken countryside? If you want to see it, it is out in the garage.'

'Thank you, Collins, that will be all for now. You may go,' Inspector Dentworth cordially instructed, sending the elderly manservant on his way once more and out of the room.

'Well, Sergeant, I do not know about you, but I think I have had just about enough of this house and its occupants for one day. The time has indeed come, don't you think, for us to rest our bodies and our minds and a pint of the local bitter would do much to aiding both, don't you think, eh, Charlie?' the inspector enquired in a characteristically jovial frame of mind directed as it was towards his well-liked and, in turn, extremely likeable associate at what was now the end of this the first day of what would be an intriguing and, to some, quite a shattering case.

'I wouldn't say no to that very agreeable suggestion, Inspector. However, we will have to hop to it quick smart for closing time is fast approaching,' responded Sergeant Charlie Jones equally good-humouredly.

'Well, let's be off then, out of this depressing house and away from these people,' stated the inspector as he took the lead in rising from his seat and, with Sergeant Jones hot on his heels, he departed this now cooling room, the warmth in the hearth having died as surely as the life from the body in the drawing room...

The day dawned surprisingly sunny and bright for this time in late September, Inspector Dentworth noticed as he absently gazed from the window of his bedroom above the bar at the Horse and Hound Inn in the act of dressing before descending a rickety set of wooden stairs to the guests' lounge and the awaiting hot country breakfast. As he put the finishing touches to his toilet for the day, by passing his much appreciated and well-used pair of tortoiseshell backed hair brushes through his neatly trimmed head of dark copper-coloured hair, Inspector Dentworth's thoughts again returned systematically to the matter at hand, that of the investigation of Lord Rupert Penman-Smythe's untimely death and a mental appraisal of the evidence so far tendered. With these thoughts lingering in his mind, the inspector quietly vacated his room and made his way along the narrow, darkened corridor towards the stairs and what, by previous experience, he knew would be the awaiting Sergeant Jones. As he approached the door of the room at the end of the corridor, closest to the stairs, it opened and out stepped a woman of considerable age and bearing, obviously heading in the same direction as himself, her face partly obscured by the large white handkerchief which she held to her constantly running and reddened nose. The inspector quickened his step slightly and easily came alongside this stout, grey-haired woman before she had reached the top of the stairs and her descent to the breakfast table. The inspector's cordial and quite innocent approach to this womanly example of the now diminishing servant class was as follows:

'Good morning, it would appear we are to be granted a lovely sunny day, today. Nothing like the weather we have had in London the last few days, is it?' the inspector mischievously enquired.

To which the elderly woman innocently replied in a wheeze, happy to explain through the folds of her handkerchief to this stranger her right to be where he had found her today, 'No, sir, when I left London yesterday, pelting down cats and dogs it was, had been for last week or so, I might add. Gave me blessed cold that you see me with now into bargain. Mistress sent me away from London to get maself bit of sun and fresh air, so I took maself off to country and came down here to visit dear friend of mine.' The inspector noted the still present Yorkshire accent in the voice and words of this still naive gentlewoman.

'Would that dear friend be one, Wilfred Harold Collins, the butler at Carlile Manor and you, my good woman, be one, Gladys Agatha Quimby?' enquired the inspector, his words striking so swift and clean as to leave this poor soul in a complete state of confusion.

'Why yes, sir, that is name of my dear friend and indeed my name, as well but what, if you please, is that any business of yours, may I be so bold as to ask?' Gladys replied having come to her senses enough to enquire quizzically of this man who still remained a stranger to her.

'That is a perfectly natural request. May I introduce myself? I am Inspector James Dentworth of Scotland Yard and the services of myself and my colleague, Sergeant Charles Jones, have been requested by the local constabulary to assist in a murder investigation here in Marlford,' the inspector quietly replied.

'Scotland Yard! A murder investigation you say, what here in inn, sir?' Gladys replied in a shocked tone.

'No, Miss Quimby, not here in the inn. The murder occurred yesterday afternoon at Carlile Manor at about the time your friend Mr Collins supposedly left his post without notice to his employer, or anyone else for that matter, allegedly to attend to your arrival in Marlford,' Inspector Dentworth coldly replied.

'I don't understand, Inspector. Was it master, Mr Carlile, or perhaps one of staff who was murdered, as you have just said?' enquired Gladys in a slightly dumbfounded manner.

'No, Miss Quimby, for your information it was the Right Hon. the Earl of Marlford himself, one, Lord Rupert Henry Penman-Smythe, who lost his life yesterday afternoon,' Inspector Dentworth replied in a most level and emotionless voice. He speedily continued, by adding, 'Now, I suggest we both continue downstairs. I take it you were in the process of descending to partake of your breakfast, as I might add so was I when I halted you in your path. I would ask that you join my colleague, who I am sure awaits us below, and myself at our table so that we may take advantage of hearing your statement of the events while we all partake of our morning nourishment. If you are so agreeable to that?' enquiringly instructed the inspector in tones most congenial.

'Well, Inspector, I doubt that I really can help any more than you appear to know yourselves already of my actions yesterday afternoon, but, nevertheless, I will do as you instruct, sir, and join you at table,' Gladys meekly replied, ever the dutiful and obedient servant that her many years in dedicated service had continually shown.

'Thank you, Miss Quimby, for your co-operation in this matter. Now, let us continue to the guests' lounge where I have said I am sure Sergeant Jones is by now eagerly and might I add hungrily awaiting my arrival, if not yours,' the inspector patiently responded, in the process commencing to guide Gladys discreetly onward from where he had abruptly halted her at their summit down the somewhat uneven, narrow and twisting stairs upon the journey to their required target.

Upon entering the breakfasting room, Inspector Dentworth was greeted by the expected sight of his assiduous right-hand man conveniently seated at a table for four positioned at the front of the room. Jones sat patiently observing the view before him through the bow window in whose alcove the table, a suitable distance from the few others scattered about this small room, peacefully reposed. As the inspector approached with his lady companion, Sergeant Jones politely rose to his feet and, at the same time, issued forth with the following hearty words to his chief and presently unknown female acquaintance.

'Good morning, Inspector, I hope you slept as well as I did last night. Like a baby, I did. It must be all this fresh country air. I know I am ready for a fine country breakfast. Listening to the comments from the other guests this morning, it would appear that the fare at this hostelry is first class indeed. Nothing like a good breakfast to set you right for the rest of the day, don't you think, sir?'

To which the inspector pleasantly replied, 'Good morning, Sergeant Jones. In answer to your enquiry, yes, I did sleep remarkably well last night and, yes, I do also believe in the benefit of a wholesome breakfast to start your day off well. You would, I imagine, be wondering at this point in time the identity of the lady who graces us with her so far silent presence at our table this fine morning? Well, I shall put a stop to your wondering immediately by way of introducing to you Miss Gladys Agatha Quimby. As you no doubt recall from yesterday's proceedings, this is the lady for whom Collins, the butler at Carlile Manor, allegedly left his post to attend to her arrival by train from London. Likewise, Miss Quimby, this is Sergeant Charles Jones, my colleague from Scotland Yard.'

With these words, acknowledgement of each other's presence

at the table came in the form of a simple nod between Sergeant Jones and Gladys. Registering this acknowledgement, Inspector Dentworth returned to the business at hand and, as he gestured to all present to take their respective seats around the white damask-clad table, he said in a strong and commanding voice, 'Let us now partake of our breakfast.'

As he gestured, the average-built man dressed at this time of the day in a large white apron, the landlord of this establishment, whom he had observed during his opening words hovering with anticipation in the background, came forward post haste to take the party's breakfast order…

The task of consuming what had indeed been a generous breakfast of porridge, followed by fried bacon, sausages, devilled kidneys, veal cake and scrambled eggs accompanied by lashings of hot buttered toast with marmalade and piping hot coffee completed, the inspector again turned his attention in the direction of Gladys and his characteristic steady calm voice issued forth with the following enquiries of this elderly and apparently compliant woman-servant.

'Now, Miss Quimby, if you would be so kind as to state for our records' (the role of keeper of which fell once more upon the broad shoulders of Sergeant Jones as he again sat with his notebook and pencil at the ready) 'your full name, address and occupation?'

'As you wish, Inspector. My full name, that being one that parents christened me is Gladys Agatha Quimby. My address is 45 Witton Place, Knightsbridge, and my occupation is that of lady's maid to Mrs Catherine Carlile,' Gladys succinctly and with a degree of respect for the serious nature of this enquiry responded.

'Thank you, Miss Quimby. I believe you have held this position for a great number of years. Could you now in your own words and good time give us a description of the life of this family as you have seen it through the years,' with the hint of an engaging smile upon his lips, Inspector Dentworth patiently commanded.

'Indeed, Inspector, if it will help, by all means I will tell you of my impressions of the life of this family. I have been in the service of Mrs Carlile for some forty-nine odd years, since her own birth, having as a mere slip of girl joined her father, Sir Frederick Bentley's, household in position of nursemaid to the new babe. As years continued and a deep bond of affection and respect formed between most beautiful young lady as she had grown to become and myself, my services were retained by old master in position of lady's maid to Miss Catherine as she was then. Then old master, Sir Frederick, tragically died in boating accident off Cowes during Regatta Week one summer and it was decided that Miss Catherine, after her father's funeral and mourning, should visit old school friend in Vienna. It was here that she met Mr Montague Carlile who was also a friend of same family. Upon returning to London, where they both resided, they courted and married and some time later they were blessed with child, Master Reginald, for whom I acted once again as nursemaid. Life was indeed fine affair in those days with much love and happiness both above and below stairs.

'Then, at what I always believed to be the Right Hon. the Earl of Marlford, Lord Rupert Penman-Smythe's, insistence, it was decided by master, Mr Carlile, that family consisting of master, mistress, Master Reginald, Mr Collins acting as Mr Carlile's valet and myself, acting as both Mrs Carlile's maid and Master Reginald's nursemaid would journey here to Marlford and their country estate of Carlile Manor one September afternoon to partake of what Mr Carlile described as weekend of pleasurable country pursuits, that was riding to hounds with the local hunt, master of which was the now late Earl of Marlford, first meet of the season and very first for Master Reginald. As I remember, mistress was none too happy with whole idea of this weekend and she told master, Mr Carlile, so in no uncertain terms. Mr Carlile had caught nasty bout of influenza during preceding week and was in no fit state to be riding on what was to be newly acquired mount. Into bargain weather was foul, windy, cold and wet all weekend. Mistress was extremely concerned for welfare of her only child, for upon Master Reginald's birth there had been no further issue. As only time would come to show that she had had due need to be concerned, for master, Mr Carlile, never finished hunt that day. They carted him back to manor, nothing more than a crumpled heap of blood and broken bones. I was told by Mr Collins that master's flighty horse lost its footing and rolled on him, crushing his legs and leaving him to this day a cripple.

'Life for all was never to be same again. I was sent back to London in accompaniment to Master Reginald, as it was deemed by mistress that the surroundings of manor were not helpful to continued growth of young lad who was at time close to going off to boarding school. At Dr Mathews, village doctor's, insistence with backing of his Harley Street colleagues, it was decided that master could not be transported back to London in foreseeable future.

'So it fell upon mistress, with my accompanying her, to scurry back and forth between London, Master Reginald's school and Marlford which, I might say, she did tirelessly in an effort to keep her family together. However, apparently master did not see it quite like that, having had great difficulty in coming to terms with losing his life of work and pleasure in London and new routine of being an invalid, he struck out at only person left under his limited control, that of mistress. I had been travelling back and forth between London, Mendrew and Carlile Manor with mistress all these years, after first having settled young master at Mendrew as had been planned whilst mistress looked after the master. I therefore thought we would settle down here at Carlile Manor, but he sent her away back to London, in process banishing me also from those I had come to respect and, dare I say, love, where both mistress and I have remained to this day. I have, for my part, as the years have rolled on, kept in what you might call fond communication with Mr Collins who has informed me of the continuing hermit-like existence Mr Carlile has kept all these years, this solitary life intensifying even more with loss of his beloved son, Master Reginald, during the last war. Might I say in ending that, in my own mind, I find it a mite unusual that master would have guests at manor. It was not as I have told you his way of dealing with life,' Gladys concluded in a perplexed voice.

'Thank you, Miss Quimby, for all that information. We will take particular note of your concerns. Now, could we move on to the proceedings of yesterday afternoon if you please. Please tell us of your movements and those of Mr Collins from the time of your arrival here in Marlford yesterday?' requested the inspector in polite and subdued tones.

'Well, Inspector, there is not much that I can tell you. Train arrived from London on time at five o'clock and Mr Collins, true to his word, was waiting at back of platform when train came to halt at platform. He greeted me in his usual discreet manner and offered to carry my valise on his bicycle for me, which I accepted readily as journey from London had tired me a good deal. Noting my apparent distressed condition, Mr Collins suggested as he escorted me down road to local inn that I should go straight to bed, which I agreed to most readily. Having introduced me to landlord whose register I shakily signed and helped me to my room door, Mr Collins then left me to myself and my bed for night,' Gladys replied with a slight wheeze edging her normally strong, clear voice standing testimony to her apparent state of incapacity.

'Thank you again for that information, Miss Quimby. I find it all most interesting. Now I have but a couple more questions which I would like to put to you, at this time. Firstly, do you have any idea how long Mr Collins would have been in your company yesterday afternoon and secondly what is your opinion of the character of Mr Collins?' the inspector enquired, now adopting a light-hearted and easygoing manner in an attempt to lure a confidential admission from this ailing witness.

To which Gladys comfortably and confidently replied, 'I may be sick, Inspector, but I am not daft as well. Yes, I can tell you exactly how long Mr Collins was in my company yesterday afternoon. As I have said, train arrived in station at five o'clock and when I turned my back from closing door of my door here in inn, having bid goodbye to Mr Collins in corridor where I met you just now, Inspector, I glanced towards bedside table and noticed that only seven minutes had elapsed since my arrival. Might I say I was not entirely surprised in this fact, as Mr Collins has always been very adept at quickly organising people around him. In answer to your question of his character, I have known Mr Wilfred Harold Collins for nigh on thirty years, having first made his acquaintance, albeit fleetingly, in Vienna when mistress and master first met, Mr Collins there in his role as gentleman's gentleman to Mr Carlile and me as lady's maid cum chaperone to then young Miss Catherine. During our subsequent years of service within same and later associated households, I have found Mr Collins to be man of most hard-working character in service of whom, as time has worn on, been most trying master in form of Mr Montague Alexander Carlile. Might I say, as testimony to the enduring character of this humble servant that, through all these years, Mr Collins chose to remain with his master of so many years simply as a mark of Christian respect to poor tortured soul.'

Having realised the depth of intense pride and respect held within these words of praise from this old woman towards her long esteemed friend, the inspector knew that no further advance in his investigation of this subject would be gained from this blatantly loyal witness. With these thoughts in mind, he brought this interview and breakfast speedily to a close.

'That will be all, thank you, Miss Quimby. You may go about your business as you wish now. In passing, might I finally ask when might you be returning to London and your duties with your mistress, Mrs Carlile? I ask this in the event that we may have some further questions to put to you in the light of our ongoing investigations,' Inspector Dentworth requested in a casual manner.

As she rose somewhat shakily to her small slightly puffy feet, Gladys replied in her usual subdued tones, 'Well, Inspector, this is Saturday. Having left London, as you are aware, yesterday afternoon, and doctor I saw there at mistress's insistence, I might add, has told Mrs Carlile that I am not to return to my duties until Friday morning. That being case it has been arranged that I will be returning to London on afternoon train on Thursday next.'

'Thank you again, Miss Quimby, for all your assistance and may you be rid of that cold before you have to return to what can often be described as miserable old London Town,' the inspector cordially responded as this gentle lady's maid slowly and silently retreated from his field of action.

Having dispensed with this none too inspiring witness, the inspector turned his attention once more in the direction of his loyal colleague, Sergeant Jones, and said, 'Well, Jones, if you are ready, we will adjourn to the manor once more. Hopefully, the cook and land agent will be awaiting our arrival, for I would like to be back in London before nightfall. The sooner we conclude our investigation the sooner we may be away from this house and its inhabitants...'

'Christian by name and Christian by nature, Inspector,' were the opening words from the full round mouth of the rosy-faced woman who sat beside the inspector as he again reposed before the warming hearth in the billiard room.

'In answer to your request, Inspector, my full name is Bressbey Voirrey Christian or, as I have been known all my years in service in England, Bridget Mary Christian. I have worked in this house all my days in service, having started as but a scullery maid. When I came from the Isle of Man as but a slip of a girl, I could not stand a life in the bustle of London so I came to the country in search of work and found it here. With patience and hard work, I rose to what God in his infinite mercy saw as my appointed station in life to sit before you now in the position of cook, with the cursory title of Mrs, though I have remained single all my days, in this fine household, a position I might add, I have held for the last twenty years and as such have resided within its four walls for all that time,' Mrs Christian proudly responded to the inspector's now familiar opening request.

'That is all very fine, Mrs Christian. Now, if we could move on to the proceedings of yesterday afternoon, if you will. I have heard from all the participants involved in the consumption of the afternoon tea of the lavish nature of the fare which beheld itself to them. Could you now tell me, in greater detail, what constituted this generous spread and who prepared it?' the inspector requested in a stern and businesslike manner.

'Why, certainly, Inspector, but I do hope that none are saying that it was cooking from my kitchen that murdered His Lordship!' Mrs Christian indignantly and instantly responded.

'Now, do not worry yourself about that, my good woman, just answer my question if you would be so good,' Inspector Dentworth commanded, his steely grey eyes beaming fiercely, leaving Mrs Christian in no doubt as to the immediate course of her actions as she speedily replied, 'My wish is to help in whatever way possible, Inspector, so as you have requested, the feast which I laid before Mr Carlile and his invited guests yesterday afternoon consisted of the following.'

In the process, Mrs Christian withdrew a crumpled sheet of white paper with obvious black ink markings upon it from the front pocket of her large white apron and, with the help of a pair of pince-nez spectacles, which she now having also retrieved from her apron pocket and perched precariously upon her snub nose, began to read.

'The guests partook of a selection of sandwiches including adelaide (cooked chicken and ham, white bread and curry butter), egg and chutney (hard-boiled eggs, estate made chutney, white and brown bread and estate churned butter), beef (cold roast beef, tomato and cress from the kitchen glasshouse and mustard), foie gras (kitchen produced terrine of foie gras, bread and butter) and clent (lean kitchen cured pork, pickled gherkins, white bread, butter and pepper). This was followed by a plate of my finest afternoon tea scones, accompanied by a dish each of strawberry jam, which I may add I had made myself last summer from berries grown in our own kitchen garden, and clotted West Country cream, a rich fruit cake and a spicy ginger cake to suit the more robust tastes of the gentlemen of the party and the lightest of creations in the form of a gateau St Honoré (concoction of choux and shortcrust pastry, filled with crème St Honoré and decorated with whipped and sweetened cream, glacé cherries and leaves of angelica) for the more refined constitution of the young lady of the party. The crowning glory of this feast came in the form of a selection of éclairs au café or coffee éclairs (choux pastry filled with stiff custard and iced with coffee-flavoured icing) and pastries such as patisserie aux fruits or apple turnovers (puff pastry, stewed apples from our kitchen garden and caster sugar), tartelettes au citron or lemon tartlets (shortcrust pastry, butter, castor sugar, eggs and lemon from the kitchen glasshouse) and tartelettes à la crème cuite or custard tartlets (shortcrust pastry, whole eggs, whites of eggs, milk from our own dairy and sugar). Finally the master particularly suggested, as a fitting finishing touch, the inclusion of a long-held favourite of his, from times long gone, the cornet de crème or cream horn or as we used to call it below stairs, the master's horn, which is a concoction of puff pastry baked in the shape of a horn and filled with a mixture of home-made raspberry jam and freshly whipped and sweetened cream flavoured with vanilla and topped with a cascade of roasted crushed nuts. All this fine fare was accompanied by a piping hot silver pot of China black tea.

'Further, in answer, Inspector, to your question of who prepared this fare, it was solely myself over a period of the forty-eight hours leading up to the arrival of the guests on Friday afternoon last, this being the case as had come the instructions from the master himself that he placed such importance on this afternoon that no one else must be trusted with its preparation. I could understand his concern for everything to be just right, as this was the first time in many years that Carlile Manor had been graced with the pleasurable activity of invited guests. Needless to say, Inspector, that I baked my heart and soul into this fare, taking as much care as possible in its preparation and presentation. Now, a tragic black cloud hangs again over this house and its occupants, the worst of it being the aspersions being cast upon me and my kitchen,' Mrs Christian concluded as an expression of dark consternation enveloped her rosy features.

'Do not worry yourself, my dear woman. No one at the moment is saying a derogatory word about your apparently fine cooking. Now, calm yourself please and let us continue. Would it have been at all possible for someone in the household to have had access to this fare after it had been prepared, but prior to it going to the table in the drawing room, do you think?' Inspector Dentworth patiently requested in an effort to continue the forward movement of the relevant testimony of this now troubled witness, as she sat nervously wringing her stubby fingered hands together.

Instantaneously, the response to this enquiry came in a searing blast from the full red lips of Mrs Christian, which took the form of a howl of indignation and the words, 'Ohhhh, Inspector, what sort of kitchen do you think I command? All the fare for the afternoon tea, as it was prepared, was locked away from prying eyes and hands in the cake pantry of which I am the sole bearer of its key. Then, as the time neared for the guests to arrive, I conveyed the laden cake trays and tea things up to the drawing room myself and laid them out on the sideboard for Mr Collins to serve at the master's instruction.'

As Mrs Christian fell silent again, the inspector acted quickly to take command yet again of the proceedings by curtly saying, 'Thank you, Mrs Christian, for that most detailed account of the lavish fare on offer to the participants of the now fateful tea. You are aware, no doubt, of the unfortunate occurrences down at the stables yesterday afternoon. Do you have any idea at what time Mr Collins returned downstairs from the stables after assisting Dr Mathews in his endeavours?'

With a decidedly sheepish expression appearing on her weathered face, Mrs Christian replied, 'I couldn't rightly say, Inspector. I know for a fact I was the only one down in the servants' hall at the time. Mr Collins had been summoned to the entrance hall by the ringing of the front doorbell just a few minutes before three and I didn't see him again until his return from the stables. The rest of the household, such as it is since the last war, were about their normal duties for the afternoon. Life in this house is fast becoming a lonely existence for those below, as well as above, stairs. What with the recent retirement of the housekeeper here of many years, Mrs Booth, gone now to partake of the pleasures of her last years upon this earth in the companionable lodgings of an old friend's house in Chippenham, my old friend Mr Hopkins the previous butler in this house having retired and subsequently gone to his maker a good few years ago now. Then that ghastly war taking poor Master Reginald from upstairs and young Bertie, the cheeky young boot boy and newly promoted footman, at the front and, if that wasn't enough, taking pretty young Ruth, the junior housemaid who decided to go and work in an armaments factory and got the life crushed out of her in an accident on the production line, so much for her patriotic efforts.

'Into the bargain, Mr Carlile gallantly saw fit to relinquish the services of his two nurses upon the outbreak of the war so they could offer their much needed experience to the poor lads in France, saying it made him feel that he was contributing something to the war effort. Then, of course, both Cedric and Angus are presently indisposed by illness and grief. If that wasn't enough, Mr Carlile instructed that the two housemaids, Emma and Charlotte, should take their afternoon off yesterday as they would not be required to serve at table and in his words not wishing to have them under his guests' feet, leaving just my two girls, Lily and Grace, whom, as was the usual routine for the afternoon of the last Friday of the month, I had sent into Hungerford for provisions and to settle the monthly accounts. I, myself, was busy preparing for the evening meal for both above and below stairs, a meal that, I must say, went to dreadful waste for those upstairs. Then, I have been waffling on a bit, haven't I, Inspector! All I know, is that as soon as Mr Collins appeared, all the demons of hell descended upon us with the master instructing Mr Collins to obtain a telephonic line to the local police, informing them that the Earl of Marlford was lying dead in the drawing room of our own fine house.'

Mindful of the inference held within this response, the inspector, his clear, grey eyes twinkling with devilment, quickly but calmly enquired further of this canny witness, 'Thank you again, Mrs Christian, for your most honest account of the proceedings of yesterday afternoon. By the way and, might I add in conclusion to this current interview, do you by any chance remember the name Gladys Quimby?'

The inspector keenly noted the effect of these simple words upon the woman who sat before him, as Mrs Christian was momentarily taken aback then contemplatively silent for what appeared to be a considerable time before she meekly replied.

'I do remember that name, Inspector. I believe Gladys Quimby acted as lady's maid to the mistress, Mrs Carlile. At least she used to when the mistress resided in this house, but that was a good many years ago now, Inspector. I could not say where she is now…'

With those last words cryptically ringing in Inspector Dentworth's ears, Mrs Christian was bade goodbye from the room with the officious words from the inspector's thin pale lips of, 'That will be all for now, thank you, Mrs Christian. However, please bear in mind that a coroner's inquest will be required to be held into this death and your testimony under oath may be required.'

Upon the hasty and hushed departure of Mrs Christian and before any conversation could be entered into on the part of either the inspector or his sergeant, a loud and forceful knock echoed across the expanse that was the billiard room, wilfully requesting immediate entry by its instigator. This sound was greeted with equal force by the now all too familiarly curt response by the inspector of, 'Enter.'

With entry having been commanded, the door flew open to reveal a mountain of a man six foot four inches in height standing comfortably upon the threshold of this masculine bastion, his frame tightly enough encased in a well-worn yet tidy tweed jacket as to show the thick broad set of his rugged and muscular shoulders and baggy cream flannel trousers. As he strode across the bare wooden floor, his footsteps loudly marking his progress, he removed from his head a slightly battered pork pie hat of matching tweed cloth to disclose to view a thin melon-shaped head with a receding hairline of mousy-coloured hair which accompanied a pair of pale, yet keenly alert, hazel eyes. Upon approaching the assembled chairs gathered around the meekly burning hearth, this ox of a man spoke in surprisingly, well-mannered tones and cultured voice.

'Mr Collins said you wished to see me, Inspector, so here I am.'

'I take it, sir, that you are Mr Thompson, the land agent or, as your master Mr Carlile puts it, the factor for this estate. Please take a seat here.' The inspector indicated with a subtle wave of his thin hand the comfortable leather wing chair positioned to the right of his own, with Sergeant Jones in his accustomed position in the chair to his left.

'Thank you, Inspector,' Mr Thompson politely replied as he followed the direction just given by the inspector.

Having noted that the witness was seated comfortably, the inspector's clear strong voice again rang out with the now familiar request.

'Now, sir, if you would for our records state your full name, address and occupation?'

To which Mr Thompson cheerfully replied, 'By all means, Inspector, I wish to help your investigation of this dastardly deed in whatever way I can. So, in answer to your request, my full name is Leonard Arnold Thompson, my address is that of 'Shady Cottage' here on the estate and, as you have already stated, my occupation is that of land agent or, as Mr Carlile is so prone to call me, his factor. As such, I deal with the day-to-day affairs of the running of this still quite sizeable estate, a position, might I add, I have held since 1907, coincidentally just before Mr Carlile was involved in his terrible accident which left him a virtual prisoner here in his country home. He had had the thought of taking more of an active interest and role in the workings of the estate to enable a better return financially on his capital investment, with a view, you see, to what he might be able to pass on to his only son and heir, Master Reginald, at a later date. Fate and circumstances after the accident, which precluded his return to his work in the city, and his depleted cash reserves with having to finance the upkeep of two permanent homes, having still retained his London residence for the exclusive use of the mistress, the estate and the revenue it generates has come to form an important, dare I say, integral part in the master's ongoing financial stability. Oh, but I do apologise, Inspector, for my digression from the original points in question. I am afraid the shock of the happenings in this house yesterday have left me with a never before experienced feeling of great unease so distracting my usual businesslike manner.'

'That is perfectly understandable, Mr Thompson. Now I wish to continue this interview by asking you to think back to the events of yesterday afternoon and in your own words and good time recount to me your record of those happenings as they affected you,' the inspector mildly requested of what he had quickly noted as an extremely compliant and, to his mind, reliable witness.

'Yes, Inspector. Well, all I can tell you of the now obviously terrible events of yesterday afternoon is that at precisely ten minutes past four, this, by the way, I am sure of as I remember distinctly consulting my watch, I closed and locked the door of my office. This room is attached to the estate store situated in a cluster of estate buildings through the woodland surrounding the gardens outside this house, where most of the non-perishable provisions for and from the estate are housed. I walked directly through these woodlands, across the lawns and up on to the terrace which gives access to the drawing room, dining room and smoking room of this house. The purpose of this journey was the routine weekly conference which the master, Mr Carlile, being the man of habit that he is, holds like clockwork every Friday afternoon at precisely a quarter past four, in which are discussed the current matters of concern with regard to the workings of this estate.

'Although I knew that he was entertaining visitors yesterday afternoon, he had said nothing to me previously during the week to indicate his dismissal on this occasion of the normal routine. So having observed from the terrace through the clear French windows the distinctive figure of the master in the drawing room at this time in the sole company of His Lordship the Earl of Marlford, I tapped upon the glass, thereby announcing my presence which Mr Carlile duly noted by coming straight to the window and bid me open it, which I did. As I did, I remember Mr Carlile turned and issued a few words by means of an apology for the intrusion and begged His Lordship's indulgence to attend to some important matters of the estate. I might add here that to my eyes the Earl at this point in time appeared to be in the prime of health and good humour. Having received a most gallant acceptance of this act by Lord Rupert, I heard Mr Carlile suggest to His Lordship, whom I might add I noticed had not completed his afternoon repast with a half-filled cup of tea still perched on the occasional table beside him, too much talking on his part I dare say, that in Mr Carlile's absence he might take pleasure in devouring one of cook's fine pastry cream horns or, as they are called in this house, the master's horn.

'Upon receiving a nod of acknowledgement for these fine words from His Lordship, Mr Carlile directed me to assist him by the movement of his chair out through the French windows, on to the terrace and along to the smoking room. Having reached the warm confines of the smoking room, Mr Carlile wheeled himself to a position beside the fireplace in which a hearty fire blazed; in doing so, I remember he made the comment that the stiff breeze along the terrace had made him cold. He indicated that I should seat myself in a straight-backed chair which allowed me to face the hearth with my back to the windows and the terrace. We then proceeded to conduct what business there was. Not that I can say that there was very much said by either of us. I must say that Mr Carlile seemed more interested in reminiscing about times past than the present or the future. The estate since the war has run quite well with the new intake of tenant farmers who were returned men and their families having settled in well and have shown a great deal of industry in their new endeavours. Having said that, our conversation still lasted the usual half-hour, as I remember the carriage clock on the mantelpiece was showing a minute or two past a quarter to five when the master indicated he was concluding the discussion and sent me on my way. I subsequently left Mr Carlile, as was his wish, alone on the terrace having assisted him there before I proceeded back along the same route I had previously taken returning to my office where I attended to a few matters before I left my office and the estate at five o'clock to journey to Swindon by train to deal with some estate matters, where I stayed overnight at the Swan Hotel returning again by train early this morning.'

'So, it is your opinion, Mr Thompson, that nothing of critical importance to the current running of the estate was discussed by Mr Carlile and yourself?' the inspector cryptically enquired.

'I would as things stand in my mind have to say no, Inspector,' replied Mr Thompson, an expression of mild concern developing upon his otherwise placid features.

'Did you, Mr Thompson, in your capacity as land agent for this estate have any dealings with the late Earl's estate, Beeches Hall, or the Earl himself for that matter?' the inspector quietly requested.

'No, Inspector, it was the policy of the laird of the manor, Mr Carlile, that this estate, where humanly possible, remains isolated from the rest of the world around it, apart from its most basic requirements, as those which I dealt with in Swindon yesterday,' Mr Thompson in an air of gracious compliance replied.

'Thank you, Mr Thompson, you may go now. However, please be aware that you may be required to give your testimony as you have just given us now at a coroner's inquest to be held at a later date. Oh, by the way, as a final statement, do you remember seeing or hearing anything unusual during the time away from your office yesterday?' the inspector requested in a parting shot as this giant of a man eased himself out of the chair to stand momentarily before the assembled pair.

'Well, now that you mention it, Inspector, a couple of things caught me as being a touch unusual. While I was sitting in the smoking room talking to the master, a cloud seemed to drift across the sun as a shadow fell across the window behind me and the room, too. However, when I looked across at Mr Carlile's face it wore an expression which to me was a mixture of relief and subtle joy, as if he had seen the leprechaun's pot of gold at the end of a rainbow. It was about this time that I heard what sounded like a cough from the direction of the drawing room. I thought at the time that maybe His Lordship had caught a cold upon his return to England. The other thing which caused me to stop and wonder was the fact that, upon the completion of our talks, I asked if Mr Carlile required my help to return to the drawing room, as I thought he would be eager to return to his awaiting guest.

'However, he sharply replied in the negative to my request and, in doing so, I remember a look of intense anger mounting on his face as he instructed me to wheel him out on to the terrace as he wished to get a breath of fresh air before returning to his guest. This, after having complained so bitterly about his feeling chilled previously and, with the sun going down to make the air even colder outside, I thought it a bit strange. However, since his injuries from the hunting accident all those years before, I must in all honesty state that Mr Carlile is not the easiest of men to work for. He has from that time on been beset by black moods of despair and depression, which he does attempt to control, but all in the household have at some time felt their effect. Oh, by the way, Inspector, this may have nothing to do with the goings-on in the house at that time, but, as I was walking to the station, I could have sworn I saw the silhouette of old Collins riding a bicycle back towards the manor,' Mr Thompson concluded with this valuable insight into the laird of the manor and its household, and with a nod of acknowledgement between witness and interrogator, heralded his departure from the room with a volley of heavy and determined footsteps, leaving the remaining two occupants of this room to ponder the evidence so far gathered… what a case this was developing into for all parties concerned…

'Alcohol! Surely, Dr Scott, you are not telling us that the simple act of ingesting alcohol killed the Earl of Marlford?' Inspector Dentworth incredulously espoused as he responded to the pronouncement of cause of death which the talented Dr Scott had just rendered to him as the two men, together with Sergeant Jones, sat in the inspector's Scotland Yard office.

'That is surely what I am telling you, Inspector. Yet I would hardly call it a simple act. Please, if I may, I will try to explain to you as Sir Garfield Pembleton explained it to me this morning when I contacted him in his rooms in Harley Street. It would appear that during his extended time in South Africa His Lordship suffered a most severe case of ague which, as a consequence of its effect upon his body, left his entire system violently intolerant of alcohol in any form. The effect upon his body was similar to that suffered by someone stung by a wasp or bee who is violently allergic to the effect of the sting. It is what we call in the profession an anaphylactic reaction. So you see, Inspector, it was the effect of alcohol actually in the food which he consumed at the afternoon tea some time between four and five o'clock which killed His Lordship. An allergy of such violent strength would have killed him all but instantaneously, as the scene of death indicated. That is not to say, though, that we are now looking at a case of death by misadventure. For I took it upon myself, having become engrossed in this unusual twist to the case, to contact the cook at Carlile Manor whom I asked pointedly had there been any alcohol added to the fare in any form which was placed before the guests on that Friday afternoon? Her reply, you will be interested to know, was in the negative. That brings us back again to the fact that someone knew of this condition of which the Earl was afflicted and, subsequently, deliberately placed what I have found through the tests I have conducted to be a concentrated dose of pure, tasteless alcoholic spirit which I found present both in the slightly damaged cream horn which remained on the plate on the sideboard and also in the remnants of the still distinguishable pastry clenched in the victim's hand. Upon further testing of the sample of blood I took from the victim, I found a concurrent concentration of said alcohol. Therefore, Inspector, it is still a case of murder which you are investigating and a diabolical one at that!' Dr Scott concluded his methodical and precise oration of his testing results.

'My word, Dr Scott, in all my years in the force this is the first time I have heard of a man dying of drink in such a drastic way. Do you have any idea how the alcohol was introduced into the cream horns?' the inspector, still a little bewildered by the evidence which had just been placed before him, enquired of the distinguished and highly professional police surgeon.

'That, Inspector, is where this person, this fiend, is truly diabolical. Through extremely careful examination of the pastry remaining on the sideboard I found a needle-sized hole. Now when I say needle, I don't mean of the sewing variety but rather one of a medical variety, that is, a hypodermic needle. It is thus my considered opinion that the alcohol was introduced into the cream horns, or as the cook described the pastry this morning to me, as the master's horn, by way of a hypodermic injection of the pure alcoholic spirit,' Dr Scott patiently replied.

'Well, thank you indeed for that most interesting information, Dr Scott. Now that does indeed open a veritable can of worms for us in this case,' Inspector Dentworth responded, his eyes glistening with the renewed challenge that this information had brought with it.

'By the way, Inspector, having completed my examinations and reached these conclusions of the death of the victim, I contacted the late Earl's family, namely his daughter and informed her that I was releasing his body from police custody this morning. Having been informed of that fact, she subsequently asked me to inform you that the funeral of the late Earl of Marlford would be held in the chapel of his country estate, Beeches Hall, on Thursday morning coming at eleven o'clock. The Lady Isabella further wished me to inform you that she and her gentleman companion, Mr Smith, will be returning to

London on the following Monday to attend to some of her late father's business affairs,' Dr Scott cordially informed the inspector and further firmly stated as he rose gracefully from his straight-backed chair in an obvious display of his wish to conclude these talks and be about the other numerous police matters of his concern, 'That is about all I can tell you for my part in this case, Inspector. If you have any further questions, you know where to find me. With that, I will bid you good luck and good hunting.'

'Thank you, Dr Scott, for all that you have told us this morning. By all means I will not keep you any longer. I know how important your time and expertise is to all here at Scotland Yard. I will let you know of the timings for the coroner's inquest as soon as they are finalised. It will be held down in Marlford most likely in the next week or so. For now though, goodbye, Doctor, and good work,' Inspector Dentworth responded as he watched the figure of the well-liked member of the modern-day Scotland Yard team acknowledge these words with the nod of his intelligent head and disappear from view behind his modest office door.

Then, turning his attention once more in the direction of Sergeant Jones, Inspector Dentworth encouragingly commanded of his painfully quiet colleague with the utterance of the following enthusiastically spoken words.

'Let's run through the evidence in this case which we currently have at hand once again in light of this new information, Sergeant, and this time let's hear your own personal thoughts on this matter, keeping in mind of course means, motive and opportunity.' As he sat behind his plain yet neat desk looking out of the window of his drab Scotland Yard office at the view of an overcast and windy Monday in London, Inspector Dentworth patiently awaited the educated opinion of his loyal subordinate.

From his position across the desk, seated in a sombre wooden chair, Sergeant Jones took from the left breast pocket of his crisply starched uniform his trusty police issue notebook and commenced his own oration of the events in his usual well-modulated voice.

'Yes, sir. Well, thanks to Dr Scott, we now know how the Earl met his death. Now the job ahead of us is to find out when exactly the alcohol was introduced into the fare and by whose hand? For that matter, who knew of the condition which afflicted the Earl with such tragic consequences? It is my opinion that we should now look at the individuals in this case one by one as you say, taking into account means, motive and opportunity.

'1. From the evidence given by Dr Robert Mathews, the village doctor, which has now been confirmed by our own Dr Scott, the deceased met his death in unnatural circumstances on Friday afternoon last, between the hours of four and five in said afternoon. His own testimony of his actions during his time at the estate have been verified by numerous witnesses such as initially, the gatekeeper and then the old groom and the stable boy, in my opinion leaving him at this point in time not an active suspect. He had a passing acquaintanceship with the late Earl. However, I do not see any motive on his part and little or no opportunity, though he would have full access to the means, that is the hypodermic syringe as the fare was served to him up to his leaving the drawing room for the stables by the diligent Collins. Not having been the Earl's personal physician, it is unlikely that Dr Mathews would be aware of the condition now at the centre of this case.

'2. Next, if we look at the actions of the Lady Isabella Penman-Smythe on that afternoon, she was observed by all participants in the drawing room to accompany her gentleman friend, Mr John Smith, out of the drawing room and to commence to stroll around the grounds. Then, by her own admission, they stopped for some considerable time to rest in the relative seclusion of the stone summer house at the extreme edge of the garden. The Lady told us that it was her understanding that she had fallen asleep for an unknown period of time. Upon realising the swift passage of time, after being awakened by her companion, the couple's return journey to the house was noted and intercepted by Dr Mathews in whose company they remained up to and including the discovery of the body in the drawing room. What motive would the Lady Isabella have for the death of her own father? The most relevant one in my view would be that of unrestricted financial stability, given the evidence from Mr Carlile that the Earl was none too happy about the forthcoming marriage of his only daughter and heir to a penniless unknown. It may well have come to the point where the Lady Isabella's allowance from her father would have been withdrawn and withheld indefinitely, leaving the young couple together penniless.

'However, with his timely demise and no other issue to which his vast estate would conceivably be bequeathed, the Lady and her gentleman are now very comfortably situated. Motive, well and truly enough there, but what about means and opportunity. Again, with her nursing experience she would probably have access to the required equipment. It would have to have occurred by her hands in the time between Mr Carlile leaving the drawing room with Mr Thompson, the land agent, and returning with the remainder of the party just after five, and what of Mr Smith, in whose absolute company the Lady Isabella appeared to reside for the entire afternoon? Does that indicate a diabolical liaison between these two young people? It must in all fairness to the truth be considered! However, the determined and independent nature of the Lady Isabella, as she displayed during her testimony leads me to the opinion that murder would not be an option considered by her. Was she aware of her father's ongoing medical condition? By her testimony, she was not, but is that to be believed?

'3. Let us now look at the man known simply as Mr John Smith, a man of mystery, one might say. I believe further investigation of his identity with the Ministry of the Army is indeed called for. Further to this matter, I believe I may be able to help in this regard as, through the years, I have retained some contacts with the Military Police and their relevant Investigation Squad, so a telephone call here and there could well produce the required lines of investigation on the army's part into this man's true identity. His actions again are somewhat dubious, to say the least. The main issue of concern is his alleged appearance across the view from the smoking room window which supposedly was witnessed by Mr Carlile and to a limited degree by Mr Thompson. Again, Mr Smith's motive for actuating the demise of Lord Rupert would be that of financial stability, having stated himself that he was indeed penniless and subsequently living at the merciful generosity of the Lady Isabella and her now late father, the Earl.

'With the Earl's early death would come marriage, a swift rise in his status in society and permanent security. By his own admission he did not see eye to eye with the Earl and stayed out of his way as much as was possible, also witnessed by the young couple's early departure from His Lordship's presence in the drawing room that afternoon. Through the Lady Isabella's testimony, we have been told that this young man is in possession of a hypodermic apparatus for his own personal administration of pain-relieving substances, thereby he had the means readily at hand. That brings us to opportunity which must have come, if we are to view him as the sole perpetrator of this crime, in some way in the time whilst the Lady Isabella was blissfully asleep in the summer house. He may have observed the exit of Mr Carlile from the drawing room to the smoking room, though he tells us his sight is not good, and gone in search of the Earl on the pretext of having a private word with him out of earshot of the Lady Isabella on the matter of their future together and the Earl's apparently most public show of discord on this issue. Which in turn begs the question, how much difficulty does this young man have in negotiating the terrain he would have incurred in his passage from the summer house to the drawing room and back? Further to this, was he indeed aware of the Earl's allergic condition? He must, in my opinion, be considered as a suspect of some considerable degree in this case.

'4. The actions of the butler, Mr Wilfred Collins, during this time between him leaving the stables, which nobody present there could precisely confirm, and his eventual return "downstairs" in the house, are, to my mind, shrouded in some mystery. Due somewhat to the wandering testimony of the old cook, Mrs Christian, who I believe has a hidden sense of affection for one of the few senior members of the household still remaining, one, Collins, and thereby instinctively wishes to support him, though I believe not through a corrupt action on her part. We confirmed, in the course of our return to London, with the stationmaster at Marlford Station that he did observe Mr Collins at the back of the platform apparently awaiting the arrival of the train from London and subsequently viewed him leaving said platform pushing a bicycle in the company of an elderly lady who had disembarked from the said train. He could not however clearly state how long Mr Collins had been waiting on the railway platform when he first observed him. Mr Collins must now, therefore, in my opinion, be considered a suspect in this case. One may ask what motive he would have for committing such a crime against the Earl? Well, one could say that as a dutiful and trusted servant of his master, Mr Montague Carlile, for many long and torturous years in virtual isolation in this country backwater, away from his friends and their intimate affection, i.e. Miss Gladys Quimby, and the joys of life in bustling London, Mr Collins had formed an opinion, this being that, over these many arduous and lonely years, the root of all their associated troubles both servant and master, had been through the actions of Lord Rupert Penman-Smythe in forcing Mr Carlile to participate in those long ago activities of the hunt and thereby took it upon himself to rid the world for ever of what he truly believed was the instigator of all their troubles.

'However, as far as we are aware, he was not alone in the room prior to the arrival of the guests, his own testimony stating that with the front doorbell having been rung, he ascended from the servants' hall to the front entrance; this testimony was attested to by Mrs Christian. There is a likelihood that he could have tampered with the said master's horn prior to his leaving the drawing room for the stables. As it surely would have been left too much to chance that the Earl received the right pastry in his absence, he must have injected all of them, but what a risk he would have had to take, the chance of being seen in the act, someone tasting the alcohol and mentioning it and the Earl dropping dead there and then with the subsequent findings leading straight back to him. The timings for his arrival back downstairs together with his sightings at the station and the inn, courtesy of the friendly landlord in Marlford, not forgetting Thompson's apparition, would seem to place him with little opportunity of conducting this act of devious ill will after his departure from the house, though he may well have obtained the means from his master's supply of needles. For that matter, where would he have found out about the Earl's condition with contact between the two country houses having been non-existent for many years, except for the recent telephone conversation between Mr Carlile and the Earl?

'5. This brings us to the host and instigator of the afternoon's festivities himself, Mr Montague Carlile. Having observed from the testimony of numerous of his employees, the sole motive which could be assigned to this person for the death of what he described himself, in what I can best describe, as sincere and emotional tones as his "dear old friend", would be that of revenge for what he may have seen as the waste of his life by the long ago actions of the now late Earl. Yet, from these same witnesses' testimony came the indication that blame was never attributed by Mr Carlile upon Lord Rupert, but rather as just a cruel twist of fate to be endured by all. As with Mr Smith, Mr Carlile would indeed have had the means of the act, stating by his own admission that he was still requiring hypodermic administration of pain relief for his long endured injuries. Opportunity, however, would be a stumbling block as far as this man was concerned. For, if we are to believe the statement of events which Mr Thompson has given us, the Earl was well and truly alive when Mr Carlile left the drawing room to hold his weekly conference with Thompson in the smoking room. If we align the timings for the return of Dr Mathews, the Lady Isabella and Mr Smith to the house, Mr Carlile, even given our opinion on his state of apparent frailty and difficulty in moving his chair, it must, given the deteriorating weather conditions, have taken all his time in moving from the smoking room albeit with Mr Thompson's assistance to the terrace and further to the gazebo alone, before the return of all to the drawing room. Would time have availed him of the required opportunity, let alone the simple act of reaching the cake tray on the sideboard from his permanent position in his chair, to commit this crime. On reflection, I think not, Inspector.

'6. If, in conclusion, we look at the testimony of Mr Leonard Thompson, the land agent, it is my opinion that we view here a man of strong character whose testimony may be believed, taking into account the confirmation we received from the stationmaster at Marlford of his comings and goings to and from Swindon and his subsequent registration for a night's accommodation at the Swan Hotel in Swindon. He, in association with Mr Carlile, upon leaving the drawing room for their weekly conference was the last person to see the Earl alive. The three points which stick in my mind from this man's account of events was, one, the expression which appeared on Mr Carlile's face when a shadow appeared to pass by the smoking-room window. What feelings within the master of the house elicited such visual responses? Two, his refusal to be helped back to the drawing room but rather to be left on the cold terrace, having already complained of the weather conditions on the earlier journey from the apparently warm room and, three, the testimony from Mr Thompson that he overheard Mr Carlile specifically make mention to the Earl of the pastries in question. This begs two questions:

'1. Did Mr Carlile indeed know of the Earl's condition or was it just a coincidence him specifically offering him the offending pastries?

'2. What, on allegedly viewing Mr Smith venturing to and from the drawing room, caused the range of expressions upon Mr Carlile's face and later his apparent refusal to enter the drawing room alone?

'However, returning to Mr Thompson himself, I see no motive for the killing of a man with whom he had no dealings and apparently no knowledge of his life-threatening condition. Further to this, his opportunity would have been all but non-existent with Mr Carlile present on the terrace until the return of the rest of the party. He would also have been limited in the availability of the apparatus of death. Thus, I place Mr Thompson at the bottom of the list of suspects,' stated Sergeant Jones, finally having come to the conclusion of his own personal scanning of the facts of the case before him, as he placed the notebook from which he had been reading on the table in front of him, awaiting his superior's response to his calculated opinions of this investigation.

Having sat with his face turned towards the dull and dreary view enclosed by his office window, in apparent disregard of the dedicated nature of the previous monologue by his worthy subordinate, the inspector now turned his attention once more in the direction of this dogged defender of justice and fair play.

'Yes, that is all well and good, Sergeant, however, let us simplify this whole problem even further,' Inspector Dentworth said as he took from the top of a pile of papers at the right side of his neat and orderly maintained desk a sheath of writing paper and from its rest at the front of his desk his well-worn and often used black and gold fountain pen and began to write quickly in a handsome flowing script the following:

1. Victim of Murder: the Right Hon. the Eighth Earl of Marlford Lord Rupert Henry Penman-Smythe.
2. Cause of Death (confirmed by Dr Scott with assistance of Sir Garfield Pembleton): severe anaphylactic reaction due to ingestion of pure, tasteless alcoholic spirit.
3. Means of Cause of Death: hypodermic injection of the said alcoholic substance into cream-filled pastry, partly consumed by victim during course of afternoon tea.
4. Time of Death: between four and five o'clock in the afternoon.
5. Place/Situation of Death: drawing room, Carlile Manor, alone.

6. Possible Suspects:	Means:	Motive:	Opportunity:
(A) Dr R D Mathews	Available	None	Limited
(B) Lady I E Penman-Smythe	Available	Limited	Limited
(C) Mr J A Smith	Available	Available	Available
(D) Mr W H Collins	Available	Available	Limited
(E) Mr M A Carlile	Available	Available	Limited
(F) Mr L A Thompson	None	None	None

7. Conclusions so far in case:
    a) Prime suspect – Mr J A Smith: suggest further investigation of identity, personality and medical and psychological condition, preferably in the sobering confines of Scotland Yard.
    b) Dismiss from investigation – Dr R D Mathews and Mr L A Thompson: confirmation of movements during afternoon and times in question have been satisfactorily verified.
    c) Room for further investigation – the Lady I E Penman-Smythe, Mr W H Collins and Mr M A Carlile.

Having placed his fountain pen gently on the desk beside his right hand, Inspector Dentworth, with a last contemplative glance at the completed work before him, passed the crisp sheet of white paper across the expanse which constituted the working surface of his drab Scotland Yard desk, delivering it into the conscientious hands of Sergeant Jones.

'This, Jones,' he said, 'is where I believe we should concentrate our endeavours in this case. Given the evidence so far to hand, it is my opinion that much more needs to be gained from and about one John Andrew Smith. To this end, as you have suggested, I would instruct you to instigate further enquiries with your contacts in the Ministry of the Army with regard to the possible identity of this young chap. Further to this, I will make the necessary arrangements for us to attend the funeral down in Marlford on Thursday morning, at which stage I will invite Mr Smith to grace us with his presence here upon his return to London on Monday next. Subsequent to that, during the course of this time in Marlford, I want you to obtain discreetly the further information from Mr Carlile and Mr Collins which our enquiries now have shown to be required. Who knows what might come to light at this time of great emotional turmoil. No point disturbing the Lady Isabella in this period of mourning and grief for I am sure Mr Smith will not venture into these corridors alone. Now what do you say to all this, Jones?'

Sergeant Jones, having spent the previous minutes during the inspector's earnest dissertation in diligent contemplation of this unusual case, now turned his gaze from the sheet of paper before him to the thin, sagacious face of his venerable superior and replied in his usual constant and even-tempered voice.

'This is truly a most unique case, Inspector, which it would appear will require a concentrated effort on all our parts. To this end I will, as you have suggested, open communications immediately with my chums at Special Investigations and see what we can turn up about this young fellow, Mr Smith, and for that matter, what further information will come to light from the lips of Messrs Carlile and Collins.'

'Good man, now let's be about our tasks and see where this whole case leads us,' Inspector Dentworth enthusiastically replied as he rose from his leather-clad chair, signifying to his companion the conclusion of this discussion and the commencement of their appointed duties, leaving each to ponder the course of this investigation... Who... Why... When?

'We therefore commit his body to the ground, earth to earth, ashes to ashes, dust to dust, in sure and certain hope of the Resurrection to eternal life...' and so with these words from the local priest drifting off into mortal oblivion on the stiff and cold westerly breeze, a small and fittingly sombre gathering bade a final farewell to the rapidly disappearing casket and the life of one Rupert Henry Penman-Smythe, the Eighth and last Earl of Marlford. It was from this respectful group that a darkly clad figure now emerged and moved in the direction of the immediate graveside.

'May I on the occasion of this most sorrowful day extend again on behalf of Scotland Yard our most sincere condolences on the sudden and untimely loss of His Lordship, the late Earl of Marlford. May I also thank you for informing me of your intended return to London on Monday coming,' Inspector Dentworth diplomatically ventured as he came to rest beside the petite figure dressed from head to toe in mourning black still lingering absently at the graveside, who upon these words now turned her finely structured head, her face veiled in a heavy swathe of black net, obscuring from view the expression held upon her delicately chiselled face, towards the instigator of these words of discreet comfort and in a voice cracking deeply with an almost physical pain responded automatically with the words she had spoken so often in the past few days.

'Thank you so much for your kindness in this very sad time, Inspector. I am sure my father would have been deeply touched as I have been to know with what degree of respect he was viewed by this, his community. Further, as you requested me to inform you of any changes such as these, it was all I could do.'

Having attended to these social requirements, Inspector Dentworth adopted yet again his most businesslike manner and turning to the figure who, throughout this dialogue, had remained as a constant and silent shadow to the Lady Isabella, the inspector now sharply enquired, 'I am of the understanding that you shall be accompanying Her Ladyship upon her return to London on Monday, is that correct, sir?'

With the utterance of these words of stern enquiry, this figure returned his attention from the trance-like observation of the grave and its contents to stare abstractedly into the face of the inspector and in a hollow voice slowly replied, 'Death is all around us here… We must get away before it engulfs us too… London, yes, we return to London on Monday morning… away from this place and all its demons…'

'Now, John, that's enough of those thoughts. We have a prosperous life to look forward to together. Think ahead to that and not to the past,' the Lady Isabella quickly intervened, in an attempt to rouse her companion out of his apparent mood of deep melancholy here in the presence of the keenly observant inspector. Then, in an attempt to divert any further undue attention away from her companion's morose behaviour, the Lady Isabella, as in previous encounters, seized control of the situation by turning to the inspector and in a voice whose politely structured words barely masked the protective aggression surging beneath their surface issued forth the following sharp volley.

'Yes, Inspector, as I communicated to you through Dr Scott, both myself and Mr Smith will be returning to London on Monday. As it would appear that Mr Smith's movements are of critical interest to you at this time, let me further confirm that we both will be residing for an unknown period of time within my residence in Chelsea. As I also explained to Dr Scott, when he contacted me on Monday last, that there are numerous and varied business interests of my late father which require my immediate attention in London, having of course now laid him to proper rest in the soil of the countryside he so loved as had been his wish. May I ask, Inspector, is there any particular reason why you have confirmed so intently Mr Smith's forthcoming movements?'

Turning his head to once again address his words to Mr Smith directly, to the obvious exclusion of the Lady Isabella, Inspector Dentworth, his grey eyes keenly observant of the mangled face now before him, brusquely replied, 'Yes, I have a very good reason for making such ardent enquiries into Mr Smith's movements. For it is my intention of requesting you, sir, to present yourself at my office at Scotland Yard upon your arrival in London on Monday, shall we say, at two o'clock. Certain developments in this case have led me to require you to answer some further questions as to your actions on the afternoon in question.'

'Oh, Inspector, surely you do not mean to say that Mr Smith is a suspect in your investigation? For if you are, then I shall certainly make the necessary arrangements for legal representation from my own firm of solicitors to be present at this meeting. I have never heard of such a preposterous suggestion as the thought that this meek lamb of a young man would be capable of such a monstrous crime against my father, of all people,' the Lady Isabella again defensively interjected on behalf of the man who stood beside her in placid bewilderment of all that was transpiring around him.

'Calm yourself, my dear young lady, there is no need for legal representation at this point in time. All I am requesting, is to have a quiet chat with Mr Smith in the peaceful confines of my office in London to confirm his recollections of the events of that fateful afternoon. That is all, for the moment at least, my young man,' Inspector Dentworth soothingly replied.

The utterance of these calm words on the part of the inspector had the effect of yet again rousing the subject of the previous brisk dialogue from his static and mute state before the graveside to action and words. As in this transformation, he took the Lady Isabella's arm in his and directed her away from the open burial plot in the chapel yard and deliberately in the direction of the main house. In doing so, he halted briefly and replied in an unexpectedly cold manner in his slow mumbled articulation to the inspector.

'Two o'clock on Monday, you say, Inspector. Rest assured… I shall be there. Now if you will excuse us… as you will no doubt be aware, Her Ladyship and I have numerous matters to attend to… before our return to London…'

With those words briskly disappearing on the ever-stiffening westerly breeze, the inspector was left to watch in silence, through the mist of rain which had started to fall, the fading view of this young couple as they languidly strolled back, accepting the condolences offered as they passed from the strands of mourners who still milled lingeringly around the chapel yard. Amongst these bearers of sympathetic comfort was one whose chance meeting with the young engaged couple would in the days to come, have such an effect on all their lives that none, not even Scotland Yard's finest, could ever have imagined. Times past… times present… times future… all entwined for all eternity…

'What have the events of today contributed to our thoughts and feelings and for that matter the information at hand on this case, Sergeant?' the inspector, displaying his usual passionate zeal for the positive progress of the case at hand, enquired of his colleague as they settled themselves opposite each other and into the peaceful solitude of an empty first-class compartment for their welcome return journey to London that late Thursday afternoon. As the sergeant commenced his monologue of the day's findings, Inspector Dentworth relieved his eyes of their aid, folding his spectacles to lie peacefully in the palm of his steady hand and turned his head to stare distractedly at the rapidly disappearing view of the autumn-toned countryside as it lay at rest in the dusk light.

'Well, Inspector, to start with, both Mr Carlile and Collins, the butler, deny emphatically that they knew anything of the medical condition which afflicted the late Earl and that neither gentleman tampered in any way with the fare before its consumption by Lord Rupert. When I further questioned Mr Carlile as to the expression which he displayed to Mr Thompson whilst in the smoking room, as what Mr Thompson described as an alleged shadow passed across the room and Mr Carlile previously ventured by way of description as the alleged passage of Mr Smith across his view. He informed me that his expression was the result of a reminiscence of a long ago and extremely pleasant personal incident involving his long-lost son as a small boy which for some unknown reason flashed into his mind upon sighting Mr Smith's transit across his field of view. Speaking of Mr John Smith, it would unfortunately appear, Inspector, that the true identity of this young chap will indeed remain a mystery as my chums at Special Investigations have drawn a blank as to his real name.

'The whole situation from what these fellows have been able to piece together was made so much more complicated by the fact that the young man had somehow lost his identification tags. The chaps at Special Investigations believe that, by virtue of the injuries Mr Smith received, they were severed from his body by the slicing action of the shrapnel which bombarded him. Further to this point, when the regimental stretcher bearer found him in the field, what remained of his tunic lay in ribbons trodden in the mud around him, with the accompanying badges having already been pilfered by the marauding Huns who thought him already dead. Consequently, the chance of finding this man's identity is like looking for the proverbial needle in a haystack. By the way, Inspector, while we are on the subject of Mr Smith, I had my chums down at the Ministry pull out this fellow's medical file. It would appear that in part he is not all that he appears to be. Indeed, though it is apparently true that he has totally lost his memory of times past and does suffer from bouts of dark depression and lapses in concentration, on the other hand, his remaining sight was noted upon discharge as being adequate in all conditions. That I am afraid, Inspector, is all that my chums could confirm about this young fellow,' Sergeant Jones concluded, an air of frustration edging his determined voice.

'That is as I thought it would be, Sergeant. Too many poor souls in the same boat as Mr Smith, so to speak, lost in the chaos of the front never to be returned to their rightful place in society. However, the medical evidence certainly places a new light upon his testimony and that of the Lady Isabella, wouldn't you say, Jones?' enquired Inspector Dentworth, his grey eyes gleaming brightly once more at the thought of another emotion-charged encounter with the fiercely protective young blue blood and her constant companion.

However, before Sergeant Jones had an opportunity to respond to his superior's enquiry, a face suddenly appeared pressed hard against the clear glass of the compartment window. Registering the required identity and solitary nature of the cubicle's occupants with a simple nod and with a swift and uncharacteristically fluid movement of the associated body, a visitor materialised from the adjacent passageway to stand before the two mildly bewildered men.

'I do so apologise for unheralded intrusion, Inspector. I do believe I am in possession of information of great importance to the case you are at present investigating,' the intruder cryptically announced.

Grasping control of the situation once more, Inspector Dentworth, returning his spectacles to their appointed place, cordially responded by saying, 'Well, that being the case, you had better sit down here and tell us immediately about this information which you state to be of such great importance to our investigations,' he further continued with the instruction,

'Please take a seat beside Sergeant Jones,' the inspector said, indicating with a wave of his thin hand the seat opposite him and beside the now keenly observant Sergeant Jones who through mechanical instinct eagerly readied himself with pencil and notebook at hand, 'and by all means let us hear what you have to say on this matter, whatever it may be.'

Having settled comfortably in the seat opposite the inspector, this new occupant of the compartment spoke again, 'Well, Inspector, you may well say I am old but I am not daft and I never forget a person, especially one I have known since birth.'

Still with a sense of bewilderment lingering in his usual sharp mind, the inspector brusquely interjected by saying, 'Come now what is all this about, Miss Quimby? Who are you speaking of? What relevance is it to us?'

Leaning forward to stare directly and evenly into the fatigued face of the inspector, Miss Gladys Quimby spoke in a clear, determined voice.

'Who am I speaking of, Inspector? It is young Ladyship's gentleman friend, Mr Smith, whom I am speaking of or, rather, I should give him correct identity least one I believe him to be, seeing as how I nursed him from wee babe to tall strikingly handsome young man before he was sent away to Mendrew. You may call me stupid old woman but I would swear Bible in any court in this land that that young man is Reginald Alexander Carlile, only child of master of Carlile Manor, Mr Montague

Alexander, and my mistress in London, Mrs Catherine Elizabeth Carlile. You could have knocked me over with feather when he walked past me this morning in chapel yard at Beeches Hall. Seeing how we all thought, master and mistress included, that although his body was never found to give proper Christian burial to in terrible days of last war, it was presumed by all above and below stairs that young lad had been tragically killed back in 1917.

'Now this poor lad appears clearly before my eyes today as clearly and closely as I see you now, Inspector, so badly scarred as to be unrecognisable by most, but not to me his old and faithful nursemaid or as he was so prone to call me in now long gone, private times shared only by we two souls, his "roly-poly pudding". As you may well observe now, as then, I have never been lithe of figure, Inspector. However many years it might have been, Inspector, since I last laid eyes on my handsome young charge, Master Reginald, or as I affectionately called him my little "jack-in-the-box" for his habit of darting from nowhere to be under feet unexpectedly, I would stake my life on fact that these two supposedly separate men are one and same. You can judge for yourself significance of this information to your investigations,' Gladys, with tears of long buried emotion welling in her tired old eyes, emphatically concluded and sat back awaiting the inspector's reply.

That expected reply came after a moment or two of deep reflection on the part of the inspector upon the evidence which had just been presented to him so resolutely by this normally reserved, elderly gentlewoman.

In a voice rich with pathos of the situation, as it was unfolding before his weathered eyes, the inspector, looking directly into the face of the woman seated opposite him, replied calmly.

'Yes, Miss Quimby, the information which you have just offered is indeed of great importance and interest to us. From the affirmation which you have so readily given that it is your sincere belief that the man known as Mr John Andrew Smith is in actuality one Reginald Alexander Carlile, I take it then that you truly believe that you could not be mistaken in this observation.' These words elicited a sudden and violent shake of the old woman's head. 'That being the case, I will thank you for bringing this matter to our attention so speedily and, in conclusion, confirm that indeed what you have told us here this evening has a great relevance to our investigations. That being the case and in light of the fact that you are in the process of returning to your duties in London, I would command you most emphatically to keep this information to yourself. Do not tell another soul what you have just told us here tonight, and that includes your mistress and Mr Collins. Keep a silent tongue in your head in regard to this matter if you truly wish to be of service to all concerned.'

With the conclusion of these polite, yet firm, words on the part of the inspector, Miss Gladys Quimby, as if having only been a spirit manifestation before the occupants of this compartment's exhausted eyes, with a curt nod of her grey head was gone as suddenly as she had appeared, leaving the inspector and his companion to consider in earnest silence all that had just transpired, their jagged nerves and whirling minds soothed by the rhythmical clickety-clack of the carriage upon the rails.

With more than a few moments and a good many miles having transpired and been traversed since the departure from their presence of the old woman, Inspector Dentworth, having during this time stared blindly at the darkened view displayed through the compartment window, his mind a whirlpool of thoughts, now turned his attention once more in the direction of his competent assistant, Sergeant Charles Jones, and contemplatively enquired, 'Well, Sergeant, what do you make of all that that old woman has told us here tonight? Do we believe what could be just the ramblings of a feeble old mind?'

'I doubt very much, Inspector, that Miss Quimby's mind is at all feeble. From what the fellows at Special Investigations have previously told me, it is well within the realms of possibility that these two gentlemen are one and the same person with such confusion reigning supreme at numerous times during that bloody conflict. What I suggest is that, upon our return to London and the office, I make some further enquiries with my chums at the Ministry about one Reginald Alexander Carlile and see what turns up. Further to this, might I suggest that we include this newly acquired information into our forthcoming questioning of Mr John Smith. With a bit of luck we may well be able to trigger something previously lost in his memory to confirm his identity as that of one Reginald Alexander Carlile,' Sergeant Jones replied in his usual steady and methodical voice.

'Yes, Sergeant, I fully concur with your thoughts on this matter and our actions for the forthcoming days. However, it has been a long and exhausting day and, for now, if you have no objection, Sergeant, I suggest we rest our bodies if not our minds for the remainder of this journey,' the inspector gently instructed as he settled himself more comfortably in his deeply padded seat, removed his spectacles from the bridge of his thin nose to the inside pocket of his sombre black jacket and closed his grey eyes, the tempered sway of the train along the tracks having the desired calming effect of gradually lulling the inspector into the state of deep and restful slumber, to sleep, perchance to dream…

'Please come in, Mr Smith. Close the door if you would and sit yourself down here beside the sergeant,' the inspector cordially instructed, waving a hand of welcome towards the man who had, upon the appointed time of two o'clock on Monday afternoon, punctually presented himself at the open door of the stark Scotland Yard office in which Inspector James Dentworth presently resided in the ever-observant company of Sergeant Charles Jones. Having observed Mr John Smith's tentative entry into the room, the inspector further encouragingly spoke in a most fatherly tone of voice.

'My dear fellow, there is nothing to fear here. We are just going to sit down, three gentlemen together, and quietly discuss a couple of matters which have come to light in this investigation since we last spoke, that is all. Now come along, the sooner you answer our questions the sooner you may be away from here. By the way, I take it, sir, that you ventured here alone this afternoon, that is to say, without the highly supportive companionship of the Lady Isabella?' the inspector enquired with an apparent air of mild curiosity edging his voice offhandedly.

As he finally settled himself none too comfortably in the straight-backed wooden chair positioned to the right of Sergeant Jones and directly across the expanse which constituted the immaculately tidy working surface of Inspector Dentworth's plain government issue desk, Mr Smith to the best of his now well-noted and limited ability replied briskly in an even voice, reminiscent to those present of a parrot reciting a well-rehearsed line of explanation.

'That is true… only in part, Inspector, for the Lady Isabella was kind enough to drop me off… here at Scotland Yard in the cab we shared from Paddington earlier. Her Ladyship has continued on to Regent Street… to occupy herself in the time-honoured, womanly pursuit of shopping… before I join her at Verrey's for tea upon the conclusion… of what you have just described so ambiguously… as our little chat between gentlemen. May I further declare, here and now… that I will require a cab to be procured for me… upon the conclusion of this interview, Inspector.'

'Certainly, Mr Smith, we will by all means attend to this act of procurement when the time comes,' Inspector Dentworth smoothly replied. Then, leaning forward slightly in his comfortable leather chair to rest his thin hands peacefully on the leather inlay of his desk top, he continued in his even, soothing voice with the following initial words of what appeared superficially to be a general, polite enquiry.

'You spoke just now of your trip up to London from Marlford. I trust that it was a pleasant trip for both yourself and Her Ladyship. In the grateful knowledge of this trip, I have in latter days been left wondering since our recent discussion held down at Marlford what your previous travel plans have been? Indeed, what for instance your course of return to this country from the front had been? How long you have been returned and for that matter what your intended course now will be, given the apparent change in your fiancée's financial circumstances upon her father's tragic death?'

The inspector's soothing words and equally calming tone of voice had their desired effect upon the current subject of his attention, as Mr Smith in a robust and confident voice replied, 'The Lady Isabella and myself enjoyed a most… smooth and relatively speedy return journey to London… earlier today, thank you, Inspector. In answer to your other enquiries… as to our past, present and future, travel arrangements… my answer is as follows. I incurred my injuries during the summer of 1917; due to the nature of those injuries... I required extended treatment... before I could be repatriated back to these shores. However, in the interim, the armistice was declared... and it was decided by both the Lady Isabella and myself that we should remain in Europe... for a time to allow me to regain some of my strength and avail me... of what medical care I could in a more temperate climate. For, both of us knew, our return to this country would herald further... extended and painful treatment, for what you can plainly observe... as most horrific wounds. Associated with this was the knowledge that I had no family's loving arms to return to, well, no family... that I could remember and, for Her Ladyship's part... she too was a free soul, so to speak, having lost her mother some years ago... and with her father away in South Africa.

'Having said all that, the plain fact is that we returned to England, that is to say London... in the summer of 1920, whereupon treatment was commenced upon my tattered body... by the best minds and hands of Harley Street... that money could buy. What you see, sitting before you... is the best result which could be achieved with what fate left me. Subsequent to all the never-ending surgery... and extended treatment being completed, and in the constant... and compassionate company of the Lady Isabella Penman-Smythe... and I might add at her insistence, we journeyed in recent weeks... to her family's country home, Beeches Hall, which provided me with... the necessary recuperative facilities having graciously in his absence abroad... been opened by Lord Rupert Penman-Smythe as a convalescence home... for returned wounded servicemen. Finally, in answer, to your enquiry as to my future, given the untimely death... of the Earl of Marlford, all I can say, Inspector... is that it is still my understanding that the death changes nothing... and that the Lady Isabella will honour me by becoming my wife... in the coming summer.'

With those triumphant and passionate words ringing out across the staid expanse of the inspector's cold and lifeless office, Mr Smith fell silent, the hint of a smile appearing on his young yet prematurely aged face, signifying to all present his pride with himself for handling the difficult situation so far. How soon the old proverb of 'Pride goeth before destruction' and 'An haughty spirit before a fall' would be brought to bear upon this young man as the inspector spoke this time in a decisive and thoroughly businesslike manner.

'With the injuries you incurred and the surgery and treatment you have apparently endured, Mr Smith, do you still suffer great pain and, if so, how do you relieve it?' the inspector suddenly and most pointedly enquired of an openly flabbergasted Mr Smith.

'Well, yes, Inspector, I do still suffer great and fairly constant pain from my wounds... and, in answer to your further question, the relief of this pain comes... via the administration by myself of a hypodermic injection of morphine... only when required,' John Smith meekly replied, in the process withdrawing from his inside coat pocket a green leather pouch which, upon being opened, revealed to the inspector's interested eyes a glass hypodermic syringe, a vial of fluid which he keenly observed as being labelled as morphine, as well as a small blue glass bottle of unlabelled liquid contents and two small squares of cotton gauze.

'What do we have here then, Mr Smith?' the inspector sharply requested, leaving Mr Smith no opportunity to reply before his thin, deft hand reached across the desk, delved into the pouch and extracted the unmarked blue bottle for his further examination. As he deftly twisted the small, ground, glass stopper and sniffed gingerly at the air above the now open bottle, the inspector's neatly kept eyebrows shot momentarily towards the ceiling and his voice released the single word, 'Alcohol.'

Finally, now finding his mumbling voice once more, the bemused Mr Smith responded by saying, 'Yes, Inspector, that bottle simply contains a solution... of pure alcoholic spirit which, in conjunction with the cotton swabs... I use to disinfect the needle of the syringe... and that part of my body before I administer... my morphine injection. That is all.'

'Mr Smith, does this pouch ever leave your person in the course of the day?' the inspector further enquired, his terrier-like instincts now enlivened to the chase.

'No, Inspector, my requirement of it comes at any time... of the day or night. So I retain it close at hand at all times,' Mr Smith responded as his countenance expressed to those about him his rising degree of concern at the unexpected course this current line of the investigation was taking.

Without publicly acknowledging this concern, the inspector doggedly continued his now sharp and unrelenting bombardment of this increasingly agitated, young fellow.

'Why, on that Friday afternoon at Carlile Manor, did you insist upon leaving the company of your host and the other guests? Was it indeed, as has been suggested to us, the simple act of a stroll around the grounds partaking of a breath of fresh air? Or, more to the point, was it really the fact that you, Mr John Andrew Smith, could not stand to be in such close confines with the man you so detested for his boorish manner and distrust of your intentions towards his daughter, that man being one Rupert Penman-Smythe, the Eighth Earl of Marlford? Further, my good fellow, please inform us here and now, for what reason you were observed crossing the view from the French windows of the smoking room in the act of moving towards the drawing room and the apparent presence of what was then the solitary Lord Rupert only to be again observed retracing your steps a few moments later? It has been forwarded to me by words from your own mouth that your limited vision restricts your mobility. This statement I now find very hard to believe and it leads me to wonder further how much more of your previous testimony will be proved to be false. Who indeed are you, Mr Smith? Is this all some very elaborate hoax which you are playing at? What indeed is your game, sir?'

With this latest, unremitting questioning of his identity and his intentions, the last tenuous thread of mental balance within John Smith's tortured mind unravelled and his composure snapped like a spider's web in the onslaught of a violent summer storm, leaving him a quivering mass of broken humanity to plead for mercy through trembling lips.

'Enough, Inspector, enough! Yes, it is true that I left the Lady Isabella... while she slept in the summer house that Friday afternoon. Yes I returned... across the lawn in the direction of the drawing room. My intention for venturing alone... back to the presence of His Lordship was to take the opportunity... of speaking with him in what I presumed to be... the gentlemanly company of Dr Mathews and... our host Mr Carlile on the subject of my future life with his daughter... hoping that he may be persuaded to see his way clear... to granting us his blessing for our union in marriage. As you may well have gathered by now, Inspector, the late Earl... did not consider me the most suitable prospect for his only child... and heir in this matter. However, upon approaching the drawing-room window... but before I caught sight of the occupants of the room... my courage suddenly evaporated and I realised that I could not muster... the strength to speak my mind to this most headstrong gentleman... whom I knew would only gather more support for his opinion... from the fellow gentlemen of his community, who were... to my knowledge gathered in the room with him. This being the honest truth, after standing for some minutes in contemplation... of these thoughts, I slowly retraced my steps to the summer house... where I found the Lady Isabella thankfully still blissfully asleep.'

At this juncture in his informative oration, Mr Smith halted more decidedly, as if battling to determine which course of explanation his further words should take; then, having come to a resolution, he continued on slowly.

'As to your questioning of my powers of sight, Inspector, I can only proffer as a rationale for the discrepancy... between now and what was recorded in my discharge papers that... in the weeks prior to my demobilisation... I had a minor improvement in the sight in my remaining eye... which the army physicians at the time attributed to the effects of a change... in my ongoing medication. However, I have since been warned by my specialist physicians... that these improvements will not be long lasting and that... due to the trauma and strain that has been and... is continuing to be placed upon this eye, I will gradually over time... lose my remaining sight. A touch of heaven, before the perils of hell... so to speak. This deterioration, unfortunately, has already commenced. You may, by all means, confirm these facts with my specialist... physician, Sir Garfield Pembleton, in Harley Street... if you so desire, Inspector. As for my identity, Inspector, it is no hoax... as you say. There is nothing that I would regard more as a precious gift... than if you or anyone else could give me back my real name... and family heritage. This anonymity is a state which it would appear... I will be burdened with for what remains of my life here on earth... man without true name or family... no better than the local wild cur, endlessly roaming the village streets... in search of a home, and a name...' John Smith's words trailed off, as he buried his head deep into his sensitive-looking hands and began to sob uncontrollably.

'There, there, Mr Smith, steady yourself, young man. Is there nothing of your younger days, your days of childhood and youth that you possibly remember?' the inspector gently requested of the obviously broken, young fellow who sat so disconsolately before him.

With this request, Mr Smith raised his dishevelled head from his still shaking hands, revealing the stain of freshly shed tears still evident upon his scarred face as he turned to look directly into the now compassionate face of the inspector and replied in a truly downcast manner.

'No, Inspector, those times which in the normal flow of life... we all treasure into our old age have... for my part been lost for ever, never again to be savoured... upon their reminiscence.'

'You remember nothing of your parents? What of your life as a small boy, think hard now? You must have been a real jack-in-the-box as most young lads with boundless energy are. Perhaps, sir, you had a nanny? What was she like, I wonder? Maybe she was tall and thin or perhaps short and stout, like a roly-poly pudding?' Inspector Dentworth covertly enquired, his astute eyes keenly watching for any response to be displayed on the tormented face before him.

However, his efforts appeared to be in vain as the face he viewed so intently gave the same appearance as the sheath of fresh, white paper which lay upon the desk in front of him, emotionless and blank.

'No, Inspector, I have tried all this, time and time again... first with the quacks at the Ministry... then with their Harley Street colleagues and now again with you here. However, nothing has come to light... then or now,' Mr Smith, with an air of increasing frustration edging his voice, savagely replied.

'Well, on that rather depressing note I will conclude this discussion, Mr Smith, with the final request to you to convey to Her Ladyship the fact that the coroner's inquest into the death of the Earl of Marlford will be conducted under the most competent supervision of the local coroner, Colonel Hicks, at the village hall in Marlford on Thursday next, commencing at ten o'clock that morning. As I have previously informed you, both Her Ladyship's and your attendance will be required at this inquest. Subsequent to that, I invite you both to again attend a gathering at Carlile Manor the following Friday afternoon at three o'clock. The only explanation for this request I will give to you at this time is that there are certain matters regarding this case which need further clarification in the atmosphere in which this murder took place. I therefore suggest that you both make the necessary arrangements to return to Marlford for those days. Having said that, you are now free to go. If you see the constable on the desk at the end of the corridor outside, he will assist you in obtaining a cab for your previously mentioned rendezvous with the Lady Isabella. I will finally take this opportunity to thank you, Mr Smith, for your continuing assistance in this investigation by coming here so punctually today,' the inspector cordially instructed with the hint of an enigmatic smile appearing upon his intelligent face.

'That is perfectly all right, Inspector. I am, indeed, most eager to assist… in any way I possibly can if it means the speedy arrest of the fiend responsible… for this ghastly act. Further to this, I think I may speak on behalf of Her Ladyship and myself… when I say that you may rest assured we will be in attendance… at the inquest as requested on Thursday and, subsequently… at Carlile Manor the following afternoon,' his composure now all but restored, John Smith earnestly replied as he rose none too steadily to his feet and initiated what he naively thought would be his uninterrupted passage from the room.

Having taken but a few shuffling steps in his longed for journey to peace and tranquillity far from these mercilessly inquisitive confines, the clear strong voice now rapidly becoming familiar to him rang out again forcing this obviously physically exhausted and mentally drained shell of a man to halt in his tracks, turn again and face one last time that day his inquisitor, as the inspector nonchalantly enquired, 'Oh, by the way, Mr Smith, before you leave us here today, one final question if you will. Whilst you were standing on the terrace outside the drawing-room door that Friday afternoon did you hear any unusual noises coming from the direction of that room?'

With these apparently tempered words of enquiry Mr Smith breathlessly replied,

'No, Inspector, I did not hear any noises or voices... for that matter coming from the drawing room... that afternoon. However, that is not very surprising... as you can plainly see and my medical file will confirm... fate has also robbed me of my entire ear and, consequently... sense of hearing on this side and a considerable degree of my hearing... from my remaining ear here.' In the process of responding to the inspector, Mr Smith in turn indicated with his shaking right hand the scarred flat area on the right side of his head where his right ear had once proudly resided and then the flushed counterpart on the left. 'Indeed, Inspector, if there had been any noises... coming from the drawing room that afternoon, they would have been lost to me... on the stiff breeze that was beginning to blow... as I stood there on the cold stone terrace. Really, all I can hear is in close conversation... in quiet surroundings, such as here today, Inspector.'

'Right, Mr Smith, thank you for that information and again thank you for your time here this afternoon. We won't keep you any longer from joining your fiancée as I see it is just a little after three now. May I, in conclusion, wish you all the best in your ongoing quest to discover your true identity. Be fearless, young man,' Inspector Dentworth encouragingly concluded.

With these final words of seemingly innocent encouragement from the inspector, an expression of childlike bewilderment suddenly dawned upon the socially grotesque features of John Smith and he was further observed to drift into a trance-like state of deep meditation. Then, as this battered and bruised embodiment of all that was so pitiful in the aftermath of the war to end all wars slowly turned away from the inspector's intent gaze and moved laboriously towards and through the stiffly opening office door, he was heard to whisper the following cascade of jumbled phrases as he finally disappeared from view.

'Be fearless, young man... fearless by name and fearless by

nature, eh, sir... roly-poly pudding... is that jam or blood... jack-in-the-box... over the top we go, lads...'

Leaving the Pride of Scotland Yard and his dutiful companion to each silently reflect upon the true course of this young man's past, present and future...

'Are you ready to order, sir?' a high-pitched voice, polite yet urgent in its manner, pierced through the thick sea of dark thoughts in which John Smith had remained floundering since leaving Scotland Yard some few minutes before and his subsequent arrival into the presence of his beloved. Forced back to the surface, to reality and to the realisation of his surroundings once more, the remnants of his thoughts still clung to him like seaweed twined around a piece of driftwood, as he distractedly replied, 'Roly-poly pudding?'

With a bemused expression appearing upon her banal and lustreless face, the smartly dressed waitress at Verrey's café, curtly replied, 'We don't serve that now, sir. That's on the luncheon menu. This is afternoon tea. Please, if you would make your mind up. I have several others to attend to.'

'Yes, we will have a pot of Earl Grey tea with milk, not lemon, a plate of ham sandwiches and one of scones with jam and clotted cream, thank you,' the Lady Isabella commanded as she swiftly seized control of the situation in an attempt to dismiss quickly from her position at the side of the table the increasingly puzzled serving woman.

'Thank you, Miss,' the waitress dutifully replied, as she returned her pad and pencil to her apron pocket and promptly departed to serve the numerous other tables under her supervision in this well-patronised and most reputable Regent Street establishment.

Turning her attention once more towards the morbid figure seated to her right, the Lady Isabella, her sapphire blue eyes burning with fierce yet tempered emotion, still blatantly mindful of the close proximity of fellow diners, quietly implored her distracted companion to return his mental faculties to the present with the following words of loving reproach and enquiry.

'Oh, John, my dearest, please snap out of this demon-possessed trance. What happened at the interview earlier? What did the inspector say to cause this malaise of the mind which afflicts you now so markedly? Speak to me, my beloved. Tell me what is troubling you so? Please come back to me, my love, from that dark abyss which so cruelly traps your mind. Come back to your treasured Isabella.'

Suddenly, upon the utterance of this name, a transformation of mind and spirit was wrought upon this morbid personage. As if by the click of a medium's fingers, the trance enveloping John Smith was lifted dramatically, returning him to an intelligent and responsive young man of his age. With a shake of his head, as if clearing the demonic spirits from their resting place, this meta-morphosis was complete witnessed by virtue of the mumbled yet observant words of response from this man's own scarred lips.

'Isabella, have you been busy shopping... while I have been having my little chat with the inspector?' he asked as his gaze cast downwards expectantly to the base of his companion's elegant mahogany balloon-backed chair in search of parcels.

'Yes. There's so much, they are in the cloakroom,' the Lady Isabella quickly replied.

'Well, it's obvious you kept yourself well amused in my ab-sence, my love. Now what are we having for tea?'

With the utterance of these light-hearted words of playful reproach and eager enquiry of the culinary delights on offer from this most fashionable Regent Street eatery and as if upon some unseen cue, the previously curtly spoken waitress silently materialised to stand again beside them. With a well-laden tray held firmly in her two thick, yet muscular, hands she again tersely let forth her words of motherly warning directed towards the previously childlike John Smith as she dextrously removed each item from her tray and gently arranged them on the table before what she had previously noted to be the horribly scarred young man and his equally beautiful lady companion.

'Mind now, sir, here's your afternoon tea, one pot of very hot Earl Grey tea with milk, one plate of plain ham sandwiches and one plate of our finest afternoon tea scones with a pot each of strawberry jam and clotted cream. Now, will that be all for now then?' the waitress hastily requested turning her attention once more in the direction of the apparent figure of authority at this table, the Lady Isabella, to be greeted by the equally curt response, 'Yes, that will be all for the moment, thank you.'

These words had their desired effect in again sending the young serving girl scurrying on her way to service the other tables in her care. Thankful of the rapid retreat of the waitress, the Lady Isabella, in the act of pouring the piping hot brown liquid from the gleaming tea pot into the stark, white, fine, bone china cups residing in their matching saucers, all of which had been placed within her easy reach on the crisp, white tablecloth-clad surface, again endeavoured to extract from her now lucent companion the content of the recent discussion in which he had just previously been involved at Scotland Yard by uttering the following simple request, 'Please, John, tell me what happened at the interview with the inspector? What further questions did he ask you and perhaps more importantly what answers did you give him, my dearest? Please, my darling, tell me all that transpired.'

'Well, Isabella, my sweet, there's not that much to tell. The inspector asked about my method... and use of pain relief, and I showed him my pouch. He asked if I kept it with me at all times and I said, "Yes," just a few matters... such as that, my love. Oh, by the way, the inspector did inform me that the coroner's inquest will be held down at Marlford on Thursday coming... commencing at ten o'clock in the village hall... under the supervision of a man by the name of Colonel Hicks... I believe, he said the fellow's name was. Further to this, the inspector has also requested our attendance at Carlile Manor... the following afternoon, that being Friday at three o'clock... to participate in what he explained as further discussion of matters... with regard to his ongoing investigation. Let's hope that the inspector and his men can clear... this whole ghastly matter up as quickly as possible... so that we may continue with our plans for the future,' John Smith diplomatically replied in the hope that his explanation would appease and divert his fiancée's attention away from what in reality had been a quite messy interview to more pleasant thoughts of their forthcoming union as husband and wife. As he graciously accepted the cup of steaming aromatic beverage which the Lady Isabella proffered to him, he further quickly continued this line of attack, not allowing her at this crucial point in their discussion to enter into the conversation.

'Speaking of our forthcoming act of marriage, what of our honeymoon… my love? Have you had any further thoughts as to where you desire… to spend this most precious time together?' John Smith gently enquired, his face now a picture of content-ment and loving pride while at the same time radiating to the Lady Isabella his intense determination to direct her thoughts away from the earlier proceedings of the day, leaving the Lady Isabella, as the conversation ventured to pleasant thoughts of faraway places and events, with a privately held uneasy feeling of ignorance of the true facts of this dreaded encounter between friend and foe. A time and a place where ignorance could never be bliss…

'Now, finally, have all the special arrangements been completed for the proceedings tomorrow and, more importantly, the following afternoon, Sergeant?' Inspector Dentworth enthusiasti-cally enquired as he sat behind his, as always, neat desk in his cold and colourless Scotland Yard office this damp Wednesday afternoon in late October. Absently twiddling his thumbs, the inspector's mind was awash with his methodical flow of thoughts of this case as he awaited expectantly the quiet and well modu-lated reply from his loyal junior.

'Yes, Inspector, I have organised for all parties required to be present at the inquest tomorrow morning and the afternoon gathering on Friday afternoon. Reservations have been made for our accommodation once more for tonight and Thursday night at the local inn in Marlford as has our transport down there by the twenty past three afternoon train and our subsequent return to London on the early evening train on Friday.'

'Good man, Sergeant. I knew I could leave these requirements in your most capable hands. Now we must wait, Charlie, and see if our earnest endeavours in this case will bear us the longed for fruit,' the inspector philosophically espoused.

Generating the simple yet respectful response from his subor-dinate of so many such cases, 'Yes, Inspector.'

As a final indication of his satisfaction for the progress of the case and his strongly held belief in its successful conclusion, the inspector, his clear grey eyes glistened in anticipation of the thrill of the final chase of their quarry to victory, encouragingly, yet cryptically, concluded, 'I am sure, Sergeant, that, if all that we have discovered since our recent discussion with Mr Smith can subsequently be confirmed, our quest for justice and the truth will find its target and the Earl of Marlford may finally rest in peace in his grave. Now, let's be away to Paddington or we will miss our train to Marlford, away to the final charge in this hard fought battle.'

'This court will now come to order,' barked the gruff, coarse voice of the crusty Colonel Hicks across the packed confines of the modest stone-walled village hall of Marlford. Thus the coroner's inquest into the untimely and suspicious death of the Right Hon. the Eighth Earl of Marlford, Lord Rupert Henry Penman-Smythe, began with the entrance into the witness box in rapid succession of Constable Stevens, Sergeant Jones and Inspector Dentworth recounting their official observations of the case at hand. The first in a long procession of such occupants to the stand, this trio was followed by Dr Mathews, Dr Scott and Sir Garfield Pembleton all adding their requested segments of medical information to this heinous jigsaw puzzle, then the likes of the Lady Isabella Penman-Smythe, Mr Smith and Mr Carlile providing their interpretations of the afternoon's events, and finally the testimony of the estate and household staff including Samuel the gatekeeper, Old Ben the head groom, Mrs Christian the cook and Mr Collins the butler as to the timing and content of these proceedings. The day finally dragged on to its inevitable conclusion with Colonel Hicks delivering to the hushed audience in the makeshift public gallery his verdict in this case in the following legally ambiguous terms.

'It is my finding in this case that upon the afternoon of the twenty-ninth day of the month of September in the year one thousand nine hundred and twenty-two between the hours of four and five, the Right Hon. the Eighth Earl of Marlford, Lord Rupert Henry Penman-Smythe, did have an act of assault by means of a hypodermic injection of pure alcoholic spirit committed upon his person, occasioning his immediate death by person or persons unknown at the time of this inquest. With the pronouncement of these findings I shall now adjourn this case.'

So, with the crash of the gavel on the bench still echoing around the cramped cavity of the stone-clad room, Colonel Hicks departed, leaving the public gallery in stunned silence at the words they had just heard and certain members in astonished disbelief of their consequence.

The rain pelted relentlessly against the French windows of the drawing room, painting a fitting grey and dreary backdrop to the equally austere proceedings which this room was upon this, another, Friday afternoon, about to witness uncharacteristically again. Turning from this drab view, as he placed the final pieces of the mental jigsaw puzzle into their rightful place in his methodical and ordered mind, Inspector Dentworth, like a conductor assembling his orchestra for the commencement of a performance with the tap of his baton, decisively cleared his deep voice bringing all assembled occupants of the room, which buzzed with the muted hum of discreet conversation, to a respectful, almost reverent, silence.

Gesturing towards the rain-drenched window glass with a nonchalant wave of his thin hand, the inspector opened the proceedings by way of the following words of polite welcome.

'I do trust that this most inclement weather, which we have been plagued with since first light, has not caused too much inconvenience to your progress here this afternoon. Rest assured, I am most grateful to all of you now assembled here in this fine room for the assiduous concern for punctuality you have displayed in such trying conditions. You may all be wondering what good your efforts in this regard could be. For that matter, why indeed have I so formally requested your attendance here this afternoon. Nonetheless, I do earnestly believe that all your endeavours and enquiries in this matter will be richly rewarded and answered by the time of our parting, later this day.'

Whereupon, before the inspector could continue any further, the calm clear voice of Dr Mathews rose in urgent interjection and simple enquiry, 'Is that to say, Inspector, that, before this afternoon is through, we will know the identity of the murderer of the Earl of Marlford?

'That well may be the case, Dr Mathews,' Inspector Dentworth succinctly yet cryptically replied, the result of which was a combined and sudden intake of air in shocked response by the drawing room's assembled occupants as – at what had been the inspector's initial request upon their recent earlier arrival in the grand room – they settled themselves into the same chairs they had occupied the fateful afternoon, some Fridays previously. The inspector, at this point of disturbance, thus cast his gaze surreptitiously across the sombre gathering, which, he noted in passing, constituted the following individuals; as host once more, Mr Montague Carlile dressed in his usual insouciant manner and seated as always in his wheelchair with the tattered red carriage rug on duty across his apparently withered legs, and positioned at the centre of the cluster of chintz-covered comfortable chairs. Gathered around him were the handsomely dark figure of the ageing Dr Mathews, the Lady Isabella Penman-Smythe still draped in her dark shrouds of mourning for her late father, Mr John Smith with a touch more of a confident manner to his clean-cut bearing and, in attendance at the side of the room, the ever-dapper Mr Collins, the butler, accompanied this day by a rather flustered Mrs Christian, the cook, and a curious Mr Thompson, the land agent. It was thus to this still astonished and silent gathering that the inspector spoke once again.

'Now, Your Ladyship, lady and gentlemen, with all of you here having been present at the inquest conducted by Colonel Hicks yesterday, you are now fully aware by what means His Lordship met his death upon the afternoon of the twenty-ninth of September last, by a most insidious mode and one which was based on knowledge which was supposedly known by only two people. The knowledge of which I speak is that of the now late Earl's total and fatal intolerance to any form of alcoholic spirit in his system, and the two people who were party to this information were the deceased himself and his Harley Street specialist physician, Sir Garfield Pembleton. In association with these two points, we must now consider the third fact: that a partially consumed pastry containing a high level of pure alcoholic spirit was found in the clenched fist of the deceased. Alcohol was also found to be present in a smaller quantity in the remaining similar pastry, but not in any of the other fare on offer that afternoon, only in the crushed remnants of the master's horn. Subsequent to this information, you have heard the postulated method for the said alcohol to have been introduced into the pastry as being that of hypodermic injection.

'Together, all these facts beg me to question of each of you gathered here in this very room where such a barbaric crime was committed, who had the means, the opportunity and the motive for this heinous crime to be committed against such a pillar of the community as the late Lord Rupert Henry Penman-Smythe? Well, let us look at this methodically.

'First Dr Mathews'– the inspector turned his gaze from where he sat in the chair previously occupied by the Earl directly upon the passive face of the reputable country physician to be pleasantly greeted by an expression of balance and steadfast honesty in his dark eyes – 'by virtue of his profession had the means, the hypodermic syringe and alcoholic spirit being common tools of his trade. I am sure that a day does not go by without his use of these implements.' The inspector received a nod of confirmation from the good doctor for the utterance of these words. 'Now let us turn our attention to the second point, that of opportunity. Did Dr Mathews have a suitable opportunity to commit the crime? Let us look at his movements upon that afternoon. He arrived here, at Carlile Manor, a couple of minutes after three o'clock. He proceeded to the drawing room where he sat in full view of all the other guests and partook of afternoon tea. Then, at some time just after four o'clock he was requested to attend an injured stable boy where he remained until approximately ten minutes to five. Whereupon he returned directly across the lawn, meeting up with the Lady Isabella and Mr Smith in whose company he remained and, having gathered Mr Carlile into this group, proceeded back to the drawing room to find the Earl dead. His movements and their timing have been duly verified to my satisfaction, thereby leaving him no real opportunity of committing this crime. Finally, if we look at motive for the doctor's part, there appears to be no possible motive for the untimely death of Lord Rupert Penman-

Smythe, Doctor Mathews having had but a passing acquaintanceship with the late Earl as physician to his estate workers. Thus I believe we may cross Dr Mathews off our list of suspects in what has developed into, at times, a most baffling but always most intriguing case,' the inspector confidently stated, in the process casting a wry smile towards the ever-composed and emotionless countenance of Dr Mathews.

Then, as he paused briefly to gather together the threads of his thoughts, Inspector Dentworth, his grey eyes glistening brightly from behind his highly polished glasses, again cast his gaze discreetly across the faces of the occupants of this gracious room. He was rewarded for his effort by a mixture of expressions from an air of disregard and indifference of the serious nature of this encounter on the parts of both Messrs Carlile and Smith to nervous curiosity on the parts of both the Lady Isabella and Mrs Christian, with Messrs Thompson and Collins showing only respectful interest in the ongoing proceedings. Having noted this spectrum of reactions, Inspector Dentworth, with his usual calm and orderly manner in place, continued his oration as he turned his attention this time towards the upright figure of Mr Thompson, Mr Carlile's long serving and competent land agent, this giant of a man who now stood with his large muscular hands clasped peaceably before him.

'Now,' he continued, 'let us look at the actions of Mr Thompson upon the said afternoon. Did he have the means to commit this horrendous crime? I would say not. What access would he have in his duties as land agent here at Carlile Manor in procuring a hypodermic syringe? I would say very little. Opportunity? No obvious opportunity, as he did not come near the main house until the usual appointed time of the weekly meeting between himself and his master and, having been observed by Mr Carlile as he sat on the terrace after the conclusion of their talks, to return immediately in the direction of his estate office. Given that he was observed on the platform of the Marlford station at around five o'clock in the process of boarding the train for Swindon, I do not believe it to be humanly possible for Mr Thompson to have committed this crime. Finally, if we look at motive, there is in my opinion, none present in this case. Mr

Thompson knew the late Earl by reputation and name only and would by that fact have had no opportunity of obtaining the knowledge of the Earl's medical condition. Further to these points, the Earl's early demise would grant to Mr Thompson or Dr Mathews for that matter no fortuitous change in the circumstance of their existence. So, again, we may cross this gentleman off our list.'

Pausing to draw breath once more, the inspector was instantly bombarded by a hail of raised and concerned voices.

'I do hope, Inspector, that all this is leading somewhere for it seems to me at this point to be nothing but a dreadful waste of everyone's most precious time. If you indeed know the identity of the scoundrel who committed this dastardly crime then let his name be known now,' Montague blasted out in a manner possessed of great acerbity.

'Yes, Inspector, I can only agree with the sentiments just expressed by Mr Carlile. I well understand that you truly wish to catch the fiend who murdered my dearly loved papa, as I am sure everyone here does, but must we be subjected to these apparently needless musings on your part,' the Lady Isabella fiercely stated, her words forging an unlikely bond between the Lady and the laird.

'Calm yourself, Your Ladyship and Mr Carlile. Please extend to me a little patience in this matter for, as I have said, all will be revealed before any of us leave this room this afternoon. Now with your kind permission, I will continue,' Inspector Dentworth diplomatically responded and, having received for his trouble a gruff grunt from Montague and an exasperated huff from the Lady Isabella, he patiently continued.

'Now, where were we? Yes, now we come to Mrs Christian.' The utterance of this name elicited a howl of indignant anguish from its possessor, which the inspector discreetly ignored. 'Where does this domestic figure in the scheme of this crime, one wonders? Again we must look at means, opportunity and motive. Firstly, means. Living her entire working life below stairs in the confines of the kitchen, I consider that Mrs Christian would have had all but no chance of obtaining both the means or the knowledge for this crime. With the lines of communication between these two great country houses having been discontinued by the occurrences of life in each home many years before, those being the death of the Earl's wife and his speedy dispatch to South Africa occurring at about the same time as Mr Carlile's tragic hunting accident. Further, the alcoholic spirit was to our knowledge only placed in two of the pastry horns which, if it had been at the hands of Mrs Christian, it would have to have been done whilst the fare was under lock and key in her cake pantry, with a two in six chance of His Lordship choosing the right pastry or indeed having the pastry at all. I think too much would be left to the demons of fate in this regard. No one else present that afternoon has mentioned tasting alcohol.'

The inspector paused briefly, noting the appropriate heads shaking in the negative to this last statement. Satisfied with this response, he continued.

'Thus, opportunity in this case would be all but non-existent. Then what of motive? Mrs Christian had no score to settle with His Lordship. It is highly unlikely that she had ever come in contact with the man, much less incurred his wrath, enough to wish him dead. If the truth be known, she probably appreciated greatly the late Earl. For indeed, if not for his insistence all those years ago that the Carlile family be resident in their country home for the weekend of sport and festivities, her life would have remained a lonely existence without the considerate companionship of her esteemed colleague, Mr Collins, for whom, over the long and at times torturous years, the lady has developed a deep and sincere fondness.' These words yet again elicited a piercing howl of indignant protest on the part of the flushed Mrs Christian which the inspector again chose to ignore discreetly. 'Given all this, it is thus my belief that we may dispense with Mrs Christian as a suspect in this case. Now let us move on.

'Speaking of Mr Collins, let us now direct our attention towards the study of his actions upon that afternoon. Indeed, was this man possessed of means, opportunity and motive for this crime? Let us examine the facts before us. Initially, what contact did Mr Collins have with the fare on offer? By Mrs Christian's testimony, the fare was under lock and key prior to her personally transporting it upstairs just before the arrival of the guests that afternoon. Then, by his own admission, Mr Collins stated that upon hearing the front doorbell he proceeded from his post in the servants' hall and having greeted all the guests conducted them to the drawing room, where he remained on view to all until his departure to the stables. The only cloud of doubt which seems to hang over this man's actions is the time between his departure from the stables and his sighting on the Marlford station platform. However, given his age and decreased level of agility, it would appear that all the unaccounted time would have been taken up with his movement from Carlile Manor to the station and subsequently back again. It could again be said that Mr Collins, having procured the required apparatus from his master's effects, could have discreetly injected the pastries prior to leaving for the stables. However, as it would appear that only two of the pastries seem to have been affected by the alcohol, it would again be leaving a great deal to chance. That leaves us finally to consider the motive for this act on the part of Mr Collins and here it runs deep and passionate. For indeed by virtue of the hunting accident caused in part by the late Earl's insistence of the Carlile family's attendance all those years ago, Mr Collins had been made to endure a long and lonely life here in the country. Cut off so drastically from his friends, including the developing affectionate companionship of Miss Gladys Quimby and life in London, his feelings towards the Earl may well have festered in his mind like a pus-riddled sore until finally it had exploded into this devious action but, again, what knowledge would this simple man have had of the Earl's condition and thereby its use in his demise. Very little, I would think. Which leaves us to once more ponder this perplexing puzzle.'

With the utterance of those polite words and before any fur-ther direction of this case on the part of the calmly acting inspector, a voice, rich with fierce emotion, suddenly interjected, 'Will you get on with it, man. You surely must believe you know who committed this heinous crime against the late Earl of Marlford. So stop playing with us all like a cat with a nest of mice and tell us,' Montague Carlile vehemently protested, a protest in which he was quickly joined by others present in the room.

'Yes, Inspector, I must agree with Mr Carlile here. It is quite unconscionable the treatment we are receiving this afternoon at your hands. Further, I feel we are well within our rights to lodge a formal complaint at this treatment to your superiors at Scotland Yard,' the Lady Isabella defiantly stated.

'I must also agree, Inspector. Have we not all suffered enough? I beseech you, Inspector, bring our suffering, to an end,' Mr John Smith, a picture of wrought-up emotion, as evidenced by his hands which he nervously clasped and unclasped as they lay restlessly in his lap, distressfully pleaded.

'Yes, Mr John Andrew Smith, I believe I may in part be able to bring your suffering to an end at this point in the proceedings,' Inspector Dentworth cryptically responded. As he turned his attention fully upon the now quivering mass which resided before him, and before any reply on the part of this shocked being, the inspector, his grey eyes gleaming stoically, continued by officiously barking out the following simple command, 'Sergeant Jones, come.'

The utterance of these three words having the effect of the drawing-room door gently opening to reveal to the assembled group three very distinctly different sights, that of Sergeant Jones as usual resplendent in his crisp policeman's uniform in the unusual role of escort to two ladies. For upon each of Sergeant Jones's two thick arms resided a lady each of diverse character and position, whom the sergeant adroitly conducted across the threshold and into the room to stand before his chief.

'Thank you, Sergeant Jones, you may now take up your position on the chair by the door,' Inspector Dentworth quietly commanded, indicating as he did to his subordinate the empty straight-backed chair by the French windows.

'Yes, Inspector,' Sergeant Jones plainly replied as he quickly moved across the room to take his requested position.

'Now, ladies, if you would be so kind as to sit here opposite Mr Smith,' the inspector politely instructed, indicating as he did two chairs situated strategically directly across from Mr Smith in the cluster of comfortable chairs.

With a nod of acknowledgement on the part of these two new members of this group and having seen them settled at ease in their chairs, the inspector turned his attention once again in the direction of the now bemused occupants of the room to be greeted instantly by a ferocious attack of bitter words on the part of the group's senior member.

'Catherine, it is you, Catherine, is it not? Yes, it is you! How dare you show your face here in my house uninvited by me, as it is. What brings you here anyway? Were you invited here? Who asked for your attendance here this afternoon without asking my permission, I might add? Why are you here, woman?'

Having taken advantage of a brief pause in this furious tirade on the part of the crusty Montague Carlile as he stopped to draw a much needed breath, Inspector Dentworth decisively counted this previous vitriolic attack by calmly stating, 'It was at my invitation that Mrs Catherine Carlile ventured from her home in London today in the accompaniment, I might add, of her trusted maid Miss Gladys Quimby, to be in attendance here this afternoon. Their reason for being here this afternoon is quite simply to return to this young man, Mr John Andrew Smith, here, his true identity in life.' At this point the inspector, with a flick of his wrist, indicated towards Mr Smith.

With the utterance of these simple words, a hush instantly fell over the assembled group, as all sat in a state of intense bewilderment, unable to comprehend fully the words previously spoken and their true significance to all concerned, none more so than Mr Smith himself.

As he struggled to the total realisation of the inspector's words, Mr Smith, in a haze of childlike wonderment edged with disbelief, turned his increasingly troubled face to stare directly into that of the inspector's placid countenance and mumbled almost incoherently, 'You know who I am? Please, Inspector, if that is truly the case, I beg of you... do not leave me in the dark a moment longer.'

With the expression of this heartfelt plea, Inspector Dentworth gestured with a slight nod of his intelligent head to the lady and her woman-servant seated beside him to take command of the proceedings. Taking up the mantel of responsibility with her usual consummate ease and sense of fierce determination, Catherine Carlile in turn gestured to her trusted maid, Gladys, who commenced to speak soothingly to the distraught young man seated opposite her.

'Now then, young sir, do you by any chance recognise me?' Gladys quietly requested of the still stunned John Smith.

'I believe, madam, that I saw you in the chapel yard... the day of the funeral service for Lord Rupert Penman-Smythe,' John Smith replied in his usual halting and breathless manner.

'Ah were partially gloppened when ah sin tha at funeral. Ow's thoo getting' on lad? Come on, yer lahtle ullert talk tiv thi roly-poly puddin' mi lalitle jack-in-t'-box,' Gladys gently cajoled as she slid effortlessly back into her native Yorkshire tongue, in an effort to jog a long-lost memory on the part of the frustrated young man seated before her.

Her efforts were instantly rewarded by the young man's sudden and unhesitating reply of, 'Now then, Gladys, what have Mama and Papa told you... about lapsing from the King's English, in my hearing... my dear old thing. Ah fain to sithee.'

With the unheralded escape of these words from his trembling lips, John Smith's battered frame slumped deep into his chair, burying his face in his shaking hands. As his precariously balanced demeanour dissolved in an outpouring of bitter sweet tears he sobbed uncontrollably for some minutes.

Then, having regained his composure somewhat, he raised his dishevelled dark-haired head from his twitching hands to stare blankly into the face opposite him and meekly enquired, his voice ringing with the profound fear born of genuine uncertainty of the proceedings occurring around him, 'I don't understand. Why should I answer... your strange mutterings as I did? I am sure I do not know you. Why should I know you? What is all this about... a roly-poly pudding, and a jack-in-the-box? It all seems such nonsense. Yet your words leave me with vague and unnerving feelings... of a lost childhood, feelings which I have not felt since before the war. I fear I must truly... be going totally mad!'

Registering the distress displayed by the terrified young man seated opposite her, Catherine, as her long buried motherly instincts surged once more to the surface casting final reassurance over and confirmation of her strongly held beliefs, now hastily interjected with the following strange mixture of maternal comfort and startling revelation.

'Do not be afraid, my dear boy. There is nothing to fear now that you are home again with your family,' immediately registering the expression of intense shock which upon the utterance of these words had enveloped John Smith's face.

Catherine speedily continued in an attempt to allay the obviously continually rising fear and confusion in this tortured young fellow's mind,

'Let me allay your fears immediately by saying it is my sincere belief that your name is Reginald Alexander Carlile,' to which a diverse mixture of exclamations and expletives issued forth from the other members of the assembled group.

Oblivious to this intense cacophony surging around her, Catherine doggedly continued with the following quietly spoken words, 'Yes, I believe you are in point of fact my long-lost son and the heir to all that your father, Montague Alexander Carlile, possesses.'

As the effect of these words settled upon the assembled group, John Smith shot a glance at the stern face of Inspector Dentworth and hesitantly enquired, 'Is this the truth, Inspector? Am I indeed finally home? Amongst my family? Do I indeed have my name and heritage... returned to me?'

With his countenance aglow with compassionate concern for the crumpled shadow of a man who sat before him, Inspector Dentworth judiciously replied, 'Well, sir, having conducted the most exhaustive investigations possible under these most extraordinary circumstances with regard to this matter, given the extensive assistance of the Ministry of the Army and, of course, this exceptionally observant lady here' – Inspector Dentworth graciously indicating Miss Gladys Quimby – 'it is truly our opinion that your identity has indeed been recovered once more.'

With these words of verification from Inspector Dentworth's thin pale lips, the identity of John Andrew Smith drifted silently into obscurity for ever to be substituted from this moment on in the hearts and minds of all those present by that of Reginald Alexander Carlile.

In the midst of all that was transpiring, the Lady Isabella grabbed Reginald's arm and was heard to whisper, as Reginald looked at both Montague and Catherine, 'Reginald! I like that better than plain John. Now I know the true name of the man whom I am going to marry.'

The final act of this confirmation came in the simple act of a mother's embrace as Catherine lent forward wrapping her strong yet elegantly proportioned arms around the skeletal and sobbing form of her only born child and placed a passionate kiss upon his badly scarred cheek. As this mother and her son, in the act of parting from their moving embrace, lifted their heads to view again the scene before them, their efforts were greeted by the unexpected sight of the previously crusty and cantankerous Montague Carlile, now a picture of uncontrollable pride and pleasure as evidenced by the heavy trails of sweet tears of joy which continued to fall like rain across his craggy features. He lifted and outstretched his arms towards them in a poignant plea to gather his family once more unto him. Without a word needing to be spoken, two became three, and individuals again became a family as, with the tears that fell away, so did the years of pain and fear for all concerned leaving in their wake a newly united family to face the continuing trauma of this life and, more particularly, this day, the horrors of which were about to descend once more as Inspector Dentworth, who had remained silent in the course of this reunion, now took command again as his rich, clear words of instruction rang out across the expanse of the humming room, bringing all those present to attention once more.

'Now then, Your Ladyship, ladies and gentlemen, much as I am pleased for Mr Smith or I should now say Mr Reginald Carlile to have been granted his wish of true identity there is, however, still the outstanding matter of the murder of the Earl of Marlford to be considered here this afternoon. I would therefore ask you all to take your seats once more so that we may continue in our ongoing investigations of this most important matter.'

Having thus observed with the hint of a wry smile upon his composed face the somewhat peculiar sight of this gathering of grown adults in what an outsider might well have described as a haphazard attempt at the children's game of musical chairs, as Catherine and Reginald moved to seat themselves beside Montague at the expense of the settled comfort of Dr Mathews, and Gladys moved to place herself between Collins and Mrs Christian, Inspector Dentworth calmly said, 'Now, if everyone is settled comfortably once more.' These words having produced a wave of murmured assent on the part of all present, Inspector Dentworth stolidly stated, 'I will now continue.'

Now turning to stare upon the still slightly bewildered countenance of Reginald Carlile, the inspector sternly said, 'Mr Reginald Alexander Carlile, I informed you a little earlier that I believed I could in part relieve your suffering. That I hope I have achieved.'

To which Reginald immediately interposed with an obviously ardent and uncharacteristically forthright response of, 'Rather more, Inspector, than I could ever have truly hoped for. I am, and will always remain... eternally grateful to you and all those concerned... for your apparently tireless efforts in regard to this most difficult matter. My family has been returned to me... and my future is now secure.'

'Yes, Mr Carlile, your family will, I am sure, be of great comfort and support to you in the times ahead,' Inspector Dentworth cryptically replied as he nonchalantly removed his wire-framed spectacles from his lean, intelligent face and, taking a starched white handkerchief from the breast pocket of his dark grey jacket, commenced to clean the already glistening lenses. It was thus into this atmosphere of subdued activity that the inspector so dextrously had created that he lobbed his most decisive volley of verbal shots in this ongoing battle, as he raised his penetrating grey eyes to stare directly into the lone green oculus of Reginald Carlile and so determinedly spoke.

'Now then, Mr Reginald Alexander Carlile, I must request you to assist us further with our ongoing investigation and recount yet again your movements on that Friday afternoon, from the time of your arrival here at Carlile Manor to when the lifeless body of the Earl of Marlford was discovered in this very room.'

'Surely, Inspector, with all that has just transpired, those investigations can now wait for a short time at least. This is indeed a time for celebration. For it is not very often in a man's life that God in His Heaven grants you a second chance by returning your family to you,' Montague Carlile purposefully interjected as he sat majestically in his newly rediscovered position of strength flanked as he was by Reginald and Catherine.

'No, Mr Montague Carlile, this matter cannot wait. Come now, Mr Reginald Carlile, the sooner you start, the sooner you will be finished. Now, what truly happened that Friday afternoon?' Inspector Dentworth doggedly enquired, displaying a perseverance indicative of his terrier reputation. As he sensed a near at hand conquest as strongly as any fox's scent, the inspector brusquely continued his verbal bombardment.

'What really did happen that afternoon? Why did you come back to the house, leaving the Lady Isabella alone in the summer house? Did you indeed stop before you reached the drawing room and turn back as you have previously informed us, or did you proceed into the room and thereupon somehow inject the fare with the alcohol, thereby causing the Earl's untimely death? Tell us what happened, Mr Reginald Carlile? Further, is it not true that you could not stand the late Earl of Marlford and had come in the few short weeks you had habituated under the same roof to despise the position of power he held over the Lady Isabella and thereby yourself? I put it to you, sir, that the late Earl of Marlford had, in the last few days before his death, issued an ultimatum that if his only child continued on her chosen path of marriage to you, Lord Rupert would withhold her sizeable allowance and disassociate himself from her in all aspects of life including her inheritance of his vast estate upon his death. You could not have that now, could you, sir? You could see your one chance for a life of privilege and position rapidly disappearing and by your own admission the war had left you without name, family or position, a precarious situation for a man with no profession and no prospects. Having given so much to your country, you saw it as your right to take something back from those who you saw to have it all, didn't you, Mr Reginald Carlile?

'The only aspect of this case which leaves me at a loss is how did you find out about the Earl's most unusual condition? As far as we were aware, from the Earl's own Harley Street specialist physician, Sir Garfield Pembleton, Lord Rupert and himself were the only two people in possession of this knowledge, but then Sir Garfield Pembleton is your personal physician as well, isn't he, Mr Reginald Carlile? How did you find out? Come on, Mr

Carlile, tell us all about it. Why did you do it, lad? You know you will hang for this.'

With those last catastrophic words reverberating around the room, Reginald was left sitting in stunned silence, as at first a look of total bewilderment and then fear etched into his increasingly contorted face. As the full realisation of the exact implications of Inspector Dentworth's words slowly dawned in Reginald's dazed mind, a cacophony of voices raised themselves in abject protest around him.

'No, Inspector, this cannot be true,' pleaded Catherine desperately.

'Here sits before you a man of peace and love, not murder and hate,' intoned the Lady Isabella passionately.

'Inspector, by your own endeavours you have just returned my son to me. Now you are telling me I must lose him again. I'll not sit by quietly and let that happen. You'll have a damn good fight on your hands if you try,' Montague Carlile ardently espoused.

'Please everyone, calm yourself. All I want at this moment is to hear from Mr Reginald Carlile in his own words what happened that afternoon. That is all. Now, Reginald, are you ready to tell me exactly what happened during that fateful escapade at Carlile Manor?' Inspector Dentworth, his voice having returned to its usual velvet smoothness, knowingly enquired.

'I have told you all my actions on that day, Inspector. There is nothing more I can tell you,' Reginald replied, his voice suddenly taking on a stubborn and highly defiant tone.

'I don't believe that is entirely the case, Mr Reginald Carlile. Now let us run through the facts as they pertain to you in this case, if you please,' Inspector Dentworth persistently requested. Having obtained for his trouble a contemptuous nod of grumbling assent on the part of Reginald, Inspector Dentworth quickly surged forth in his quest by commencing his own oratorical interpretation of the events of the afternoon.

'Now, Mr Carlile, please correct me if I am wrong in any detail. You arrived here in the company of the late Earl and his daughter, the Lady Isabella Penman-Smythe, at a few minutes before three o'clock on the afternoon in question. Upon the all but immediate arrival of Dr Mathews you were, after some passing introductions, escorted to this room and your awaiting host for the afternoon's festivities, Mr Montague Carlile. Thereupon, further more formal introductions were conducted and all parties were settled in this ring of most comfortable chairs and afternoon tea was commenced to be served by Collins, the butler, from his domain of the amply covered sideboard. You and the Lady Isabella were observed to consume your tea and fare on offer at a quite prodigious rate. Why was that, Mr Carlile? Was there indeed somewhere else you wished to be? At whose instigation did you leave the room so early in the proceedings?'

'Yes, Inspector, there was somewhere else we wished to be. By mutual agreement, we wished to be alone... together and away from the stuffy confines of this room... and the suffocating influence of that most bombastic of men... the Earl of Marlford,' Reginald angrily resounded, the inspector's simple enquiry acting as the lever of a floodgate as Reginald continued in his bitter tirade.

'You see, Inspector, upon our return to Beeches Hall from Europe recently... the late Earl was at first a most gracious host, considerate... and most accommodating of my many and varied needs. However, when we subsequently informed him of our intention to marry... in the summer of next year, his demeanour changed completely. He became obstinate in his refusal to cast upon... our forthcoming union his blessing and, more pointedly, badgered and bullied... my beloved Isabella to the point where he threatened her that... if she continued upon her chosen course, he could and would see that she and I... were forced out of society and into poverty.'

'I see, Mr Carlile, that is most enlightening. Now, let us continue. You strolled around the grounds for a short time and then pleading tiredness suggested to the Lady Isabella that you both retreat to the relative seclusion of the summer house. Once settled there, you suggested to us that you remained there talking for some considerable time during which the Lady Isabella fell soundly asleep. At first, you told us that you had both remained in the summer house until your eventual return to the house. However, evidence as tendered to us by Mr Montague Carlile, and later verified by your own admission, suggested that whilst the Lady Isabella was apparently soundly asleep in the summer house, you ventured back to the main house with the intention of having it out once and for all with Lord Rupert Penman-Smythe for the offhand manner in which he was conducting himself towards his only child, perhaps in an effort, I might suggest, to come to some mutually beneficial arrangement for all concerned.'

'What do you mean by that last statement, Inspector? If you are implying that I would act as Judas... and renounce my love for some pieces of silver... then you are very mistaken,' Reginald angrily exploded. Then as if having exhausted all energy in this outburst he resumed his usual composure and continued.

'As I have confessed to you, I left the summer house and returned to the main house, leaving the Lady Isabella sleeping... with the sole intention of asking for His Lordship to have a compassionate change of heart... in this most delicate and desperate matter. However, as I have told you before I lost my nerve... before reaching the drawing room, standing in motion-less contemplation... for a number of minutes on the terrace before retracing my steps... back to my beloved fiancée, who remained sleeping in my absence. As I have told you before, having ascertained the swift... and extended passage of time, I woke Isabella and we returned across the grounds... where we met Dr Mathews and, subsequently, joined Mr Montague Carlile on the terrace... and returned to the drawing room... where we found Lord Rupert dead,' Reginald impassively concluded.

'That, again, is very interesting, Mr Reginald Carlile. How long do you think you were away from the summer house that afternoon?' Inspector Dentworth smoothly enquired. Then, as a casual adjunct to the proceedings, he added, 'By the way, Reginald, when you enacted your return to the house, did you have in your possession that leather pouch you have previously shown us containing your pain relief medication and apparatus?'

'Firstly, in answer to the timings of my actions, I don't think I could rightly say, Inspector. Perhaps ten minutes... at the most. I did not look at my watch at the time... I left the summer house and it was some minutes after my return... that I consulted my watch before waking the Lady Isabella. Secondly, Inspector, by some strange stroke of chance... I did not have that pouch with me at that time. My dearest Isabella, so concerned for my welfare as she is... had deemed that I had been a little heavy handed with my self-prescribing... of my medication, as I must admit, I am prone to do when feeling anxious... and had, whilst we sat in the summer house, asked to act as its caretaker... for the rest of the afternoon,' Reginald thoughtfully replied.

'Thank you for that, Mr Carlile. In passing, you mentioned that the Lady Isabella was asleep when you left the summer house and was still asleep when you returned. By your own assumption, the Lady Isabella remained asleep during your entire absence from the summer house. Yet, can you indeed be sure of that fact, young fellow?' Inspector Dentworth, his grey eyes gleaming with an inner fire of dark knowledge, meaningfully enquired of the now dumbfounded Reginald Carlile.

'I don't understand, Inspector. What are you saying?' Reginald naively enquired, his thin voice echoing the childlike innocence of his pure heart.

Suddenly from across the room came a gentle laugh, halting Reginald in the midst of his confused mumblings, allowing the following amused words of reproach to be aired.

'Oh, do be quiet, my dear foolish boy. You don't understand do you, my love. You never do.'

'No, Your Ladyship, he does not understand and, by the faces I see before me, neither does anyone else in this room. If you have no objection, I will place before you my interpretation of the events of that afternoon, events which I believe saw you murder your own father.' These words having generated an expected wave of shocked expressions and a frenzied buzz of whispered comment on the part of the other occupants of the room, Inspector Dentworth sat and patiently waited for the initial excitement to fade away before he thoughtfully continued.

'Please feel free to correct me at any time if I am wrong in any detail.' With a nod of polite assent from the perfectly coiffured head of auburn-coloured hair, Inspector Dentworth commenced upon his tale.

'Now, let us methodically proceed through the afternoon in question, as it unfolded itself. You arrived at Carlile Manor at a few minutes before three o'clock in the company of your late father, the Right Hon. the Earl of Marlford, and the man whom you then knew as Mr John Smith. With the subsequent and timely arrival of Dr Mathews, you were conducted by Collins to the drawing room. Once there and with formal introductions having been completed, you were invited by your gracious host, Mr Montague Carlile, to partake of afternoon tea.

'It has been noted by all others present that afternoon that both you and Mr Reginald Carlile consumed your tea and your selection of the fare on offer at a most prodigious rate, thus allowing you to bid easy leave of the rest of the party for what you explained as a breath of fresh air while they completed their own consumption of the said fare. However, it was more than that, you had had as much as you could bear of your own father's pompous manner. The thought of yet another repeat oration on the topic of his recent and protracted exploits in South Africa filled you with dread. This feeling, being compounded by the thought that he may throw into the open forum of this social gathering your current personal problems for general discussion by virtual strangers, as he had on previous occasions in your life been prone to do, his already having discussed the matter at some length previously with your host for the afternoon.

'Having escaped from the drawing room, you deliberately walked at a brisk pace up and down the grounds and gardens in an effort to tire your companion whose stamina you knew to be still greatly depleted. With your aim readily achieved, Mr Reginald Carlile proclaimed the need to rest in the conveniently near at hand summer house. Then, having settled yourselves in the relative peace and seclusion offered by this slightly out of the way structure, you adroitly steered the conversation from the reminiscences of your first meeting, touching on the deep and affectionate bond which developed between you in those times of great adversity during the war to the more pleasant experiences you shared during your subsequent excursions in the countryside of Europe, all the while consolidating your effort to reinforce in Mr Reginald Carlile's mind, as it teetered precariously on the precipice of mental imbalance, the thought that all your worries for the future stemmed from one man and no other, one Lord Rupert Henry Penman-Smythe. Yet, having observed that day the fluctuating state of Mr Reginald Carlile's mind you knew that that mental imbalance was indeed a very suspect instrument in which to place your trust for your entire future happiness. Having planted the seed of intense discontent through these simple musings over your past, present and future times together, you knew Mr Reginald Carlile would finally break and confront the Earl once more; however, you could not be sure what the end result this confrontation would secure.

'In passing, might I also add that from your prudently chosen vantage point in the summer house, a well-known place of hiding and adventure from the summers of your childhood, you had observed the departure from the drawing room of Dr Mathews and Collins and, subsequently, Mr Montague Carlile, thereby leaving your target free for your mark. With you feigning sleep, Mr Reginald Carlile conducted himself slowly back across the unfamiliar terrain to the house, in the process and unknown to you being observed directly by Mr Montague Carlile and by inference Mr Thompson as they sat in the adjacent smoking room. Having seen him on his way and remaining on his blind side, you, the Lady Isabella Penman-Smythe, lithely scampered across from the summer house and entering the house via the side door quietly ventured along the darkened and empty corridors until you reached the drawing-room door.

'I further make the assertion that you then gently opened this door' – the inspector indicating with a dramatic wave of his thin hand towards the ornate drawing-room door – 'before you. Finding the Earl still seated in his chair, thankfully for your purposes with his back turned to you, you quietly slipped into the room and using the hypodermic syringe, belonging to Mr Smith which you had earlier confiscated from his control and subsequently before leaving the summer house had quickly loaded with alcohol from the bottle he carried in the same pouch, injected the fatal doses of alcohol into what you observed to be the two remaining and final samples of fare your father would partake of, that of the crowning glory, the master's horn. You then slipped back out of the drawing room and quickly returned to the summer house, thereby transferring any blame which may ensue on to the weakened shoulders of the man then known as Mr

Smith, in the misguided knowledge that given his current and documented mental state he could and would not be found guilty of the crime of murder. Thus your future happiness and financial security was secured.' Inspector Dentworth having arrived at his ultimate conclusion then fell silent, his keen grey eyes surveying and noting the elegant and totally composed nature of the face before him, those piercing sapphire blue eyes still mesmerising as they lay like shining pebbles in a calm and crystal clear pool.

As all present waited with veiled yet eager anticipation of the expected response, the tempest of wind and rain which had continued to rage unabated outside during these discussions suddenly heightened further as a percussive symphony of thunder reverberated through the lingering silence, providing a macabre fanfare to the final act in this protracted drama. Against this tympanic backdrop, a clear modulated voice rang out in a laughing tone.

'A very interesting interpretation of the dreadful events of that afternoon, Inspector. I am sure if you took the trouble to write those words down on paper you would have a best-seller on your hands, purely fiction of course,' the Lady Isabella Penman-Smythe jocularly stated to the room in general. Then, adopting a more serious intent in her manner, she continued.

'Seriously, Inspector, if I wished to dispose of my late father for whatever reason, I feel sure I would not do it in such a public manner. Nonetheless, I do admit that some of what you have just stated is quite true. Since my return to Beeches Hall with Mr Smith or, as I should now rightly call him Mr Reginald Carlile' – at the mention of this name the Lady Isabella flashed an affectionate and sincere smile towards her fiancé and then determinedly continued – 'there had been an increasing degree of animosity displayed by my late father towards us upon his being informed of our intention to marry. Yes, it is quite true that he bullied and badgered me constantly about the unsuitability of Mr Carlile as my future husband and what subsequently would be the administrator upon the Earl's death of his vast estate. Yes, we were eager to free ourselves of the stuffy confines and overbearing company of the drawing room that afternoon. Yes, Inspector, whilst we sat in the tranquil peace of the summer house I did, by carefully chosen words, encourage Mr Carlile to confront the late Earl. Like any woman, Inspector, I wanted the man that I intended to marry to be prepared to fight for my honour. My beloved had once been prepared to fight for king and country, so why not now for love? Yes, I whipped his spirits into a frenzy, then sank into apparently deep and somniferous repose. Whereupon Mr Carlile, as if upon some unseen cue, rose and ventured forth back towards the house.

'Having seen my love on his way, I sat for a fleeting moment to reflect upon my actions and instantly decided that I had been in dreadful error. What course might Mr Carlile's intentions take in his, at times, confused state of mind? I decided anything was possible. It was in this instant, Inspector, that I decided to follow Mr Carlile to remain within hidden earshot of what occurred, ready to step in if necessary. It was for that reason, and that reason only, Inspector, that I gained admittance to the house through the side door and hurried along the corridor to wait at the drawing-room door. As I held the door only partially open so as not to disturb the room's occupants, the identity of which I was in point of fact not entirely sure, I observed my late father seated alone as you have said in his chair with his back towards me and his head slightly lowered as if in deep contemplation. Beside him, I noticed sat one of the cake trays and upon the top plate of that tray resided a single, slightly crushed cream horn. The minutes ticked by slowly. Then I caught the barest glimpse of what I deemed to be Mr Carlile as he stood lolling on his heels at the extreme edge of the drawing-room window. Again the minutes seemed to tick by as an eternity before he turned and disappeared from view in what I presumed correctly to be a characteristic change of heart on his part. Further, I assumed that he would be in the act of returning to the summer house, thus I, too, turned on my heels, closed the drawing-room door and speedily retraced my steps, resuming my previous position of gentle slumber before Mr Carlile's breathless entrance into our retreat. The rest as they say is history. There, Inspector, you have the real truth of this horrible matter and not as you propose some makeshift concoction of half-truths,' the Lady Isabella scathingly concluded, her sapphire blue eyes blazing with a blatantly obvious and totally unyielding determination of her right in this issue which caused the inspector to pause briefly in earnest contemplation.

Roused from his reflection by the distant buzz of the front doorbell, Inspector Dentworth instinctively commanded, 'Collins, stay! Sergeant Jones, go and see what that is all about, will you?'

To which in the characteristically calm and well-modulated voice came the familiar response of, 'Yes, Inspector,' as he dutifully rose from his seat by the window, manoeuvred his way deftly through the cluster of chairs, grouped as they always were beneath the dazzling Venetian crystal chandelier, and disappeared from view into the relative gloom of the dark, panelled corridor.

Having observed his subordinate's dextrous departure from the room, Inspector Dentworth doggedly returned to the matter at hand, as he turned his attention once again upon the still upturned face of the Lady Isabella Penman-Smythe and sternly enquired, 'Your Ladyship, were you aware of the nature of the condition which afflicted the Earl of Marlford to what has been shown to be his fatal detriment? If so, please tell us, by what means did you come by that knowledge?'

'Well, Inspector, strange that you should ask those questions in such a roundabout way. For it was in just such a roundabout way that I indeed became party to that knowledge. However, let me say firstly that my late father was not a man to confide in others, even his own family, in such matters as his own state of health. That is what makes the information I am about to tell you so hard for me to understand.'

Hesitating briefly as if in an effort to gather together and correlate her thoughts and the correct order in which these events happened in her astute mind, the Lady Isabella without further prompting on the part of the now appetent and attentive inspector then surged on in her informative narrative.

'It all came tumbling into my lap, so to speak, by what I now see as sheer coincidence: right place, right time, sort of thing, if you see what I mean. Oh dear! I don't seem to be explaining this at all well, but I'll keep going and hope it comes good in the end. Well, as I was saying, pure coincidence. It all happened on the Monday morning before that Friday, Inspector. For some reason, known only to God in His Heaven, I rose early that particular morning. It must from memory have been a little after half past nine when, having dressed and in the process of descending the stairs on my way to breakfast, I overheard a conversation being conducted between my late father and at that stage an unknown party via the telephone which is situated directly below my position on the stairs in the entrance hall. I admit it was terribly bad manners on my part but, like a child listening for family secrets, I halted in my tracks and whilst remaining on the stairs out of view of my late father I listened to the somewhat one-sided conversation taking place below me. It was during the course of this conversation, the instigation of which took the form of an invitation, that I heard for the first time the nature and extent of my late father's state of ill health. It was also during this telephonic exchange that my late father's derogatory opinion of my choice of a husband was confirmed publicly by his own lips. The conversation having come to a close, my father conducted himself upon his many and varied pursuits around what is the rather vast expanses of Beeches Hall and I, for my part, continued on to breakfast. Oh, by the way, Inspector, I mentioned earlier an invitation. I assume there is no need to assert from whom this invitation was proffered?' the Lady Isabella incisively concluded as she gracefully turned her neat head and glanced nonchalantly in the direction of the laird of the manor.

'Ah, Mr Montague Carlile, the final player in this most intriguing mystery. What part did you indeed play in this whole hideous affair? Let us now, in the light of this new information from Her Ladyship here, again examine your actions leading up to and upon that fateful afternoon, shall we, sir?' Inspector Dentworth courteously commanded as he turned his gaze upon the insouciant form before him. Not allowing Montague time to respond by way of the inevitable protest of innocence, the inspector speedily continued with the following, calmly stated request.

'Now then, Mr Carlile, did you, as has just been stated, indeed learn of the late Earl of Marlford's most unusual illness via the telephone conversation you held with him on the Monday morning prior to the Friday afternoon in question?'

'I am an old man, Inspector. As I have told you before, my mind has a habit of playing tricks with me. The matter of the late Earl's medical condition may have been touched upon during our conversation, however I cannot now remember. The late Earl of Marlford was, Inspector, prone to monopolise such conversations as this one to his own benefit, which from memory I believe he did in this particular case. Much time was spent on the subject most dear to his heart that of the recent return from Europe of his treasured daughter, the Lady Isabella, her past exploits and her proposed future adventures being foremost in his thoughts,' Montague diplomatically replied in a vain attempt to divert attention away from himself.

'So, you are telling us you knew nothing of the most serious nature of His Lordship's illness, Mr Carlile?' Inspector Dentworth doggedly continued in this modern-day inquisition.

'That is correct, Inspector. I simply contacted the Earl to invite him for tea after reading in the local newspaper of his return from abroad. When he subsequently informed me that his daughter and her companion were in residence at Beeches Hall it was only natural that I should extend the invitation to include them as well. In her obviously exhausted state of mind and body after her extensive exploits abroad, might I venture to propose the thought that Her Ladyship was mistaken in what she thought she heard that morning,' Montague smoothly replied.

These final words instantly elicited a highly defiant and staunch response from the Lady Isabella's full red lips.

'I know exactly what I heard that morning, Inspector. If you are truly looking for the murderer of my dearly loved father then look no further than this man,' the Lady Isabella Penman-Smythe indicated, with a flick of the long sensitive fingers of her left hand, the old figure seated in his wheelchair.

'How dare you! I had no good reason to murder my old and dear friend, the Earl of Marlford, unlike some others here. Money and position are powerful catalysts to murder, Inspector,' Montague indignantly yet philosophically responded.

'That may well be, Mr Carlile. However, you must agree that, if not the motive, you did have the means and the opportunity to conduct this heinous act?' the inspector stoically countered.

'By means, are you implying my personal use of the hypodermic syringe and the accompanying morphine and alcohol which I carry with me at all times, Inspector? If so, on that particular afternoon in question, I left the pouch containing this various apparatus on the occasional table beside my chair when I left the room in the company of Mr Thompson, leaving, I might add, a very much alive Lord Rupert Penman-Smythe alone. As has been documented by the other members of the party present that afternoon, we all subsequently returned to the drawing room together. Strangely enough though, Inspector, when I returned to the drawing room, I retrieved my pouch not from where I had left it, but rather on the occasional table beside the body of His Lordship. As for opportunity, Inspector, this would have had to come in the short time between dismissing Mr Thompson and the return of the Lady Isabella, Dr Mathews and Mr Smith or, as he should rightly be called, my son, Reginald Carlile. Time enough perhaps for a healthy man to have accomplished the task, but me, I think not,' Montague evenly responded as he tenaciously clung to his rock of innocence in the surrounding sea of conflict and doubt.

Suddenly, as the room fell silent once more, intently awaiting the inspector's next words of stern command, a crisp knock resounded loudly upon the drawing-room door, instantaneously shattering the recondite concentration of the room's occupants and initiating within them a wave of startled disquiet within their number.

In expeditious response to this request, Inspector Dentworth's rich, deep voice barked out his characteristic encouragement of, 'Enter.'

The strength of his effort had, in passing, the efficacious outcome of calming his cohabitants of this still gracious room to circumspect silence once more. All sat in eager anticipation as the door slowly opened to reveal the thickset figure of Sergeant Jones in accompaniment to the now familiar personage of young Constable Stevens standing in silence on the darkened threshold.

'Oh, it's you, Constable Stevens. What brings you here today in such foul weather?' Inspector Dentworth courteously enquired of the likeable country policeman, indicating as he did the highly inclement weather which was still plainly evident as the rain and wind pounded mercilessly against the glass of the French windows outside.

'Good afternoon to you, Inspector. In simple answer to your enquiry, sir, it is the delivery to you of this portfolio of documents that brings me out in what you so aptly describe as foul weather. The information I have here came straight from Scotland Yard, by personal courier off the last train no more than twenty minutes ago, with the strict instruction for its immediate delivery to you, personally, Inspector. That's why I asked Sergeant Jones here to see you myself,' Constable Stevens, displaying his usual conscientious manner, solemnly replied.

Little did the inspector realise as he accepted the portfolio proffered now to him from the steady hand of Constable Stevens with austere thanks that the words he was about to read would change totally and irrevocably the complexion and direction of the investigation which still lay unanswered before him. Promptly, he tore open the plain, buff-coloured envelope marked 'urgent and confidential' and quickly read its contents whilst the rest of the room looked on in confused silence. Then, Inspector Dentworth looked up, removed his spectacles, rubbed his lean nose then replacing his spectacles said, 'I think I should read this entire correspondence to the whole room.

'Received the following information at approximately eleven o'clock this morning from the office of Picklewood, Picklewood and Whit-field of Chancery Lane, London, solicitors to the late Earl of Marlford who acted as overseers in his absence for Lord Rupert Henry Penman-Smythe's financial interests abroad.

Inspector Dentworth,

Pursuant to our recent conversation of the tenth of October last and your wish for my office to inform you of any further information in the matter of the late Earl of Marlford's financial standing, the following, most important and I believe most relevant correspondence has this day been placed before me courtesy of the early morning post, the envelope having been marked with the instruction that I open it and act upon its contents only in the event of the Earl of

Marlford's early or untimely death.

Kindest Regards

Augustus Picklewood
Senior Partner of Picklewood, Picklewood and Whitfield

(The original of the following transcribed letter received by Mr Augustus Picklewood has been duly confirmed by Mr Picklewood, the late Earl's solicitor of long standing, as having been in the personal hand and style of the late Earl of Marlford.)

Beeches Hall
Marlford
Wiltshire

29 September 1922

Mr Augustus Picklewood
Senior Partner
Picklewood, Picklewood and Whitfield
Solicitors at Law
Chancery Lane
London

My Dear Augustus,

Please forgive what will become apparent as you read on, the somewhat bizarre nature of the following correspondence. However, let me waste no time by stating initially my most fervent desire that you execute the subsequent commands that are expressed in this document as has always been my brief to you in our numerous business dealings.

My command to you, my dear and trusted friend, is simple; read the following words and upon their comprehension please forward this letter immediately to the relevant authorities. You always told me you thought I was a bit of a dark horse; you will find now in these words the confirmation of your long held impressions of my character. Now read on, Augustus.

This letter is by way of a confession, a confession that I have led all those present at Carlile Manor on the afternoon of the twenty-ninth of September last, a merry and most disturbing dance. You might even say that I have had the last laugh on all those around me. However, I must now explain and by way of that explanation we must return to the morning of the twenty-fifth of September last. That was the Monday before I received and accepted the invitation from Montague Alexander Carlile for myself, my daughter and her gentleman companion to attend tea at Carlile Manor the following Friday afternoon.

It was upon that early Monday morning that my resolve to carry out the actions I am about to disclose was cast. With the customary act of attending promptly to the first morning post, my future hopes and dreams were irrevocably shattered. You may well ask what missive of despair was contained in this postal delivery, none other than a concise and completely damning confidential report of operations from the conscientious hand of my mine manager in South Africa. This action was, on his part, in accordance with my direction upon leaving South Africa that if such a dire situation as this was to occur he was to correspond its nature and extent to me personally to the exclusion of all others, yourself included, Augustus. The content of this report confirmed my worst held fears, with its conclusion stating emphatically that mining operations had been forced to cease due to the unheralded evaporation of the diamond seam, further explorations of the surrounding terrain having subsequently yielded no replacement.

With this grave knowledge in hand, the innocent invitation came from Montague Carlile. Here was the man upon whose so-called expert advice, through the instrument of the Barland Bank, I had invested all those years before all my quite substantial working capital into this now doomed venture. In the desperation of the moment, I saw and grasped the perfect opportunity which was afforded to me through this social act of 'welcome home' to wreak my rightful revenge upon the man whom I saw to be at the centre of my disastrous situation. Therefore, during our conversation, I took it upon myself to allow him to become party to my most unusual medical condition. It was also during this conversation which, by a stroke of fate, was held for my part in the relatively public arena of the front hall of my country home, Beeches Hall, that I became aware of the fact that I was being observed from above by my daughter, Isabella. Thereby, she was also made aware, through the course of this conversation, of my determination as I expressed it to Montague Carlile, whom I pointedly addressed clearly by name, not to allow the marriage between herself and Mr John Andrew Smith to proceed, mentioning in passing my suggested action of withholding her financial support and changing my will for the eventual distribution of what all believed to be my very sizeable assets. These actions, towards my daughter and her companion, were again prompted by revenge to, in part, dig the grave even deeper for Montague Carlile as my daughter stood as a witness to what transpired between us on that morning and also to encourage this young couple to become players in my elaborate game.

What, you may ask, my dear friend, could possibly have been my motive for the inclusion of what had always appeared to be my devoted daughter in this dastardly plot? The simple motive was yet again, revenge, revenge, for all the pain that that young woman had put me through over the years. She never loved me and, after the unexpected death of her treasured mother, we tolerated each other's company even less. Let me say that I always fulfilled my responsibilities as her father. However, when she returned home from Europe with that vagabond of a man riding on her coattails, I could take no more. I was determined that all that I had worked and striven for throughout the years would not eventually fall into the control of such a misfit as my daughter's intended. So, as a witch stirs her cauldron of doom, I constantly poked and prodded at this young couple in the hope that they would separate. Ironically, then came the devastating knowledge of what little there would be left for my life, let alone upon my death; my life was ruined. As a final parting shot, I intended to take all those around me who had caused me such pain down with me into their own grave. Knowing of both Montague Carlile's and John Smith's reliance on hypodermic injections for pain relief, I devised my plan of action as follows:

1.   To insist that the Lady Isabella and Mr John Smith accepted the invitation to accompany me to Carlile Manor.

2.   Then, whilst at Carlile Manor, avail myself of the hypodermic

syringe and alcohol of either Montague Carlile or John Smith and then at a suitable point in the proceedings discreetly inject a lethal dose of alcohol into the fare on offer to me, thereby causing my death in what could only be viewed by the authorities as highly suspicious circumstances, in the process casting a grave shadow of guilt over the major players in my drama and thereby causing them to share in the pain that they, in their turn, had each caused me.

Having gradually arrived at this decision in the days leading up to the Friday afternoon, I obtained a certain degree of peace of mind. I would die as I had lived with dignity, still in a position of strength and power in the community and not as a pauper which I would soon become. It was during this final period of tranquillity of mind that I wrote this confessional missive to you, my stalwart friend. Given the wandering path that this letter would travel in its long journey to you (the details of which are one secret I do carry with me to my grave), I deemed that sufficient time would elapse for suspects to be gathered, but not for the hangman's noose to find its mark before this correspondence fell into your most efficient hands, my final caustic joust with the demons of my life before I showed my majestic benevolence and released them from the terrors of the gallows.

Thus, in conclusion, I formally state that I, Rupert Henry Penman-Smythe, Eighth Earl of Marlford, did upon the afternoon of the twenty-ninth of September last take my life by the actions of my own hand and mind by way of a lethal injection of alcohol into a portion of the fare on offer during the course of the afternoon tea. Thus, by way of its consumption and in the clear knowledge of the final effect of my actions, I brought upon myself my own timely death. Only God himself may now sit in judgement of my actions. However, let me finally say here and now I feel no sense of remorse at the course of action which I chose and the macabre game I played. Sweet is revenge...

Yours faithfully

R H Penman-Smythe
The Right Hon. the Earl of Marlford'

'Well, I'll be blowed. It was suicide then, Inspector,' exclaimed Sergeant Jones in a most uncharacteristic display of emotion.

'We will, of course, have to confirm the late Earl's financial situation. Still, that would appear to be the case, Sergeant,' Inspector Dentworth candidly replied. Then turning to face the Lady Isabella, the inspector continued.

'During the course of attending to your late father's affairs, were you not aware at any stage of the now apparently disastrous state of his investments abroad and his subsequent financial ruin, Your Ladyship?' the inspector calmly enquired.

'No, Inspector, I was not aware of his disastrous situation. As I told you, on the day of his funeral I was returning to London to attend to his affairs which, as you also know, I subsequently did. However, at that point in time Mr Picklewood had not received the routine monthly report from Piet Uys, the mine manager in South Africa, which was not unusual, given the vagaries of the postal service in that country, let alone abroad, and since there were numerous other matters to concern ourselves with here in England we were content to wait our time. Now, I know that communication would never have arrived anyway. Where does all this leave me, Inspector? Am I too left without a future?' the Lady Isabella soberly enquired of the inspector as she clung valiantly to the last semblance of composure.

However, before he could reply, a voice possessed of a clear and determined manner rang out with the words, 'Do not worry, my dear child. We, your new family to be, will look after you always,' espoused Catherine in the most loving of tones as she stretched out her hand in an act of benevolent comfort to the forlorn creature before her. As Catherine did so, she glanced towards Montague for a sign of reassurance that her own hopes for the future would not be dashed.

'Can't quite understand how that old blaguer could blame me for his financial woes. Yes, I advised him to invest in the mine, but not every penny he owned. He always was very impulsive. Putting all his eggs in one basket was a very foolish idea. However, you could never presume to tell him what to do. He never really listened to a word of advice on any matter. Very headstrong was Lord Rupert Henry Penman-Smythe. Anyway, enough of the past. We have a bright future to look forward to as a reunited family away from this house of doom and disaster. Given my stronger condition these days, Dr Mathews, would it not be possible for me to return to London and resume my life of peaceful retirement in the bosom of my family once more?' Montague pleadingly requested of the previously silent country doctor.

'I see no reason, given your improved state of heath in these past years, why that cannot be the case. You are indeed a fortunate man, Mr Montague Carlile, for it is not often that one is granted a second chance at life. Never let it be said that I stood in the way of your seizing this most golden opportunity,' Dr Mathews heartily responded as the glimmer of a smile dawned upon his dark features.

'Yes, indeed, Dr Mathews, I am a fortunate man,' Montague reflectively replied.

'Most of you here are fortunate. For I am well within my rights as an officer of the crown to charge you with contempt of court and misleading the true course of justice in this case. I doubt that there would be many among the lot of you who had not told me a mistruth during this investigation. So consider yourselves jolly lucky. Now, I suggest you all to go home,' Inspector Dentworth bluntly instructed.

As Montague sat and absently watched the people who had assembled around him shuffle silently out of the room and his life once more, his mind drifted pleasantly to a collage of thoughts of family... London... home... all once lost but now found... to be once more master of his own London family home... He had finally been exorcised of the demons of his life... By the Master's horn he had lost his past and by the master's horn he had been granted his future... but at whose hand had it truly been? No one would ever know...